For Phil,

HIGH FIVE

An Anthology of Fiction from Ten Years of *Five Points*

May these stories bring you joy.

Warmly,

EDITED BY
MEGAN SEXTON

Megan

CARROLL & GRAF PUBLISHERS
NEW YORK

HIGH FIVE
An Anthology of Fiction from Ten Years of Five Points

Carroll & Graf Publishers
An Imprint of Avalon Publishing Group, Inc.
245 West 17th Street, 11th Floor
New York, NY 10011

All stories in this publication were first printed in *Five Points*,
a publication of Georgia State University

Library of Congress Cataloging-in-Publication Data is available.

Cloth edition ISBN-13: 978-0-78671-845-0
Cloth edition ISBN-10: 0-78671-845-5

Trade paperback edition ISBN-13: 978-0-78671-846-7
Trade paperback edition ISBN-10: 0-78671-846-3

9 8 7 6 5 4 3 2 1

Interior design by Maria Fernandez

Printed in the United States of America
Distributed by Publishers Group West

CONTENTS

INTRODUCTION

The great storyteller Isak Dinesen said "without repeating life in imagination you can never be fully alive." So for the writers and readers of short stories a work of fiction is a gift, a way of wringing the truths out of life long after experience has fled from us. This need to relive our lives through story is a very basic human trait. Try to think of any civilization since the beginning of time that did not seek to find itself again and again in the sagas of war, the ballads of love and death, and the fairy tales of childhood initiation. There are no exceptions; stories are as common throughout the ages as fern fossils. So it is not surprising that we are still looking for stories to illuminate our lives today. Call me old-fashioned, but even though we have witnessed the rise of so-called experimental forms like flash fiction and the advent of the blog, and despite the dire news that less than 50 percent of us bother to read them at all, I think the well-made short story structured into meaning still serves us well. No other form can capture the vector of reality and freeze-frame life's consequences the way it can.

We might look to Coleridge, that renegade Romantic poet, when considering the essential function of story in our lives. Coleridge reminds us of the countless possibilities of narrative to edify and restore ourselves. His "The Rime of the Ancient Mariner" serves as a kind of primer on how to tell a story as the mariner recounts his tale to the "spellbound" wedding guest. Although Coleridge emphasizes the usefulness of an exciting action-driven plot, the real story evolves in the telling between the mariner and the wedding guest amidst the chaotic backdrop of his ill-fated voyage. It's the journey to the interior—the individual life—that becomes his main concern and the main concern of the modern short story as well. The poor unsuspecting wedding guest, eyeing the open bar over the mariner's shoulder pleads, "I fear thee ancient mariner." Somehow he knows the tale will change him. It will provide him with knowledge, the kind of knowledge Eudora Welty was talking about when she said that all of Chekhov's stories asked: "What will you do with the knowledge this story has provided you?"

I have assembled the stories in this collection with the notion that these writers previously published over the course of ten years in *Five Points* are participating within a tradition of storytelling rooted in the belief of human meaning. This assembly of stories offers us the infinite regress of human existence as moments of our lives unfold in their many permutations and reflections. With an editor's urge to organize, I have chosen three categories by which these stories may be read but in no way seek to limit the interpretation of these works, for all of them exceed the boundaries of classification. In *Five Points* we have been fortunate to pursue the mysteries available to us and uniquely encountered in short stories. May we all be spellbound and enlivened by them.

—*Megan Sexton*

SELF

Ha Jin

In the Kindergarten

Shaona kept her eyes shut, trying to sleep. Outside, the noonday sun was blazing, and bumblebees were droning in the shade of an elm. Time and again one of them would bump into the window's wire screen with a thud and then a louder buzz. Soon Teacher Shen's voice in the next room grew clearer.

"Oh please!" the teacher blubbered on the phone. "I'll pay the money back in three months. You've already helped me so much, why can't you help me out?"

Those words made Shaona fully awake. She moved her head closer to the wall and strained her ears to listen. The teacher begged, "Have mercy on me, Doctor Niu. I've an old mother at home. My mother and I have to live. . . . You know, I lost so much blood, because of the baby, that I have to eat some eggs to recuperate. I'm really broke now. Can you just give me another month?"

Shaona was puzzled, thinking how a baby could injure her teacher's health. Her grandmother used to say that babies were dug out from pumpkin fields in the countryside. Why did her teacher sound as though the baby had come off from her body? Why did she bleed for the baby?

Teacher Shen's voice turned desperate. "Please, don't tell anyone about the abortion! I'll try my best to pay you back . . . very soon. I'll see if I can borrow some money from a friend."

What's an abortion? Shaona asked herself. Is it something that holds a baby? What does it look like? Must be very expensive.

Her teacher slammed the phone down, then cried, "Heaven help me!"

Shaona couldn't sleep anymore. She missed her parents so much that she began sobbing again. This was her second week in the kindergarten, and she was not used to sleeping alone yet. Her small iron bed was uncomfortable, in every way different from the large soft bed at home, which could hold her entire family. She couldn't help wondering if her parents would love her the same as before, because three weeks ago her mother had given her a baby brother. These days her father was so happy that he often chanted opera snatches.

In the room seven other children were napping, one of them wheezing with a stuffy nose. Two large bronze moths, exhausted by the heat, were resting on the ceiling, their powdery wings flickering now and again. Shaona yawned sleepily, but still couldn't go to sleep.

At two-thirty the bell rang, and all the nappers got out of their beds. Teacher Shen gathered the whole class of five- and six-year-olds in the corridor. Then in two lines they set out for the turnip field behind the kindergarten. It was still hot. A steamer went on blowing her horn in the north, and a pair of jet fighters were flying in the distant sky, drawing a long double curve. Shaona wondered how a pilot could stay inside those planes that looked as small as pigeons. In the air lingered a sweetish odor of dichlorvos, which had been sprayed around in the city to get rid of flies, fleas, mosquitos. The children were excited, because seldom could they go out of the stone wall topped with shards of dark brown glass. Today instead of playing games within the yard as the children of the other classes were doing, Teacher Shen was going to teach them how to gather purslanes. Few of them knew what a purslane looked like, but they were all eager to search for the herb.

On the way their teacher turned around to face them, flourishing her narrow hand and saying, "Boys and girls, you'll eat sautéed purslanes this evening. It tastes great, different from anything you've ever had. Tell me, do you all want to have purslanes for dinner or not?"

"Yes, we want," a few voices cried.

The teacher smacked her lips. Her sunburned nose crinkled, a faint smile playing on her face. As she continued walking, the ends of her two braids, tied with green woolen strings, were stroking the baggy seat of her pants. She was a young woman, tall and angular, with crescent eyebrows. She used to sing a lot; her voice was fruity and clear. But recently she was quiet, her face rather pallid. It was said that she had divorced her husband the previous summer because he had been sentenced to thirteen years in prison for embezzlement.

When they arrived at the field, Teacher Shen plucked a purslane from between two turnip seedlings. She said to the children standing in a horseshoe, "Look, its leaves are tiny, fleshy, and egg-shaped. It has reddish stems, different from regular veggies and grass. Sometimes it has small yellow flowers." She dropped the purslane into her duffel bag on the ground and went on, "Now, you each take charge of one row."

Following her orders, the children spread out along the edge of the field and then walked into the turnip seedlings.

Shaona lifted up the bottom of her checked skirt to form a hollow before her stomach and set out to search. Purslanes weren't difficult to find among the turnips, whose greens were not yet larger than a palm. Pretty soon every one of the children gathered some purslanes.

"Don't stamp on the turnips!" Uncle Chang shouted at them from time to time. Sitting under an acacia, he was puffing away at a long pipe that had a brass bowl, his bald crown coated with beads of sweat. He was in charge of a few vegetable fields and the dilapidated pump house.

Shaona noticed Dabin, a rambunctious boy, sidling up to her, but she pretended she hadn't seen him. He nudged her and asked, "How many did you get?" He sniveled—two lines of dark mucus disappeared from his nostrils, then poked out again.

She lowered the hollow of her skirt, showing him about a dozen purslanes.

He said with one eye shut, "You're no good. Look at mine." He held out his peaked cap, which was full.

She felt a little hurt, but kept quiet. He turned away to talk to other children, telling them that purslanes tasted awful. He claimed he had once eaten a bowl of purslane stew when he had diarrhea. He would never have touched that stuff if his parents hadn't forced him. "It tastes like crap, more bitter than sweet potato vines," he assured them.

"Not true," said Weilan, a scrawny girl. "Teacher Shen told us it tastes great."

"How can you know?"

"I just know it."

"You know your granny's fart!"

"Big asshole," Weilan said, and made a face at him, sticking out her tongue.

"Say that again, bitch!" He went up to her, grabbed her shoulder, pushed her to the ground, and kicked her butt. She burst out crying.

Their teacher came over and asked who had started the fight. Shaona pointed at Dabin. To her surprise, the teacher walked up to the boy and seized him by the ear, saying through her teeth, "You can't live for a day without making trouble. Come now, I'm going to give you a trouble-free place to stay." She was dragging him away.

"Ouch!" he cried with a rattling noise in his throat. "You're pulling off my ear."

"You'll have the other one left."

Passing Uncle Chang, Teacher Shen stopped to ask him to keep an eye on the children for a short while. Then she pulled Dabin back to the kindergarten.

Shaona's mouth fell open. That boy would be "jailed" and he might get even with her after he was released. On the second floor of their building there was a room, an unused kitchen, in which three bedside cupboards sat on the cooking range. Sometimes a troublesome boy would be locked in one of them for hours. Once in a while his teacher might forget to let him out in time, so that he had to go without lunch or dinner.

About ten minutes later Teacher Shen returned, panting hard as though she had just finished a sprint. She counted the children to make sure nobody was missing.

Shaona soon forgot Dabin, immersed in looking for more purslanes. For most of the children this was real work. Few of them had ever tasted anything gathered by themselves, so they were searching diligently. Whenever their little skirts or caps were full, they went over to unload the purslanes into the duffel bag, from which their teacher was busy picking out grass and other kinds of herbs mixed into the purslanes. The children were amazed that in just one and a half hours the bag was filled up and that they had almost combed the entire field. Their teacher kept reminding them of the proverb they had learned lately—"Many hands provide great strength."

When they had searched the field, they were lined up hand in hand behind the pump house, ready to return to the kindergarten. But before leaving, for some reason their teacher gave several handfuls of purslanes to Uncle Chang. With grudging eyes they watched her drop almost a third of their harvest into the old man's wicker basket, but none of them made a peep. The old man went on smiling at the young woman, saying, "All right, enough, enough. Keep the rest for yourself." As he was speaking, spittle was emitted through his gapped teeth.

Shaona's mind was full, and she couldn't wait for dinner. She thought, If purslane tastes real good, I'll pick some for Mom and Dad. She knew a place in the kindergarten—inside the deserted pigsty—where she had seen a few purslanes.

To her dismay, dinner was similar to other days': corn glue, steamed sweet potatoes, and sautéed radishes. There wasn't even a purslane leaf on the table. Every one of her classmates looked upset. Not knowing what to say, some children were noisily stirring the corn glue with spoons. Shaona wanted to cry, but she controlled herself. She remembered seeing her teacher leave for home with the bulging duffel clasped on the carrier of her bicycle. At that moment Shaona had thought the green bag must have contained laundry or something, because it was so full. Now she understood, their teacher took their harvest home.

Shaona liked sweet potato, but she didn't eat much. Anger and gas filled her stomach. Despite their sullen faces and disappointed hearts, none of the children mentioned purslanes. Everyone looked rather dejected except for Dabin. He had kept glaring at Shaona ever since he was let out of the cupboard for dinner. She knew he was going to take his revenge. What should she do?

In the dusk, when the children were playing in the yard, Shaona caught sight of Dabin. She called and beckoned to him. He came over and grunted, "What's up, little telltale?"

"Dabin, would you like to have these?" In her palm were two long peanuts. Her father had given her six of them when she was coming back to the kindergarten two days ago.

"Huh!" he exclaimed with pursed lips, "I never saw a peanut with four seeds in it." He snatched them from her hand and without another word cracked one. His eyes glittered and his mouth twitched like a rabbit's while he was chewing the roasted kernels.

Within a few seconds he finished the peanuts off, then he asked, "Do you have more?"

"Un-un." She shook her head, her slant eyes fixed on the ground.

He touched her sweater pocket, which was empty. She had hidden the other four peanuts in her socks. He said, "You must be nice to me from now on. Remember to save lots of goodies for me, got it?"

She nodded without looking at him.

Standing below a slide, she watched him running away with his bowlegs to join the boys who were hurling paper bombers and imitating explosions. Behind the cypress hedge, near the closed front gate, a couple of children were playing hide-and-go-seek, their white clothes flickering and their ecstatic cries ringing in the twilight.

That night Shaona didn't sleep well. She was still scared of the dark room. One of her roommates, Aili, snored without stopping. An owl or a hawk went on hooting like an old man's coughing. A steam hammer in the shipyard on the riverbank pounded metal now and then. Unable to sleep, Shaona ate a peanut, though the rule didn't allow her to eat anything after she had brushed her teeth for bed. She took care to hide the shells under her pillow. How she missed her mother's warm, soft belly; again she cried quietly.

It rained the next morning, but the clouds began lifting after nine o'clock, so the children were allowed to go out and play. In the middle of the yard stood a miniature merry-go-round, sky blue and nine feet across. A ring of boys was sitting on it, revolving and yelling happily. Dabin and Shuwen, who was squint-eyed, were among them, firing wooden carbines at treetops, people, birds, smokestacks, and anything that came into sight. They were shouting out "rat-a-tat" as if the spinning platform were a tank turret. Shaona dared not go take a spin. The previous week she had ridden on that thing and had been spun giddy, sick for two days.

So instead, she played court with a bunch of girls. They elected her the queen, saying she looked the most handsome among them. With four maids waiting on her, she had to sit on the wet ground all the time. Weilan and Aili were her amazons, each holding a whittled branch as a lance. The girls wished they could have made a strong boy the king, but only Dun was willing to stay with them. He was a mousy boy, and most of the girls could beat him easily. He should have been a courtier rather than the ruler. Soon Shaona couldn't stand remaining the queen anymore, because she felt silly to call him "Your Majesty" and hated to obey his orders. She begged other girls to replace her, but none of them would. She got up from the ground, shouting, "I quit!" To keep the court from disintegrating, Aili agreed to be a vice-queen.

Because of the soggy ground, many of the children had their clothes soiled by lunchtime. Teacher Shen was angry, especially with those who had played mud pies. She said that if they were not careful about their clothes, she wouldn't let them go out in the afternoon. "None of you is a good child," she declared. "You all want to create more work for me."

After lunch, while the children were napping, Teacher Shen collected their clothes to scrub off the mud stains. She was unhappy because she couldn't take a nap.

Too exhausted to miss her parents, Shaona fell asleep the moment her head touched her pillow. She slept an hour and a half. When she woke up, she was pleased to find her sweater and skirt clean without a speck of mud. But as her hand slotted into the sweater pocket she was surprised—the three peanuts were gone. She removed the toweling coverlet and rummaged through her bedding, but couldn't find any trace of them; even the shells under her pillow had disappeared. Heartbroken, she couldn't stop her tears, knowing her teacher must have confiscated the peanuts.

The sun came out in the afternoon, and the ground in the yard turned whitish. Again Teacher Shen led the twenty-four children out to the turnip field. On their way they sang the song "Red Flowers," which they had learned the week before:

> Red flowers are blooming everywhere.
> Clapping our hands, we sing
> And play a game in the square,
> All happy like blossoms of spring.

When they arrived at the field, Uncle Chang was not in view, but the water pump was snarling, tiny streams glinting here and there among the turnip rows.

The sight of the irrigation made their teacher hesitate for a moment, then she said loudly to the children, "We're going to gather more purslanes this afternoon. Aunt Chef couldn't cook those we got yesterday because we turned them in too late, but she'll cook them for us today. So everybody must be a good child and work hard. Understood?"

"Understood," they said almost in unison. Then they began to search among the turnips.

Although most of the children were as high-spirited as the day before, there weren't many purslanes left in the field, which was muddy and slippery. A number of them fell on their buttocks and had their clothes soiled. Their shoes were ringed with dark mud.

Yet the hollow of Shaona's skirt was soon filled with several puny purslanes, and some children had even dropped a load into the duffel, which began to swell little by little. Unlike the silly boys and girls who were still talking about what purslanes tasted like, Shaona was sulky the whole time, though she never stopped searching.

In front of her appeared a few tufts of wormwood, among which were some brownish rocks partly covered by dried grass. A swarm of small butterflies rested on the wormwood, flapping their white wings marked with black spots. Now and then one of them took off, flying sideways to land on a rock. Shaona went over to search through the grass; her motion set the butterflies in flight all at once like a flurry of snowflakes. Suddenly a wild rabbit jumped out, racing away toward a group of girls, who all saw it and broke out hollering. The animal, frightened by their voices, swerved and bolted away toward the back wall of the kindergarten. At the sight of the fleeing creature, Teacher Shen yelled, "Catch him! Don't let him run away!"

All at once several boys started chasing the rabbit, which turned out to have a crippled hind leg. Now their teacher was running after it too, motioning to the children ahead to intercept the animal. Her long braids swayed from side to side as she was dashing away. Within seconds all the children except Shaona joined the chase.

The turnip field was being ruined, a lot of seedlings trampled and muddy water splashing from the running feet. Shrieks and laughter were rising from the west side of the field.

Shaona was not with them because she wanted to pee. Looking around, she saw nobody near, so she squatted down over the duffel, made sure to conceal her little behind with her skirt, and peed on the purslanes inside the bag. But she dared not empty her bladder altogether; she stopped halfway, got up, and covered the wet purslanes with the dry ones she had gathered. Then with a kicking heart she ran away to join the chasers.

The rabbit had fled out of sight, but the children were still excited, boys huffing and puffing, and bragging about how close they had got to the animal. Dabin swore that his toes, caged in a pair of open-headed sandals, had touched that fluffy tail. Shuwen said that the wild rabbit tasted much better than the domestic rabbit; a few children were listening to him describe how his uncle had shot a pair of wild rabbits in the mountain and how his aunt had cut them to pieces and stewed them with potato and carrot cubes. Their teacher stopped him from finishing his story. Without delay she assembled the children and led them out of the field, fearful that Uncle Chang would call her names for the trampled turnips.

Before dinner Shaona was worried for fear the chef might cook the soiled purslanes for them. To her relief, dinner turned out to be similar. She was thrilled. For the first time in the kindergarten she ate a hearty meal—three sweet potatoes, two bowls of corn glue, and many spoonfuls of fried eggplant. The whole evening she was so excited that she joined the boys in playing soldier, carrying a toy pistol, as though all of a sudden she had become a big girl. She felt that from now on she would no longer cry like a baby at night.

Michael Downs

Elephant

I was thirteen when my father told me he once shot a circus elephant.

"Through the eye," he said.

We sat in the dim light of Gray's Tavern. It was pay day, and on most pay days we killed afternoons at Gray's. My father chased vodka with Knickerbocker beer and smoked his Marlboros. I sipped cola from a glass bottle.

"With a Colt forty-five, semi-automatic," he said. "Civilian issue. A tiny gun for such a big animal."

My father is dead now. Emphysema. He'd smoked since he was a boy in southeastern Poland, hauling lumber out of the woods, which was a dangerous job. Africa and Italy during the war were dangerous, too, but what eventually got him were the two packs a day. He enjoyed cigarettes and he enjoyed his factory job. He loved my mother.

"I love her more than God loves her," he once said, as we sat around the dinner table, eating stuffed cabbage and meatloaf.

Mama frowned and said, "Your papa is a simple man."

When she spoke that truth—and she spoke it often—she was describing the man who rocked in a chair on our front porch, listening as the Yankees played at 1080 on the AM dial, tossing bits of stale pumpernickel bread to blue jays and starlings and calling them sweet names. "I'm out to feed my chickens," he would say as he stepped onto the porch, and the birds would swoop to our yard from neighborhood rooftops and branches. This was Mama's simple man.

Mama wanted not to be simple. She kept secrets. She spent afternoons alone in her sewing room with the door closed. Sometimes at Sunday Mass she cried but would never say why. My friends and the parents of my friends talked about her. My mother cleaned houses, but she should have been an actress. From her I learned that the redeeming currency of old pain is drama.

Our family's pain is young, but old enough to allow for a dramatic history. Not long after my father left for the war, there was a fire in Hartford that killed nearly two hundred people. The fire is famous not so much for the horrific deaths it caused, but for where they occurred. A circus tent burned that afternoon. No one knows for sure how the fire started, but it consumed the tent so quickly that the crowds inside were trapped. Flaps of flaming canvas fell from the sky. There was black smoke. Panic. Screaming circus animals. A famous photograph shows Emmett Kelly, the saddest of clowns, carrying a water bucket, which, given the scale of black-and-white ruin around him, holds nothing but its own inadequacy. His clown pants are shredded and his hand bats the air, obscuring his face so all you can see is his bulbous nose and his frown. My mother and I went to the circus for that matinee. We spent weeks in St. Francis Hospital after. Her scars included half a butterfly on her forehead that she never attempted to hide. Mine cover much of my body, but not my face or hands. People who see my scars ask how I got them, and then they ask what it was like to be inside the tent. They are always disappointed when I admit that I can't remember. In truth, I'm disappointed, too. When I asked about the fire, my mother would only say I was blessed to have forgotten. She saw no reason to interfere with God's plan for my memory.

I remember Gray's Tavern, though. It's still there: a little hole in the sidewalk down Maple Avenue near Goodwin Park. It's an Irish bar, and I think my father liked it because he felt supremely Polish there. Surrounded by all the Gavins and Carraghers and Bolgers, his difference shined—the whisper of his Slavic accent, his Slavic eyebrows, his flat, round face. Each time we walked through the door the bartender and proprietor—Eddie Gray, who served with my father in Italy—greeted Papa with the opening line of a joke.

"Hey Charlie, how many Polacks does it take to tie a shoe?"

"Hey Charlie, did you hear about the Polack and the cabaret singer?"

"Hey Charlie, what's the difference between a Polack and a platypus?"

"Zip the lip, Mick," my father would say, and Eddie Gray would laugh and so would anyone else in the bar. It was their way of saying hello, how the hell are you, it's good to see you and we love you, you Polack son-of-a-peasant. Come have a drink.

Behind the bar, a baseball trophy: "Gray's Tavern, Twilight League Runners-up, 1948." Their best season ever. Eddie Gray throwing strikes from the mound one game and stabbing line drives at short the next. A year later, his arm went bum and without him the Grays couldn't even beat Traveler's Insurance. In the corner of the tavern, a map of "Irlande" hung from the wall, and superimposed over it was a shirted man with his collar open and a rifle in his hand. Below him, the clarion whoop, "They may kill the revolutionary, but they will never kill the Revolution." Jimmy Williams always sat beside the poster. Jimmy, who was not so old but had the pleading, helpless eyes of a spaniel, and who fingered tunes and hymns on a recorder for coins. "Danny Boy," of course. But also "When You Wish Upon A Star" and each version of the memorial acclamation of the Roman Catholic mass, proclaiming the mysteries of faith. Only slow tunes, and each note arrived on the air weak in the knees, as if Jimmy first had to think before letting it go. Papa used to tell me not to stare at Jimmy. He always gave Jimmy a dollar.

This was 1954, ten years after the fire.

It was the early, wet April of that year when I heard about the elephant. The thermometer said it wasn't cold, but the wind and the spitting rain gave the air a bite. My nose stung and dripped. Papa waited for me outside the school gate. He never liked for me to walk anywhere alone.

When I drew within range, he spread his arms and scooped me into them. He cupped my head and kissed my brow with cold lips. Without a word, we splashed through puddles to Gray's.

At the bar, a man with grease-blackened hands and a bandage on his forefinger was introducing himself and a friend to Eddie. "This is Brendan, my birthday buddy," said the man, and he lit a cigarette. "We've got the same birthday, and it's today."

"Charlie," Eddie shouted to my father, "how do you sink a Polack battleship?"

"Same as a Mick ship. You put it in water."

"Have I tried that one before?"

"A year ago February."

Eddie slid the vodka and the beer across the bar, and the fizzing cola for me. Papa and I sat at our regular table, which tilted my way if he lifted his elbows. He sipped his vodka, his smiles lasting only a moment. He swirled the glass so ice sang on the edges, then sipped again. I still try to remember whether he chewed his lip or blinked too much, or suffered from some twitch that, had I been paying attention, would have shown me that my father was not himself that day. Nothing comes to mind. I wasn't paying attention to him. Not yet. It was a pay day afternoon at Gray's, like so many others.

"Do kids tease you still?" he said.

"Sometimes they want to touch my skin," I said. "I don't mind."

In the corner, Jimmy Williams played his recorder, each note squeezed to life.

When
you
wish
u-
-pon
a

"In Italy," my father said to me, "I had POW duty. You know what that is, POW? Prisoners of war."

He rapped his knuckles three times on our table. Eddie brought him another round.

"I was like a guard in a jail," Papa said. "It was easy most of the time. But we had one fascist—solid-as-bone that guy—kept yelling at us, 'God damn GIs. Bastard GIs. God damn GIs.'"

My father never swore when I was around. Yet now he spoke forbidden words casually, as if they had no power. But they did. Dark, gristly power. I leaned nearer.

"He had a mouth, that guy," my father said. "Over and over. Like a mynah bird. The kind of thing that would drive you crazy, like someone on a Saturday morning trying to start a car, turning over the engine six, seven, eight times. 'God damn GI. Bastard GI.' This fascist, he's on us like that until this one fella, this one fella, he picks up a chunk of brick from a bombed-out building, and he breaks all that fascist's teeth. Bashed him right across the chops. That son-of-a-gun kept on, though: 'God damn GI. Bastard GI.' Grinning at us with his mouth and tongue swollen. Blood all over his lips. I watched, wishing he'd zip it, you know? Because he was stupid, because all that happened was he got smashed in the mouth again, then again. I hated him for that. Now, I don't know. Now he's just a fact of life."

Brendan's birthday buddy at the bar was explaining his bandaged finger, how he'd cut it to the bone at the typewriter factory where he worked. He offered to show Eddie the stitches. I had stitches in my chin when I was eight after falling from my bicycle, and of course, I knew all about scars from flame. But I had never seen a man whose mouth was shredded by a brick. I ran my tongue over the fronts of my top teeth between the gum and the lip. I imagined my mouth like the stringy inside of a pumpkin, all bloody. Street water from the rubbers covering my shoes pooled with the grime under my chair.

"I read about the fire in an Army newspaper," my father said. He wouldn't let go of his vodka glass. Now, he tapped its bottom against the table. "But I didn't worry. Your mama and me, we didn't have much money, not enough to spend on circus tickets. I read about the fire, and I wrote your mother a letter. I asked if we knew anyone who had been there."

He shook a cigarette from his pack, but didn't light it. He took off his eye glasses and chuckled, but the sound was small and sad. He rubbed his eyes and then the bridge between them. My father had deep indentations in his nose because the lenses of his eye glasses weighed so much. When Papa died, Mr. Liszak at the mortuary suggested masking the indentations with make-up, but I said leave them and have Papa wear his glasses instead.

"There was a fella. A PFC from Waterbury. We never talked much, but his sister had gone to the circus. She'd been burned, but not bad enough for him to get compassion leave. Not like your mother and you were burned. But I didn't know that yet. I just knew about this fella's sister. So I bought him a beer. Patted his shoulder. He showed everybody her picture. She was eighteen. Good looking. A lot of the fellas made jokes about her afterward because she was so pretty." Papa looked at me suddenly, as if remembering who sat across from him. "You don't make jokes about pretty girls, do you?" he said. "You and the other boys at school? Your mother was a pretty girl. Never make jokes about pretty girls."

I nodded that I wouldn't.

"Your mother's not a girl anymore," he said.

He loved her. I believe this. Yet many times, I woke to find Papa on the couch downstairs. "I snore," he told me. "Keeps your mama awake." His answer never sounded whole. Nor did my mother's, when I asked why I had no brother or sister. She would kiss my nose and whisper, "God gave us one perfect child."

Brendan's birthday buddy tossed peanuts into the air and caught them in his mouth. He suggested Eddie buy a pinball machine to add some whiz-bang to the place. "Whiz-bang's out that door," Eddie said. "We like peace and quiet in here."

Papa lit his Marlboro and shook out the match. He hadn't looked away from me.

"How was I supposed to know how badly you were hurt?" he said. "I don't . . . Jesus. I'm in Italy. A goddamned bastard GI. It took a while for the nurses to get your names. Your mama's English wasn't so good then. You . . . I hate to think it. About a week after

I read about the fire—must have been more than a week later—a Red Cross woman took me aside. She held my hand. She told me that you and your mama had been inside the circus tent that day with all those people and all that fire."

The army sent my father home. He arrived on a hot, hazy afternoon, stepping out of the Union Station into a city that seemed to him strangely serene. No mortar fire. No screams. No bombed-out buildings. "Queer" is how he described it that day in Gray's Tavern.

Now when I imagine my father home that first hour, I imagine him walking through the working streets of downtown, amid secretaries and switchboard operators, lawyers and bookkeepers. He pauses at the corner of Trumbull and Pearl to stare at the old Hartford Insurance Company building, at the stone stag over its door. His khaki uniform is crisp, and he squints into the stark July sun at the building's cornices and window panes that stand intact. An Italian man in a white T-shirt tries to sell him a newspaper. My father breathes cologne and perfume. Women smell clean. It's a good day to live. It makes no sense. An ocean away is a fascist with his mouth stuffed full of blood-soaked cotton, and my father understands why. But here in this familiar and alien place, this place so at peace it seems not of the world, his wife and son lie alone in hospital beds, their skin peeled. He is home, and he staggers at the horror.

Years later at Gray's, my father stared at the grain of our table top and traced a knot with his hard, thick thumbnail.

"I didn't visit you for three days," he said. "I stayed away for three days."

Then he looked at me as if I would accuse him, as if a thirteen-year-old, knowing only the sting of cola on his tongue and the smell of stale beer and cigarettes, could pass judgment. I was too young to understand what three days meant. All I understood was that my father was tattling on himself, confessing something that made him seem small.

He told me of those three days.

First, he returned to the apartment. It was mostly as he remembered, though my mother's jade plant sat rootbound in its pot, and the landlord had painted the windows black in case of air raids. In the room where I had slept, he opened dresser drawers and lifted out shirts and jumpers and shoes that were too large for the baby he remembered, and—having been gone those two years—he could not imagine the boy who might fit into them. Instead, he turned his hand to chores. He swept and mopped the floor, then dusted window sills and the small shrine my mother had built to the Virgin Mary. He watered the victory garden she had planted in the back yard and had marked with a small penciled sign that read "Ania Turosz" to distinguish it from other tenants' gardens. He changed a washer in the bathroom faucet to stop a drip, and he patched a torn window screen. He moved from chore to chore as if one depended on the other, as if everything hinged on his labor. Still, he failed. He dropped a light bulb and it shattered. He knocked over an end table and left a gash in the floor. He worked past dark, past midnight, until he couldn't help but sleep, leaning in the corner where he had yet to finish mending a crack in the plaster. Not until the next morning would he dare step into their bedroom to run his fingers along the sheets where she had slept, to smell her pillow, to touch the hair still twined in her brush.

On the second day he shopped, telling himself he couldn't visit the hospital empty-handed. He took most of the morning and all of the afternoon to find just the right gifts, wandering shop to store in awe and confusion. He discovered that time and distance had made him uncertain of what his wife and son would most want.

Would his boy play that board game? Could he look through that magnifying glass? Would she wear such a fancy blouse? He settled on a box of colored pencils for me; for Mama, he chose a frame for a family photograph. To wrap these gifts, he bought silver paper and red ribbon.

Though he wasn't hungry, he forced himself to stop at the downtown five-and-dime where he sat on a swivel stool at the counter. He ordered a root beer and fried egg sandwich. As he ate, he overheard in the booth behind him a woman in a flowered hat talking to a friend. She was talking about the circus. He listened more closely. The woman in the flowered hat told her friend that most of the circus was still in Hartford—right up there on Barbour Street. Yes, the circus! It can't leave, she said. There are so many law suits already, and no one knows how the circus will pay. Gorillas and lions as collateral, she laughed. It's true! All the animals survived! I read it in the *Times.* Not a singed whisker. Why, they've even got elephants in Sponzo's Meadow!

My father left his root beer and a few coins on the counter. He walked out to the sidewalk, surprised by the bright sun. That night at the apartment, he drank too much vodka. And then he lay awake imagining me and my mother sitting in the grandstands as fire flashed around us, the animals outside and safe from the flames, and because he did not know the neighborhood a few miles north where the circus tent had burned, he saw instead a war-wrecked Italian countryside where elephants and lions stepped softly through the dust. Twice he left his bed to vomit, but his stomach was empty and the heaves brought no relief.

On his third day home, Papa caught a bus downtown and another north on Main Street. From there, he walked.

The smell struck him first. The wind carried it, the smell of dry, sweet ash mixed with animal stink, rich and nauseating, and Papa spit but couldn't get it out of his mouth. Then he came to the field where the Big Top had burned.

"It was like an army camp," he told me. "Except it was like the sloppy camp of troops who'd been beaten. Tents with walls flapping loose—not a proper tie-down to be found."

He stubbed the butt of his cigarette in one of Eddie Gray's tin ashtrays.

There were trucks, he told me, parked and rusted and caked with mud. Railroad cars painted red, though the paint had bubbled and split, the fire had been so hot. One railroad car smelled like the kitchen, and another was obviously the latrine. Rough characters lounged all over, their shirts unbuttoned and untucked, their T-shirts stained yellow under the arms. Only a few of them worked, carrying hay by the armful for the animals.

"Gorillas. Lions," my father said. "Amazing, yes. But I'd seen gorillas and lions at zoos in cages, and this wasn't so different. But I'd never seen an elephant. Only in picture books."

He lit another cigarette, letting the smoke ease out of his nostrils before he spoke again.

"These elephants they kept staked and crowded into a meadow, with just a man or two to watch them. You could hardly see the stakes, and it didn't take much to imagine the elephants running from the lot, trampling a bunch of neighborhood kids playing hopscotch. But all the elephants did was stuff their trunks into these banged-up barrels full of water and sometimes drink and other times spray themselves like they were their own garden hose. Geez, it was hot. My shirt stuck to my back. I found a shade tree, but it didn't help. Shade didn't help.

"The elephants were all the same color—like ash," he said. His eyes grew wet, and he blinked, his voice quiet as if steadied by certainty. "And they were giants. Bigger than the piles of hay. And those piles were as big as cars. Mountains of hay in front of them, mountains of shit behind them. The stink would make you dizzy. Flies, too, zigzagging near your ears, your eyes. All you could hear was that buzzing. Louder, then quiet; louder, then quiet. And then, those elephants would sound off. Raise their heads, their trunks, then blast away. Even on a day hot as that, it'd turn your spine cold."

Papa told me that he walked around the meadow a dozen or more times, waving off flies and staring at the elephants. He drew close enough to study where their pigmentation spotted and the flesh became pink or dull white. "Like they had been burned," he said. "But they hadn't." He wagged a finger. "You had, though. You had. I tell you, Teddy, they seemed like something born when the mountains came up from the oceans. Something that survived everything."

Papa drew close to the elephants, so close that he could see even the bristle of hairs along the bottom of a jaw, the stunted tusks hidden inside an elephant mouth, the depression above and behind an eye.

"But over there was a block full of three-family houses, one with a porch swing. And power poles up and down the street, their lines running from house to house. And there, a forty-one Oldsmobile. Sheets hung out to dry. It didn't make any sense." His eyes sparkled with the monstrousness of it. His voice grew loud. "Those elephants, you know, they were just wrong. There weren't supposed to be elephants in meadows in Hartford. Everything was wrong. Every last thing was wrong."

I glanced to Eddie Gray, who wiped the bar with a caramel-colored rag. He saw me—it was plain on his face—but he turned aside, started working down the other way.

My father grabbed my arm and hissed, "Look at me when I'm talking to you."

"Yes."

"Do you understand? Their stink would peel paint. The inside of my nose was burning."

He pinched his nose. When he let go, the skin was pink.

Jimmy had stopped playing his recorder. The bar seemed too quiet, as if everyone were listening. But I didn't dare turn to look.

"You understand, Teddy? These were elephants right here in Hartford. Lounging in a meadow as if this is the way the world is supposed to be. But it's not. It's not.

"So I shot one. I walked up close to an elephant at the end of the row, away from the circus workers. It was so easy. So slow. Its head swung toward me. I fired right into its eye."

He reared as if I would challenge him.

"There was blood," he said. "Elephant blood on my uniform."

Now Eddie approached our table.

"Hey, Charlie, maybe it's time you headed home, huh?"

"I'm talking to my son," Papa said. "I'm explaining things."

Eddie snorted. He took the empty glasses, wiped our table and left the smell of dishrags.

"Did the elephant die?" I asked.

"Maybe," my father said. "I'm not proud to have shot an elephant. I'm telling you that everything was wrong, and that all I could do was shoot the elephant. And then I ran. I'm not proud of that, either, Teddy. I ran."

I nodded.

"It was a Colt forty-five, semi-automatic," he said. "I think the elephant would have been blinded, but not killed. No, not killed."

I nodded.

"They're big animals," he said.

Eddie came back with another cola.

"Here kid, on the house."

My father acted as if he didn't notice. "Time to go," he said.

In less than an afternoon, my father had become new, different, strange. I wasn't yet ready to be alone with him. I pointed to the full bottle. "I haven't finished my soda," I said.

"Drink fast."

He stood and walked back to the toilet, his steps sure and deliberate, leaving me alone, heavy with responsibility and adolescent grief because he had shot the elephant on my behalf. Because of an injury I couldn't even remember, an elephant had been blinded.

Brendan's birthday buddy said something then, about the tears and soft lips of a sad woman. "That's what I want for my birthday," he said. He swiveled on his stool to face me. "Kid," he said, "never forget that a crying woman is a beautiful thing."

Papa and I walked home through a dark drizzle. Headlights rushed past, and splashed gutter water over the curb to the sidewalks. When we got home, he turned on the radio, then sat in his rocking chair and wiped his glasses clean for a long time.

He never again spoke to me of the elephant he had shot. Even when I tried to bring it up, he changed the subject. Eventually, he did tell me of his first visit to see us in the hospital, how I protested that no, this stranger was not my papa, until a nurse vouched for him. But the nurses wouldn't let him touch me, and they wouldn't let him give me the colored pencils. Neither my father nor the pencils were sterile. My mother, my father told me, wept when she saw the family portrait in its wood frame painted gold. When he told me this, it had been years since we'd spent afternoons at Gray's Tavern. I saw an opportunity and asked him why he took so long to visit. He shrugged and said, "All I know is that I love you and your mother more than God loves you, because He burned you, and I'd never do that."

Time passed. My grief for the elephant disappeared with my pimples. I graduated high school, studied art and design in college, and I learned to embrace the elephant story as I would a favorite gift. Now and again, I'd pull it out, turn it over, admire it, enjoy pride in owning it. Who else could claim such a thing? I couldn't remember my own circus fire story, so I would tell my father's. I'd reveal it to friends late at night after too many shots of tequila made my tongue dry and loose. I shared the story with women in hopes that my escape from the tent combined with my father's dangerous history would impress them. Oftentimes, it did.

But there was one woman who asked, "If the gun was civilian issue, where did he get it?" I couldn't say. He never kept guns in the house. She peppered her salad, said, "I'm surprised he wasn't hurt. You'd think the elephant would have gone crazy and him standing right next to it. It might have trampled him or grabbed him with its trunk and smashed him against the ground."

"Maybe it couldn't see him," I said. We both shrugged. She asked, "When he went to have his uniform cleaned, wouldn't someone have asked how he got all that blood on it?" and "Aren't you angry that he left you in the hospital bed for three days?" She was a persistent, questioning woman who challenged everything and accepted nothing, and maybe that's why we're no longer together. But her questions made me wonder about the story my father told me on that brittle afternoon in Gray's Tavern. I believed him, but I doubted his story.

In the basement of the Connecticut State Library, there are thousands of documents that tell the story of the circus fire. Letters, photographs, government reports on onion-skin paper copied with carbon. I spent days there turning fragile page after fragile page. I suffered headaches and nausea from spinning microfilm. My father's story had brought me into the library, but I let myself lose him in the larger history of the fire. This was as close as I had ever come to knowing the world in which I burned and later became patched together by skin grafts. In the end, though, even what the library held was not enough. It was cold and lacked life. So I turned back to my father's story, which felt closer to my own truth than any government record.

I learned that the circus did remain in Hartford with its elephants—but it rolled out of town on the railroad ten days after the fire. If it is true that my father left Italy more than a week after reading the news, traveled across an ocean, then spent two days in Hartford before visiting the circus grounds, how could he have made it in time to see the elephants? Perhaps my memory is faulty, or his was, and he left Italy earlier than he remembered. But I never found an account in any newspaper of an elephant being shot. Nor could I find any such report in police records.

I asked my mother once. It was a slushy winter day, and we sat in the living room drinking tea and eating kryszczyki—a fried confection powdered with sugar. "To remind us how beautiful is snow," Mama said. She had retired from cleaning houses, but Papa still worked, and he was at the factory that day. I asked about the circus elephant. She smiled as if pleased and surprised. "No, of course not," she said. When I told her the story, she laughed. "What magic! I wish he had told me."

Now I wonder about everything. Or, more accurately, I work to decide which parts of Papa's story are true. Because some of it is. I add to the story, and I subtract. Some days, I believe he lied to distract from his failing: the three days he let us linger. On more generous days, I put him at the circus grounds, weeping beneath a shade tree because all he sees is an empty field, and how could a tired meadow have caused his family such pain? Some days, I set him in Italy, and I put a bloodied brick in his hand. Other days, I bury the fascist in a grave, and I imagine a hole in his skull, opposite the eye socket.

My parents came together in the age of marriage and not in the age of divorce, and so they lived. I believe she came to love him—I saw hand-holding and gentle smiles as they aged—though how they survived those years before I don't know. I think she never wanted to love a simple man, and he knew that. Perhaps in telling me his story, he tried on the cloak of mystery and found it didn't fit, even if it was true. But he was patient, and when my mother's love eventually embraced him, it was not a love of bodies or of mystery. It's naive to think my telling the elephant story made any difference to my mother. It seems more likely that her love grew from need and proximity and time's slow unfolding.

My mother died a little over a year ago. She slipped on ice outside DiPietro's Market and broke her hip. Despite the shattered bone, or maybe because of it, she met each morning with new joy and vigor, yet she lasted only a few happy weeks. That last burst of vivacity reminded my father of the teenager he'd married, and he missed her even more. His depression was acute, and because he was already crippled by the emphysema I had no choice but to move him into a nursing home. I wanted him to move to North Carolina, where I then lived (a woman, a job), but he wouldn't leave Connecticut. "Whose games will I get?" he asked me. "The Braves? That's the National League!"

A mediplex in Rocky Hill was as sane a place as I could find in Greater Hartford, but pastel prints of flowers and a jukebox in the game room couldn't disguise the small unbearable ways in which residents conceded their lives. Because of broken vertebrae, Papa's roommate shrieked with every simple shift in his bed. A woman in a wheelchair stopped most afternoons at the door of their room to curse my father and accuse him of adultery. And the Yankees seemed to lose every day.

He called me one summer evening in North Carolina to ask that

I come home. I had not seen him for three months. He could barely summon breath enough to speak. In words interrupted by coughing fits, he told me to fly to Connecticut right away. He told me he wouldn't last past the next night.

But the doctors had said Papa would live another few months at least. And I already had a plane ticket that would bring me home in a week and a half.

"You're not dying yet," I said. "I'll be there in nine days."

"Too late," he said. "Too late."

I told him I couldn't arrange for the time off. I insisted that he wasn't dying the next day. I told him it would cost too much to reschedule the plane ticket.

Those excuses hung on the line.

"All right," he said, and he coughed awhile.

"Good night," he said.

Then he hung up.

Here is the real reason I did not go home when he called me.

I was afraid.

I did not want to see my father deformed and grotesque among all those others who were deformed and grotesque. I did not want to see him, bloated from the steroids, wheezing through an oxygen mask, the purple capillaries in his face mapping age and pain. I was afraid to see him as a body on the verge. I was afraid to see him when he was not my father. I would visit in nine days. It would take that long to muster the courage.

The sins of the father become the sins of the son. Papa did die the next day. He did die. Just like he said he would. In a fluorescent-bright room, with a pitcher for his urine on the stainless steel tray beside his bed, my father tried to suck life into his lungs and life refused him. At the moment of his death, I was driving along a beach in North Carolina, replaying in my head the latest argument with my boss, taking for granted the pretty girls stepping out of the ocean.

Papa was buried beside Mama at St. Joseph Cemetery. Rain threatened, but never fell. The reception was held at Gray's Tavern. Eddie Gray has retired to Florida and he won't fly so he missed it, but his nephew Tom opened the doors. It's the same bar in a lot of ways, except now there's a television with cable mounted on the wall over where Jimmy Williams used to sit. Tom Gray likes the financial news, and he left the TV on with the volume muted during the reception.

Some of the workers from the mediplex came, and a few old men who said they knew my father. I recognized some names, but except for Father Harvey, I received condolences from a group of strangers. When the older ones finished shaking my hand, they retreated, backs bent, to other tables. They whispered then, and I overheard as they recalled my father's ailments and then the ailments of others—bleeding ulcers, ruptured spleens, tumors in the testicles.

I wish I could say that my sorrow got the better of me that afternoon and that in a rage against how the world is not supposed to be, I smashed the face of a drunk with a brick, or that I shot a bullet through that television screen. I did neither. Instead, I listened to the old men talk of prostates and bile, their voices sounding distant almost to absence, and I wondered about my father in the mediplex that day when he hung up the phone and let his head fall to the pillow, knowing that I had refused him and that he would die alone. Did he trust that this end was just? I worry that he did. The sins of the sons too often punish.

It was a short afternoon. Toward the end, two laughing young women walked in, their skin tanned, hair bleached and voices aged by cigarettes. They shouted out drink orders before Tom Gray could let them know they'd stumbled into a funeral reception. Then each of them hugged me and told me how sorry they were, and they asked about my father. I told them he had been a poor logger in Poland and a Polack factory worker in America. I would have told them more, but the shorter one squeezed my hand with hers, and the blonder one stood and wished me well. They left me there, at my very small table, and finished their drinks at the bar, now leaning away from each other, now leaning near, whispering, their quiet laughter cutting through the cigarette smoke that swirled high and silver in the tavern's dull light. I wanted them to stay, to laugh louder, and when I noticed the shorter one set down her empty glass and stub out the butt of her cigarette, I signaled Tom to bring them another round on me.

Peter Ho Davies

King of Fruits

A mother leads her son down a dirt track. He drags a large rattan basket, bumping along behind, until she takes it from him and carries it on her back. The boy runs ahead and snaps off stems of lalang grass, almost as tall as himself. He stops to peel back the flesh of the grass at the tip, then pulls down sharply and the spine flies ahead of him like an arrow. "Look," he calls to his mother, running to break off another stem. She follows him slowly, smiling. They are on their way to collect durian, his father's favorite fruit.

"Why do we have to go so far?" the boy says a little later and his mother tells him the best trees are a long way from their village.

"Why does Father like durian so much?"

"Because," she tells him mildly, "durian is the king of fruits."

The boy pulls a face. He hates the rich, strong-smelling fruit with its thorny hide and glutinous seed pods.

"You'll see," she says. "One day you'll like it."

"Never," he says. "I'll never like durian and I'll never leave home and I'll never get married." She laughs at him and he is happy to have pleased her.

Suddenly, he says, "Why did you marry Father?"

She tells him to hush. Her husband is a rubber tapper. Whenever he touches her, his hands are sticky with latex.

"When I'm big I'm going to plant my own durian tree," the boy says quickly. "Right in the garden. So you won't have to walk so far, Mother."

They walk on in silence after this. The boy embarrassed and his mother unable to speak for love. The sun is high overhead and the sky is white.

They walk for two miles and then she leads him off the track and through the grass, until they come out into a small clearing. The trees here are tall and thin, with gray trunks and small frail leaves that tremble in the breeze. She points out the dark green fruit, as big as a child's head, heavy and spiked. She warns him to run into the open if he hears a tearing in the branches above him. They begin to collect the fallen fruit, carrying them awkwardly away from their bodies, wary of the thorns, until they have a full load.

The boy stands by the basket and counts them slowly.

"How many does Father want?"

She tells him, "Ten."

She thinks of her husband kneeling over the fruit at dusk with his iron parang. The way he chops a blunt triangle out of its thick skin and pries it out, with a sharp ripping sound. He pushes a filthy thumb into the soft white flesh of the fruit and if it leaves a mark, he knows it's ripe. She holds the fruit she picks, one at a time, up to her nose, and hopes they're ripe. Her husband is skilled with a knife. He carves the spiral channel in the bark of the rubber trees to guide the sap into his collecting cup.

The boy pulls on one handle of the basket with both hands. He can raise it only slightly. When they start out, his mother takes one side and he the other and they walk home slowly, taking quick short steps, weaving a little under the weight.

"Tell me when you need a rest," the boy says, and a little later, "Are you tired yet?"

"Yes," she says, and they set the basket in the track. The boy moves a little way off and keeps his back to the basket. His mother watches him. The smooth brown skin of his arms and legs. The way the fine dark hair lies damp against his neck. When he sweats, she can smell him. It reminds her of when she used to hold him.

"All right," she calls after a few moments, and the boy comes back slowly. They walk a hundred steps and stop. They walk fifty and stop. Twenty. The boy counts out loud, panting, and his mother tells him how well he's doing. His feet scuff in the dust. After they have come one mile, she takes his hand and wraps a bright cotton handkerchief she carries around it. Her own hands she finds will not open fully.

They take another two hundred steps and the boy begins to cry softly. It is oddly peaceful. He dips his head to his shoulder and rubs the tears away. The basket rocks, and the mother says she needs a rest. The boy throws himself down and watches as she searches around in the basket. She takes out one of the fruit, cups her hand lightly over the sharp spines, puts her nose in the gap between thumb and first finger and inhales deeply. She sits and puts it by her feet in the road. She studies her feet for a moment. They are white with dust.

"I'll tell you a secret if you stop crying," she says.

"What secret?"

"How to grow good durian."

He rubs his eyes again.

"A good tree," she says, "must be neglected. You know what is 'neglected'?"

He nods.

"If you tend it, pull up weeds, give it water, it will only give you poor fruit. You have to treat it badly to make it bring forth its best. That way it has to try harder."

She gets to her feet and puts her hand on the basket and he joins her. They walk away from the fruit in the track without a word. The basket is a little easier and they go another hundred steps before they stop again.

"Some people even say you should cut your tree," the mother says. "Wrap it with wire. Make it suffer a little."

"Why?"

"So when the tree swells the wire digs into it. You make its own growth painful. Then it must put all its energy into its fruit."

"Do you think Father will let me hold the parang?" the boy says suddenly.

"I don't know," she says, and then because he wants it so much, "perhaps."

At the next stop, she takes out another fruit and rolls it into the grass by the path.

A line of ants has formed before it stops moving. By the time they are in sight of the village, there are six durian in the basket and she carries it on her back alone. No reason, she thinks, they should both suffer. The boy walks behind her and counts them aloud.

"Will Father be angry?"

She shakes her head slightly. Her neck aches from the weight on her back.

"I'm going to tell him how to grow a durian tree," the boy says. "Then when he eats these all up, we can plant the seeds. How long do you think it'll take to grow?"

"Your father knows already," she says impatiently. She feels a sudden sharp regret, as of clumsiness, for telling him this nonsense. She sees her husband in the distance, sitting on the steps of their home, in dirty shorts and singlet, smoking. The parang is stuck in the wood of the steps. He is waiting for them.

The boy is tugging at her. "How long?" he insists and she looks down at him and says, "A long time."

"Perhaps I'll like durian this time," he says. "Do you think so?"

She stops at that and leans to one side until the basket slides off her shoulder. She makes him take one handle and they walk the last two hundred yards with the fruit between them.

Heather Sellers

Water Safety

My mother and father were fighting in the dining room. This was the year we faced the Atlantic Ocean and all of Daytona Beach. The year we lived on the twenty-third floor, in a condo, Pleasure Towers. The building seemed to sway. I could see the ocean between them. I thought he was going to hit her.

"What do you want me to do? What do you want?" He held his drink in front of her face like a citation.

She marched through the sharp bright light in the dining room and braced herself on the glass table with her arms as if she was holding that plate of glass down, keeping it from slipping off. Sid and I went and sat under the silk sheflera. We were brought together as a family like this every afternoon. My father, an accountant, was not working. He'd been sent here to teach. It was summer. He hated his ex-students all day and went out all night. Sid and I were dizzy all the time. That condo was all one big room once you got out of the kitchen. I crawled past my yelling parents on my hands and knees, across the white shag, and folded myself in the credenza, which was nearly empty, because we were just staying here, we weren't really putting down roots. I sat there crunched up among other people's tablecloths, our boardgames, Battleship and Trouble. Sid was supposed to make sure I didn't get locked in. I opened the door to the exact right place. From this vantage point, I had a new view of my family's legs. My father's, bare, because he was in his usual outfit, black dress shoes, thin white socks, and his tight green bathing suit, a bikini. It seemed to me his legs were missing a lot of their hair. They were bare, skinny, and shiny, as if he were a woman, or diseased. The skin was pink and spotty, like a leopard shell.

My mother's legs were cricked up under her on the dining room chair, where she had collapsed mid-sentence.

"Buck, I cannot live this way. Can you even begin to imagine how I worry?"

"Jesus, Mary Carolyn."

She wore support hose because carrying us two kids inside her body for a total of eighteen months (that's almost two years) caused a serious problem with varicose veins and she could never again stand for long periods of time. Her legs were otherwise hidden in khaki workpants, wrinkled and thick. My mother hated being inside. She hated being stranded in the sky. She wanted to be back in our regular house. I think it was being foreclosed on, though. In the afternoon, when my father was home, they fought about equity, a concept I could not figure out for anything. What was it. Where was it. They weren't really great explainers, these parents.

I needed to be around dirt, my mother said. She would have liked a tractor and fields and hills to bicycle up and down when she was done planting trees. She maybe would like an orange soda late in the day, when she came in from the clear cut to check her sourdough's second rise. That was my mother.

Kelly the bird was on top of me, on the credenza. This was a condo bird. Happy to sit in one place, green bird on white cuttlebone. I could hear eating. I could imagine her little legs, those green scales, her knees bending backwards as she scratched her back.

Sid was on the floor and he was picking the scab on his knee, making it bleed. He had the pale yellow legs of a blue-eyed person, the skin translucent, and to me, a dark hairdo person with green-brown tan skin, Sid was creepy. He had white hairs sticking out of his legs. Some like baby hairs and more and more like goat hairs—thick, coarse wires. His legs were noodle-like and difficult to look at for a length of time. He had the scab off in a perfect sheet—I could just feel it between my own fingers like a little mat from Mars, a wonderful strange alive/dead thing to pick apart, taste, multiply, save, bury, plant, drop over the edge of the balcony. He had the scab off completely, and he was going around the edge with his mouth, that hard edge. And then the soft middle part would be free. We liked them, scabs.

"What was that woman doing here?" my mother said through her teeth. Her feet were planted hard in the white carpeting under the inch-thick dining room glass table. "What was she doing here? What was she doing in my house? My house," my mother said.

"Condo," Sid said.

"MC, you know damn well. You insist on making misery. You fucking insist!" He swatted the chandelier, and one of the teardrop crystals flew into the sliding glass doors. Kelly Green went nuts. I slammed my cupboard door shut and wished I had a pillow in with me, a bolster cushion from the sectional. The front door banged behind my dad.

When my dad told us he was leaving he put it like he'd just been month-to-month the whole time. "I'm giving you my notice," he said at five P.M. the next night. My mom and Sid and I were sitting at the table picking the shells off shrimp and slaking them through ketchup. Even my mom liked her shrimp that way.

Suddenly there he was, standing behind me, with a lit cigarette, and the dining room suddenly silvery with smoke. I scooted like a spider, out from under him because those ashes were headed for my bare shoulder. I sat at the head of the table, in his seat, right by the bowl of shrimp on their big mattress of ice cubes in my mom's mixing bowl. Now that we lived at the beach shrimp was just a regular dinner, not such a dressy dinner.

"What about the children, Buck. What about them? I can see why you hate me and that's fine, of course you hate me, but what about the children?" My mother kept peeling her shrimp. Now she had a village of them, naked, stranded, little pink hooks all along the edge of her plate. She wasn't eating anything. She wasn't moving her lips. Those words—*the children, the children*—just came out and hovered with the little white pink shrimpers and the pyramids of translucent shells. And then she toweled her hands, squirted the lemon on them, folded her fingers, her hands, folded her arms, and seemed to simply put herself away.

I started screaming.

My mother was turning to wax.

Sid said, "We don't need him anyway. He's never here." Sid had just popped a shrimp with its shell and tail on in his maw. He was crunching away, and I was so afraid. I was afraid the shrimp would come back to life and swim inside of him. I was afraid my dad was going to wallop him, I was afraid my father would want to marry me and take me with him because my housekeeping skills were so useful and polished, I was afraid I was going to throw up and never like shrimp again. My father was leaving us. I couldn't look at him.

"Go if you are going," I said softly.

"Everyone hates you," Sid said.

My dad started to go after Sid with his fist, but Sid was out on the balcony, through the open sliding glass doors, out of our Daytona Beach condo in about a half a second, over the edge, hanging there like a little monkey on the outside of the railing—I am not kidding. Twenty-three floors up. It wasn't the first time he'd done it, but it was the first time he'd done it real showy like this. And my mother started screaming, and I thought this was pretty scary, because it was Safety Week and we had learned so much, but nothing like this.

"You all hate me, you hate me," she kept saying without moving a single facial muscle. Then, she did move—she dug at her hair with her hands, pushed her poor hair into one big tall gray fan around her face. I was thinking Madame Tussaud's.

"Honey, come in, come in," she said to Sid. "Get some candy, Georgia," she said. She wouldn't step out there onto the balcony, into the wind.

I sat there getting nothing out of this. Sid was swinging twenty-three floors up, and my dad was glowering at my mother there with his gin and tonic, using the shrimp lemon to flavor it! His fingers were wet with shrimp juice—he'd just been standing there grazing—and he was ignoring Sid.

Sid did a little banshee screaming. He dropped himself from the balcony again, over the other side, his feet down into the Cooper-Pickett's on twenty-two, kicking their impatiens baskets, and hung on with just his hands. I tried to see if his knuckles were white. Behind him, the Camelot sign was flashing way up the beach, the hotels looked fake like in *Godzilla,* and the sky was wrecked with clouds.

My dad made himself another drink in the kitchen while Mother stood by the sliding glass doors, not going too close to Sid, who hung still like a monkey over the edge. Dangling.

"Mom, don't push him. Don't go out there," I said. "That's just what he wants you to do." I looked at Sid, who was only about four feet away, listening like a little demon child.

My dad stood there, stymied.

"You are not leaving me, mister. You are not leaving these children. You are not. I will not let you."

"I'll come in, Mom. When he goes." Sid faked like he was crawling back over the balcony and my mom made the sign of the cross and ran through the kitchen and grabbed the car keys off the counter and ran to the front door, and slammed it shut. I thought she was gone. But when I got to the hallway myself, there she was—with herself on the inside of the door, facing us.

Sid didn't come in, but I could tell he wanted to. I ran up to my mom, who was gripping her purse and keys in an unnatural way, and the whole time I was hoping my own brother would fall, so at least my parents would have to stay together for my sake, for the sake of the memory of the smushed Sid-man.

She plastered herself across the door like an X, and my dad threw his drink down on the carpeting and ripped her off. It was like she was wrapping paper. He just threw her down.

"You are going about this in the wrong way, MC."

"I'll wrong way you, mister," she said from the floor.

Then she grabbed her purse from behind the silk bougainvillea, where it was lodged, and she ran out. My dad went out into the hall where you were only supposed to use your whisper voices. He bellowed after her, "There's nothing you can do, MC, I am leaving this cracker factory once and for all!"

But she was the one leaving. She was like a football player running down the red carpet hall, running to the elevator, her purse tucked deep into her gut.

"You haven't seen anything yet, Mr. Let-me-tell-you." The elevator came and she flung herself in. "You don't know who you are dealing with, buster. If anything happens to these children."

My dad and I tentatively walked halfway down the hall. I wondered if Sid had come in yet. The bronze doors closed around her, and you could see my dad and me reflected all the way down that hall in those elevator doors, only we were tall and thin and wavering, not like real people at all.

"For pity's sake," Dad said. "All hell's broken loose and there's no reason for it to be like this."

I grabbed his leg, and cried and said *please please please please please.*

He kicked me. He actually kicked me with his shoe and left a black mark on my thigh. I couldn't believe it.

"Daddy," I was crying. I cried and cried and cried. I couldn't believe how our lives were turning out. I couldn't believe this was my family. I felt this enormous crushing sense. It was never going to be any different. It was never going to be any better. It was never going to be a good family. It was going in all directions, my family, like a man-o-war after you poured sugar on it in the sea. It was tearing itself apart and leaving me.

I hated Pleasure Towers and the beach, and I was the kind of person who loved the beach; when we used to come as kids I never threw up, ever. My dad pounded the wall. He smoked two cigarettes. I cried and cried and cried and I hadn't ever cried like that before. I could tell my face would be permanently altered after this cry. I wished people would come out of their condos and rescue me, intervene. No one did.

"You guys, come quick," Sid yelled. We could hear him way out in the hallway, the tomb-like hall of the Towers, and we ran back into the condo, over the thrown-down drink in the hallway, and into the dining room. He was on the balcony firmly anchored by a super-size bag of M&M's which were supposed to be for baking, not eating. He was just standing there, popping them in, staring down at the beach, like he was at the races.

"Look," he said.

He pointed down toward the beach, and right at the edge of the water was our aqua blue Plymouth, like a Tom Swift underwater search submarine, about to be launched. And that's what she was doing. She was driving it into the water. There were some flares on the beach behind her, I don't know where from. And our family's car was slowly driving in, into the Atlantic Ocean, my favorite body of water! And then it stopped in the sand that is soft right before the wave sand. My mother, she hopped out. Her ankles were in the breakers, her support hose would be getting really wet, carrying that water up her legs—it was too awful to imagine.

"For God's sake," my dad said. "You don't get an engine wet. Is she out of her mind?" He threw his cigarette over the edge. Sid watched it float down, and made bomb noises the whole way.

"Shhh," I said. I didn't want a lot of freak-out movement up here. I didn't think we should be distracting my mother. Pushing her over the edge.

She motioned the people clustering behind her on the beach to get back, get back, her white vinyl purse clutched like the space capsule she was taking to Atlantis the lost city, and she hopped back in, and hit the gas, because the Plymouth lurched and launched and went out into the water.

"Oh, Jesus Christ, she has to do everything the goddamn hardest way," my dad said. He wasn't going to be able to leave us though, you had to give my mom credit for that. What was he going to do, walk?

"Sid, get your ass off the railing, son." He slammed his drink down his throat. Now that Sid was inside the balcony, just flopped over it, my dad suddenly got parental. I wanted to say that, but I knew I'd get hit. Plus, I had the altered face from my big cry a few minutes ago, and it hurt to talk. Plus, my mother had just driven a car into the Atlantic Ocean, and I really didn't want to get sent to my room at this juncture.

People were down there watching our ocean-born Plymouth in greater numbers. Buffy, who lived on the thirteenth floor of our building, and Angie, the girl who was the daughter of the gate man, they were there. The dog walkers and the retired people were there. The car kept going out. Bobbing like a toy. I pretended the ocean was tiny.

"We should go help her out, man," Sid said. "It's a scene."

A man with white hair, a guy who looked like Santa, waded in after the car and waved his arms in the rescue-me-rescue-me SOS signal.

When the breakers hit, the car nosed up, and then down, pointing down, and it lost ground—that is, from our point of view. It came back towards shore a good two waves' worth. Everything was going to be okay, the car was moving back towards the beach, and the windows were down—she could get out. I knew she wouldn't leave her purse.

"She won't leave her purse," said Sid.

Sid was just peeling fronds off the palm on the balcony, my dad was drinking, and I was just crouched there, bars of the railing between my big toes and their neighbors, just sitting there like I was watching television.

"Could I have a sip of that?" Sid said to my dad. Now that Sid was fully planted inside the balcony, not hanging over, now I had the urge to push him over. This was my mode: When Sid was in danger, I wanted to rescue him. I wanted the wind to be perfectly still when he hung over the edge of the balcony and sat on the rail like that. I wouldn't even breathe. When he was on the Astroturf, begging my dad for a sip of his liquor, not even watching my mom in the Plymouth, I wanted to shove him off the twenty-third floor.

Really, I wanted Sid to be arrested and us visit him at Boys' Town. There would be organized activities, and I would visit so often I would become the Dean of Boys when I grew up, and kids everywhere would want to come to this place, to be in my command, and to be safe from their parents. I could learn to sew. Why did I have a brain like that? Who wanted to save their family and kill their family at the same time?

But when we were all scattered like this, I wanted us to be back like we were, although I couldn't remember what that would have been like.

Some of the men on the beach had waded in, but they stood way off leeward, out of the way and when they pointed, you couldn't tell if they were talking or not. You couldn't tell if they had a plan. And she was still in it, at least I think she was. Had she swum away? Had she somehow slipped into the water, and swum to the bottom of the sea? The light was getting shifty and blue, and I couldn't see my mother anymore. Was she lying down on the front seat? Two dogs had broken loose or had been set free and they were racing each other to the car. But the light was different, and everything was flat and unreal like a movie, though I had never actually seen a movie. And my mother would not be rescued because this was not an accident. It was on purpose.

Sid was now back to straddling the balcony, like it was a horse. My dad pretended to shove him.

"Jesus, Dad, kill me why don't you."

"Are we going down there? What are we going to do, Daddy?" I said. I tried not to sound whiny.

"Fuck her," he said. "We are going to fuck her."

With that the car turned sideways and lunged back towards us, back to the sand, the shore, the tiny miniature onlookers in their red and black and pink bathing suits; all cattywampus our family car hooked itself back onto the beach and rested on the sand sideways, listing.

The three of us stood on the balcony like the Swiss Family Robinson without the Swiss part, without the Robinson part. We were just up high. And we huddled by Sid, my dad's glass of vodka gleaming like a steady light, my hands around his waist. I pressed my stomach into his back so my guts wouldn't launch. And slowly, as the sea water turned pink all around the aqua blue Plymouth in the last little bit of sunset, she climbed out of the window on the driver's side and came back at us. People cheered and came up to her but she didn't look at them, and they slowly dropped off. She just kept walking toward us, her eyes purple with fire—you could almost see them. She marched over the dunes, ignoring the restraining fences. She stalked across the shuffleboard courts, and she headed toward Pleasure Towers. She walked fast. She was wet. She came back.

I watched from the balcony, my fingers in my mouth, chewing. It was that taste again, the taste of blood, and my throat tightened and I leaned over the edge. This was my only weakness that I knew of.

Nancy Reisman

No Place More Beautiful

Sophie rises in darkness; twelve, her body pale curves, she rises only to fall. She's shaking, her mother is gone—four months dead—the rest of us are just kids. It's night in a cabin in Northern Ontario. We don't know what to do when she falls and starts shaking like that, her honey-colored hair in tangles, her face white.

Sophie's quilt slips off her bed and as the rest of us notice her silence, one by one we hush. Someone snaps on the lights and calls for the Night Watch counselor; someone else runs down the path to get the doctor, an unnaturally skinny man with blinking eyes and black-framed glasses. He's awkward, too clumsy to be a real doctor, nonetheless we trust him. We wait, silent, for him to stop Sophie's shaking. What he does is ready a hypodermic. He asks the counselor to make sure Sophie is as still as possible—hard for anyone to do, Sophie's like a dog hauled out of North Bay: chilled muscles, chilled lungs, chilled blue map of veins. We watch from our bunks while he gives her the injection. Our counselor kills the lights and stays there, holding Sophie's hand until she knows Sophie's asleep and she's convinced the rest of us are calm. After an hour, the counselor leaves. She'll be back—the doctor told her to keep checking on Sophie—but for now she's on the back steps smoking a cigarette. The cabin is full of sleep breathing, and I whisper to the dark air. *Anyone awake?* No one answers. I slip out of bed, over to Sophie's bunk. She's a small head poking out from a pile of blankets. Perfectly still, lips slightly parted. Sleeping like an ordinary person.

The next day Sophie is excused from all activities, but in the afternoon she and I take showers and sit by the lake and let our hair dry in the breeze. Sophie perched on a rock: small hands, small feet, toes short, almost stubby, but lovely, pink and white, everything about her petite and curvy, everything except the paralyzing grief, the repeating, stricken nights when the world vanishes to her. Then she's untouchable, even though I want to touch her. In daylight I bring her to the best places I know: the rock jutting from the eastern bank of the lake, a clearing in the birches on the far shore, the fringes of the playing fields, thick with raspberries. At night I bring cool washcloths for her forehead. Watch her.

The watchfulness lasts a couple of years, consecutive summers. Her sadness is a limb, an arm she leans on when she compares clothes with the other girls in the cabin. When they brag about sex, no one pressures her to talk. They can feel the sadness like a radiating wave: she is luminous in all her grief. The boys treat her gingerly, the girls pet her hair and offer to stand watch for her when she smokes cigarettes. I share my candy bars with her and lend her my books. I don't have clothes to swap, as mine are ordinary, T-shirts and sweatshirts, not the silky stuff the Toronto girls bring. She doesn't care, she tells me. Before she falls asleep at night, we read books by flashlight on her bed. I stay there until I hear the Night

Watch walking up the path. Once or twice Sophie says "Becca. Stay," and I do. The Night Watch counselor nudges me and points to my empty bunk. *After Sophie falls asleep.*

Most of the year we write letters. My mother buys me air mail stamps: Sophie lives in London, Ontario with her father and her wild older sister, Debbie, the one who painted her own name in huge red letters up on the rafters of three different cabins, the one who was kicked out of camp after a compromising incident behind the woodshop. Debbie and a visiting tennis pro, naked in the storage shed. Or so went the rumor. Sophie and wild Debbie and their businessman father huddle and fight in an oversized house, for a while anyway, until their father remarries a woman with two little girls. Sophie describes the wedding in neat cursive, on stationery with butterflies.

~

My mother reaches through the mess on the kitchen counter—egg shells, vanilla, brown sugar, cellophane bags of chocolate chips—scoops up a fingerful of cookie dough and eats it.

"You're wrecking my diet," she says, happy. She licks her index finger.

I'm baking a double batch. "Raisins?"

"Mmm, yes. In half?"

My brother Richie won't eat raisins. "Right," I say, and dump half the dough into another bowl.

I'm greasing cookie sheets when the phone rings. My mother picks up, her voice bright: *Hi, sweetheart!* My sister Laura, calling from college in Wisconsin. But the cheeriness drains away almost immediately. My mother hunches over the phone, curling the cord around her waist. I drop chunks of dough onto the first sheet and pretend not to notice her tightening jawline, her fingers pressed against her lips. Finally she says, “Honey, have you been drinking?” and there’s a burst of sound on the other end of the line, loud static: yelling.

My mother pulls her cardigan tighter across her belly, fills her hands with blue wool. “I see,” she says. “Umm Hmm . . . I’m sorry you feel that way.”

On the message board she scribbles a note, big letters. Points at me. *Get Your Father.*

Other phone calls follow, most of them muffled—behind the closed door of my parents’ bedroom, from my father’s study. Every time my parents emerge from the study, my mother seems smaller, more condensed, shellacked with worry. Her lipstick wears off. My father pats my head, calling me Rebecca instead of B.; he tells me he loves me and wanders away, only to repeat himself an hour later. I bake sheet after sheet of cookie dough and the house fills with a sweet, buttery smell. When I knock on the study door with a plate of cookies, my parents, both of them pale, begin speaking to each other in a code of prepositions and hand gestures, punctuated by the word *Madison.* In regular English they mention airline tickets, but won’t say more.

“I’m not stupid,” I say. I’m fourteen.

“We know,” they tell me. “Do you want pizza for dinner? Ask your brother if he wants wings instead.”

My brother and his three best friends are immersed in APBA baseball, their own imaginary league. I bring them cookies without raisins. “Pizza or wings?” I say.

Richie shushes me. He’s recording third-inning statistics. “What?”

"Pizza or wings?"

He closes his eyes and rubs his lips together. "Pizza."

By dinner time, my father has left for Wisconsin. The next morning, a woman named Etty shows up at the house in a cream-colored Oldsmobile. She's wide and copper brown, and the frames of her glasses sparkle along the top. My mother gives her a long list of instructions, tells my brother and me to behave, then drives off to the airport. Etty lights an unfiltered Camel and suggests we go out for brunch.

They've gone to help your sister Laura, Etty says in her Oldsmobile, in the Your Host parking lot, in the blue naugahyde booth. In the convenience store, where she buys more Camels, chocolate bars, lemon drops: *They're in Madison with Laura. You like Milky Way?* In the living room, during commercials in the Buffalo Sabres/Detroit Red Wings game: *They'll call us later.* Only after I ask eight times does Etty let the word 'hospital' slip: *They'll call after hospital hours.* This narrows the field. Laura's an artist, a bohemian. I suspect she's done something artistic and bohemian, like gotten herself pregnant.

"Watch this replay," Richie says.

"Mmmhmm," Etty says, "those boys can skate."

My two closest and only friends from school, Jessie and Abby, speculate about drugs. *Bad microdot?* Abby says. This is her usual response to mysterious hospitalizations: she's already experimented her way into an emergency room and had her stomach pumped. Jessie, who is obsessed with mysticism and poetry, asks if I've read Carlos Castaneda. She suggests I write about my feelings.

That night, and every night all week, my parents call. Laura is going through an emotional time, they say. They use the words 'stress' and 'exhaustion.' I'll be able to talk to her soon, my mother promises. Be patient, my father says. Don't forget to go to school.

Meanwhile, Richie and I make a string of cards for Laura, his with drawings of dolphins and talking fish, mine collaged from magazines. I send a letter to Sophie, whom I haven't seen for six months, and at the end of the week, Sophie calls long distance and invites me to London. I picture our lake, Sophie on the rock.

"Ontario?" my distracted parents say. "Good idea, sweetheart."

Etty makes me pack extra sweaters, counts out eighty dollars from the stash my parents have left, and fills a paper bag with Swiss cheese sandwiches, oranges, and Almond Joy bars for the trip.

Southern Ontario spins by beyond the dirty bus window—an hour to go before the train station and my connection to London. I work over the Laura clues: *Stress. Exhaustion.* Fainting spells. Anemia, I think. *Emotional time.* Hysteria. Sedatives. I start another card, this one store-bought and pink, covered with roses, "Get Well Soon" in elegant script. The bus jiggles and lurches, my handwriting alternately lumping up and skidding like cartoon volts. I draw stick-like daisies around the roses, a stick figure version of myself in high-top sneakers, a dialogue bubble surrounding "Get Well Soon." The bus makes a stop. I write knock knock jokes in the card's corners. A broad man-boy in a lumber jacket appears, enormous, and drops his cap on the seat next to me.

"Okay if I sit here? Nice card," he says, and eyes my drawing. His body bulges over the edges of his seat, onto mine. The bus starts back on the road. "Someone sick?" he says. I nod. He comments on the passing scenery, tells me he lives in Peterborough, asks me where I'm going. "London, is that right? I'm going there too." He knows the area like the back of his hand, he tells me. His hands are sausagy and rough and after a while he picks up one of my hands in his.

"What are you doing?" I say.

"Can I hold your hand for a little while?" he says. "You don't mind if I hold your hand, do you?"

I don't answer. But he touches my palm anyway, says my hands are little and soft, so nice, such soft little hands. I turn my head and gaze out the window; when he pauses for a moment I pull my hand away, pretending to sweep hair out of my eyes. Then I keep my hand hidden away from him.

"Don't you want to talk to me anymore?" he says. "I thought you liked me."

"I just want to look out the window."

"Listen," he says, "don't waste your money on the train." He's going to hitch from the train station, he tells me, it's much cheaper. I should hitch with him. "I'll get you where you need to go," he says, "I'll get you there fine." After all, he's a standup guy. There's nothing to worry about, not a thing.

"I already have my ticket," I say. Lying, which Laura would call "bad karma."

"You could cash it in."

I pull my down jacket tighter around me and stare at the chipped yellow road lines. Finally he gives up. When the bus stops, he lets me get off ahead of him, and I run to the Canadian Railway information booth. For a few minutes he stands on the bus platform, watching me, his army duffle as thick-bodied as he is. I move on to buy my ticket and when I glance back, he's melted off into the crowd.

At London, I step off the train into a jumble of bobbing hats and fat winter coats. Sophie is not Sophie. No jeans, no blue sweatshirt, no pensive gaze. Instead: a rabbit fur jacket, wool pants, a lilac silk blouse. She's layered her hair; gold jewelry hangs off her ears and neck and wrists. Lipstick, bubblegum-pink, nail polish to match. Lilac eyeshadow beneath brows as thin as spaghetti. She touches my arm, leans in and kisses me on the right cheek. Then a woman's hand, gloved, reaches toward me from a mink coat: puffy frosted hair, sunglasses, white skin, ginger-colored lips.

"My mom," Sophie says. I picture graveyards, decomposing bodies, the frog I'm dissecting in Biology. A few seconds pass, Sophie smiling her candied smile, Sophie's stepmother holding out her gloved hand. I drop my suitcase and shake the soft leather.

"Mrs. Steinhart," Sophie's stepmother says.

Light beads off her sunglasses; her pencilled eyebrows seem to melt. "Nice to meet you," I say.

As we pick our way over the ice in the parking lot, they make consoling remarks about Laura—*verry sore-y*—and cautiously ask if I'm still a vegetarian. Last year, Laura convinced me that cows have souls and tomatoes do not.

"I hope you don't mind us roasting chicken," Mrs. Steinhart says.

"No," I mumble. "Of course not."

Sophie ruffles her bangs with her free hand. "I told her you'll eat fish."

"Fish. Right," I say.

"We'll make salmon patties," Mrs. Steinhart says.

We pull into the U-shaped drive of an enormous columned house and unload my suitcase from the Mercedes, which Mrs. Steinhart leaves running. She has more parental errands: groceries to buy, daughters to pick up from gymnastics. After she drops us off, I plop down on a loveseat in the high-ceilinged front hall, waiting for

Sophie to revert to herself. She opens a compact and offers me her hairbrush.

"She seems nice," I say, waving at the empty driveway. "What's her first name?"

Sophie runs pink lipstick over her bottom lip. "Helen."

"Is that what you call her?"

A sugary comic-book pout. "Let me show you the house."

I can't keep track of the rooms. Downstairs, they are all silver-blue—carpets, upholstery, wallpaper—trimmed with mirrors, blue-curtained windows, photos of Sophie and her stepsisters. Upstairs is easier: the colors frequently change. Pale yellow, creamy orange, light pink. It's like walking through bowls of sherbet. I count six bedrooms, four baths, a living room, a dining room, a family room, a recreation room, a study, a summer porch. In her bedroom, Sophie shows off the canopy bed, the extra twin bed where I'll sleep, the makeup she's acquired: nailpolish bottles, a paintbox of eyeshadow. She opens her own closet full of clothes, as nice or nicer than what she's wearing: more tailored pants, more silk blouses, knit dresses, lambswool cardigans, corduroy skirts. She fingers garment after garment, so obviously pleased I can't help but feel depressed.

My own clothes—blue jeans faded at the knees, cable knit fisherman's sweater—have turned against me. In every mirror I look lumpy and oafish.

Sophie holds a pale yellow sweater-dress in front of me and touches my arm. "You can borrow anything you want," she says. "Anything."

"I brought American cigarettes," I say. "Is there someplace we can smoke?"

Outside, I feel better. Snow has been cleared from most of the sidewalks, but the roofs and lawns are still white, the larger trees a mix of white and gray. The wind has died down and the cloud cover has thinned, patches of blue opening up to the west. We walk for blocks, and the houses become newer, the trees smaller. As Sophie navigates the streets, she waves in the directions of her school, downtown London, the train station, Toronto, Windsor, camp. Sophie can be like that, I remember, *she likes geography.* But then she switches to describing her London friends. Shauna, who Sophie keeps saying is 'fantastic,' and a brazen girl named Dina, and a guy named Perry, who is in grade twelve, gorgeous and hilarious and very rich. His father owns hotels. She waves in the direction of one of the hotels Perry's father owns.

"There's a Bar tomorrow night," Sophie tells me, "with a big reception." She means Bar Mitzvah. "Shauna's brother. We'll go to the party. You can meet everyone."

"Fantastic," I say.

We slow when we reach a street of new homes and empty lots. Fields of straw grass and graying snow spread to the west. Behind a house under construction, we smoke cigarettes and eat mints.

"About your sister," Sophie says. "Have they told you what's wrong?"

I kick at a patch of dirty ice. "My dad says to be patient," I say.

Sophie's mouth puckers into a pink scowl and she drops her cigarette butt into the snow. Then she offers me another mint.

Without her mink, Mrs. Steinhart seems much smaller and more ordinary looking; without her sunglasses, more worried. She bastes the chicken and murmurs to Art Garfunkel's breathy love songs, while the little girls cartwheel around their play room. The relief I feel in the presence of competent mothers begins to take hold. Sophie and I set the table for six, while Helen washes the salad greens, scores and slices a cucumber. At seven we hear the garage door close, and Mr. Steinhart pops into the house, sighing and round—round-headed, round-bodied in his suit, eyebrows one thick line across his forehead. He kisses Mrs. Steinhart in an automatic way and, for reasons I can't name, my relief vanishes.

Mr. Steinhart nods to me, "Hello, Rebecca," pours a gin and tonic, pinches Sophie's cheek. His peppery scent mixes with the odor of damp wool and lunchmeat, and he stands close enough that I see a tiny razor nick beneath his jaw. "Buffalo," he says, "What shul do you belong to? What kind of Jewish? Rebecca a family name? How long have you known Sophie?"

I answer, say all the polite things I can think of, and ask after Sophie's grandmother and sister Debbie. Too late, Sophie makes a cutting gesture across her neck.

"Debra's at boarding school," her father says, his tone sharp. He raises his eyebrow.

"That's nice," I say.

"You think so?"

Mrs. Steinhart clears her throat and sets a tray of crackers and pâté on the table. "Becca said her sister will be in the hospital for a while."

"Yes, I'm sorry," Sophie's father says. "What did you say it was?"

"I don't know."

"What?"

"Well, no one's sure."

"They must have some idea."

Sophie frowns at me.

"It's probably pneumonia," I say. "With complications."

"Ah," he shakes his head. "Bad business." Then he turns away from all of us, and calls in the direction of the playroom. "Where are my girls?"

"Here," the little girls yell in squeaky voices. "Here." They rush at him, still in their pink and purple leotards, their hair in ribboned braids. He sits in a wide-armed kitchen chair and they climb onto his lap.

Later, while I brush my teeth and Sophie washes her face with Noxema, Sophie tells me, "It's a girl's school. Strict." She shrugs and caps the blue jar. "Debbie likes to party. She got caught."

In high school, Laura was a walking party. My parents discovered a fraction of her transgressions: smoking, drinking beer while babysitting Richie, using Mom's Mastercharge to buy albums, taking the station wagon without permission, visiting a heartthrob dope dealer at Attica State Penitentiary (station wagon, no permission), visiting an unnamed friend at 3:30 A.M. (Dad's car, no permission), smelling like pot, smelling like sex. This led only to shouting, slammed doors, and weeks of Laura moping in her bedroom.

So far, I've been caught cutting class, twice.

Sophie falls asleep quickly, one arm flung over her head. No novel-reading, no conversation. Her breath comes slow and even, and the air smells of vanilla lotion. I listen to the kick and wheeze of the furnace. Beyond that sound, nothing. As if no one else exists: not the Steinharts, not my family. I close my eyes and try to synchronize my breathing with Sophie's, which is too slow. I hold my breath, exhale, inhale slowly, hold it again, and suddenly I'm pinned down, miles from air and light, crazy white spirals racing under my closed lids and back through my temples. I open my eyes, the spirals swimming in the room now, between the dark hulks that once were the bureau and desk, the bookcase, the canopy bed, Sophie. The spirals spawn more spirals, elongated, serpentine, too close, as my breath speeds up to a shallow, spastic huffing. *Hysteria. Hospitals.* Spirals swallowing flecks of light, careening past the bed. *Fourteen years old. Nearly fifteen. Stop it.* Finally I stand, shuffle across the room to the door, the hallway dotted with night-lights for the little girls, the bathroom with its Bambi-faced night-light. I flip the wall switch. The spirals vanish.

Back in Sophie's room, I drift off and wake in time to watch the dawn shift the air in the room from black to gray. My heart beats in my throat. I believe that 'exhaustion' is code for 'nervous breakdown.' Eventually, Sophie sits up and stretches, pink nightgown the color of the dustruffles. "I wish we were up North," I say.

"Buried? You know what it's like there now? The snow started in October, maybe even September. No one lives there now."

"There's a town," I say. "Haliburton." A little town, with a diner and a grocery, a post office, a laundromat. A hockey camp. Small houses tucked into the woods. Beyond the woods, lakes and more lakes, more woods—maples, birches, pines. Dirt roads winding off to other lakes. Here and there, gas stations that sell coffee and cigarettes and Cadbury toffee.

"Well. Those people."

Then the lakes and woods evaporate; I picture instead a rutted parking lot, a greasy shack, tables of heavy-set boy-men, their fingers shaped like sausages.

Before breakfast, I dial Wisconsin. *I feel exhausted too,* I plan to tell my parents. *Maybe you should bring Laura back. Home. Now.* I promise myself I'll say yes to whatever they want. Yes, I'll leave school and move to your hotel in Wisconsin. Yes, I'll bring Richie. Yes, I'll babysit. But already they've left their room. I ask the desk clerk to tell them "Hi."

I drink orange juice, wash my hair with Sophie's strawberry shampoo, rub her vanilla lotion on my skin. I wrap myself in thick towels and walk barefoot over her bedroom carpet, calm, the day off-white and glassy, as if the light is laced with codeine.

At her desk, Sophie rubs the color from her fingernails with toxic smelling cottonballs. I dress in blue jeans and a white turtleneck; she sizes me up and drops the cottonballs. From the closet, she pulls out a pale green lambswool cardigan. "Wear this."

"Okay," I say. Okay to Cherry lipstick, okay to matching nails. Okay to modeling Debbie's clothes, all of them—the dozens of dresses and skirts she hasn't taken to boarding school, her shoes—heels, platforms, leather boots. Sophie picks out a black, V-neck cashmere dress for me to wear to the Bar Mitzvah reception. In the afternoon, we go to the mall; I spend most of my money on a pair of black suede pumps to match Debbie's dress. In Eaton's, Sophie lifts a bottle of Love's Baby Soft cologne. *Bad karma.* We spray it on in the Volvo's back seat. By the time we leave for the Bar Mitzvah reception, I am Sophie's twin, training my attention on hair gel, lip liner, and earrings.

It's like meditation, I tell myself. Be a Ming vase.

In the hotel ballroom, I take the rum and Coke Sophie hands me and drink it too fast. We wander between the tables of plastic-looking fruit and tables of gigantic desserts. The thirteen year olds disco in the far lounge; the adults foxtrot in the ballroom. Shauna—an auburn-haired girl with perfect teeth—hugs Sophie and kisses her on both cheeks, leaving lipstick marks. "Isn't it fantastic?" she says, waving at the tables of flowers and food. She mentions Perry—at table nine, his uncle boring him stupid—then falls into a spasm of gossip about several people I've never heard of. She whispers dramatically and ignores me. A photographer snaps several shots in our direction, and white balls of light begin to blotch Shauna's face and rain on the buffet table.

"Becca brought American cigarettes," Sophie says, and I become visible again.

"Becca, you're going to love this," Shauna says. "Let's introduce you around."

In a dim bathroom two floors up, I hand out cigarettes to girls named Rhonda and Sandy and Jodi, Sarah, Lisa, Dina—Sophie's Dina, the one she called brazen. From what I can tell, this means showing cleavage and knowing how to blow smoke rings.

After my second drink, Shauna's friends become pink-faced insects. We're in the ballroom eating strawberries. They use the word *schvartze.* They joke about the insanity of dating Catholics. *Pure craziness. And why would you want to?* I think of the white spirals and of beautiful Eddie Santora, a sophomore I've fantasized about.

Sophie catches me frowning. "Oh Becca, it's not the States here, it's different for us."

I nod, but I'm queasy: Sophie's giddy, she likes these girls, she's dropped into relentless, idiotic happiness. I want the old Sophie, the tragic one, the one who remembers her mother is dead. This, I realize, makes me a pervert.

"You're worried about your sister, aren't you?" Sophie says, and the queasiness spreads.

"She'll be okay," I say. "Let me get us some refills." I head off to the bar with the least vigilant bartender, away from Shauna and Sophie, into a swarm of laughing adults.

When Laura was in junior high, she'd climb the oaks in our cousin's backyard, hang from her knees and swing like a pendulum—face red, hair a brown-black horsetail whipping four feet off the ground. Summer cook-outs, Halloween parties: Laura in the trees. The last time, she wore a smock top and jeans, and when she hung from her knees, the smock bunched up at her neck, exposing her stomach and white cotton training bra. In magic marker, she'd drawn rainbows over her belly, all the way up to the bra. You could see green and blue lines under the cotton, red bulls-eye nipples. Laura played deaf when Mom ordered her to get down. The swinging and the ordering went on for twenty minutes, until my aunt threatened Laura with the garden hose.

If Laura were here, we'd escape together.

When I return from the bar, a guy in a gray Italian suit is spinning Sophie across the kids' dance floor. Olive-skinned, stocky, handsome despite the extra weight. Perry. They jitterbug until Sophie's face flushes red and thick strands of hair cling to her skin. When they move off the dance floor, he palms an ice-cube and rubs it on the back of her neck. It occurs to me that he won't be easy to get rid of. In fact, he's invited Sophie and Shauna for a ride in his mother's car. The three of them round up a boy named Leon, big-chested Dina, and me. I finish my rum and Coke in the elevator to the parking ramp. A momentary blast of cold air gives way to the leather-lined interior of a BMW.

Through downtown London, Sophie's snug against Perry, Shauna beside her, the three of them waving Tiparillos and mouthing inaudible jokes. Perry drives fast and smooth, tobacco smoke rising in fat rings, his shoulders bobbing to the too-loud Earth, Wind, & Fire cassette. Cold air streams from the windows back to Dina and Leon and me. Dina uncaps a bottle of apricot brandy; I hand out more Marlboros. We pass through the night-dark business district, the neon and flash of restaurants and bars further on, the music loud enough to prevent conversation. We're heading to a park they all know, and after we've passed the densest city traffic, Leon pulls a small wooden pipe and a film container out of his pocket. Hash.

The lead singer's high tenor weaves through the steady, pounding beat of *September.* "I love this," Dina says, rocking up against me. A swatch of Sophie's hair falls over the seat, sways against the black leather. Leon passes the pipe to me, holds the lighter over the bowl while I inhale a light sweet stream of smoke. My body seems to fill with feathers. Dina takes the pipe, inhales, still rocking, and starts singing along to the tape. Her eyes close. Sophie's voice mixes in, and then I feel a lifting, the silky speed of the car, my skin tingling. We begin to move through neighborhoods, the black night softened by snowclouds, snow on the ground, fuzzy rays of light from houses. Everything becomes slinky—Debbie's cashmere dress, the car, Dina's husky voice, Sophie's soprano, Perry's hand slipping over Sophie's neck. Leon lights another bowl, and Dina skips a chorus to ask Perry to stop for fast food. I watch the sunroof: streaks of white and yellow light, beyond them the quilted sky. The houses in this neighborhood seem as large as Sophie's—perhaps it *is* her neighborhood—but I don't recognize anything, not a street name or an intersection. Most of the houses are dark inside, as if they are empty, abandoned, as if the owners have vanished on yet darker streets, their bodies dissolving into particles of static. Above the sunroof, white spirals appear, puncturing space, circling a cartwheeling stick figure girl, her lines splitting off as she tumbles—an arm spinning away, a leg. White lines, yellow lines, chipped highway paint, the pink card for Laura, the man pawing my hand on the bus, tracts of weeds smashing into half-built houses. *Get Well Soon.* Dina elbows me and offers the apricot brandy, its wafting smell sickeningly sweet. I shake my head.

"What do you see?" she says, waving toward the window.

There's nothing out there, I want to tell her, *Do you realize?*

"I don't know," I say, and lean back into the window, the sense of death thickening, the fear that something catastrophic is happening, then the sudden conviction of it. That yelling on the phone: hysteria before the shaking sets in. An overdose. A brain tumor. Laura shrouded, propped in a wheel chair, her head a white turban; Laura on some other abandoned street, dead animals in the trees, a scattering of ice, and my parents pacing the blank corridors of a hotel then shrinking away, smaller and smaller, the city evaporating with them in it, the land beyond, until the States is nothing but sky, London, Ontario adrift in space.

"I have to go back," I say.

"Back?" Dina says.

Home. "The hotel."

Dina leans forward and whispers to Shauna, who turns down the music.

"Not *yet,*" Shauna calls over her shoulder. "We have an hour before anyone will start looking for us. Dina wants french fries."

The car speeds on, the windows pressing in, impenetrable; my fingertips are slick with sweat, my breath fast and shallow. Perry lights another Tiparillo and turns down a wide boulevard, a road with no other traffic. I picture us spinning out, the BMW skidding on black ice, flipping over the median, bashing the row of blue spruce and speeding on, into a ditch, into a lake, into a field of straw-colored hypodermics, finally into the ocean of space that once was New York, Ohio, Michigan, Wisconsin.

"No," I say. "I have to stop."

Finally Sophie turns around. "What is it?"

"Yeah, what is it with her?" Perry says.

"I'm going to be sick." I cover my mouth.

"Oh," Shauna says.

"Uh oh," Dina says.

"Poor Becca," Sophie says, and reaches back to touch my forehead.

"I'm pulling over," Perry says. "Right here."

The car stops. I grab my handbag and stumble out, onto the snowy street, the cold seeping fast through my black suede heels. Air. Around me the sudden quiet of the sleeping neighborhood, the houses solid, the trees immense. I walk a few yards from the car, hold the collar of Debbie's borrowed coat, bend over, pretend to gag. Stick my hand in the crusty snow then hold it to my face. A few houses down, a light goes on. I straighten up, and the back door of the BMW opens for me, yawning panic and Tiparillo smoke. Shauna rolls down her window. "You finished? Come on."

"You go ahead."

"Don't be ridiculous," Shauna says.

"Really."

She turns to Sophie, and Sophie leans out the window. "Come on, Becca."

"Don't be a suck," Shauna says.

I walk away, picking over patches of ice to the shoveled stretches, the ruts from cars in the driveway, while Perry and Sophie call from the car. Snow melts through my off-black hose: ice-water down my ankles.

Finally Sophie gets out, stumbling. "What's the matter? It's freezing."

"I have to go back."

"But Perry doesn't."

I picture his hand on her neck, the fat padded fingers. Something snaps. "I can't believe you like him," I say. "I can't believe this is what you like."

"Nobody asked you," she says, and she's right. But flecks of light are still skittering, and the lawn seems like an island in space. She ought to know.

"I'm not getting back in the car," I say.

"Sure you will," Sophie says. "I'm getting back in the car and so are you. You have to."

"I don't have to do anything."

"What do you think my Mom and Dad will do? You want me to go to boarding school?"

"She isn't your Mom," I say. "Her name is *Helen.*"

"Shut up," Sophie says, her voice sharp, a stranger's.

"Do you even remember your Mom?"

"Just shut up." Sophie stares, pale, then flees to the car, which has already become toy-like and remote. My hands and arms are almost as distant, my shoes curiously blotched and misshapen. *Monster feet.* I take one step, another, further from the car, over the flat spread of snow.

Perry beeps the horn. "Some American Princess," he calls. "Get back here, princess."

In my coat pocket, I find my last American $20; in the borrowed handbag, an array of Canadian bills. Enough for a cab. The BMW drives slowly behind me, until I turn up the walk of the house with lights on. Then Perry takes off, and Sophie is a blur of black sedan.

A woman answers the door of the brick house, a brunette with shoulder length hair, blue ink stains on her hands. Three little boys leapfrog around in their pajamas. I need a taxi, I explain. "I had a fight with my boyfriend." I gesture at the snow. The woman sizes me up, nods, calls "Honey?" She leads me to a chair in the front hall. There are footsteps upstairs, a man's voice calling the little boys. She brings me a glass of water. I tell her my name is Debbie.

In a short while, the taxi drives up, bright and empty: a momentary surge of hope. A few snowflakes fall on the road, large ones that hit the windows just long enough for me to glimpse their structures before they melt. The interior smells of coffee and vinyl cleaner. There is no music. I give the driver Sophie's home address, and he shrugs. At the end of the street, we turn, stop at a traffic light, drive five more blocks. Turn again. "Here we are," the driver says.

I tell the Steinharts I'm exhausted and stressed.

Where is Sophie? they want to know.

"The hotel. With Shauna."

Shauna and who else?

"I don't know," I say. "I don't know people here."

Once, when Laura and I were at an arts festival in Buffalo, an ordinary looking man began shouting the soliloquy from *Hamlet.*

"A street actor," Laura said, but the crowd near him immediately thinned, and the artists whispered and shrugged. For several minutes we didn't know if his performance was a planned or spontaneous outburst. I kept waiting for the point.

A guy in a festival staff t-shirt yelled, "Hey, could you do that someplace else?"

The man ignored him, reciting louder, enunciated lines. My stomach knotted and I relaxed only after a police officer arrived and escorted Hamlet to a patrol car.

"Pig," Laura muttered. Then we bought slices of pizza and she let me try her cigarette.

At two in the morning Sophie returns, reeking of rum and cigars. I sit up in bed while she pulls her clothes off and drops them in a pile on the floor, her body startlingly white and pink and blonde, even her pubic hair blonde. She pulls the pink flannel nightgown on and climbs into the canopy bed. She won't look at me. I lie back and gaze at the dimly lit ceiling, which breaks into delicate patterns. Sophie brushes her hair—brisk, drunken strokes.

"I'm sorry. What I said," I tell her.

She keeps on brushing and turns off the light.

In the morning, Mr. Steinhart interrogates Sophie at breakfast. She stares, wretched, at her tea. "I'm sorry, Daddy," she says. Her voice is quavery and penitent, but she won't answer him. He says what every other Dad would say: sorry isn't good enough, this can't happen again, he won't have it, she's grounded for a month. Then he announces he's sending me home.

He waits, as if she'll protest. As if that's what he wants her to do.

"We were just going to read," she says.

He sighs and leaves the room. Mrs. Steinhart pours us more orange juice.

"I know you're not yourself," Sophie tells me.

Of course, no one wants to explain to my parents—the Steinharts to admit there's been a problem under their watch, me to admit anything. We agree my parents have enough to worry about, and when Mr. Steinhart calls the hotel, he tells my mother that Sophie has the flu: he's afraid I'll catch it, he'd prefer to send me home. Then he hands me the receiver.

"Sophie's feeling pretty crummy," I tell my mother. "How's Laura?"

"I'm sorry about your visit." Her voice sounds watered-down. "Etty can pick you up. I'll be back tomorrow."

"And Laura?"

"Soon," my mother says.

"Soon what?"

"Have a good trip, sweetheart."

Mrs. Steinhart puts me on a train: the mink again, the sunglasses.

She checks to make sure I have my ticket and money, a note for Customs, my bag of snacks. She climbs on with me, claims a window seat, tells the conductor I'm traveling alone—could he keep an eye out? Mom things. The sorts of things Mrs. Steinhart does for Sophie, daily acts that keep Sophie afloat, prevent the shaking, that cap off Sophie's grief and allow her the foolishness of pink nails and rabbit fur and Perry. At this moment, what I want most is for Helen Steinhart to ride with me on the train, escort me through Customs to Buffalo, to stay with me until we've found my parents sipping their percolated coffee, proclaiming Laura healthy, Laura herself at home, batiking in the laundry room, Richie and his friends creating baseball dynasties. Mrs. Steinhart gives me a quick hug, says goodbye, and waits on the platform until the train pulls out.

Heading east, I watch the flat snowy fields broaden and contract, thumb my novel. I try to sleep, which seems better than panicking, better than guessing what other freakishness and cruelty lurks inside me. Something ahead is dangerous, that much I believe. But in a few hours, I'll cross the border, fish out my parents' letter, tell the customs officials I've been visiting a friend from summer camp—the words themselves a door to the maple woods and the lake and the cabins, that other me, that other Sophie. In a few hours, Etty and Richie will find me at the bus station, we'll order pizza, we'll watch TV. My parents will fly home. Soon.

After a month, my sister Laura moves back to Buffalo. The first time I see her again, she is bloated and strange: an imitation-Laura, skittish and white-faced, almost mute. We sit at the white formica table and I offer her things to eat, as if she's a guest. She shakes her head at carrot soup. She shakes her head at pie. Finally, I stop offering. She glances around for my mother, who is deliberately busying herself on the other side of the kitchen.

"Becca's glad you're back," my mother says, and I pull my chair closer to Laura.

"I missed you," I say.

Laura gazes at me and chews at her lip, and I wonder if she's going to cry, or worse, shake without crying. I don't yet know her diagnosis, which will change and change again, as she visits different psych wards. I don't know she's lost her ability to read. Or that the Laura who resurfaces will for many years be a foreigner.

I know to mix lies in with the truth. It's already becoming habit.

"I went up to Canada," I tell her. "No place more beautiful."

Stephen Gibson

Dooley's G_ill and Tavern

Dooley's G_ill and Tavern was missing an r, but it had loud talk, loud music, beer and whiskey smells, the Clancy Brothers on the jukebox and Mel Allen on the TV over the bar giving the afternoon Yankee starting line-up. I was nine. I sat on a red plastic-covered stool that swiveled whenever I got down to go to the bathroom, watching for my glass of Coke on the bar with my dollar bill next to it as soon as I came out. The dollar bill was my step-father's, Harry Keiser's. A dollar bill for all of the Cokes I could drink, all the pretzels and peanuts in the bowls I could eat, and all the ham salad or tuna salad white bread sandwiches that were cut into triangles and had the crusts cut off. Quarters weighed down both front pockets of my dungarees for the pinball bowling machine. I was tops at pinball bowling. I racked up nearly perfect games every Saturday. Men would drift over from the bar on their way to the bathroom and rub my head. They rubbed my head for good luck. They also rubbed my head because I was tops at picking out who would be the next Miss Rheingold. Whether anyone was looking or not, I would go off by myself to the corner booth in the back past the bathrooms and the jukebox and fill in all the ballot slips from the pads. I stuffed the ballot box with my favorite. The next Miss Rheingold always had to have a round face and dark hair just like my mother. Then I returned the ballot box to the side of the cash register that was never used, the one sitting against the wall at the end of the bar under the crossed Irish and American flags where the big mirror and the duckboard ended. I liked walking along the duckboard. When Dooley's wasn't too busy in the morning, Dooley would tie an apron at the back of my neck and around my waist and put two glasses running over with foam into my hands to take to someone at the bar. I made a game of getting the glasses over to the cork coasters on the bar without spilling any and before any of the foam dripped off the bottoms of the glasses. The tip that went into the tip jar would be mine.

In the afternoon, Dooley's was thick with men and women and overflowing ashtrays. My unofficial job was to go around the bar, step up onto the foot-rail between the stools, and empty the ashtrays without anyone noticing I was doing it. I carried a metal mop bucket which had water in the bottom of it and tape on the outside that said "For Butts." I liked stepping up on the rail next to the women and quickly dumping their ashtrays. I liked the smudges of lipstick on their teeth, the way they turned their heads up when they laughed, the way they flicked their ashes into the ashtrays without even looking, or knowing I'd gotten their ashtrays back under their cigarettes without them noticing. I liked being next to the women, the way they sat sideways on the stool with their legs crossed over each other, the way the smell of perfume and beer and cigarettes all mixed together on them—the way they sometimes didn't know an extra button on their blouses had opened. The men they talked to and who bought them shots were men who had been through the war against Germany and Japan, just like my father. When they weren't in Dooley's, they drove bread trucks and were mailmen and hot-type typesetters for newspapers and cabbies who always parked in front of Dooley's so they could watch through the window so that nobody tried to pry off a medallion with a screwdriver. The men wore white short-sleeved shirts and black or brown pants and white socks and black or brown shoes and they had pale white skinny and hairless forearms, or thick, meaty, hairy forearms that had tattoos on the insides and outsides of them. Sometimes the tattoos under the dark hair were pictures of the face of Jesus looking up to heaven with the crown of thorns pressed into his head and little droplets of blood hanging off the tip of each thorn just before the drops were about to go into Jesus' eyes. Usually, the men had more than just one tattoo on their arms. Red hearts with banners flowing across them with a girl's name, like "Rose" or "Catherine" or "Peggy," written across the banner that scrolled up on either end. Sometimes there would be "Mom" written across the banner in place of a girl's name. Tim Murphy, who drove a *Daily News* truck and who was also in the union, had a naked hula girl in a grass skirt that wiggled on the outside of his left forearm when he moved his fist up and down. *The Daily News* did a story about Tim. He was on the Hornet when the Hornet was sunk. It was only the first time or maybe the second time when the Japs sent kamikazes into our ships. But Tim got his job driving the truck because he knew someone in the union. The story about him watching the rest of the battle while he was in the ocean, that only came later after he got the job.

But most of the time, the men didn't talk about the war. If someone who wasn't a regular did, you could count on the guy on the next stool getting up, digging into the front pocket of his pants, pulling out his money clip, and leaving more than enough next to his glass to cover the tab. Most of the men kept their money folded in half with a silver or gold clip in the front pocket of their pants. When they took their money out, they laid the bills neatly next to their glasses or under the ashtray when they got up and left. The regulars I listened to didn't talk about the war. Sometimes they got loud, but that was always because of the booze, not because of the war, not like the ones who weren't regulars at Dooley's, the ones who sometimes stopped in and then you never saw again. The men talked loudly because of the booze and because they couldn't be heard above the jukebox or the television, but they always knew what they were talking about—about Whitey Ford being taken out of the starting rotation because of his elbow, the left one, the only one that counted; or why no one would ever pitch a perfect game in the Series again; or why Ingemar Johansson's foot kept twitching on the canvas at the Stadium after Patterson caught him with that left hook. His foot kept twitching like that because there are nerves that still stay alive for a few seconds in your body, not only after you've been knocked unconscious, but even after you've just been killed because some of those nerves don't know yet that you're already dead.

Dennis O'Toole didn't fight in the war, but that's all he ever talked about. Just like he was there. He got drunk so he could talk about it—and anything else. O'Toole got drunk just so he could talk. And he was a filthy liar. Those were my mother's words. Even when I was really little, before Patrick was born and Michael was still a baby, all I remembered was that whenever my father would sign himself back into the hospital. O'Toole would always be upstairs in our apartment. He lived with his older sister Margaret, who also wasn't married. They owned the corner candy store in our building. I would be in the bathroom in the tub and my mom would be washing Michael in the kitchen sink and then I would hear someone talking to her, and by the time I came out in my pajamas, there would be O'Toole in our kitchen. The tea kettle would be on the stove, not yet whistling, and there would be two cups and saucers and two plates with forks and napkins next to the plates and there would be a box of Drake's coffee cake sitting in the center of the kitchen table. I would be sitting on the couch in the living room and I would watch O'Toole sitting there in the good chair by the kitchen window, the chair that didn't have gray tape on the seat and back like the two others. He'd be talking to my mom while she was washing Michael in the sink. O'Toole would put his feet up on the side of the stove and smoke a cigarette, waiting for the tea kettle to whistle. Then he'd pour the boiling water over the tea bags while my mom wrapped Michael in a towel and carried him into the bedroom to go to bed. There was one bedroom. The big bed was for my mom and dad, when he wasn't in the hospital. Michael and I shared the fold-up cot. When Michael was a baby, he slept in the bottom drawer of the big dresser. The drawer was filled with towels instead of my dad's pants and shirts. Then when Patrick was born, he got the bottom dresser drawer. When my father didn't come back from the hospital, Michael and Patrick and I slept in the big bed and my mom slept on the cot.

I hated Dennis O'Toole.

He thought he was a big shot just because he could light the pilot light under the stove when it went out with only the first match. He thought he was so smart. I didn't want to see him try standing an egg up on one end on our kitchen table. I didn't want him in our apartment. So he broke the egg on the bottom. So what? It was a broken egg that my mom had to wipe with a dish cloth into the garbage. He was a sneaky, skinny man with red hair that stood straight up on his head like wires. He had a pale face with red freckles all over it, and he wore thick, black-rimmed glasses that were as thick as the bottom of Coca-Cola bottles. The thickness of the glasses made O'Toole's eyes look like two tiny cat's-eyes marbles behind them. When I walked into the kitchen, I would always look at those cat's-eyes behind those glasses and my eyes would go to the pocket of his white short-sleeve shirt where his black eyeglass case stuck out, then to the silver pocket watch chain hooked to a belt loop on his black pants, then down to his pants pocket. I had the feeling he had stolen something from our kitchen. After the first ten seconds, O'Toole wouldn't look at me. He'd pull out his pocket watch, snap the case open by pressing his thumb, look at the time, then shut it and return it to his pocket. He'd look up at the clock over our stove, or up at the ceiling above his head, or turn around at the table and begin dunking his tea bag up and down in his cup or else maybe open the lid of the box and begin picking at the top of the cake. If I stared at him too long, he sometimes got angry and would suddenly jump, telling me, "Didn't your mother teach you it's impolite to stare at people?" and he'd go into the living room and plop down on our couch. He'd sit there in the dark with both arms stretched over the tops of the cushions. Waiting for my mother to come out and waiting for me to go to bed.

O'Toole was always up in our apartment.

The last time, when my father was home—it was a couple of months after Patrick was born—I tried to tell him about Dennis O'Toole always coming up. I wanted to tell him about O'Toole being in our apartment almost every night to have tea, and the box of Drake's coffee cake that he would always bring with him, and the Hershey bars I found in the refrigerator in the morning next to the newly opened container of milk. I hated those Hershey bars. I would never eat them even though my mom said they were left for me. One time, I threw them in the garbage right in front of her. I told her O'Toole shouldn't be coming up to the house every night.

"Dennis just keeps me company while your father's away," she said.

I hollered at her that he shouldn't be keeping her company. He shouldn't be bringing up Drake's coffee cake or containers of milk or Hershey bars—and she shouldn't let him press up against her when she was washing Michael in the sink. (On that occasion, my mother had asked O'Toole to get down the cups and saucers from the cabinet overhead because her hands were soapy.)

My mother smacked me when I said that.

So every time my father came home, I wanted to tell him about Dennis O'Toole. When my mom said I was too old to go to the hospital with her, I would look out the front window, waiting for the taxicab to pull up, and my father would get out with Michael in his arms, and then my mother, and the cabbie would take the single brown suitcase out of the trunk and I would hold open the door as I waited on the landing, listening to them come up the stairs. Then when Michael was too old, the both of us watched for the taxicab.

The last time he came home—I didn't know it was to be the last time—I made up my mind to tell him about Dennis O'Toole. Patrick was only a couple of months old. But I couldn't tell him. My father had taken the steamer trunk out of the bedroom closet and he had spread out all of his war souvenirs on the big bed. There was a gun and a bayonet and a big German flag that he had spread out on the big bed and laid the gun and bayonet on top of it. And the same pictures were spread out everywhere. Pictures my mother stuffed back into their envelopes and put back into the steamer trunk, along with the German flag and the bayonet and the gun and the letters that she tied into bundles with rubber bands and put back into the trunk and put the trunk back into the closet the day after she took my dad back to the hospital in the taxicab. They were pictures of my dad smiling, relaxed, with his hands behind his back, in his army uniform, squinting into the sun. Pictures of him and my mom on the stoop of our building, my mom standing on the second bottom step, my dad on the bottom one. Pictures of them at the Bronx Zoo, my mom turning away, making a face, her hand behind her as a llama's head leans down over the fence. Pictures of the both of them leaning together against the front fender of a black car, my dad's left arm over her shoulder, my mom with her dark hair worn up above her forehead, two big scrolls of shining dark hair with a flower between. (It's an antique. A two-by-three black-and-white one with serrated edges that's faded to oatmeal. It's the one photo of them I keep in my wallet, behind the picture of Kristen getting her degree from Tulane and Andrew's high school graduation. My dad's got style. The end of his tie is tucked between the third and fourth button of his uniform and his hat is folded through the epaulette on his right shoulder. My mom's wearing a polka dot dress and is laughing—she's leaning down with her arm because the wind is blowing up the bottom of her dress as the picture's being shot.) And letters—piles and piles of letters scattered all over the German flag. It was the middle of summer but the bedroom was dark. My mom was crying. She told me to take Michael and Patrick across the street to aunt Helen's. When I ran back upstairs, my mom was sitting on the steps in the stairwell in the hallway. She was blowing her nose into her hankie and looking up at a big New York City cop who was standing over her, talking quietly to her with one of his hands on her shoulder. The cop turned around to tell Mrs. Malloy across the hall, who opened her door, to shut it. "Mind your own goddamned business," he said when she tried to come out. I ran inside before the cop or my mom could stop me.

There was a big cop in our kitchen, standing there, leaning with his arm out against the doorframe like he was holding the wall up, looking into our bedroom. I pushed between him and the door. My dad was standing there in his boxer shorts and undershirt by the cot. All of the pictures and the letters and pistol and the bayonet and the German flag were all over the big bed. My dad had his head down, and he had his arms over the shoulders of two other big New York City cops. They were helping him get his pants on. The big black cop was saying over and over, "It's okay, Frank," as my dad's other foot tried to find the other opening. My dad looked up at me as he got the leg into the pants. I don't think he knew who I was. . . .

Like I said, I hated Dennis O'Toole.

Until the day Harry Keiser married my mom, I used to go into O'Toole's candy store and steal. Candy, gum, packs of balloons, balsa wood airplanes, cheap metal cap guns, boxes of rolled caps, boxes of plastic model tanks and ships and airplanes, even a big box with an aircraft carrier in it, the tubes of modeling glue, the safety pins you used to poke holes in the tubes, quarters, nickels, dimes, dollar bills from the cigar box outside on top of the newspaper on the paper stand in front of the store. It didn't matter what, just so I could get my hands on something and then later on throw it down the sewer. And when Michael was old enough, I taught him how to steal with me. I let Michael keep the caps because he liked to unroll them on the sidewalk and make them snap with the soles of his shoes. And gum. I let Michael chew the packs of gum I snuck into my pockets, but then give it back to me when he finished so that I could leave his and mine in front of the newspaper stand or inside the newspapers or on the street or inside the entrance of the candy store, and sometimes even on the seats and the edge of the counter where people who sat down would lean on the gum with their arms or their elbows. Whenever O'Toole and Margaret weren't paying attention that I'd come into the store, I did whatever I could get away with, taking whatever opportunity presented me with. If it was only a pack of gum, then I wanted people who went into the candy store to get gum on their shoes and on their pants and on their dresses and on their elbows when they sat down at the counter. And if O'Toole or Margaret looked up and saw me, then I'd go outside and wait and sneak gum inside the newspapers or take whatever I could grab from the cigar box. But never all of it. Never too much of anything at one time. I wanted him and Margaret to know money was missing from the cigar box or a model airplane box had suddenly disappeared from the front window or gum had again gotten on a seat, but I didn't want them to know for sure that it was me. Michael was too little to understand. He didn't understand why O'Toole's sister Margaret always shouted for us to get out whenever she saw us come in, or why O'Toole and his sister always got into arguments when she did, Margaret always shouting and O'Toole shouting back at her, customers or not in the store, about him and that "shanty Irish whore who thinks she's lace" or her "shanty children" and that "good for nothing husband" who "can't even say his own name anymore."

I didn't care. It didn't bother me. In fact, O'Toole's sister's shouting at me to get out didn't embarrass me at all—it only made me happy—because then she would start shouting at him and then they would begin shouting at each other and would still be shouting even when customers started walking out. I was glad. Michael was too young to understand. Like he was too young to understand why we always ran around the block to the empty lot in the alley between the buildings, or why I would tear open the boxes and snap apart the plastic models and stomp on the tubes of glue until they splattered all over the broken cinderblocks. Or when I took stick matches from on top of the stove, why I would set the boxes with the model airplanes in them on fire, or destroyers or aircraft carriers, or P-51 Mustangs, just like I set the balsa wood airplanes on fire, and if O'Toole and Margaret's candy store wasn't in our building but was in the building next to the lot, I would have set the building and their candy store on fire by starting a fire in the mattresses by piling the tires and the newspaper and old chairs against the building, hoping the bricks would collapse into their store from the flames. Instead, I opened the candy bars and the snack cakes and threw them down into the sewer and burned plastic models and balsa wood gliders instead of burning Dennis O'Toole and his sister Margaret. Michael was too little to understand, so I always let him have one candy bar or a package of balloons or the rolls of red paper caps so he could scrape them with his shoes on the sidewalk because the caps made him happy making loud noises and he liked the black smudges and the burn marks the caps left on the sidewalk.

O'Toole had been sneaky and mean by always coming up to the house to smoke and to have tea and eat Drake's coffee cake, waiting until after my brother and me were in bed. So I was being sneaky and mean to him for him being mean to my father.

In Dooley's, if O'Toole just sat at the other end of the bar and didn't make a peep, everything was all right. Everyone watched the ballgame, the men talked to the women and bought shots for them, I played pin ball bowling and filled in the Miss Rheingold slips and learned to tilt the glasses under the tap and then carried them over to the bar, and then later walked back to the apartment with my arm across the back of my step-father's, Harry Keiser's, gray suit jacket as he walked crookedly on the sidewalk like he was going to topple over, but never did. My stepfather, Harry Keiser, winter or summer, always wore a gray suit and a white shirt, open at the neck, no tie, a gray fedora to cover his bald head, and always the same black pair of high-top shoes with white socks, the left shoe with the metal toe in it and metal through the sides because of the polio. In all those years before I stopped going to Dooley's with him, Harry Keiser never once said one word to Dennis O'Toole, not even on those times when O'Toole got big and brave after he'd had too much to drink and would shout at the bar so Harry could hear it, that Harry Keiser was a fool "for buying the cow when the milk was free." Not even when the other men would tell O'Toole to shut up and pull him off of his stool and throw him out the door—when Dooley himself more than once would take the baseball bat out from behind the bar—Harry Keiser never said anything.

And it wasn't because Harry was afraid of Dennis O'Toole, because he wasn't.

But I didn't understand.

How could a woman, almost right after her husband died in some hospital way down in Florida, marry a sixty-one year old man like Harry Keiser—who never fought in the war, who was partially crippled from polio, who took me to Dooley's, who filled my pockets with quarters, who drank too much on Saturday, never on Sunday, and got up every morning to go to work. How?

And how could he have married a woman with three kids who were someone else's?

I didn't understand.

I was a kid.

FAMILY

Leslie Epstein

Malibu

1.

The sun was where it always was, high overhead, though on the particular Sunday I have in mind it had to force its way through a thin layer of cloud that stretched above us like a sheet of wax paper. I assume it was Sunday: we weren't in school, Barton and I, and it wasn't warm enough yet for summer. In spite of the cool weather, I'd put down the top on the Buick we owned back in the Fifties. As we made our way in traffic along the Pacific Coast Highway, Sampson, our spaniel, leaned out from the back seat, nose up, ears blown inside out. My brother hung onto his leash, lest at the sight of a skunk or a cat or—rising out of the haze-hung ocean—a silvery dolphin, he leap into the opposing stream of cars. Lotte, our mother, sat beside me, clutching a scarf over the permanent wave she'd set in her hair.

"It's going to be a nice day," she declared; as if in obeisance one corner of the milky overcast peeled away. At once the windows of the houses atop the right-hand hilltops began to shine, winking down on the sudden checkerboard of the sea.

"No, it is not," said Bartie.

I glanced back in the mirror: his face was buried in dog fur, the wind socks of the animal's ears twirling just above his own. He wasn't, I knew, referring to the climate.

"Why are you being so negative?" Lotte replied, though I doubted Bartie could hear her in the rush of air. "René is looking forward to the afternoon and so am I and you should be too. He is a wonderful cook. He is going to a lot of trouble to make a special treat. And his house is a little dream."

"A little dream on stilts," I muttered.

"Well, of course it's on stilts, Richard. It's a beach house. I hope you're not going to be in a negative mood too. Let's relax. Everybody just relax. We're going to have a good time."

I pulled around a Bekins van and was able to speed up after Carson Canyon. Lotte twisted her pale green scarf under her chin, and in that clamp fell speechless.

Bartie, in back, said, "It's too soon." Which might, from him, have meant anything: *Slow down,* we're getting there too soon; Too soon for the three of us to start fighting; or, and here's where I put my money, Too soon to have a good time.

I took a quick look over my shoulder. Barton stared back at me, grinning, a little gap-toothed, a little buck-toothed, which is what he got for sucking his thumb. "They don't have a King of England anymore. Everyone there wears black clothes. I saw it on the Zenith. They are sad because there isn't a king."

Lotte: "Yes, they have been very sad. But now they are going to have a queen, Bartie. The Princess Elizabeth. You can watch her coronation next month on television. No one will be wearing black, I promise you that. Isn't that how things should be? The king is dead. Long live the queen."

"But they waited a year. More than a year. That was February. Next month is June."

Our mother didn't answer. In Barton's mind, she knew, our father was the king—king of Hollywood, king of comedy—and it was a scandal not to mourn him for at least as long as the English had George VI. Instead, she pointed through the windshield. "There it is. Slow down, Richard. We'll go by."

The row of beachfront properties fell away on the left, caught between the highway and the public beaches. I coasted past the Sweetwater turnoff, trying to distinguish one of the sagging shacks from the other. None looked as if it had been painted since before the war: faded pastels, cheek by jowl, like a tray of melting sherbert.

"It's that one!" said Lotte. "See? That's his car."

She meant, I saw, a blue Plymouth coupe parked in front of what looked to be little more than a cabin of *creme de menthe.* I swung in behind it and turned off the ignition. A dog was barking nearby. A piece of tarpaper on the place next door was slapping against the rooftop. And of course there was the thump of the waves on the hidden beach below. I opened my door at the same time Rene stepped out of the little house and made for us.

"Ah, Lotte, I have been waiting. You are late, just like today the sun. Welcome! Hello, boys! *Comment allez-vous?* All is well?"

He had, as always, his thin Frenchman's moustache and his thin Frenchman's hair, slicked down with brilliantine we all could smell when he leaned over the passenger door and gave our mother a Frenchman's double kiss.

"We got a late start, darling," Lotte began, though René had already moved to the rear, where with what I knew was called *bonhomie* he was kneading Bartie's neck.

"And how is this one, eh? My sailor! My marine!"

Barton's lashes dropped over his eyes, which when open were a startling blue. He smiled. "We brought Sampson," he said.

"I see! *Bonjour, monsieur,*" he said to the dog, patting him once on the head, so that his eyes closed reflexively too. "What a fierce beast. That is why I have put Achille on the rope. You hear him? Barton, what is he saying?"

"I want that spaniel for lunch—" That was my contribution, which I covered with a chuckle.

René laughed aloud, with his head back, so that his short-sleeved shirt, circles of yellow, circles of blue, split over his belly. "Ha! Ha! But no! Ha! Ha! Lotte? You heard? *Pour le déjeuner!*"

"He didn't ask *you,*" said Barton. A button of flesh, a red-colored welt, rose on his brow. "Why did you answer?"

Lotte slid off the bench cushion to the gravel of the drive. "And you wouldn't believe the traffic. At least, I can't believe it. Norman and I moved out here in 1935. Practically with the covered wagons! There was hardly a car on the road back then. Honestly, you blink once and the population doubles. We were the pioneers."

I got out the driver's door and turned toward where our mother's lover—I hadn't much evidence for that, aside from his diplomatist's kisses and a single embrace that I had spied through the wind-blown curtains of our living room window—now approached me, his pink hand out. The lids of my own eyes dropped at his touch, so that I found myself staring at the wrinkle-free material of what people were beginning to call Bermuda shorts; his bowed, tanned legs; and the oddly pale and oddly small feet, crisscrossed by the leather straps of his sandals. "Richard," he said, "I feel embarrassment because I am going to show you my latest paintings. I mean, I cannot hide them, eh? They are not in your style. They are more—what do you call it, chèrie? More of *l'expressoinisme.*"

My mother had leaned back over her side of the Buick, to fish out her beach bag, which was woven from the same washed out colors, in straw, as the dwellings along the shore. "Darling, why do you apologize? There's certainly no reason for *that.* Your work *is* expressive. Did I tell you that Betty is considering the new oils for her gallery? She has the best taste of all my friends."

"What do you mean, *pioneers?* You and Daddy came out on the Super Chief! With an observation deck, for Christ's sake, Mom. Do you know what the real pioneers, the ones who *did* have covered wagons, went through?"

"Well, I wasn't suggesting that we were cannibals."

"Why do you have to put yourself—I don't know, at the head of the line."

"Richard—" This was René. "You must not speak with this disrespect toward your mother. I implore you."

"*Disrespect?* I am just trying to make a point. Have you read *Grapes of Wrath?* It's a great book. A John Steinbeck novel. The Okies, the people from Oklahoma—do you even know what that is?"

"It is a province of the country. I know that of course."

"A province! Ha! Ha! Ha! Did you hear that, Bartie? I bet he couldn't be a citizen, even if he wanted to. No French guy is going to know who signed the Declaration of Independence."

"Richard, you are always so smart. Do you know that we wouldn't even have our independence if it weren't for the help of France? Lafayette, we are here!"

Lotte beamed at René across the cooling hood of the automobile. Then her smile disappeared. "Oh, no, Barton," she cried. "Not now! Please don't!"

Bartie had donned a pair of dark glasses, wire-rimmed, and now he put a cold corn-cob pipe in his mouth. "I shall return," he intoned, in a voice deeper than his own.

"Ha, ha! This boy: he makes for us a masquerade?"

"I'm so upset. Oh, René. I don't know what to do. He's had that pipe for a year. And he has a cap too! *Barton! Please!* He keeps pretending he's that terrible MacArthur."

As if on cue my brother took out a visored cap and placed it over the mop of blond curls that, with his blue eyes, reinforced the romance that he was not from our dark-haired, dark-skinned family, nor from any other line of Jews. He got to his feet and through some kind of trickery—jutting the jaw, sucking in his plump, pink cheeks until they sank in like the septuagenarian's—transformed himself into the great man, the darling of the Republicans, as he drove down Fifth Avenue.

"Old soldiers," he declared, around the pipe-stem, "never die—" Then he threw out his arms, as if to catch the streams of ticker tape, the snow storm of the confetti, the roaring crowds that were simulated by the cymbal crash of the oncoming sea. But in that instant the dog's leash slipped though his boy's-sized hand; Sampson flashed over the side of the Buick and disappeared yipping and yapping down the side of the bluff that separated René's green house from the plum-colored bungalow next door. A howl went up: the beast on the rope!

"Sammy!" cried Bartie.

Lotte: "Stop him! René!"

"I'll get him," I shouted; but I knew, from the torrent of animals growls, the two different pitches of the barks and bays, that I was too late.

René's cabin was indeed supported on stilts, four long iron poles sunk into the sand. Achille, a big German shepherd, black and brown, was tied to one of them. He lunged, gasping from the pressure of his collar, at our little spaniel. Each time he did so, the rope caught him, standing him upright, so that the saliva flew from his mouth. Again and again Sampson, his fur standing upon his back, dashed forward, teasing and taunting. The din, in that cavern, was tremendous.

"It's a Nazi dog! A Nazi dog!" Barton was screaming the words. He scooped handfuls of sand and threw them at the crazed Alsatian. The breeze blew them back in his face.

"Richard! Richard!" cried Lotte, from atop the bluff. "Can't you do something? Catch him!"

I tried, hurling myself full-length at the darting dog. But Sampson dodged easily and came at his antagonist from a different angle. Achille turned, rearing, only to have the spaniel run beneath him, nipping at his hocks. After a series of feints I saw, or thought I saw, a method in this madness. Sampson kept moving to his left, which meant that each new stand that Achille took tended to wind him clockwise around his iron pillar. It took less than a minute for his tether to be cut by half. His breath was shorter too, coming out in human-like groans. The fierce barking had stopped.

"Don't cry, Bartie," I shouted, glancing back at my brother, whose face was covered by a mask of sand crystals and zigzagging tears. "He's going to win!"

It seemed, for an instant, to be true. The big brute was strangling himself. He breathed now with the hacking, wheezing cough of a smoker.

Barton saw this. He thumped his chest with his balled-up hands. "It's David," he cried. "David and Goliath!"

But this time the giant was the clever one. Sammy came in at five o'clock, like a Spitfire attacking a lumbering German Stuka. Achille didn't leap; instead he remained in a crouch close to the ground, and Sammy in amazement tumbled to a halt before the snot-smeared snout. In an instant the Alsatian shot forward and took the spaniel in his open jaws.

Lotte screamed. Bartie cried, "No-o-o-o!" For a heartbeat I thought that Achille like a python would swallow him whole.

Then René strode forward. *"Assez! La ferme!"* Without breaking stride he kicked his dog in the belly, not with the leather toe of his sandal but with the much harder bone of his shin. The shepherd buckled, spitting out his prey, who dragged himself off, whimpering, whining. *"Cochon!"* cried the Frenchman. He kicked the animal again, this time against the heaving ribcage.

Bartie ran toward his own dog, who stood slick and shaking, like a miniature of a newborn foal. He took him in his arms.

"Don't kick him anymore," I said, fighting tears myself. "Please."

"What? You ask me to spare him? This pig of an animal? It will be as you wish. We will show mercy."

Lotte came down the bluff, stumbling a little. "Is everyone all right? Is anyone bitten?"

"Wasn't Sammy great, Mom?" said Barton. "He's a brave boy!"

"What is this?" asked René, pointing to his nose.

"A nose," I answered.

"*Le nez. Oui.* And it smells something. Wait. A moment. Ah, it is the crust of the saucisson. Come. Up the stairs, my friends. Our luncheon is burning."

The Frenchman led the way up the wooden planks that served as the back staircase. Bartie followed, holding Sampson against his chest. I moved to the first of the unpainted steps. Lotte touched my arm.

"I didn't mean anything," she said. "You and Bartie, you're the real Angelenos. The natives of the land." Then she leaned closer, though her lover, I realized, was still close enough to hear. "You mustn't worry. You know I'd never do anything you didn't approve."

2.

The smoke filled the whole of the little house. René opened all the windows and pushed up the skylight. A column of soot corkscrewed from the open door of the oven and out into the pale patch of sky. René stooped to remove an aluminum pan, at the center of which lay the charred log of our feast, a log with juices spurting from it in little golden arcs. The truth was it smelled delicious. "Ah, we have arrived just in time," declared the chef, an oversized oven mitt on either hand. We three guests applauded. He grinned. "It is only necessary to peel from the top a bit of the dough." He leaned over the dish, expertly flaking away the burnt layer, like a scab from a healed wound. "Ah, it is as I thought. Only the butter was burning. We shall eat! Lotte, you will toss the salad?"

Our mother went to the sink, where the greens were waiting in a colander. She poured oil from one bottle, rose-colored vinegar from another. René, meanwhile, had laid out the sausage-filled crust on a platter and was slicing it into sections. "You notice here the pattern of the ingredients: the veal; the pork; here the pistachio, the strips of the ham; the darkness, it is the mushroom and the chicken livers. What you see with the eye, this helps us with the sensation on the tongue."

"That's why you are an artist, darling," said Lotte. "Everything you do is a composition."

"The funeral-baked meats," I said, giving my brother a nudge. But he looked up, entirely blank.

"I tell you what, Barton," said René, holding up a chunk of the paté. "You may give a taste to *le chien.*"

Bartie took up the saucisson and shifted the hot meat—gray and green, pink and red, swirling with steaming black bands—from hand to hand. He brought it over to where Sampson lay trembling in the corner.

For a moment everything was calm. The last of the smoke whisked out the windows. The haze over the ocean was lifting too. A sailboat went south to north on the horizon; another side-slipped the breeze a little closer in. I could make out the fisherman throwing their lines for mackerel at the end of the Malibu Pier. A few hardy swimmers were testing the waters. The breakers crashed to pieces before them and rolled sizzling about their feet and ankles, like animal fat. Lotte, heaping salad onto each plate, hummed, a little pointedly I thought, *I love Paris in the springtime;* and René, standing directly behind her, arranging a line of mustard at the rims, came in on *I love Paris in the fall.* You couldn't turn on the radio without hearing the lyrics. I moved from the kitchen area and walked the walls, white and stucco, to examine the paintings of our host.

"Mommy! What's wrong? He won't eat!" Bartie was kneeling on the floorboards. He was pushing the meat at Sampson, right up against his nose.

"Perhaps he is a true Jacobi, eh?" said René, with a belly laugh. "Ha! Ha! Ha! He must not eat what is forbidden."

Bartie wheeled to face him. "That's not my name. *Jacobi!* My name is Barton Wilson."

"Don't say anything," said Lotte. "It's a phase."

"But why? Is it because he has shame?"

"That is the one thing I am thankful for. That Norman didn't see this behavior in his son. He wasn't a religious man; he just laughed at the rabbis. But he was proud of his family, and of his people too."

"To change your name, this cannot be allowed." René pounded a fist into his turned-up palm. "It is I think terrible."

Lotte replied lightly, so that her laugh mingled with the tinkling knives and forks she set at the table. "Oh, it's not so terrible, sweetie. Didn't I change my name to Jacobi? And what *about* the

Jacobies? That wasn't their name when they came to Ellis Island. Richard, you know: didn't Grandpa Leo take the name of the man who was ahead of him in line?"

"Hee, hee hee! Ha! Ha! Ha!" I couldn't control my laughter. It had nothing to do with the old family joke—how Leo had exchanged the family name, *Ochsenschwantz,* ox tail, itself bestowed upon *his* father's father by a jesting German; and why couldn't the stranger in line be a Belmont, an Adler, a Vanderbilt even. Ha! Ha! Ha! I burst out again at the sight of René's paintings—a half-dozen canvases on which the paint had been laid out on the blade of a knife, a thick, multicolored impasto out of which emerged something like daisies or magnolias or meadowlands, a tree, a horse.

"Why are you laughing, Richard? It's impolite."

I only half knew myself. I turned toward the last painting in the row. I glanced from it back to the painter: *this cannot be allowed.* I saw how his little moustache was suddenly drenched by the sweat on his lip. His hand, as he screwed the cap on the bottle of mustard, was shaking. He could not bear the thought of changing a name. This last work was of a sad-eyed clown: chalked face, reddened cheeks, lipsticked smile. The great thing was the nose, not the red bulb of a Bozo but a long, pointed schnoz, *le nez,* which literally grew out of the canvas, layer upon layer of dried, stiffened paint that thrust precariously a good six inches into the air.

"Ha! Ha! Ha!" I couldn't control myself. I knew, and I saw that René knew too, that this was a self-portrait: a picture of a name-changer, a fraud. Impasto? Impostor! But I only said, or rather bellowed, a single word: "Pinnochio!"

"Ah, it is a pity. Richard does not like my effort."

"Of course he does. He wasn't laughing *at* them. Were you, Richard?"

"Not exactly."

"No, no, no—I see that I have in your eyes made a failure. This makes me sad."

"René, darling. Don't be silly. Betty loves your paintings. Richard likes to be a know-it-all. Mr. Know-It-All. Mr. Snob. But he's only a boy."

"A boy! Yes, a boy who has sold his paintings in that same gallery whose patron, this *Betty,* only talks with repetition of hanging mine."

"Oh, those were just drawings of our neighbor—"

"Mademoiselle Madeline. *La petite jeune fille.* I have seen all the series. I have no choice but to bow to the critique of such a *master.*"

I didn't like the French word *Mademoiselle.* It didn't fit Madeline. I remembered the patch of dark down at the nape of her neck and the thin line of hair—not like Sampson's, more like a shadow—that ran down her spine almost to the flesh of her buttocks. I didn't like *petite jeune fille.*

My mother laughed. "A *master?* Richard? Those were nothing but charcoal sketches. Betty only—"

"Lotte, *tais-toi!* Eh? I warn you."

"What does that mean, *tais-toi?* Shut up? Don't tell her to shut up!"

"Richard, it's all right. He's upset."

"Don't you see he's a fake? *René?* Is that your name? *René Belloux?* Joe Blow I bet!"

"But what are you accusing me of—?"

"I bet he didn't make this—what is it? *Saucisson en croute.* Where did you get it? At the Farmer's Market? At Chasen's?"

Now it was René's turn to laugh. "I assure you this recipe has been in my family, the family Belloux, for generations: yes, and we did not change this name for the Germans or for the immigration. We are not ones to wander the earth. But believe what you wish, my young friend. I am happy to see that the repast is being enjoyed by Monsieur Wilson."

He waved toward where Bartie had taken his seat at the table. He was stuffing the food into his mouth with both hands. He grinned, so that the crumbs fell from the corners of his mouth. "*Oui! Oui!* Mr. Barton Wilson. *Oink! Oink!* A Jew wouldn't eat all this pork."

"Now look," said Lotte. "I want everyone to sit down. There is no reason to continue this bad temper. We have a lovely meal. And I happen to know there is going to be a special dessert. Isn't that so, René?"

"Yes, the éclairs. About this I confess they are from the store. We can have them after our swim. Do we agree to this plan?"

Lotte took her place at the table. "That would be wonderful. And the sun is burning brighter and brighter. It's almost like a summer day. Richard, aren't you going to eat? Come sit next to me."

I did as she asked. I cut into the warm meat with a fork. We passed around a pitcher filled with the halves of lemons. The ice cubes bounced musically off the glass.

"I can't wait to get out on the beach," said Lotte. "There hasn't been any sun since I don't know when—since last fall. I've no color. You'd think I was a character in Tennessee Williams. A pale Southern belle."

"Richard and I will go out in the boat," René declared. "Would you like that?"

"Oh, I know he would."

"It is just a modest rowboat."

"What about Barton?" Lotte asked, smiling; there was a trace of lipstick on the white of her teeth. "Bartie, would you like to go too? Or would you rather stay here with your paper and pencils and write?"

My brother had put down his knife and fork. I saw the rouge-colored welt rising between his eyebrows. Tears formed a bell of light over the blue of his eyes. "Why did I do it? It's wrong for me to eat. Poor Sammy! He's sick. He won't eat. He's going to die. The big dog killed him!"

We all turned our heads to the corner where Sampson lay flat on his side. For an instant it seemed he was no longer breathing. Then he sighed, with a great heave of the ribs, and slapped the floor with his tail. I would have thought he was dreaming, but his eyes were wide. Again, the pause; again, the slap, the sigh. *Brrr* was the sound that he made through his vibrating lips, like a man who is warming himself in the midst of a snowstorm.

Our mother was the first one onto the beach. She didn't put on a swimsuit. "This is a sun suit," she announced. "The rays come right through and the wind stays away." Then, as she sometimes did, she said something odd and striking. "I can't think the last time I went into the ocean. It's so unconscious." With her scarf tight over her head and her straw bag over her shoulder, she clutched the handrail on her way down the weatherworn steps.

From that same bag she'd pulled trunks and T-shirts for my brother and me. René, at the sink, had his back turned; Bartie dropped his pants and his shorts, and hopped into his trunks—blue with a white stripe down one side. When he struggled with his shirt, arms upraised, I saw the remains of the baby fat that puckered his chest and hips; then his head, with his buck-toothed grin, popped through the V-neck.

"What's so funny?" I asked.

"You," he answered.

At the exchange, René turned around.

"I have to use the bathroom," I told him. "To urinate."

He gestured with his head and his shoulder, over which he wore a checkered dishtowel. "It is there. Past the bedroom."

I took up my things and headed down the short corridor. The bedroom door was open and the bed itself, more expressionism in confused blankets and sheets, was on the floor. The bathroom had a stall shower surrounded by opaque glass. A pedestal sink stood beneath a flat mirror. Toothbrushes, hair brushes, a shaving brush too, along with a soapy razor and a bottle of the sweet-smelling pomade, were scattered across a single shelf. Over the toilet hung a smaller version, a study, of the clown painting I had seen before: sad eyes, crimson mouth, eggshell skin. I stripped off my clothes and stood before the bowl. Nothing came out. I ran the water in the sink. Nothing still. I closed my eyes, to shut out the gaze of the clown, with his pointed, protruding nose. But of course I knew the painting was there, like a man in an adjacent stall. I turned my back altogether and pulled on my swimsuit and elbowed my way into the shirt. When I stepped back to the living room, René and Bartie were gone.

3.

The belated sun had brought a small crowd to the public beach. People lay on their blankets, in couples, or families, or quite alone, but always each equidistant from each. Here and there a radio played snatches of popular songs: *Baubles, Bangles, and Beads; Wheel of Fortune; Ebb Tide,* though I saw that in reality the tide was coming in. Small children ran from each other, screaming. The breeze came hard off the ocean, stringing out the fringes of the beach umbrellas and kicking up little whirlwinds of sand. A lifeguard stared out to sea, though no swimmer had dared venture past his knees. I trudged steadily ahead in my unlaced sneakers until I saw Bartie digging not far from where the last wave had coughed up a bellyful of kelp.

He squinted up from what was already a hole the size of a sailor's trunk. "Want to dig too?" he asked.

"Sure."

He stooped and with a little green shovel—had he found it? swiped it?—tossed a new helping of sand onto the barrier he was erecting against the oncoming sea.

"That won't work," I said.

"Yes, it will."

"Don't you see? You started too far down."

"You don't know anything."

"But the water will come around the sides."

Even as I spoke there was a thud, I felt it through the rubber soles of my Keds, and in no time a wave came snarling and snapping to within a foot of the redoubt.

"No, it won't!" shouted Barton, standing upright and pointing skyward with the blade of his plastic shovel. As if he were Neptune, the sea retreated.

I shouldn't have been surprised. Bartie had always been an imperious god. Ten years before we'd driven out to the pier for a Sunday brunch, only to find all the restaurants closed and barbed wire strung clear across the dock. At the end, hundreds of feet away, barrage balloons bobbed upon thick wire cables. More of the anti-aircraft devices were tethered well out to sea. A trick of the light, the perspective of a three-year-old child, the taut lines gathered on buoys or barges, made it seem that these fat blimps, a mile off shore, were streetcorner balloons. "Want one! Want one!" Bartie cried, stamping first one foot then the other. Down he went, rolling on the planks of the pier. Norman plucked him up and ran for our

Packard sedan. A terrible wail trailed the fleeing figures, so loud, so piercing, and adamant too, that I half-expected the whole of the fleet to nose about and follow him dutifully home, like a herd of cows that were lighter than air.

There was another thump, hard enough to send sandslides down the walls of Bartie's excavation, and the next moment the wave came rushing up, biting at the bottom of the barricade with its slick white fangs. Bartie jumped from the pit and began inexplicably to scoop at the mud that the wave had left behind and pile it up on the untouched sand. "What are you doing?" I asked. "What are you making now?"

"It's Jolie's pyramid," he answered. "You know, at the cemetery!"

"You mean his shrine? It's not a pyramid."

"It is too! The same as in Egypt."

"Well, how do you know that?"

"How do you know it isn't?"

He had a point. Neither of us had gone to our father's funeral, yet like almost everyone in Los Angeles we had a vague impression of the Jolson Monument, which could be seen on the hillside, white and blazing, by those driving to the airport on Sepulveda. "What is this?" I asked, with foreboding. "This hole in the ground?"

"A grave."

"A grave. For who?"

"For Sampson. He died."

I stood for an instant, shivering in the sea spray. "What do you mean? What are you saying?" But I had understood clearly enough. I suddenly realized that he had not been at the house when I left it. Poor Sammy! Where was he? In the garbage can? Waiting for the garbage truck?

Bartie was patting down the sides of the singer's memorial. "He did it. The Nazi dog."

I turned toward the highway, where I could just make out the brown and black Alsatian, prowling at the end of his leash. Then I turned seaward again and dropped quickly to the floor of the grave. On all fours, dog-like myself, I pawed at the hardened sand. "Dig! Dig deeper!" I cried. "We've got to bury him! Before the sea comes in!"

Bartie squeezed in beside me. Like a slave on a chain gang, he threw shovelful after shovelful onto the top of the embankment. We kept at it for a minute, a minute more, though the thunder of the surf seemed to be clapping directly over our heads. Then we glanced at each other and broke simultaneously into laughter.

"Not a pyramid!" Bartie guffawed.

"No, a tower!" I answered.

Then we both yelled together: "The Awful Tower!" You would have thought that the strength of our shouts alone would have brought down the walls of Sampson's tomb. "The Eye-Full Tower!"

We were both thinking of the great monument in Paris, down the stairs of which we'd seen the actor Alec Guinness come running. That is where we were during Norman's funeral, at a movie, a comedy, where we laughed our fool heads off. Everyone in Hollywood, a thousand people, was at the cemetery; they all saw how Lotte had jumped into her husband's grave.

The oncoming sea covered us with its spume. We hadn't much time. Frantically we dug until with a boom like artillery a final wave seemed to break at point-blank range, eradicating the retaining wall and, with a torrent of water, collapsing all four sides of the grave. "Oh, Sampson!" I cried, as if the poor spaniel had actually been disinterred. I pushed the meat of my palms into my eyes to damn the welling tears. Then, with a sucking sound, the wave retreated and the water drained from what was now no more than a shallow depression.

"Look," said Barton. "Listen." About our covered feet and

across the sodden landscape there now opened a hundred thousand tiny holes, inside of which we thought we could hear the faint clicking membranes of the buried animals, the crabs, the clams, the periwinkles, unhappy insects and spiders, each of them gasping for light and air.

4.

It was already mid-afternoon. The haze, which had only half-lifted, holding itself in a thin suspension, now began to drop like a curtain on our matinee. The bathers retreated from the edge of the ocean. Outward, toward Malibu Point, a surfer rode a large wave, green and milky, like water in a glass of absinthe. A second surfer paddled seaward, windmilling his arms. I walked the beach, zigzagging about in a fruitless search for our mother. People had begun to pack up, calling in their children, shaking the sand from their own beach towels onto those of the groups farther inland. A biplane flew by, dragging a banner for Zesto.

On a nearby blanket two men, both shirtless, with barrel chests and hair-covered bellies, had the ballgame from Gilmore Field on their portable radio. The Stars were playing the Beavers. I stopped to listen. Portland was up 4-2, but we had Gene Handley on first and Ted Beard at the plate; only a few weeks before he'd hit four home runs in a single game against the Padres and right after that tied a league record with twelve straight hits. On this Sunday, however, he went down on three pitches. Frank Kelleher, my favorite, hit a long foul and then grounded to short. How Lee Walls got on base I didn't know, because the biplane had banked round and buzzed so low I could see the streaming hair of the pilot; but when the noise of the propeller had faded the bespectacled outfielder was on first, Handley on third, and Dale Long had the count against him, one ball and two strikes. He sent the next pitch over the left field wall. The roar that went up from the radio was much like the sound of the surf. I gave a little jump, instinctively mimicking the leap I used to take from my seat to hug my brother, my father, the perfect strangers in the rows before and behind.

There would be no embrace of these two fans. Neither of the men had reacted at all. They didn't even seem to hear the crowd as the hero circled the bases. Each remained propped on an elbow, looking northward to where a woman in sunglasses lay flat on the sand. Her dress was hiked over her open knees, and her head was pillowed on the woven straw of her basket. It was Lotte. I walked over and knelt next to her sleeping form. She lay parallel to the coastline, one arm by her side, the other flung outward. In sleep, all the lines had disappeared from her cheeks. A sheen of perspiration clung to her cheeks, her brow. I saw that she had slipped both straps of her bodice from her shoulders. When the wind puffed in off the sea it lifted a flap of her sundress, so that the pink nipple was plainly visible on her breast. The breeze lost its grip, the cotton dropped down, only to rise upon the next breath of air. Behind my back, I knew, the two men still lay on their haunches, unabashedly staring.

I ran. First uphill, toward the house, the highway, the car; then to the left, along the rows of pilings; then back, at an angle toward the ocean. All too soon my chest, my throat were burning; I could barely lift my high-topped sneakers from the sand; I staggered to a halt.

"Richard! Hello! Have you come to assist me? That is admirable." It was René, dressed now in an old-fashioned black swimsuit, clinging tights and sleeveless top. He was dragging a rowboat from the inland lagoon toward the sea. Its brown wood was slathered with lacquer. The oars were stowed inside. "You are strong? *Fort,* eh? Let us carry her together. It is not good, you know, the friction of the sand." He threw the rope into the boat and strode from front to rear. For some reason the nautical terms came to me: the prow, the stern, the painter. I gave a little laugh: *more of a painter than you are.* He squatted and without straining lifted the heavy back. "Now you. Not with the torso. With the muscles of the thigh." I wanted, now, to laugh out loud, to walk away, as a spectator might from the strong man in a circus. Instead, like a zombie, I did exactly as commanded: moved to the front of the rowboat, took hold of the—*gunwale,* was it?—and raised my half of the craft. The two of us walked crabwise to the foaming shore.

Timing the breakers, we made our way out to where the boat floated freely. The Frenchman, up to his waistline, steadied her while I climbed aboard and took the seat at the rear. Then he hauled himself over the side. Without a word he grasped the oars, turned our prow to the open sea, and began to row. Immediately I felt seasick, though I did not know whether the wave of nausea was caused by the motion of our little boat across the troughs and swells, or by the fact that each time the rower raised his oars from the ocean, I smelled the brilliantine upon the head of hair that thrust nearly to my lap. I bit my lip. It may be that I had turned a shade of green. For beneath his furrowed brow René glanced upward. "Ha! Ha! Ha!" he laughed. "The *mal de mer.*"

He did not break his rhythm. If anything he rowed with more determination. Sweat dripped from his hairline; droplets of it formed on his shoulders. His black shirt was soaked through. I heard how, at the start of each stroke, he grunted. It was as if he were in a race, rowing against others, and not on an outing for pleasure. Suddenly, as if we'd crossed a finish line, he slipped the oars, so that the shafts lay at the waterline and the blades rose on either side of me, neck high. For a moment he panted. His fingers, I saw, were curled, as though he were still gripping the wooden poles. Then he turned and reached into the prow, where an oilskin pouch was hanging. He took out a pack of Chesterfields and a book of matches. What was left of the breeze blew out the flame in his hooked hands, repeatedly. But just as I was about to bark with derision, he drew the flame into the end of his cigarette.

"Lotte," he said, with the Gallic shrug. "She does not permit me cigarettes. Her opinion is that it was the habit of smoking that killed your father." I did not reply. The boat remained motionless amid the whitecaps, like a decoration upon a frosted cake. René exhaled a blue, diesel-like cloud from his nostrils. "Richard, I did not know your father—except, naturally, through his work. During the war it was not possible to see American cinema. *Les Boches,* you know. And then we had our hands full, as you say. But I remember, in Nineteen Thirty-Nine, and also in Nineteen Forty, how the laughter rang out in the theaters of Paris. Not to mention these last years, when according to my taste he created his finest films. Well, I have not had the opportunity to tell you I am very sorry at your loss, which is also I understand very well a loss for all the world."

I had, at these words, to fight back a surge of tears. I turned my head. I brought my fist down on my knee. "Selfish!" I said out loud. But I kept to myself the source of this sorrow: *Poor Stanley,* those were the words I was thinking, furious that the pale, pudgy attorney, Norman's pal, had been forced to drag Bartie and me all around the city, to the museum, to the movies, when of course he wanted to be at the funeral of his friend. "Selfish!" I said once again, this time without tears, and perhaps even with some gratification that the Frenchman was bound to misunderstand.

With a quick motion he flicked his cigarette over the side. "*Oui.* Selfish. It is true. Your loss, it was also my opportunity. I have been enabled to meet Lotte. Yes. Ironic." A pause. The waves slapped and sucked at the watertight boards. René took a deep breath, as if upon his abandoned cigarette. "Richard, it is important that you know something. Allow me to tell you I love your mother very much. She is the delight of my life. My intention is to marry her. I offer you the promise that I will do all in my power to make her happy. As she makes me happy now." Another pause. Another inhalation. "In this case I will be for you and Barton a kind of father. I do not speak of Norman. I know what he meant to you. But you should know this, Richard: I will work to make up this loss, and I will make the attempt to be for you a good parent. I hope that in the course of time we shall perhaps respect each other and experience love among the members of our family."

"What do you mean, *respect? Love?* Don't make me laugh!" All I could think of was his arms on my mother's back, she leaning into him, the blowing curtains that had exposed them. *The Kiss,* by Rodin. "I know you're living in sin!"

At these words René plucked up the oars, leaned forward once more, and dipped both blades into the ocean. I felt the same thrill of triumph that I supposed Dale Long must have sensed when the sweet spot of his bat struck the fastball. I had won! Humbled, defeated, the Frenchman was taking me back. But then I noted that he had swung the prow westward and that, more leisurely now, effortlessly even, we were drawing still further from the coastline. I peered ahead, to the horizon, only to discover that there was no longer any demarcation between sea and sky. I wheeled to look over my shoulder. The very continent had disappeared! The hills were gone and so was the highway, with its stream of cars. There was no bluff, no row of houses. The beach itself was dissolving, as if inundated by a great, gray wave. Here and there I could make out a figure, half dismembered, or an article of clothing: a bathing suit in red; a parasol, orange; a scarf, green or greenish, held aloft. Was that Lotte? Waving a greeting? Signaling danger? In a few more strokes even those shreds had vanished. It was dead calm. There was nothing but fog on every side. Soon even the tips of the oars, the dripping blades, grew blurred. René rowed on.

"This is far enough." The words, my own, in that bell jar, sounded like a shout.

René, not halting, glanced up. "Far enough for what?" he answered.

I had no idea why I said what came out next. "For whatever you want to do."

He did not respond. He pulled the oars six more times. Then he sat upright, letting the shafts dangle in the water. "Yes. It is far enough."

I did not dare speak, because I feared my voice would tremble, not so much from fear as from the force of an inexplicable sadness. René spoke instead.

"It is a pity. I have offered you friendship. But you make a mockery. I row, you know, to release the anger in my arms." I stared at those arms, which hung at his sides, and at his fingers, which once more remained tense and curled. "You are a boy, a child, nothing, Richard: there is in you no experience of life. But in your work, that is where you are already a man. Poor René, eh? He looks in the mirror. He paints a clown. Much life. Little talent."

Now, as he spoke, he began to pull on one of the oars. The boat turned on its axis, and kept spinning about in its own little whirlpool. Then, singlehandedly, he removed the Chesterfields from his tightly stretched shirt top, popped like magic a single cigarette from the pack, and placed it in his mouth. Another trick: he struck with one hand a match on his matchbook and in the calm allowed it to burn. "So, Richard, if you will attend my words. This Mademoiselle Madeline. The *petite jeune fille,* eh? The little neighbor girl. You will tell me how you persuaded her to take off her clothes."

That was the instant I realized René was going to kill me. I had read with absolute certainty the contents of his mind. The movement of the boat in a dizzying circle; the match that burned in the gray and gloom; his voice, *you will tell me, attend my words*—it was all a form of hypnotism. And I was the one sleeping, nodding, willing to obey his command: *squeal like a pig! rear like a horse! throw yourself into the water!*

René drew up the oars. He got to his feet, towering above me. One by one, I understood, he was going to kill us all. Starting with poor little Sammy. Then me, the hurdle, the obstacle: *I'd never do anything you didn't approve.* Next crazy Bartie. Poor crazy Bartie. And Lotte too, though only after he'd married her. For her money. Norman's money. His Oscar that looked as if it were made from gold.

He raised the oar, streaming with the wet of the sea. "*Ecoutez!*" he commanded, continuing the fiction that he was a Frenchman. "On your feet." I obeyed. "Turn around." I followed those instructions too, turning my back upon him. I had no idea whether I was facing Malibu Beach or the islands of the Pacific, MacArthur's Philippines, the far off lands of the East. He moved directly behind me in the tipping boat and grasped my shoulders. I took a breath, to prepare for the moment I hit the water. Now I wanted to live. Not for myself. To warn the others. Could I swim for it? But in what direction? And would he not beat the life from me, as one might club to death a swimming rat?

"Don't budge yourself," he said, his grip like iron. Then I smelled something familiar. The sweet wisps of tobacco. He had lit his cigarette. Suddenly he was by me, sitting in my place at the stern. "Hold these," he said, extending the grips of the oars. He gestured for me to take his empty seat. "You will teach me from your knowledge, all the secrets of art. Perhaps one day, in a future we cannot know, this Betty will also hang a work by René upon her walls. And I? I will teach you. My friend, you have much to learn. So. Straighten your arms, if you please. Lean from the waist. Up. Lift the oars up. Now dip them. Pull! Pull! Pull for *la Californie!*"

5.

I rowed us in. The breeze, ever capricious, started up again, easing my task. The sun, well down in the sky, began to burn through the thinning haze, like the bulb of a projector scorching a strip of film. We caught a wave into the shallow water, than carried the boat over the gravel and across the beach to its mooring in the lagoon. René headed off to the pastel cabins along the highway. The hills were again in plain view, brown even in springtime, with patches of white yucca. There were still a few people lingering on the beach. I trudged back along the shore. Before I reached the spot where I'd left Bartie, he came running toward me, trailing a dancing and darting maroon-colored kite.

"Where'd you get that?" I asked.

He looked up to where the kite tugged at its taut, white tether. "It was under the house. He's got a box of stuff down there."

Just then a dog came rushing out of the surf and made for us. "It's Sammy!" I exclaimed. The spaniel, half normal size in his wet coat, leaped at me, happily barking. Then he shook the salt water from his body. "You said he killed him!" I screamed at Bartie. "That Achille killed him! It was a lie!"

My brother was still looking up, to where the kite was diving toward the ground. He pulled on the cord, which sent it scooping skyward again. Then he turned the wet and glittering marble of his eyes on me. "I didn't lie. You don't know the truth. It's possible to come back from the dead."

"Oh-hoo! Yoo-hoo!" I knew that cry. Lotte was making her way toward us from the foot of the tumble-down house. Behind her, René followed, carrying a small four-legged tray, like a Japanese table for tea. He'd changed back into his shirt of concentric circles, blue and yellow, and had on a pair of white, tennis player's pants.

"Éclairs!" he shouted. "Éclairs!"

Lotte waved her grass-green scarf. "Well," she exclaimed as she drew closer. "If Mohamot won't come to the mountain—"

I saw that she'd washed out her hair, which now hung loose and dark to her shoulders. Sampson dashed by her, making for René. He leaped three feet in the air, hoping to snatch one of the cream-filled pastries.

Bartie grabbed my arm. He put the spindle of string into my hand. "It's you who made the mistake," he said, starting up the beach to get his dessert. "It was all inside your head."

I remained alone for a moment, while the three of them, the four counting Sammy, arranged themselves around the lacquered tray. Motionless, I stared across the ocean. There was no way I could know that just two months later René and Lotte would be married. Or that, after another two months, she would discover that he had looted all her accounts. In the British comedy Alec Guinness is led off in handcuffs. In real life René and my mother only divorced. But by then much had irrevocably changed. Bartie and I were sent off for a few months to a private academy; when we came back we discovered that Sampson, irascible, not to be reconciled with Achille, had been put to sleep. He had seen clearly what, on that far-off Sunday, I could only imagine.

At Malibu, on the empty beach, the kite continued to jerk back and forth above my head. At my feet a wave broke into pieces, like a hundred thousand beads of mercury that soon reassembled themselves beneath the shining mirror of the sea.

Alice Hoffman

The Wedding of Snow and Ice

In 1957, on the very rim of the Cape, a small town often didn't feel small until the first snowfall of the season. In those muffled first moments, in the hush and stillness before the flakes began and the anticipation of the mess there'd be to dig out afterward, people congregated in the general store, there to stock up on candles and flashlights, franks and beans and loaves of bread. People regularly knew each other's business, now they also could recite what was in their neighbors' refrigerators and cupboards. Then and there, the world shrank and became a smaller thing, simple as a driveway, a red wicker basket filled with bread and milk, a cleared road, a light in a neighbor's window, a snowglobe on a child's shelf.

At the Farrells', they were taking down the barn, and when the first big flakes began to fall all work had to stop. There was no point in risking a slip on the roof and the possibility of a broken arm or leg. The Farrells, after all, were a cautious breed. The father, Jim, and the two boys, Hank and Jamie, trooped into the kitchen, their faces ruddy, hands frozen in spite of woolen gloves. Grace Farrell had been listening to the weather reports on the radio and had made soup from the canned tomatoes left from last August's garden. The bowls of rich broth were so hot and delicious it made tears form in Jim's eyes, although, frankly, the boys preferred Campbell's.

Still, at fourteen and seventeen, the Farrell brothers knew enough to compliment their mother's soup. When they'd foolishly made their preference known in the past, their mother, most easy-going but with occasional frightening spikes of passion that surprised one and all, had spilled the entire contents of the pot down the drain. She, who liked things homemade and was known for her grape jam and Christmas pudding, announced she didn't know why she bothered with any of it. She might just get herself a job and then where would they be? Eating bread and butter and soup right out of the can. She'd been a nurse when Jim Farrell met her and she'd given it up to take care of them and did they even appreciate what she'd sacrificed? Why, next summer she might even let the garden go wild if that was how little they thought of the work she put in. The garden was a trial anyway, a constant war against the naturalized sweet peas, vines so invasive Grace Farrell yanked them out by the handful. In the early fall, she'd had the older boy, Hank, hack down the vines with an axe, then build a bonfire. The smoke that arose was so sweet Grace Farrell wound up crying. She said there was smoke in her eyes, but she got like that sometimes, as if there was another life somewhere out there she might be living, one she might prefer despite her love for her husband and sons.

The sweet peas in the field were thought to have been set down by the first inhabitant of the house, Coral Hadley, who lost her husband and son at sea. Coral was said to never look at the ocean again after that, even though it was little more that a mile from her door. She dug in tightly to the earth, and there were people who vowed that her fingers turned green. When she walked down Main Street acorns fell out of her pockets so that anyone following too closely behind was sure to stumble. Coral certainly did her best to cultivate this acreage. All these years later her presence was still felt; odd, unexpected specimens popped up on property, seeming to grow overnight. Peach trees where none belonged. Hedges of lilac of a variety extinct even in England. Roses among the nettle. The two-acre field rampant with those damned sweet peas, purple and pink and white, strong as weeds, impossible to get rid of.

Grace Farrell had stated publicly that she would swear that Coral Hadley came back from the dead just to replant anything that had been ripped up. Surely a joke, considering that Grace was one of the most sensible individuals around, the last woman you'd ever expect might believe in ghosts, the first a body could depend on in times of strife. She'd had her hands full with the boys of hers: Hank was the dreamer who didn't pay attention to his schoolwork. Jamie was the wilder one who simply couldn't sit still. In grammar school the fourth-grade teacher, Helen Morse, had tied Jamie's left arm to the desk in an attempt to force him to improve his penmanship by using his right hand, but Jamie had simply walked around the room dragging the desk along with him. He remained victorious, stubbornly left-handed.

He certainly had energy, that boy. He had to be kept busy, for his own good as well as for the peace of mind of those around him. Thankfully, they didn't have to think up projects. There were endless tasks around the house. The shaky old barn pulled down for safety's sake, for instance, though the boys had loved to play there when they were younger, swinging from the rope in the hayloft, nearly breaking their necks every time. New kitchen cabinets had just been put in, and Jamie had helped Jim with that job as well. He'd been just as helpful when the dreadful stained carpeting was at last taken up, exposing the yellow pine floors that were said to be soaked with Coral Hadley's tears.

There was always something gone wrong with a house as old as this one. Maybe Grace should have said no when Jim first took her to see the place. It was the week before their wedding, and Grace was still living with her parents up in Plymouth. She had recently given up her job at the hospital. "Isn't it gorgeous?" he'd said of the farm. It looked like one of those tumbledown places you saw in the news magazines, with hound dogs lazing around the front door. The fields were so thick with milkweed back then that a thousand goldfinch came to feed every spring. Anyone wishing to reach the pond had to use a scythe to cut a path. All the same, the look on Jim's face had made Grace say, "Oh, yes." It had made her throw all good sense away. For an instant the house did look beautiful to her, all white clapboards and right angles; the milkweed was shining, illuminated by thin bands of sunlight, an amazing sight if you looked at it in the right way, if you narrowed your eyes until everything blurred into one bright and gleaming horizon.

Jim Farrell had grown up in town. His father had been a carpenter, and Jim, wanting steadier work, was the chief of the public works department, the chief of three other men, at any rate. He was a good man, quiet, not one to shirk responsibility. People said he could smell snow, that he could divine a nor'easter simply from the scent in the air. The biggest storms smelled like vanilla, he'd confided to Jamie, the small ones like wet laundry. Tonight, Jim seemed antsy. He got like that when he simply couldn't tell what the snow was up to, when the whole damn thing seemed like a mystery. His job, after all, was a cat and mouse game against nature and fate. Did he get the town plows out early? Did he conserve sand and salt for the next snowfall? Would the storm carve away at the dunes, which were already disappearing all along the shore?

When Jim finished his soup and had taken his bowl to the sink, he stood at the window facing west. The field of sweet peas was already dusted white. Snow made him feel like crying sometimes—just the first flakes, the purest stuff.

Behind the hedge of hollies, the Brooks house next door was dark.

"Do you think I should go over there with some soup?" Grace had come up behind her husband. She liked the way he looked at snow, the intensity on his face, there when they made love, there whenever he was concentrating and trying to figure things out. "Hal might be away. I think he might still be working on that house in Bourne. She might be alone there with Josephine."

The Brooks were their closest neighbors, right there on the other side of the field, but there was no camaraderie between the families. Hal Brooks was a shit, there was no other way to say it, and even Grace, who was offended by bad language, would nod when someone in town referred to her neighbor that way. Lord, he'd been a mean snake all his life, the way Grace had heard it. Even as a boy, he'd shoot seagulls for sport, and once or twice a stray dog had disappeared on his property, only to be found strung up from one of the oak trees. Hal hadn't changed with age, and people in town all knew what was going on over there. You could see it when the Brooks name came up. A nod. A stepping back. Some people had seen what went on with his wife, some had heard about it. The rest would simply cross the street when the Brooks were in town.

"If she needs something she'll come and get it, won't she?" Jim said, although they both thought this probably wasn't true.

The boys were in the living room watching the new TV; they would watch anything that flickered up in front of them, and for a while at least Jamie, always so restless, would settle down. The boys didn't need to know what went on at the Brooks'. When Grace and Jim had first moved in, Lionel Brooks was the only occupant, a widower, a hard-working fisherman who kept his boat out in Provincetown. Hal had inherited the house from his father and had come to claim it after the old man died. He'd arrived home from the Navy with this wife of his, ready to make enemies left and right no matter how many welcome baskets were brought over and how many women in town sent over pies, Jim Farrell didn't want his wife next door for any reason, not even to take over a pot of soup.

"Stay away," Jim told Grace. "We all decide our own fates, and what they do is their business."

"Well, of course I won't go over. But I might send the boys to shovel snow."

Jim couldn't say no to that. Just last year, Mattie Hammond, eighty-four years old and all on her own, had been snowed into her cottage during a blizzard. The drifts had been so high, Mattie couldn't open her front door and had nearly starved to death before Jim came to plow out the street. Thankfully, despite the blanket of white that could cause semi-blindness in some men while they were at the plow, Jim had noticed the square handkerchief Mattie had taped up in a window to signal her distress. There were some things Jim Farrell couldn't deny a neighbor, particularly on a snowy night, and other situations Grace couldn't turn away from either, and because they didn't like to argue with each other, no matter their differences, they left it at that.

Jim went out to his truck at four in the afternoon, headed for the department of public works. It was the hour when everything turned blue—the snow, the white fences, the white clapboards of the house—that luminous time when the line between earth and sky disappeared.

"I want you boys to go shovel over at Rosalyn Brooks'," Grace called into the living room. She had ladled out a separate pot of tomato soup despite what Jim had advised. "Take the shovels and bring this soup with you."

When there was no response Grace went into the living room

and stood in front of the TV. The boys would watch just about anything, but their favorite show was *You Asked For It,* on tonight at seven. There were the most amazing things out there in the world, and all you had to do was ask and you'd see it right in front of you, on your very own screen.

"I'm turning this off," Grace announced, then did so. "I want you to shovel."

"At the Brooks'," Jamie said. "We heard."

"Can't. I've got a history paper," Hank said. "Sorry, Mom, but it's due tomorrow."

Hank was having his troubles in school, so Grace let him stay and sent Jamie on his own, making sure he bundled up, handing him his hat, which he often managed to forget, watching to make certain he pulled on his scarf and his leather gloves. The pot of soup was under one arm, the shovel carried over his shoulder. He was a quiet boy, not much of a student, but loveable to his mother in some deep way, so that she worried about him as she didn't anyone else in this world. Perhaps it was true that mothers had favorites, at least now and then. Grace watched Jamie disappear into the blue of the field and felt a catch in her throat. Love, she presumed. A moment of realizing exactly how lucky she was, of being grateful that she was not Coral Hadley, that her son was not out on the ocean, but was instead traipsing through the snowy reaches of their own familiar acreage.

When he was alone, Jamie tended to hum. His mother was a fan of musicals, particularly *The King and I,* and Jamie found himself humming "Getting To Know You." His mother loved Yul Brenner, for reasons Jamie couldn't understand. The king he played was bald, for one thing; he was bossy as all get out for another. All the same, the song stuck. Sometimes when Jamie walked though this field, in winter, at exactly this hour, he would see deer. There were wild turkeys too, crazy birds that have very little fear of humans and would run straight at you if you invaded their territory. There was a short cut to the Brooks', through the winterberry vines. The berries were shiny and red; sometimes you'd happen upon a skunk as you made your way though the brambles, and that skunk would just go on feeding, calm as could be, rightfully assured that no creature on earth would be stupid enough to interrupt or attack.

Jamie was in the winterberry, thinking about deer, singing softly to himself, when he heard it. A clap of thunder. A snowplow on the road. A firecracker. He stopped for a minute and breathed in snowflakes. When he breathed out it was a like a steam engine. It melted the snow off the winterberries. He listened. He was good at that, but heard nothing, so he went on. He was that sort of boy, intent on his task at hand. He knew what his mother wanted him to do: shovel the Brooks' front door to their driveway. He and Hank had done it before, last year. Mr. Brooks hadn't been at home, but Mrs. Brooks had made them hot chocolate, which they drank out on the front step. Now, alongside the Chevy there was Mr. Brooks' truck, a wreck of a thing, battered as all get out, leaking oil into the snow.

Jamie tried to balance the soup on the front step, but the step was made from of an uneven piece of stone. He went up to the door then, to deliver the soup before he started to work. His breath did the same thing to the glass window set into the door as it did to the winterberries, melted off the snow, then fogged it up. But even through the fog he could see Rosalyn Brooks, right there on the floor with no clothes on and something red all over her face. He should have backed away; he should run home, done something, anything, but he had never seen a naked woman before, and it was as though he was hypnotized, frozen in place while his breath kept melting the snow. One minute he had been a fourteen-year-old boy with nothing much on his mind. Now, he was someone else entirely.

He was still holding on to the pot of tomato soup when he opened the door. People didn't lock up much in their town; there was nothing to steal and no one to steal it. Jamie walked in as though he'd been drawn inside by a magnetic force. The Brooks' house was an old farmhouse, like the Farrells', but it hadn't been updated. It was cold and empty and the only light turned on was in the kitchen, all the way down the hall. Everything looked blue inside the house, except for the thing that was red. It was blood that was all over Rosalyn Brooks, but when she looked up and saw Jamie she seem most panicked by the fact that she was naked. She let out a strange sound and grabbed a rag rug, trying to cover herself. It was a sob, that's what Jamie realized. That was the sound.

"I brought you soup," he said. "It's from my mother."

Mrs. Brooks looked at him as though he were crazy.

"She makes it herself." Jamie felt like running, but he didn't seem capable of turning away. He had the feeling he might be paralyzed. "Are you all right?"

Rosalyn Brooks laughed, or at least that's what Jamie thought it was.

"Just stay there," he said. "I'll get you something."

He put the soup on a tabletop and went to the hall closet, grabbing for the first thing he felt, bringing back a heavy black woolen coat.

"It's okay," he said, because of the way she was looking at him. As though she were scared. "It's a coat."

Rosayln Brooks stared at him, then took the coat and put it on. Jamie Farrell looked away, all the same he glimpsed her breasts, blue in the light of the house, and her belly, which was oddly beautiful. She had bruises all over, that much he noticed as well, on her legs and shoulders especially. He now saw that her lip was split open and she could barely see through the slits of her eyes.

"Do you want me to heat you some soup?" It was so cold in the house that Jamie's breath came out in billows, and he was embarrassed by his own heat. When Mrs. Brooks didn't answer, he figured she wanted him to take the pot in the kitchen, but as he turned to head down the hall, Rosalyn lurched from her prone position and grabbed his pant leg.

She did it so hard and so fast he almost fell over. She looked at him in a way that convinced him that something really bad had happened. Somebody else might have taken off running, back through the winterberries, snagging his clothes as he raced through the bushes, but Jamie crouched down beside Mrs. Brooks.

"Where's Josephine?' he asked.

That was the Brooks' five-year-old daughter. Josephine liked to pick the sweet peas in the field. She liked the pears that dropped to the ground from the big tree in the Farrells' yard. Rosalyn looked up the stairs.

"Is she in bed?"

"Asleep."

At least Mrs. Brooks could talk. That was a relief.

"My husband had an accident."

"Okay," Jamie said. "Should we call my Dad? He could help."

"No. You can't call him."

He could tell that whatever happened was bad from her tone. Still, he stayed. Maybe Jamie felt he owed Rosalyn Brooks his allegiance because he'd seen her naked, or maybe it was all that blood, or the way his breath was so hot and the house so very cold.

"In the kitchen?"

Mrs. Brooks nodded. She was not yet thirty, a young woman, pretty under other circumstances.

"I'll just go in there and get a dishtowel to stop the bleeding," Jamie said, for her lip and her scalp were oozing.

But when he rose, she grabbed his leg again.

"It's okay," he assured her. "I'll be right back."

The hallway was even colder. The old houses had no insulation and the kitchen was especially chilly. There was even more blood on the floor, especially around Hal Brooks' body, which was right in front of the stove. Jamie tried not to look too closely. He grabbed a dishtowel, ran cold water over it, then brought it back to Rosalyn. He wondered if he had stepped in blood and if it was on the soles of his boots, if he'd left tracks down the hall. Then he stopped wondering. He put those thoughts aside. Rosalyn was sitting on the floor now, the coat buttoned; when he handed her the dishtowel, she held it up to her lip.

"What do you want to do with him?" Jamie said.

Outside, the blue was turning into darkness. A black night. So quiet you could hear the cardinals nesting in the hedges outside the Brooks' window. The snow fell harder. Jamie figured his father was up on the main road with his plow by now.

They sat there in silence in the cold house.

"I'll shovel your path, and then I'll come back," Jamie said. "You think about what you want to do."

"Okay," Rosalyn said. "I will."

Jamie went out and shoveled hard and fast. It was heavy snow, thick and dense, the kind he would have thought was good for snowball fights on any other occasion. He wasn't thinking that way now. He was thinking of the pond beyond the field. In the old days food could be stored in the summer kitchen right up until July if enough ice was stacked against the walls. He'd heard the old woman who'd lived in their house a while back had hauled blocks of ice from the pond until her horse, the one who'd lived in the barn they'd begun to tear down, slipped through the ice and drowned.

The kitchen floor at the Brooks' was already clean when Jamie came back inside. Rosalyn Brooks had mopped up, then washed her face and pulled back her honey-colored hair. There were still streaks of blood in her scalp, but Jamie Farrell didn't have the heart to tell her. Rosalyn went to check on her daughter, then came back downstairs and put on her husband's workboots. She looked even more delicate wearing them. She didn't bother with gloves. At least there was a blanket around Mr. Brooks, and Jamie was grateful for that. They tried to pull him along the floor, and when that didn't work, Jamie went and got the wheelbarrow from the garage. He was so hot he felt like taking off his hat and scarf, but if he misplaced them, his mother would have his head.

It took all their combined strength to push the wheelbarrow through the snow. The thick, heavy snow that they quietly cursed. They stopped for a break halfway across the field: they both looked up at the falling snow. Rosalyn put her arms out, and tilted her head back. Jamie had never thought about the future, who he was, what he would do. It had all been a haze. Now he saw that blood was still seeping through Rosalyn's hair and he thought she probably needed stitches. He saw that his future was almost here.

There were pine trees and holly around the far side of the pond, and that's where they went. They had to drag him along over the frozen weeds. They had put stones in his pockets, heavy black stones, the kind Jamie and Hank liked best for their slingshots. Rosalyn took off the workboots she'd been wearing and filled them with stones as well, then put the boots on her husband, laced them and carefully tied a knot, then a double-knot.

"Your feet will freeze on the way back," Jamie whispered.

She did not seem to care. She closed her eyes and when she opened them they were still slits. The snow was making things quieter all the time. They pulled him into the pond and watched him sink. There was a gulping noise at first, then there was nothing. Only the quiet.

"You go home," Rosalyn said to Jamie. "Go on. Your mother will be worried."

He hated to leave her like that, barefoot, bleeding.

She leaned over and kissed him, on the lips, in gratitude.

Jamie Farrell ran the rest of the way, his hot breath rattling against his ribs. His boots and pantslegs were wet and mucky. There was pond water in his boots, fetid, cold stuff. He was shivering and couldn't stop. Worst of all, his mother was waiting for him.

"What took you so long?" Grace demanded. "It's after eight. You missed your TV show." Then, looking at him carefully. "Where's the shovel?"

"I forgot it." Jamie turned back to the door. "I'm sorry. I'll go get it if you want."

His mother stopped him. She looked at him harder still. "I'll go. You do your homework and get ready for bed."

"I can get the shovel in the morning," Jamie offered, an edge of panic inside him, but Grace was already getting her coat. She had stepped into her warm black boots. After she left, Jamie went up to the bedroom he shared with his brother. It was as though he'd just walked out of a dream and here he was, melting in the overheated second floor of his family's house. He thought of all the wounded people there were in this world, people he'd never know, and he felt helpless.

"What if I was an accessory to murder?" he asked Hank, who was already in bed, more than half-asleep as he gazed at his history book.

"What if you were the biggest moron that ever lived?" Hank shot back, a question for which there was no answer, at least not on this night.

It was nearly midnight by the time Grace came home. The snow was tapering off and she brushed the flakes from her coat and stomped on the welcome mat to dislodge the ice from her boots. Usually, Jim didn't get back until dawn, but tonight he'd come home earlier. The storm wasn't as bad as the meteorologists has predicted. His men could take care of the rest and clean up.

"Where were you? The boys are in bed, and you weren't here, I didn't know what to think."

But that wasn't true. For a moment, what he'd thought was that she'd left him. Just disappeared into that other life she seemed to be thinking about sometimes. They stared at each other now, their breath hot. Outside the drifts leaned against the house; winter here stayed a long time.

"I went over and heated up the tomato soup for Rosalyn."

"Did you?"

Grace sat down at the table. Everyone had known what was going on, and no one had done a damn thing about it.

"Hal up and left. No money, no warning, nothing. She thinks he might have re-enlisted."

Jim was looking out the window; two deer had just now wandered into their field. Hopefully, the snow wasn't so deep that it would prevent them from unearthing the last withered sweet peas, thought to be delicious by anything wild. "I guess it's none of our business," he said. From this distance, the winterberries almost looked tropical, the fruit of another place entirely.

"So you say."

Grace Farrell still had snow in her hair, but it would melt when they got into bed and she'd never even know it had been there. When she thought back to this night she wouldn't even remember it had been snowing, she'd only remember the look on her husband's face, the concentration she loved, the man she could turn to, even on a night as cold as this.

Alice Elliott Dark

Maniacs

Silent sound, vivid absence, pressure from beyond the quilts and walls, the taste of pennies on the tongue; several miles apart two sisters awoke within moments of each other and instinctively knew it had snowed. Diana, the little sister at thirty-four and still known as the pretty one, didn't even have to confirm it by looking; she smiled; hadn't she prayed for this? She had, all week, and her prayers had worked! The children wouldn't have to go now, not today at least.

Thick mugs of melted chocolate, a fierce, popping fire, Scrabble, a pillowy camp in the Irving room—Margaret had the same picture in mind as she hurried to the window and snapped the curtains open, her toes curling away from the bitter floor. She was the type of slender, well-proportioned blonde who made a good figure and platinum hair seemed prim and unassailable rather than desirable and obvious. She was capable of feeling a secret wildness, though, and the thought of the storm that had come through overnight stirred her. She leaned her forehead against the cold glass and looked out.

It was still snowing, albeit gently now, just the final fat, ineffectual flakes. A fresh coat of white covered the frozen crust that had covered the ground in Wynnemoor for weeks, and the lower branches of the old pine were buried except for a smattering of green-black fronds that emerged yards from the tree, looking freakish and disconnected.

There was a girlish second when Margaret swayed a little, imitating the drifts on the windward side of the house, but she couldn't allow herself to think of the potential pleasures for long; the skies were calming, the children would go. She dialed the airline and pulled her navy-blue christening-wedding-funeral suit out of the closet. If there was any problem about the girls' reservations or seats, Margaret believed she could prevail more easily if she were respectably dressed. Duncan Abbott, her ex-husband, had always compared her to Princess Anne when she wore this particular item. Good riddance to him, she thought as she laid the suit on the chaise and picked bits of lint off the pleats. At least now she could enjoy her clothes.

She'd just run a bath when the telephone rang. Probably Duncan, she thought; she wouldn't put it past him to be up at four in the morning, calling with a last-minute request for the girls to have some obscure piece of equipment with them when they arrived. In the past couple of weeks she'd bought snorkels, in-line skates, rubber swimming shoes. She wished she could trust him to purchase safe equipment, but as always, if she wanted it done right, she had to do it herself. She certainly couldn't get out to a store this morning, though. She'd have to send it express, whatever it was.

She grabbed the receiver, irritated, hoping the ring hadn't woken the girls. She wanted to let them sleep as late as was practical; she doubted they'd have a bedtime at Duncan's.

"What now?" she asked, without even saying hello.

It wasn't Duncan, though.

"Hurrah, hurrah," Diana cheered. "Let it snow! Now the girls can stay home."

Margaret wondered at Diana's perpetual wishful thinking. "No, they can't. Their plane is three hours late, that's all. They're going."

"You're not going to let them fly in this weather!"

"Why not?" Margaret crossed to her dressing table and picked up a nail file. She had a whole list of ways to use the time she spent on the telephone.

"It's dangerous. Think of all the planes that have crashed because of icing. You're giving a lot of credit to the greedy people who make these decisions."

"Oh, Diana." Margaret looked at the trees, the glassed branches, and hoped the gardener would remember his promise—she'd make him promise before signing a contract with him—to always plow her driveway first.

The girls were flying to visit their father at his new place in California, their first extended stay with him since the divorce. The night before, as she read in the living room, Margaret heard sounds she thought were squirrels in the walls; but as she approached the staircase, she realized it was the girls, tiptoeing back and forth to each other's rooms, whispering. Go to sleep, she called out, and the footsteps stopped. Later she'd wanted to look in on them, watch them sleep, but they'd reached the age when they'd taken to shutting their doors. "Anyway, I couldn't postpone the trip if I wanted to. There's a legal agreement, remember."

"Laws are made to be broken."

"Not this one. I can't afford another court battle."

Diana gave an exasperated sigh. "All right. I give up for now. Maybe you'll change your mind when we get to the airport and you see the condition of the planes."

"When *we* get to the airport?"

"I'm going with you," Diana said. "I promised the girls I would."

"When did all this happen?"

"Yesterday. When I was helping them pack. They're nervous about seeing Duncan, Marg."

"You should have asked me first."

There was a pause. Margaret heard a match strike.

"You'll be glad I came when the car gets stuck in the snow and I'm there to help shovel," Diana said.

Margaret considered whether or not it was worth arguing about this. She had to pick her battles with Diana the same as she did with the children. Little did Diana know how much she'd helped prepare Margaret for motherhood.

"All right. We'll pick you up at eleven. Be outside, please, and *please* don't repeat your paranoid plane crash fantasies to the children."

"I'm not an idiot."

"No comment."

"See you," Diana singsonged and hung up.

In the bathroom, Margaret hung her nightdress behind the door and plunged swiftly into the water. The bottom of the old cast iron tub was cold against her back. She picked up her loofah and went to work, scuffing her pale skin and coaxing the blood to the surface. Scrub, scrub, scrub, until she ached. Of course the children were nervous about seeing Duncan. He'd made Margaret nervous for fifteen years. Diana always thought she was so insightful, especially when it came to the girls. Margaret wished Diana would hurry up and get married and have children of her own, so she wouldn't be so obsessed with Allie and Evie. She'd drifted for long enough. She was probably back in bed right now, sleeping the morning away. Never mind, never mind, Margaret told herself. She had enough to worry about. In just a few hours, the girls would be gone.

"Looks like we have some time to kill. Shall we play *I Spy?*" Diana asked as they got into the long check-in line.

The girls glanced at each other in mute consultation. They were only a year apart but they looked nothing alike; Allegra was narrow and dusky while Evangeline was freckled and fair. But they were very close, like an old married couple, and alternated between bickering and putting up a united front against the rest of the world. At eleven and twelve, they'd reached the stage when people such as the man in the booth at the parking garage addressed them as "young ladies," and they were consequently wary of backsliding into the leagues of mere children. Margaret half expected them to reject Diana's suggestion, but Allie cocked her head and nodded, signaling that this situation was an exception to whatever their current rules might be.

"All right," Evie said, announcing their silent consensus.

"Good!" Then Margaret headed off a predictable squabble between the girls by insisting she go first. "I spy something blue."

Diana rolled her eyes.

"Not interesting enough for you?" Margaret challenged.

Diana raised her hands in a defensive gesture. "I didn't say anything."

"You don't have to."

"No fighting, no biting," Evie said.

"We're not fighting," Margaret and Diana said simultaneously. Diana laughed. "One-two-three-four-five-six-seven-eight-nine-ten you owe me a Coke," she said.

"What does that mean?" Evie asked. Margaret always marveled at Evie's femininity. She was the kind of girl Margaret always envied when she was little, the kind afraid of spiders and disturbed by dead birds and mud. Margaret hadn't been, and when she'd tried to fake that range of sensitivity, she thought she came across as a jerk. She couldn't believe she'd produced a daughter who could shriek with the best of them.

"It's what we used to do after we said something at the same time," Diana explained. "Except both people are supposed to participate in the race. Margaret is a party pooper."

Diana wrinkled her lip at the girls, who took the cue and giggled at Margaret's expense. Great, Margaret thought. It hadn't taken long for Diana to get on her nerves. During the drive to the airport she'd prattled on *ad nauseam* about a man she'd met at a party the weekend before. As usual, her fantasies were way ahead of reality, to the point where she engaged the girls in a silly, in-depth discussion about possible bridesmaid dresses. Evie wanted gingham and a big bonnet, and Allie said she'd seen a fashion spread on black bridesmaid dresses in a magazine and thought they looked cool.

"Your mother would never were a black matron-of-honor dress," Diana said. "Would you, Marg?"

"Not even in hell," she'd answered.

She hadn't meant to be funny, but the girls roared.

She laughed, too, in an involuntary burble that caused a pain in her chest. Finally she brought the conversation back down to earth by asking Diana a few practical questions about this prince, such as what he did for a living, what his last name was, and why wasn't he married at his age. Diana didn't know the answer to any of them.

"He was nice," Diana said. "And cute," she added, winking at the girls. "What more is there?"

An hour later, Margaret was still annoyed by that exchange. She wished Diana wouldn't fill the girls' heads with romantic garbage.

Especially not when they were about to spend time with their father, about whom she wanted them to have some perspective.

"I spy something blue," Margaret repeated. "Any guesses?" She pushed the girls' suitcase—her big old suitcase—forward with her foot. Kicked it, really.

"Is it that man's scarf?" Evie asked, pointing at someone a few check-in lines away.

They all turned to look. Margaret wasn't sure of the order in which things happened next—whether she spotted Jerome Strauss before Diana gasped or vice versa. Either way, there he was.

For a long time—too long—Margaret had looked for Jerome wherever she went. She had no right to, he'd never been her boyfriend; he'd like Diana from the moment they met him at a proper old hotel in Florida where he was on spring vacation with his parents as they were with theirs. Diana had seen him on and off for years. Everyone assumed they'd get engaged sometime after college, but their relationship continued much as before, on-again, off-again, and befuddling to all observers. When you asked Diana about Jerome, you were as liable to hear that she was over him and seeing someone else as you were to hear his news. He disappeared from her conversation for months at a time; then, suddenly, Diana would be obsessing over him again, in her own, utterly self-referential way.

"What do you think he's going to give me for Christmas?" she'd ask. Or, "He's going to love me in this dress."

Margaret inured herself to Diana's patter as best she could. It was difficult not to blurt out the truth, though, difficult not to shout out loud that she was the one who really loved Jerome, deeply, constantly, and so truly that she had the strength to keep it to herself. She continued to love Jerome for years, even after he and Diana broke up for good and he moved to Texas, which—to her—was the equivalent of disappearing from the face of the earth. It wasn't until somewhere between the births of her two daughters that Margaret had stopped looking for him, stopped imagining she'd spotted the back of his head, that it was him a few rows ahead in the movie theater or that he was the man who had just rounded the corner and slipped out of sight.

She didn't forget him, however. After Duncan moved out she reread her old diaries, searching for the passages about Jerome. They were even more intense than she remembered; she was tempted to make copies of a few particularly avid passages for Duncan, who'd accused her of lacking passion. She didn't do it, though—her feelings for Jerome were none of Duncan's business. After her reading had buoyed her she'd put the diaries back in the attic. They were like money tucked in a mattress, insurance for bad times. For a while, in her shock and loneliness, she obsessed over the memory of Jerome, but even at her lowest, she never actually believed she'd seen him again.

Now, here he was, standing just a few airline check-in counters away. She found herself alternately straining to get a better view and foolishly glancing around at her fellow travelers—she didn't want to look at Diana—to see if anyone else was showing signs of the amazement she felt, as if he were universally recognizable. She noted the ironic flair with which he reached into the inside pocket of his jacket for his ticket, making fun of big shot types. The woman behind the counter began her work perfunctorily, but was soon leaning forward, offering him private smiles that she no doubt ordinarily withheld; so, Margaret thought wryly, he hasn't lost his touch.

Instinctively, she looked up at the overhead monitor and wondered which flight he would be taking. She didn't see any flights to Texas listed; perhaps he was making a connection somewhere, like Atlanta, or St. Louis, or. . . . Margaret stopped herself. In the present case, such calculation was particularly pointless, as there was no chance that she might be on his flight, no chance of it at all. The children were flying to California. Margaret wasn't going anywhere.

"Do you see what I see?" Diana said in a low voice, as if he might somehow hear her.

"I do," Margaret said.

"He hasn't changed." Diana continued to stare. "He's exactly the same. Even his hair."

Jerome's hair was the clear shimmery gray-brown of a pond in the fall. He wore it loose and long. He looked like Jesus.

"Who are you talking about?" Allie asked.

"An old friend of Diana's is here," Margaret said.

"Oh. An old boyfriend," Allie said knowingly.

Diana gave a pained smile and lay her hand on Allie's shoulder.

"Am I the only one playing this game?" Evie asked.

"I'm sorry. Take a guess."

"I just did. Is it that woman's shoes?"

Margaret said that was indeed what she'd had in mind. She'd actually been thinking of the navy uniforms on the airline personnel, but what difference did it make? Diana was right: blue was everywhere. "So it's your turn."

"Let me think for a minute," Evie said self-consciously.

"I can't believe it's really him," Diana said, mostly to herself. Neither can I, Margaret thought, feeling the same queasy lift in her stomach that used to overcome her whenever she thought of him. It was so easy to hide her own emotion; she'd always done so. Diana had never had any idea how Margaret really felt.

"Which one is he? I want to see," Allie said.

Diana pointed. The girls raised up on their toes.

"You liked him? He looks like a hippie." Allie fixed Diana with a gaze that combined curiosity with disapproval. In her consternation, Margaret was sorry to note, Allie resembled Duncan Abbot.

"I think he looks nice," Evie said. "And looks aren't everything anyway. How old were you when you knew him?"

"I met him when I was in eleventh grade, then we saw each other during college."

"Did you love him?" Allie asked.

"Uh huh."

As if! Margaret thought. It had driven her nuts how casual Diana was, how she toyed with Jerome and took him for granted. Apparently Diana remembered it differently. The sight of Jerome rendered her features young and sweet, and gazed at him wistfully, the way Margaret had at the girls when they were babies, when she was both happy and pained to see them getting bigger.

"I loved him a lot more than I understood at the time," Diana said.

As if picking up on Diana's nostalgia—he wouldn't pick up on Margaret's, he'd never picked up on any of her feelings—he suddenly stared in their direction. Diana waved, but in an uncharacteristically small way, and he didn't respond. She'd been up on her toes, but sank back down when he turned away again. "I guess he didn't see me," she said. "I wonder what he thinks of me now?"

Typical, Margaret thought with great disgust. Diana didn't even consider that he might not recognize her, and she assumed she was on his mind. What would it be like to be so sure of oneself?

"Do you think I should go talk to him?" Diana asked.

"I thought you were here for the girls."

"It would only take a minute."

Margaret shrugged. "Do what you want." You will anyway, she thought darkly.

She couldn't stand watching Diana trying to make up her mind whether or not to reopen old wounds so she turned her attention to her handbag and the girls' tickets. She'd had them in her desk for the past two weeks and had checked them daily. She'd always been like that: the person chosen to take the roll call, keep the score, be the treasurer. Someone had to. The tickets were there, of course, between her checkbook and wallet. She pulled them out and held them in her hand.

"Maybe if I talk to him I could finally get some closure on this," said Diana.

"Whatever," Margaret said, steeling herself for the old, painful picture of Jerome and Diana together, their heads bent close. "Allie, help me with the suitcase, will you?"

The girls hovered near her as she handed in their tickets and made the final arrangements for their flying unescorted. For a moment she forgot all about Jerome and thought only of the children, the safety of the children, and of how empty their bedrooms would be for the next couple of weeks, how still the house. This was where her proper suit came in handy, and her proper tone of voice. The man behind the counter was both deferential and protective. When she was all set, she turned around and saw the girls—all three of them—watching Jerome Strauss disappear into a spidery leg of the terminal.

"So you decided not to accost the poor man after all?" Margaret said.

"I'll find him. I just need a few minutes, to think of what I want to say."

"Maybe you need a cigarette to steady your nerves," Evie said.

"See the kind of example you set?" Margaret accused Diana. She turned to the girls. "No one ever needs a cigarette for any reason. We'll go get something to eat."

"Speaking of reasons—there's got to be a reason why Jerome and I are here, together, now," Diana said.

"I'd hardly say you're here together."

"Maybe not literally, but you've got to admit it's an amazing coincidence. I didn't see a ring on his finger, did you?"

Margaret didn't answer. She didn't want to admit she'd looked.

"Don't get anything heavy," Margaret said. They were in line in the cafeteria. "Just a salad or some soup. The flight can be hard on your stomach."

"Oh, let them have whatever they want," Diana said. "This is a special occasion."

The girls looked at Margaret uncertainly.

"All right. Within reason. I'm sure your father will let you eat anything you want anyway." She heard the harshness in her voice, but she couldn't help it. She was still nonplussed by how afraid the children had been to walk through the security checkpoint. Diana was the one who figured out what was bothering them. She guessed that they were under the sway of the schoolyard wisdom that predicted the metal hooks in their bras would set off the alarms on the metal-detector gates. They were both in training bras, way before Margaret would have thought them necessary, but for once, she'd given in to their pleas for conformity; they claimed all their friends had them, and that the boys were merciless to those who didn't. In her day, it had been the other way around, but she took their word for it. What harm could it do? She hoped that allowing them to wear bras would be her latest triumph in reverse psychology; they would feel secure, at one with the other girls, which might preserve their childhoods a bit longer.

When they didn't set off a slew of alarms, they slumped with relief. Evie became a little girl again, smiling and curling her fingers into triumphant fists, while Allie grabbed her knapsack off the conveyor belt, located her hairbrush and whipped it fiercely through her hair. Margaret wanted to hug them but restrained herself.

Diana, though, had thrown her arms around them both and made a few intimate, jokey remarks about the trials of being a woman that they hadn't minded at all.

"Wow," Diana said as she watched the girls choose yogurts and rolls. She looked at Margaret. "You've certainly got them well trained." She turned to Allie and Evie. "Eat like that and you'll be beautiful forever."

They smiled hopefully up at their aunt. Diana poured two cups of coffee while Margaret paid for everything. When they commandeered a vacant table, Evie used a napkin to brush the crumbs left by the previous occupants into her hand. Diana sat down, shook her arms out of her coat, and took a bracing swig of coffee. "That's better. God. I really thought I was going to fall on the floor right there."

Margaret drummed her fingertips against her mug. "That would've been just what I needed."

"He looked cute, didn't he?" Diana fished.

"You sound like a teenager."

"Hey, you were a teenager once upon a time yourself. At least biologically. Although I have to say it didn't seem to make much of an impression on you."

"I bet she was the same as she is now, right?" Allie said.

"You got it. A Girl Scout all the way."

"At least I wasn't insanely boy crazy like some people I know."

"This sounds *good.*" Allie rubbed her hands and scrunched up her face in a typically exaggerated performance while Evie merely widened her eyes. In spite of the difference in pitch, they were equally interested.

"Tell," Allie said.

"It was truly sickening," Margaret began. "All Diana talked about were boys, boys, boys, all day, all night. As you would say, Allie, yuck city."

"But I wasn't a shrinking violet. You can't accuse me of that," Diana said.

The girls burst out laughing.

"What's so funny?" Diana asked.

"A shrinking violet," Allie giggled.

"I think that's an expression way before their time," Margaret teased.

Diana grimaced. "Are you calling me old?"

"Did I say that?"

"At least I don't act old. Not like some people I know." Diana pointed to Margaret under cover of her palm, making the girls laugh again.

"Ahem," Margaret said, playing along. "Weren't we talking about Aunt Diana?"

"Right!" Evie said. "What did she do?"

Margaret leaned closer to the table. The girls instinctively copied her, encouraging her confidence.

"She always had a crush on one boy or another. I think the first one was Tommy Duffy. That was fourth grade, right, Di?"

"Tommy Duffy," Diana said dreamily. "He stole a bracelet from his mother and gave it to me."

"How romantic," Margaret drawled. The girls loved sarcasm, and she didn't mind pandering once in a while. They giggled right on cue. "Then, if memory serves, there was Chauncey Biddle."

"Chauncey!" the girls shrieked.

"If you'd seen how cute he was, you would have learned to ignore the name, too," Diana said with mock defensiveness.

"Then who?" Evie asked.

"I think that brings us to Billy Bell," said Diana. "He was a surfer."

"A New Jersey surfer," Margaret amended.

"What's that?" Allie asked.

"Never mind," Diana said. "Your mother's just jealous. Billy was very blond, very skinny, very tough. I used to follow him around and he'd pretend he didn't see me until all of his friends peeled off to their houses or wherever. Then, when he was sure no one was looking, we'd kiss. After him I met Blair Warren. . . ."

Diana took over, to the girls' delight, embellishing the stories way beyond Margaret's bald recitation of names. And stories they were, for half of Diana's fun had been to describe the blow-by-blow, the he-said-I-said, and to show around her love letters. When Margaret was sixteen, she'd written in her diary one night that if she died right then, the life that passed before her eyes would be a series of scenes of Diana appearing in the doorway of Margaret's bedroom, saying she just had to talk about some boy or another or she'd faint! Diana was always in love, full of schemes and wishes, and went back and forth between the two, as if they were of equal strategic value. She couldn't understand why Margaret didn't try harder to attract the opposite sex and took it upon herself to instruct Margaret on every tip garnered from the teen magazines she bought after school with her baby-sitting money. Want a wide-eyed look? Draw extra lashes beneath your lower lid. A pouty mouth? Put a dab of concealer in the center of your lower lip. Enhance your bosom? Wear ruffles!

Diana still followed such advice. Just recently she'd come across a reminder that keeping the muscles around her mouth as still as possible could forestall the development of laugh lines and decided it was time she paid attention. For a few days afterward she ate like one of those self-conscious aging beauties who manage to slide their food off their fork, chew it and swallow it, all with their faces in utter repose. But this was one trick that eluded Diana; she looked stiff as a robot and about as attractive. "You'd better check that out in a mirror before you make it a permanent part of your repertoire," Margaret had advised. Diana said plastic surgery would take care of the problem anyway.

Margaret witnessed Diana's adventures and heartbreaks and, in the manner of sisters, carved out an opposing identity for herself. She has a reputation for reliability and decided her best course would be to expand on that and similar qualities. She'd done everything she could to make herself immune to boy craziness, which was easy after she met Jerome, and knew she'd never love anyone but him. She thought she'd never marry when, just as she was about to go to law school, she met Duncan Abbott. Diana had always thought it funny that he'd picked Margaret up in a museum.

"He knew exactly where to find a girl like you," she said.

None of his lines had been particularly good, but his interest was clear though appropriately restrained. Their courtship was equally fathomable. Nothing he did disqualified him, and he was straightforward about his desire for children, a longing she shared. There were even moments when she adored him. Over time, she compared him less and less frequently to Jerome.

One day she realized she was going to plunge ahead with him, so there was no point struggling against the inevitable. She, who had always had some sort of job since she was nine years old, even accepted that he had family money of a magnitude that he didn't have to work and didn't. Nor did she—terrible, terrible mistake. At least she could make up for that now. She was going to start law school in the fall and go ahead with a career, better late than never. She couldn't do a thing about her bad judgment over Duncan—except raise the girls to be as unlike him as possible.

"And then, of course, there were the Beatles," Diana was saying.

The girls looked at each other and shrieked.

"You mean you were on of those Beatles nuts?" Allie winced. Evie clapped her hand over her mouth and bounced up and down.

"A Beatlemaniac," Margaret instructed.

"Really? How about Mom?" The girls looked at Margaret.

"No way." said Diana. "Can you really imagine her getting carried away like that? No, she didn't fall in love with them. In fact, one night when I was driving her crazy playing the same record over and over—"

" 'Day Tripper,' " Margaret grimaced. "Aunt Diana destroyed that song for me."

"Allie does that to me!" Evie said. "She made me hate Madonna."

Diana was unperturbed. "Well then you'll be glad to know that Margaret got her revenge. She made lists of all the girls we knew, divided onto four pages, with the names of each of the Beatles at the top. Then she told me what it revealed about each of our friends that they liked a particular Beatle the best. It was scary, because she was right, at least for the most part. How did that go again, Marg?"

"Oh, I don't know." Margaret glanced at her watch. They had plenty of time, really.

"Of course you do. Start with John."

"John. All right." She paused and automatically folded her napkin as she gathered her thoughts. "He was the coolest one, and the girls who liked him were cool, too. They usually wanted to be artists and were the first to start smoking."

Diana nodded. "You see? She remembers. Do Paul."

"The girls who liked him were the ones who dotted their *i*'s with little hearts and said aw! whenever they saw a puppy and never had to go on a diet because they never went off of one. They thought they deserved the cutest boyfriends."

Diana slapped the table happily. "Right! And the Ringo fans knew they wanted to be mothers when they grew up," Diana said. "They were goody-goodies who went caroling at nursing homes and practiced their posture by walking with dictionaries on their heads. Recognize anyone?" she said mischievously.

"Mom!" the girls said, and Margaret didn't deny it.

"One-two-three-four-five-six-seven-eight-nine-ten you owe me a Coke!" Allie looked pleased with herself.

"Remind me to get one for you in California." Evie could be droll when she wanted to.

"And then there were the girls who liked George," Margaret said. "They were imaginative and very romantic. They sat in their bedrooms writing poetry by candlelight and went for long walks in the rain. They tended to marry the wrong person."

"Who did you like, Aunt Diana?" Evie asked.

"George." Diana shook her head. "It's all true, except I never got married."

"Why didn't you marry that guy we just saw?" Allie asked.

"Jerome. Good question. At the time, I thought there were probably better guys out there, and I shouldn't get tied down so early on. But as it turned out, sometimes you meet the best one first." Diana fiddled with her armful of silver bracelets. "Now I really do need a cig."

"Funny. You've never said a word about him since then." Margaret pushed her coffee to the center of the table.

"I'm saying it now. I made a big mistake. Now I'm going to find some scuzzy corner of this damn place where people are still allowed to smoke. If you're not here when I get back I'll meet you at the gate."

She's going to look for him, Margaret thought.

"What if she can't find us?" Evie asked.

"She will," Margaret said automatically.

Evie didn't look convinced. Margaret thought that if Diana made this situation worse for them, she'd never speak to her again.

In the departure lounge, the girls immediately grabbed a row of seats by the window and settled in, as if they were going to be there forever. Margaret tried to read, but she couldn't concentrate. "How about a game of Rummy 500?" She located the deck of cards in the bag. Allie grabbed it and began to shuffle.

Evie raised her hand, as if she were in school. "May I deal?"

"I'm dealing," Allie said. If ever there was a person who instinctively understood that possession was nine-tenths of the law, it was Allie.

Margaret settled the matter by saying they'd take turns.

"Diana must have smoked a whole pack by now."

Allie organized her hand efficiently, her cards snapping.

"She's probably in one of the shops," Margaret said.

"Maybe she found Jerome again and they're still in love!" Evie's face was bright, shining within.

Margaret frowned. "I doubt it."

"Like you doubt that you and Daddy could get back together again," Evie said.

"Right. That's very doubtful."

"You really don't love Daddy anymore? Not even a little bit?" Allie asked.

I can't think why I would, Margaret thought. "I'm afraid not, honey." She had promised herself she wouldn't lie to them.

"Do you think he's changed since the last time we saw him?" Evie asked.

"I hope so!" Margaret said automatically and laughed. But Evie just stared intently at her cards, and Allie blushed.

"I'm sorry. That was a bad joke," Margaret said. "So what do you think you want to see in Los Angeles?"

"Nothing," Evie said.

"Ditto," said Allie.

It was small of her, she knew, but Margaret was pleased that the girls weren't projecting much fun. "The beaches are supposed to be nice."

"Daddy said he would take us to Disneyland," Evie said neutrally. She was holding the lead and growing more serious with each hand she won, tamping down her excitement and hedging her bets in case her luck ran out. It bothered Margaret to see this cautiousness, and she tried to offer subdued encouragement. Subdued, because she never knew which girl to root for. Allie was so able and so competitive that Margaret often neglected to cheer her on, but she identified with mild Evie. Margaret had been raised to be a good loser—at her school, the best sportsmanship award had always been given to the girl who was literally the best sport rather than the best athlete—but was it right to impose this view on her daughter? Especially as it would be such a struggle for Allie to learn, a denial of her nature.

Yet Margaret was glad to see Evie winning. It was so rare that she could do anything tangibly better than her sister. Her strongest point was a deep moral acuity, but who knew if the world would honor that? Margaret would never forget an incident that had taken place when Evie was eight. A friend of Margaret's was describing her rather brutal efforts to train her dog. "I would never hit a dog," Evie told Margaret later, her smooth forehead furrowed with concern. "It would be like if I went to Europe and everyone hit me when I couldn't understand what they were saying." It was a clear, sharp perception that left Margaret in awe.

"Earth to Mom, earth to Mom, where are you?" Allie asked.

Margaret grew serious. "Remember I'm going to call you at seven o'clock, California time. Don't let you father take you anywhere before I talk to you and know you got there safely."

They nodded.

"And you can always call me. Collect, if you need to."

Allie picked a card and lay down her hand.

"Congratulations, Al," Evie said.

Allie shrugged. "It was like I got great cards. Anyway, I have to go to the bathroom," Allie said. She began to walk off.

"Wait a minute," Margaret said. "We're coming with you."

Allie turned around. "Oh, I can go by myself."

Her tone was so reasonable that for a moment Margaret considered it. She wanted to stay close to the gate; she was afraid of having their tickets given away to standby passengers. Then she came to her senses.

"No, you can't."

"Mom," Allie wheedled.

"No." Margaret stood up decisively and inured herself to Allie's ongoing pleas that included the people around them and begged for the sympathy of reasonable minds. Well, I'm not reasonable, Margaret thought, not when it comes to the prospect of young girls being allowed to wander the corridors of airports on their own. Or to look at it another way, she was utterly reasonable in the face of all the potential craziness out there. She could not explain this angle on reasonableness to Allie, who was impatient to experiment with independence.

The truth was the substance of nightmares, so she let her strictness be interpreted as one of her own inexplicable quirks. If the girls were properly policed now, with luck, soon enough, they'd know how to protect themselves. It hurt to have Allie throw sullen glances her way as she tried to convince strangers to align themselves against her, but someone had to be the adult. She shuddered to think how Duncan would handle such instances; it was too disturbing to contemplate; she pushed it out of her mind.

Then Evie wanted to remain behind to wait for Diana. She was worried that they wouldn't find her again.

"We're all going together," Margaret said, her tone accepting no negotiation. Then her hope broke through; perhaps, as they passed by other gates, she'd see Jerome.

"What about our stuff?" Allie asked.

The three of them looked at the children's array of things, which lay used and scattered around their seats as at the end of a day of play.

"I'll watch everything for you," offered a man who had been sitting across from them for quite some time.

"No, thanks," Allie said coolly and hastily packed up. It depressed Margaret to see that the girls understood how to watch over their property better than they knew how to protect themselves. They stuck close to her until they had turned the corner. Then they stepped ahead and strode along the shiny floor together, ignoring her watchful presence, pretending they were free.

The bathroom smelled of a combination of disinfectant, cigarettes, and stale perfume. A thin man was desultorily swabbing the floors with a frayed gray mop while a chestnut-skinned woman fed hot dog chunks to an exhausted child who lay on the plank that served as changing table. Allie and Evie, subdued by the ugly atmosphere, shuffled wordlessly toward the stalls, casting glances at Margaret to make sure she would be standing guard. She felt a flash of satisfaction at their need. In her mind, she challenged their father to match this. He'd never changed a diaper, never taken them to school, never done any of the scut work unless other people were around whom he might be able to snow into thinking he was a good father.

It had amazed her when he pushed for a very precise visitation schedule; she'd imagined he wouldn't care, particularly as the girls had reported that he had a girlfriend in tow the last time he came to visit them in the city, someone closer to their age than hers, the descriptions of whom had ranged from okay to cool. The children did not like to talk about the girlfriend; they had absorbed enough of the culture to know that younger women had more currency than did mothers with crinkly lines around their eyes, and they did not want to make Margaret jealous. She was jealous, but not in the way they thought. She was jealous that this stranger would be with her children when she couldn't be.

She looked at the mirror, dismayed at what Jerome would see if she found him. She was a sweet-looking woman in her late thirties who seemed to wither beneath even her own scrutiny. She pulled out her lipstick and did what she could. She still looked haggard, she thought, and divorced, but when the girls came out of the stalls, Evie's eye lit up at the effort she'd made, which would have to do.

"That's an old lady color," Allie said. "Can I get a magazine to read on the plane?"

"I think you look pretty, Mom. I need some gum so my ears won't pop," said Evie.

Margaret looked at herself in the mirror and saw that the children had spoken true to type: Allie was right and Evie was considerate.

"If you promise you'll spit it out as soon as the takeoff is over," she said.

She wiped away the lipstick with a piece of paper towel and surreptitiously loosened a few strands of hair from her ponytail. Breezy, she decided as she took a quick last look at herself. Drab is more like it, she thought as they walked back out to the concourse.

She reminded herself that it wouldn't matter either way.

Even among the restless travelers Diana created a stir as she loped into the newsstand, her hair billowing. Just as she entered, the first boarding call for the girls' flight was announced, but she didn't seem to notice. She looked driven and shell-shocked and self-absorbed. Damn, Margaret thought as she watched the spectacle of Diana unselfconsciously commandeer the attention of everyone in the shop.

Diana spotted her and rushed over.

"You talked to him," Margaret said.

Diana slowly began to smile.

"Well?" Margaret heard herself sound shrill.

"His plane is delayed for an hour. I'm going to meet him for a drink."

"How are you going to get home then?"

"You're going to come have a drink with me." Diana was flirting already, warming up.

"No way."

"Yes way. Come on, Marg. You always liked him."

"That has nothing to do with it, Diana."

"What's the problem, then?"

Margaret gave an exasperated shrug.

"What? What?" Diana said.

"The problem is that today isn't about you. We're not here for you and your love life." The girls had spotted them together and were walking over. Margaret lowered her voice. "Just focus on the girls for five minutes, will you?"

"Aunt Diana!" Evie gave Diana a hug, as if they'd been separated for months.

"You saw him again, didn't you?" Allie said knowingly.

Diana grinned.

"What happened?"

"Nothing—yet!" Diana said. She told Allie about the "date" she'd made.

"He's not married?" Margaret asked pointedly.

Diana shrugged. "He is. I established that right away. But I got the feeling he isn't very happy."

Of course you did, Margaret thought.

"Can I have this one, Mom?" Allie asked, proffering a copy of *Mademoiselle.*

Margaret scanned the table of contents. Careers and cramps, as usual. "I guess so," she said. Any other response might lead to a fight, and it was no time for a fight.

"Why isn't he happy?" Evie asked, taking Diana's hand.

"That's what I plan to find out."

"Would you stop filling their heads with this garbage?" Margaret said.

"I'm just trying to lighten things up a little bit. Jeez!"

"What a classy way you have of doing it," Margaret said coldly.

Diana shook her head. "Anyone want some candy?" she said and led the children over to the cash register, leaving Margaret alone to wonder at the florid covers of the paperbacks.

"We have to pick up the pace," Margaret said. "It's going to take us a few minutes to get back to the gate."

"I don't want to go," Evie said. "Please, Mommy, let me stay home."

Great, Margaret thought. Diana had stimulated them, pierced the calm; now they'd balk. And she wouldn't think she'd played any part in their unwillingness. She walked alongside them, perusing her own thoughts, a small, faraway smile on her lips.

"That can't happen, Evie. The judge ordered this visit."

"But can't you explain to him that we want to stay home?" Allie said. She had her arms crossed over her chest, looking just like Duncan even as she struggled against seeing him.

"No," Margaret said. "I can't. I know you're nervous," Margaret soothed, "but you'll be fine. He's your father, remember."

"That's the problem." Evie said. "I hardly remember him."

Their helplessness was palpable and entered Margaret at every pore. As the children's flight was called again, she felt her nerves gather into a hard, swollen lump in her throat, an ice cube swallowed whole. She watched herself from an unfrequented place so deep inside that it may as well have been the point of view of a stranger. There, she wanted to run away with the children, to hold on to them with a desperate ferocity that would vanquish laws and agreements and everyone else's rights. Instead, she coaxed them down the corridor, a hand on each of their backs, pushing, pushing, all the while enveloped in a rush of raw feeling that made her heart seem to expand, then stop.

The sensation was by now familiar, yet it still overwhelmed; for a second or five or ten she was suspended in a parallel universe with a very real sense that she might not return to this one unless she willed herself to do so. It seemed up to her to get her system working again by reminding herself not to worry, that she knew what was happening and it was nothing serious. It was just that very ordinary feeling she had several times a day when she was utterly taken up with her children; seeing them; thinking of them; hearing their voices so clearly that every other sound was muted. It's only that, she reminded herself, thankful that she had explanation for such a cataclysmic physical event. Otherwise, if her heart were as disturbed, she would think she was dying.

"I'll talk to you tonight," she said as they reached the gate.

"Are you sure Daddy knows when to meet us?" Evie asked. "What do we do if we get there and he's not there?"

"Someone from the airline will be with you until he meets you. If anything goes wrong, just call me. But you have nothing to worry about."

"I think I might have told him we were coming tomorrow," Allie said.

"He knows it's today," Margaret said firmly.

"Please don't make me go," Evie said. She squeezed Margaret's hand and bounced gently up and down, then let go and clung to Diana. "I want to stay home!"

"Hey," Diana said. "Did I ever tell you what happened on the day you guys were born?"

"We weren't born on the same day," Allie said.

"I mean the days, wise guy, the days. Both times your dad called me from the hospital and said 'I have the most gorgeous baby girl in the world right here who needs the most beautiful name. Got any ideas?' "

"You mean you named us?" Evie asked.

"No, no. I made a few suggestions. Your dad chose the names. I think he did a pretty good job, don't you?"

"You're just trying to make us feel better," Allie accused, but with no malice.

"Your dad loves you," Diana said. "He's your dad, the one and only."

The girls leaned on her and all three of them cried. Margaret stood by and watched for what she felt was a decent interlude. Then she stepped forward and took command.

"We have to say good-bye now, girls." She could barely breathe.

Sniffling, they all straightened up.

"Write me a postcard," Diana said. Like a kid, she wiped her eyes on her palms. Margaret fought for the composure to get through the next few minutes.

A flight attendant approached. "You're the Abbott girls? Are you ready?"

"I'm their mother," Margaret said.

The woman lay a soft, consoling hand on Margaret's arm. "Make it brief. It's easier for everyone that way." Then she took a few steps backward, just enough to suggest she understood the concept of privacy but not enough to provide it. Margaret tried to ignore her. She hugged and kissed them quickly, as per instruction, and then stepped back in favor of the lurking stewardess. The girls hoisted their backpacks onto their shoulders with resigned expressions on their faces that made them look eerily middle-aged.

Margaret leaned against the cold glass, her eyes fixed on the runway, waving stubbornly at the inscrutable pewter-colored windows of the plane long after there was any chance that the girls might see her. As it lifted into the air, Margaret imagined them chewing their gum, gradually loosening their tight, anxious grip on the arms of their seats. She turned around. Diana was standing behind her.

"What's wrong?" Margaret said automatically.

"I'm sorry, Marg. It's awful, truly it is."

Margaret looked back at the disappearing jet. It was just heading into the clouds and the swirling snow was obliterating the smoky trail it had drawn in its wake. It had snowed the day she and Duncan got married. He had surprised her with a sapphire guard ring, which he guided over her knuckles along with the wedding band. Something blue, he said aloud, right during the ceremony. Her heart had squeezed small as a sponge, then puffed back up with all the life she had in her. She had loved him when they married. The plane disappeared completely but she kept her palms pressed against the cold windows for a few moments more. She had loved him on many occasions, more genuinely that she'd ever admitted to either herself or to him. Part of her still did, albeit a small, maverick aspect of her heart that she found incomprehensible and would rather have done without. She did not know how to reconcile that residual affection with all the sorrow. "I guess we might as well go," she said.

"Jerome's waiting in the VIP lounge. Come have a drink with him."

Margaret stared resolutely out the window, enveloped in the shroud of separation. The clouds were thick, low, and utterly obscuring. Flurries swirled up off the runway in blustery cones that raced across the ground for a few dizzying yards before imploding into miniature blizzards. The departing planes disappeared into the cloud bank upon liftoff; the girls' was long gone.

"Maybe I shouldn't have let them go. It really is nasty out there."

"They'll be fine. If the plane were going to crash, you'd have sensed it." Diana touched her shoulder. "You must be exhausted."

Margaret registered the word and immediately succumbed to it. "Yes, I am."

Bed. Sleep. Oblivion. Snow piled on the windows, snow and the quiet of it. She'd have to know the girls were safe before she could rest, though. She'd have to wait up.

"I'll drive you home," Diana offered.

"What about Jerome?"

"We'll stop and tell him we have to go."

"All right."

But when they got to the lounge she said she had to go to the ladies' room. In the stall she rested her elbows on her knees for a moment, then went to the sink and pressed her face with a wet washcloth.

"Ready?" Diana said, startling her.

"That was fast."

"He wasn't there." She looked . . . not young.

"Oh well," Margaret said. "You could have a drink at my house."

"That's okay. I want to go back to sleep myself."

Sure enough, as soon as they got in the car, Diana dropped off.

Margaret watched a plane climb the sky and wondered if it was Jerome's. The girls were probably arguing over whether or not to pull the shade against the sudden sun. Evie would want to look out at the sky and Allie would be forced by the logic of their preferences to give up her window seat. There would be other little squabbles and negotiations all through the flight, right up until they walked along the cordoned passageway to meet their father. At that moment they would close ranks, at least until they knew where they stood with the rest of the world. Thank God they had each other.

"What are you thinking about?" Diana asked.

"Duncan." It just came out.

"He's a jerk." In an instant, Diana was asleep again.

The girls called at ten sharp.

"There was a really gross man next to us on the plane, Mom," Allie reported. "His shirt kept coming untucked, and you could see his hairy butt."

"Daddy told us we look like teenagers," Evie said.

As she hung up, Margaret felt her heart twist. Silent sound, vivid absence, the ache of adoration and devotion in every cell of her body; she missed her girls. She called Diana and went up to bed—but when she couldn't sleep, she made a search of the attic, found her passionate diaries, and burned them in the fieldstone fireplace.

Stacy Grimes

Trouble

I worked with Trouble till she knew who was boss. It took a lot of work. A lot of time and a lot of work. She listens because she knows I'll kick her little ass across the floor if she doesn't. Froggy got her from some people in Columbus and took her home but he couldn't take care of her. He's got Baby and Lucky and Shooter. He's got enough to take care of. He brought her over here one day and he said, "I got her but I can't take care of her," and he put her in my arms and she was just as cute as she could be. I said, "You leave her here." I said, "I'll take care of her." But I said I'm not gonna have a dog that doesn't listen like all these dirty hounds around here chained to their doghouses and yowling all the time. I worked with her every day until she knew who was boss and I never had a bit of trouble with her. So I decided to call her Trouble.

Johnny takes care of her while I'm working at night. And he lets her in the house. He does the dishes and he cleans the house so I can't really complain. But he made me madder than hell on New Year's Eve. I went to work and then Pam told me I could go home at eleven o'clock, but when I got home, Johnny wasn't there. He went to the bar with Burns but I didn't know where he was. I sat there and I got madder and madder. I was ready to throw all his stuff out the goddamn door. It was New Year's Eve. Finally, I said to hell with it and I went to bed in the spare room. When he came home that night, he didn't even know I was there he was so drunk. He thought I was out all night, and when he got up in the morning, he said, "Where the hell were you?" I said, "You dumb sonofabitch. I was sleeping in the spare room. Where the hell were you?"

I told him I won't put up with it. He came in to work the next night and handed me a bunch of weeds, which was better than nothing. He said, "Are you really that mad at me?" I said, "You're damn right I'm that mad." He said, "I thought you were working all night. You could've come out to the bar." I said, "I'm not gonna chase you to the bars!" I said, "You could've picked up the goddamn phone."

He told me he'd make it up to me. He said he'd take me out to dinner. And he did and we had a very nice night together. I know the man loves me because he said to me the other night before I left for work, he said, "Do you have nose blowers?" He knows I have a cold and have to blow my nose and it's a long drive. He said, "Because if you don't there's a box of Kleenex in the drawer." It melted my heart. He does love me and he takes care of Trouble and he cleans and he goes to work so really I can't complain.

But I've got all his goddamn brothers here all the time because Shelby's down there dyin. They come down here from Columbus and they think this is headquarters. You can't get out of bed and put a pot of coffee on till they're knocking on the door. I told him I'm not gonna put up with it. Henry was already drinking by ten o'clock this morning. Johnny said, "Well, then tell them to get the hell out." But you can't do that.

There's thirteen of them. Johnny and Shelby and Frog are the only ones worth anything. They're the only ones that stayed on the farm—if you can call it a farm. Yvette went to town and all the rest went to Columbus. Johnny's the baby and poor little Shelby's the oldest. Sixty-four years old and the cancer's done eat her up. Poor little Shelby's layin down there dyin. She's layin down in that trailer with a temperature of a hundred and six point four. Johnny said this morning before he left for work, he said, "If she dies what should I do?" I said, "You don't need to come home because she'll be dead." I said, "You need to work."

Johnny and I *will* get married one day and then I'm gonna be the executor of this property because he'll put me right on there with him. I'm forty-four years old and I'll be goddamn if I'm gonna let anyone run over me anymore. His brothers can't come back here from Columbus and think they can tell us how to run this property. Johnny tells them. He says, "*She* runs the show around here." And they all think: *well who the hell is she?* They think: *this was Mom and Dad's place.* But this is Johnny's place now. He's the executor of this property. I told them all this shit out here is gonna be cleaned up this spring, and I'm gonna put ten head of cattle in there and I'm gonna get a horse. And I told Henry he needed to sell us the other trailer or I was gonna put a match to it because it's not doin nothing while he has it but goin to the dogs. He said, "You ain't got enough money to buy that trailer," and I said, "Henry, that trailer ain't worth a shit. The floors are falling out, the windows are falling out. . . ." I told him I'll put a match to it and by God I will.

Earlene wants to move into Henry's trailer. She wants to fix it up and rent it but I said no. She would have to tap into our water and I'm not gonna have that. No way. Earlene likes to start trouble. We don't need her here. She's not right in the head. I put up with her for almost a year down at the crossroads and I had enough. I can't believe I stayed with her as long as I did. Drunk all the time and Wayne beating the hell out of her and all those messed up people she associates with. She's got another roommate now and the girl's only been there for two months and Earlene's already badmouthing her. No, we don't need people like her around here.

Earlene thinks because she's fuckin Frog she can leave her Rott mutt runnin loose up here all the time. You live in the country you shouldn't have to tie your dog up, but all the female dogs around here are in heat and she should have Duke on a chain. Frog's dogs could get pregnant. And I don't want Duke puppies. Trouble's not a Rott she's a coonhound. I don't want to ruin her. As soon as some mutt breeds with her she's ruined. Her titties'll hang down to the ground and her stomach will sag . . . the puppies would be born real big and she'd probably have six or seven of them. No, I can't have that.

Earlene came over here looking for him and I said, "You're gonna have to tie him up or take him." I said, "Trouble's following him. They're hunting. They're going over across the road and when I call her, she won't come. She's following him and I can't have that."

Earlene had *my* chain in her hands. She looked about as skinny and twisted as the tree trunks behind her. She said, "I'm not gonna tie him up. He needs to run."

People just want to run all over top of you.

Frog can't even park in his own driveway. He's got a driveway over there and he's gotta park in ours. Frog is a hell of a nice guy but I don't know why he has to park in our driveway. Every day I have to back my car up to get around his. Johnny and I are gonna have a talk because I won't put up with it. This is just as much my house as it is his. I said your brothers and sisters are trying to run your life and I said it's about time you showed them who's got the reins. I said because I won't put up with it, and Johnny listens to what I say.

Yvette called me up last summer after I moved in and she said, "I heard you're bossing my baby brother around."

I said, "That's between me and Johnny."

She said, "If we find out you're mean to Johnny's kids we're gonna throw you out of there."

She had me so upset. I said I take care of those kids when they're here and I love Johnny's kids dearly but I said I'll be goddamn if I'm gonna let a five-year-old and a two-year-old walk all over me. It's not gonna be like it was with Kenny's brats. I'm not raising anyone else's kids anymore ever. I'm not gonna do it. They've got a mother. Let her raise them. If she thinks she's gonna drop them off every weekend she's got another thing coming. Johnny and I have a life too. And little John is two years old and there isn't anything he doesn't break. He broke the glass out of the front of the stereo. There isn't anything he doesn't get into. It's because no one has ever told them not to. It's because *Mommy* lets them go. She don't give a shit. Lazy bitch can't even clean her car. That car is so dirty you can't even get the kids in it because of all the McDonald's trash. And every time they come here they're sick. That comes from dirt. From filth. And I keep getting *her* mail. I'm gonna pile it up and take it over and throw it in her face one day. I'm tired of looking at it. And I'm gonna say change your goddamn address. Are you that lazy you can't change your address?

She's trying to get this house. But she ain't gettin a dime from him. She left him. She abandoned him. And why—because he drank a little bit? She never should've married him, because he drank when she married him. She thinks she's so high and mighty. Every weekend just comes and drops her kids off and takes off.

Don't they think I get tired? Shelby says, "Well, they're Johnny's kids. This place will be theirs one day."

Well, Johnny and I are gonna have a talk. I'm not gonna put up with it. I rule the roost here. I sleep with Johnny and I pay the bills and if they don't like it they can get the fuck off the property. I'll have what I want. I want a double car garage and I want a barn and a horse. And I want all this junk out of here. They all think this is the Gainer junkyard. There's fourteen junk cars out here. Fourteen fucking vehicles. It's like walking through a snake pit to get to your front door. Every morning I get up and look out my window and look at the junk cars. He just put another truck out here and every day I have to go let a bird out of it.

But it's going this summer. I told Frog it's going. Johnny and I are tired of it. We want to have cattle and you can't have cattle with all that shit out there. I just want Johnny and I to have a nice life. If we don't do anything about it they'll all bring every piece of junk they can back here. Like Burns says, the people around here don't give a shit about how much junk you've got layin around. They don't care. But that's no way to live. I never had to live like this ever.

Henry said, "You can't move nothin out of here. This ain't your land." He was sitting there at my table with some straggler he brought in who looked like a drug addict. I thought I don't even know this man and here he is sitting at my table. I said, "This ain't the Gainer junkyard." I said, "I'm tired of you bringing all your stragglers in here." He said, "This was my father's land." He said, "*You* pack your bags and *you* leave." I said, "Johnny owns this land." I said, "You can't even pay your taxes. Johnny's name's in the paper because you all can't pay your taxes. So it all comes down on Johnny." I said, "If your daddy gave it to you you should have the respect to pay the taxes. You're not a brother. You're nothing but a drunk. Shelby's down there dyin and you all gotta get drunk." I said, "You all think this is Gainer headquarters but it isn't. This summer Johnny and I are gonna clean up this whole property and if you don't like it right there's the door. Your fuckin ass can hit it." I said, "When you get a better attitude, you can come back."

Later on Yvette called here and she fuckin got all over top of me. Henry went over there and ran his mouth. She said, "If I ever hear of you telling my brother off again I'm gonna come over there and kick your ass."

I thought here's a sixty-year-old woman telling me she's gonna kick my ass. I said, "Johnny and I are sick and tired of you all comin in here and trying to rule the roost. You don't rule nothin here. We do." I said, "I don't want anything from Johnny. I just want to be with him. If it wasn't for me he wouldn't have made it through last winter. He would've drank himself to death."

They don't give a fuck about him. I'm the one that saved his life. They should see what a good woman I am to support Johnny and to take care of his kids and his house. I have taken my last ten dollars to go out to the grocery store and get him something to eat. And they all call me a bitch. Well I am a bitch. I'm the biggest fucking bitch they ever want to run into. Johnny needs a bitch to help him run his life.

I said to Johnny, "One of your family says one more thing to me I'm gonna leave." He said, "You can't leave." I said, "I can do whatever I want." He said, "What did she say?" I said, "She told me off!"

Johnny got on the phone right away. He made me so happy. He said none of them will ever say one bad word to me again. He said if they have anything to say they better say it to him.

He said, "This is your home." And it is. Johnny and I, we want cattle and we want horses and a garden. We want all these things and we're gonna work together to have them. Work together, not against each other. Isn't that the way life's supposed to be?

But everybody is in everybody's business around here.

It's like the other day—Janie was taking her mother's morphine pills and everybody was hollerin about that. Johnny and I told them to leave her alone. She's got enough on her. That woman has been through hell. It's not right.

Yvette called and said, "I hate that little bitch. I'm gonna have her thrown out of there." She said, "Janie's not taking care of Shelby right." But the bedsores are the fault of the hospital. I blame that on the hospital. Poor little Janie couldn't even move her mother. Yvette said, "I'm comin down there for a week and things are gonna be different."

I said, "Keep it down there. Don't bring it here."

I said to Johnny, "If I stay with you there's gonna be a fuckin gate at the end of the driveway." I'm gonna cut them all off.

Thursday morning I got up and made a pot of coffee and the lid wouldn't go down and I pushed it and the coffee went all over me. It splashed up and burned my eyelid. Then I couldn't find Trouble and I was worried. These people are the type that if they don't like you they don't like your dog. I said if anyone does anything to my dog I swear to God I'll go to jail over it because I *will* kill someone. And Johnny told them. He said, "Anyone does anything to her dog she *will* go to jail over it."

Trouble was running with Duke again. The hot water heater busted down at Frog's so he was knocking on the door. *Can I take a shower?* The next thing I knew Earlene was taking a shower too. I said, "If my dog gets pregnant it's gonna be your fault." She said, "Why don't you get your dog fixed?" I said, "Because I don't want her fixed yet. I might want to breed her."

Earlene was wearing my robe. She flipped on the blow dryer and flipped her head upside down and started blowing her stringy hair around. "Well then it's your fault," she said.

When she said that, it was like a bomb went off in my chest. I pulled the cord out of the socket and grabbed ahold of her arms and threw her up against the wall, and as soon as I did it I couldn't believe I'd done it. Wayne used to explode on her like that.

I used to take care of her black eyes and her busted lips. I even beat that drunk sonofabitch off her once. We used to sit on the porch and wait for the train. We'd just sit and watch the train go by and listen to it and act goofy like teenagers and it was great. But none of that meant anything to Earlene. I thought Earlene would be like a sister to me. Someone to holler at and scream at and cry at. Like family. But I found out what she was. I'd find fifty dollars missing from my purse or half a bag of weed gone. Then my ring came up missing. I had to keep my money under my pillow at night. And when I found out she was badmouthing me, I couldn't believe it. It broke my heart. But that's the way she does people. She don't care.

Froggy's too nice a guy to be messin around with trash like that. But I guess a piece of ass is a piece of ass. I went in the living room and turned up the TV real loud. Frog never said a word. I will give him credit for that.

Then Shelby died at four thirty. Janie's teenage daughter Missy has a bunch of birds down there and Henry walked in the trailer and looked at the birds and started hollerin. He said, "Missy, you need to water those birds! You need to feed those birds!" Janie said, "This is my home and that's my mother layin there dead. You don't come in here and yell at her like that." Poor little Janie could barely talk.

I told Johnny about it later and he said, "You should've called

911." I said, "What is wrong with these people?" He said, "They've always been like that."

On Friday night Johnny and I went to the viewing and his ex-wife was there with her mother and the kids. We were standing around with the family, and people were talking quietly. Johnny squeezed my hand and he looked at me and nodded and then he went up to the casket. I watched him touch Shelby and he said goodbye to her and then he left the room.

As soon as he left the room, his ex's mother came up to me. She was smiling and acting real nice. She said, "Have you ever seen two more beautiful children?" She said, "Little John is the spittin image of Johnny, and Tammy looks exactly like her mother." Her old man was standing back against the wall looking at me. He was standing there staring at me. I thought Oh God. What am I in for now? She said, "You know, it's really a shame about Johnny and Angie."

I gave her the same sickly sweet voice she was giving me: "Well," I said, "it happens to the best of us."

She said, "But you know it's just a temporary split up. They're working on getting back together."

I said, "Oh, really?"

She said, "Yes, they're trying to work out their problems and get back together." And then she said, "I'm sorry, and who are you?"

She knew who I was. I said, "I'm Sharon. I'm Johnny's girlfriend. We've been together for eight months now."

She said, "Oh."

I said, "Yeah, it's a shame that Angie left him. He was really upset when she took his kids. It almost killed him." I said, "But these things happen." I said, "Excuse me. I have to go to the bathroom," and I walked away.

Later that night I said to Johnny, "So I heard you and Angie are trying to get back together." I told him what happened. He said, "Angie put her up to that." He said, "Fuck her. I wouldn't go back with her for all the money in the world." And I know he wouldn't. They just have to start shit. They're all like that. Johnny and I don't get any rest.

Shelby's in a much better place now than we are. But life goes on. Janie and her old man are shacking up in the trailer, and Missy's pregnant. Seventeen years old and pregnant. Missy's the kind of girl who walks through your bedroom and opens up all your jewelry boxes and looks in your drawers. She's always comin in here asking me for a joint. I ain't feedin it to her cause I ain't dopin up the baby.

I was back in the bedroom the other night folding clothes and she snuck up on me and scared me. She said, "You got a joint?" She saw the bag of weed layin on my bed. I said, "No, I don't have a joint." She picked up the bag and said, "Ooo ooo ooo!" Well, it's mine. It's not anyone else's. She said, "Oh come on. *Pleeease?* I've got six people out in the car." I said, "That ain't my problem." Do they think the stuff grows on trees? It cost me fifty-five dollars for that bag of weed.

Then I caught her little punk boyfriend in the hallway. I said, "Back up, Bud." Froggy warned me about him. Said he was nothing but a little thieving bastard. I don't want none of them. If I have to put rattlesnakes out here to keep them off the property I will. When I start planting dope, none of these stragglers are gonna be comin around here. I'm gonna set all kinds of fuckin traps. I told Johnny he's gonna go get an alarm system to put on this house because I don't trust nobody. It's worse out here than it is in the city. It's nothing but a bunch of thieves and rutters that don't have jobs. People that live in old dirty trailers and houses and don't take baths.

Froggy and Janie are the only decent ones left. I love Froggy like a brother. He's been good to me. Johnny always accuses me of fuckin him. But that's only because Froggy drinks too much and when he drinks, he says little things and sometimes if I've had a couple beers I say little things. But it's innocent. It's like the other day—Froggy was out here cleaning up the driveway and I said, "Ooo, look at Froggy out there workin." I stuck my head out the door and I said, "What are you doin?" He got a shit-eating grin on his face and he said, "I'm workin."

But I told Johnny if we don't make it I won't ever try again. I said if you ain't the one you better tell me now cause I'm gonna get up and get out. I don't want somebody to use me all up and throw me aside. I'm too old for that. I always wanted a home. I always wanted to get married and to have a home and children but I could never find someone to help me get that. I think to myself: *why am I here? Why was I born?* Am I just taking up space, breathing up someone else's air? I keep thinking about when I was living with Kenny and he was at work and the brats were at school and I would get on the horse and go for a ride out the road. It would be the duck, the cat and the dog and they would follow me. That's the way I want to live my life. But you can't paint a picture like that because that's not the picture.

I said to Johnny, "Things are gonna have to change because I won't put up with this anymore." I'm going through change-of-life and I'm worried about everything. I'm going through some really bad mood swings and sometimes I feel like I could kill someone. I mean literally kill someone.

And I told him I'm too old to be raising a couple of kids that I didn't even have. His kids are terrible. It's the way that bitch is raising them. She lets them rule her. They eat like they've never had a bite to eat in their lives. And if it ain't sweet they won't eat it. It's because *Mommy* won't make them eat anything good. She don't eat anything good herself. Tammy's five years old and all her teeth are rotten. I want to give them water for their meals, but Johnny has to give them pop or milk. And that boy spills everything.

One Friday night Johnny was gonna take me out for a beer. He said after supper we'll let Janie watch them and we'll go out for a beer. But little John knocked his pop on the floor. I said, "Now I gotta scrub the floor!" I said, "Is this a bed of roses or prickly pines?" I don't know if I'm cut out for this. I said they're your kids and I love them but I didn't have them. Don't give me the responsibility of raising your kids. I'm not a nanny goat. I told him it'll be my way or no way. If he wants me to do this I'll work part time and he'll *pay* me to stay home and watch the kids. I said I am not little-Suzie-miss-homemaker and you're not pullin this on me. No one's ever pullin that on me again.

I had them the other day and they were pullin the pots and pans out and tearin this place up. Little John broke everything he put his hands on. Tammy was eating donuts like they were going out of style. She wanted to sit on the kitchen counter and I said no, but she kept climbing up there. I said, "You get your ass down and you sit at the table and eat like a normal person!" and I picked her up and slammed her little ass down in the chair. I'll be goddamn if a five-year-old girl is gonna tell me what she's gonna do. She was eatin those donuts like she never had a bite to eat in her life. I said, "Slow down before you choke!" Her hands were nothing but sticky donuts and she was climbing around in the chair and dropping stuff all over the floor. I said, "Do you have to put your hands all over the back of the chair? You will sit at the table and eat like a young lady should!" When they're with me, by God they're gonna listen. Or I told Johnny he can kiss my ass goodbye because I ain't never gonna let anyone walk over me again. I've had my fill.

Little John ran out to the living room to break something else. You can't let your eyes off them for one second. I ran after him and grabbed him up and took him back to the kitchen and there was Tammy back on the kitchen counter. I said, "Goddamn it get off the counter!" and she jumped and landed right on Trouble and Trouble yelped and I dropped Little John and ran over and smacked Tammy right across her sticky mouth and her little ass hit the floor. They were both screaming and I heard something rattling behind me and I turned around and there stood Earlene in the doorway with a smirk on her face and my chain in her hands.

She said, "What does Johnny think about the way you slap his kids around?"

I could've walked through a wall. That's the way I feel sometimes—like I'm invincible. I went over to her and I said, "That's *my* chain," and I ripped it out of her hands.

It was night when I came home and the moon was full. Trouble met me at the mailbox. She was totally excited. I was trying to get the mail and she jumped in the car and she jumped out. And she jumped in the car and she jumped out. She was all over me. I thought, what the hell have you been eating that's making you so hyper? I thought, maybe it's the moon.

I went in and took my clothes off and turned the TV on and I got something to eat. Trouble kept jumping on the sofa and jumping off and putting her paws in my lap. I played with her and she kept running to the door but she wouldn't go out. I thought, what the hell is wrong with you?

I did the dishes. The phone rang and it was Janie. She said, "Did you know Henry's trailer burned down?"

I went out on the porch and sure as shit it was gone. I thought, that's what's wrong with Trouble. Janie said they were over there cleaning it out. Frog and Earlene, and Henry had a couple of his stragglers helping, Tom and his old lady. Well, Tom's a fucking drunk and a wife beater. He's a woman beater. Janie said they were moving some stuff out and Tom and his old lady got into a fight and he was kicking her ass. Frog and Janie broke it up. She said she told him he wasn't going to beat on any woman in front of her, that she'd cut his belly open. They all left and when they came back, the trailer was in a blaze.

She said, "Somebody said your car was here."

I said, "It wasn't."

She said Henry said I had threatened to burn the trailer down because he wouldn't sell it to me. But she told him she didn't believe I would do that.

She said, "A cigarette could have dropped while they were fighting."

I said it's a blessing in disguise.

She said Johnny had talked to Henry about the water, that they were gonna tap into the water line. I said no—oh. Johnny didn't agree with that. Johnny and I already talked about all this. Earlene won't move in with Frog because she's afraid Wayne will kill him. They're trying to keep it hush-hush, but how long is that gonna last? Wayne's crazy. And when I say he's crazy, I mean he's crazy. He's already pulled a twelve-inch blade on me. I said to Johnny, suppose Wayne finds out and he comes and beats Earlene up and kills her over there? Then what? We're gonna have a fuckin murder on our hands. I said I'll be goddamn if I'm gonna live here and have to worry about Wayne killing Earlene over in that trailer. I said Earlene's just another piece of junk they all want to bring in here. And Johnny agrees with me. He don't want the riff-raff here either.

Johnny's the baby but he's got more power than any of them. He's the executor. It's like Johnny's the sheriff of the town and I'm the deputy but we can't get the people of the town to abide by the rules. What's it gonna come to—a gunfight in the middle of the road?

Sometimes I feel like I was raised on the other side of the fuckin universe. How do these people get the gall to do the things they do? Just let Henry try to accuse me of burning down that trailer!

Now I can look out the window and see the front road and I couldn't before. I can sit here and look across the field and see the light in town. It's miles away but I can see that and I like it. I know what lies ahead of me. I know what kind of a woman I am and I don't regret anything. There's such a life here that I'm dreaming of, like a fairy tale book. I gotta keep wanting more every day and getting it because if I don't then there's no purpose.

Trouble puts her paws in my lap. She loves to have her head rubbed. She puts her head in my crotch. She's afraid of the fly swatter.

Her titties look awfully big.

Ann Hood

The Language of Sorrow

The bus from Logan Airport pulled in with a heavy sigh. Dora's grandson was coming from New York City, via Kennedy Airport. Gate one. She considered getting a box of doughnuts to bring home with them. A Dunkin' Donuts was right inside the terminal, Dora had recognized the familiar smell before she even saw the shop. Her children had always loved doughnuts, especially the messy ones like powdered sugar or chocolate frosted. A long ago morning shot through Dora's mind: Tillie and Dan at the old metal kitchen table, the one with the green rooster on top, their mouths dusted with white sugar, with smears of chocolate, their teeth small and smooth, the sunlight sending dust particles dancing in the air, and Dora pouring purple Kool-Aid from a pitcher with a goofy grinning face on the front.

She remembered it and it was gone. As if she could somehow pull it back, Dora raised her hand, surprising herself. The hand looked like her grandmother's used to—wrinkled, spotted, gnarly. The noisy arrival of a bus right in front of her forced Dora to put all of this nonsense aside. It was the bus from New York City. On that bus was her own grandson, Dan's boy, who she had not seen in over five years. People spilled off the bus. Giggling girls and boys who looked like they were in gangs, young women with small children and older women dressed in clothes from Lord and Taylor or somewhere like that. Dora met each person's gaze with her own expectant one. Her lipstick felt waxy on her lips. Fleetingly she remembered how the undertaker had put a thick coat of lipstick on her friend Madeline Dumfey's lips, in a dreadful shade of pink. He thought it made her look healthy, as if someone who'd been killed by cancer could look healthy. What an idiot, Dora thought. The flow of people slowed, then stopped. Dora stood on tiptoes, trying to see inside the bus. Was it the wrong day? The wrong bus?

But then a boy stepped off. He was not like the tattooed and pierced teenagers who Dora saw on Thayer Street. This disappointed her for reasons she did not quite understand. He was more like the private school boys, the ones who dragged lacrosse sticks past her house every afternoon. Except for the dark shadows beneath his eyes and the defeated way in which he slouched off the bus, he could be one of them. Sad and ordinary, those were the words that sprung to Dora's mind. His hands clutched a piece of bright red American Tourister luggage, the one meant for women to carry their curlers and things. With his fair hair and pale skin, his light blue eyes and perfect pouty lips, he looked exactly like his mother. This disappointed Dora too.

"Peter," she said, stepping through the crowd waiting for their luggage.

He barely looked at her. "I've got another bag," he said, and joined the others waiting.

"Let's get it, shall we?" she said, though he had already gone to do just that.

The last time she had seen him was five years ago at her son's funeral, a hot bright sunlit day, even though it was February. That was Houston, she supposed. Relentlessly sunny, even in winter, even at funerals. She had not paid much attention to Peter that day. She'd had enough to deal with. The news of Dan's death and the way in which he'd died. The flight to Texas in the middle of the night, stopping and changing planes in Newark and then Chicago and then Dallas. Arriving just in time to get to the church, unable to even change her clothes. Peter seemed hardly there that day.

"I've got it," he said.

Dora blinked as if he woke her up.

"Welcome to Providence," she said, hoping he didn't notice her voice trembling.

His eyes looked like some kind of monster's eyes they were such a light blue. Dora found herself remembering a little albino girl who'd gone to school with Tillie.

"I don't want to be here," Peter said. He swung his other bag, also bright red, the kind men hung their suits in, over his shoulder. The weight of it made him stagger slightly.

Before Dora could think what to say, he was walking ahead of her, his shadow stretching between them like a bridge.

She put him in Tillie's old room. It still had the pink and white striped wallpaper from her childhood, and a bureau decorated with ballerinas. Even though he frowned when he saw it Dora couldn't let him stay in Dan's room. He didn't seem to deserve it, the smell of boy things, the stamps and coins carefully collected or the models of ships and race cars assembled over many lost Saturday afternoons. This boy seemed removed from any of that, a sullen stranger plunked into Dora's life.

Peter tossed his bags on the bed. "Thanks," he said. Dora heard sarcasm in that one simple word.

"I could get us some doughnuts," she said without much conviction. "We could have some doughnuts and chat a little."

He wasn't even looking at her. His eyes flitted around the room, searching. "Is there a phone I could use?"

Dora hesitated. His mother had told her he wasn't supposed to call the girl.

"There's one in the kitchen," Dora said carefully. "And one in my room. But I'm afraid you can't call . . ." What was the girl's name?

"Rebecca," Peter said. "But I have to." He walked right past Dora and pointed foolishly like the scarecrow in *The Wizard of Oz*. "Which way to the kitchen?"

Dora put her hand on his arm. Startled, she dropped it just as quickly. She didn't expect muscles under the shirt. And standing close like this she saw that he was taller than he'd seemed at the bus station.

"Your mother gave me so few restrictions. Calling Rebecca is one of them. I'm sorry."

He looked at her and she knew that really, she couldn't stop him.

"You love her, I suppose," she said.

He laughed, a barking sound that Dora didn't like one bit. "No. But I don't think I should have deserted her. I don't think I should have been sent away for the entire summer to live in this podunk town with an old lady."

Dora took a step back, away from him, rubbing her arms up and down.

"I mean," Peter said, "who are you, you know? My father kills himself and you vanish. Do you know what I've been going through for five whole years? You have no idea."

She did know, of course; Melinda had filled her in. But what Dora said was, "I hardly think your father killed himself."

That bark again, then Peter stuck his face in hers. "What do you call it when someone smokes so much cocaine that they jump out a fifth-story window running from imaginary monsters? Huh?"

Dora reared up to her full height, five feet, eight inches. She had always believed in the benefit of calcium and as a result had not shrunk like other women her age. Why, Madeline Dumfey had died a full three inches shorter than she had lived.

"An accident," Dora said. "I call it an accident."

Dora did not see the point of dwelling on her losses. But often, at night, they seized her and shook her awake. Sometimes she found herself groping for Bill on the other side of the bed, reaching and reaching as if her life depended on finding him there until, finally, panting, she had to remind herself that he had died on April 14, 1983, from lung cancer. A picture of him taking those last gasping breaths in a hospital bed would come to her and she would close her eyes and press the lids hard until it vanished.

Other times she awoke thinking she had to call Madeline about one thing or another and then a strange uneasiness took hold as Dora remembered that Madeline was dead. They had known each other since 1943 when they worked side by side as secretaries at the army base in Quonset Point. Dora wore her hair in a Veronica Lake peekaboo cut back then; Madeline favored more of a Gene Tierney wave. They went together every Friday afternoon after work to Isabella's Parisian Hair Salon in Wickford to get their hair done. Both of them had slim hips, good legs, a wide collection of shoes. They shared nylons, a real commodity back then, and lipstick. They double-dated, covered for each other when they wanted to give a guy the bum's rush. They stood up for each other at their weddings; Dora wore a deep maroon velvet for Madeline's and Madeline wore an icy blue satin at Dora's. Those were the things that came to mind when Dora woke up with an urgency to call Madeline: the smell of the chemicals at their beauty parlor near the base, the feel of a nylon stocking sliding on her leg, the crush of velvet against cool skin on a November morning.

Since Peter had arrived, what woke Dora was the feeling that she needed to check on the children, the way she would when they were young. She used to walk through the darkness of the house and slip into their rooms and make sure they were breathing. First Tillie, a neat sleeper, on her back with her covers tucked under her chin. Then Dan, often upside down in his bed, his sheets and blankets a tangle around his waist and feet. Dora would stand and count their breaths before climbing back into her own bed, satisfied.

Peter sat in the kitchen, ate entire boxes of Oreo cookies, drank milk straight from the bottle, and talked to Rebecca. At first Dora reprimanded him, reminding him of her promise to his mother. But Peter would just stare at her with those practically albino eyes, popping whole cookies into his mouth while she explained. Really, Dora didn't care if he talked to the girl. Talking wasn't going to change anything. So she gave up and let him do it.

". . . so Polly's coming over a lot? Her mother lets her?" Dora heard him say one afternoon.

Dora was making baked scrod for dinner, with parsley potatoes. He didn't like anything she cooked but she continued to make complete meals for the two of them despite that. Over her roast beef and mashed potatoes he'd asked her if there was anyplace around to get a good burrito. The night she'd made leg of lamb he'd requested fish sticks. Last night he'd described something called Hot Pockets, a frozen bread type thing stuffed with meat and vegetables. Dora had nodded and taken another pork chop from the platter.

"I'm surprised her mother lets her. Really surprised. Her mother's like so uptight. She's a Republican, you know."

Dora glanced at him. *She* was a Republican, after all. But she would have let Tillie visit her pregnant friend. She would have considered it a positive experience for Tillie, to know that there were consequences for actions.

"What?" Peter said, cupping his hand over the mouthpiece of the phone.

Dora spread the crumbled Ritz crackers over the scrod and put the pan in the oven. "I think you have foolish ideas, that's all," she said, and set the timer.

"Excuse me," Peter said. "But I wasn't talking to you."

Dora shrugged.

"You're eavesdropping," he said.

"I'm making dinner," Dora told him.

"Anyway, I think Polly is probably sick of Jen and Justin and that's why she's hanging around so much," Peter said, presumably not to Dora.

Dora took out two of the blue and white everyday dishes and began to set the table around Peter. She tried to picture the girl on the other end, but could only come up with an image of Melinda at that age, a sullen girl who always looked like she was not to be trusted. She'd slunk into their home during dinner one night, Dan's arm protectively around her waist, dressed in torn jeans and brown suede Indian moccasins. Those shoes had bothered Dora. Earlier that day she had commented to Madeline Dumfey that it seemed loose girls wore those. Then right in her kitchen, hanging on to her son, Melinda appeared with that very type of shoe. "That girl's trouble," Dora had announced as soon as Melinda and Dan had gone. And of course she'd been right. Before Melinda he had never even gotten drunk. After Melinda's appearance in their kitchen Dan had started with marijuana and who knew what else. The school was calling every other day about his absences. One night the police brought him home, stoned, confused, and with Melinda.

Dora sighed. She was holding two forks, the timer was buzzing, and Peter was staring at her hard.

"Gran?" he said.

She shook her head. "I'm fine." She went to the oven for the scrod, her heart twisted in grief. In her own lifetime she had taken chances. When she was only twenty she'd fallen foolishly in love with a married man. He had taken her to a lopsided ski cabin he and his wife owned in Maine and Dora lost her virginity on the floor there; he felt too guilty to have sex in his marriage bed. The next morning, feeling reckless, Dora took two runs down the bunny slope, then boarded the chair lift to the top of the mountain where she promptly fell and broke her leg. The man drove her home in a stony silence and never called her again. My how she had carried on! she remembered now, making Madeline drive her past his house, her leg stuck in that awful cast for two entire months, a reminder of her indiscretion.

She'd told servicemen on their way overseas that she loved them when she didn't, sad young men who did not always come back. Dora had enjoyed the way they used to cling to her, as if she mattered more than anything else. She remembered one young man from Pennsylvania who was headed to France. He had cried after they'd made love because he was so afraid to die. So she knew about risk, how any of those trysts could have resulted in pregnancy, how the wife could have discovered the affair. And worse. When her own children were small she'd had an affair with Bill's partner, an affair that lasted almost two years. She'd even considered leaving Bill for him. Talk about risk. There were dinners with the man and his wife, even a week long vacation together in Puerto Rico with all of their children. Like the foolish people they were, Dora and the man had met every night on the beach and made love while Bill and Gloria looked over them from the twenty-eighth floor of the Old San Juan Hotel.

But all of that was nothing compared to Dan. Dora liked to blame Melinda for what happened but she knew the truth: it was drugs that took her son from her. He and Melinda drifted around a world that Dora could not even imagine. They moved from job to job and city to city so much that entire months passed when she couldn't even find them. Landlords had no forwarding address, operators had no new numbers. Finally the night came when Dan called Dora, waking her from a fitful sleep. He was leaving Melinda, he'd told her. He was checking into rehab. "I have to save myself," he'd said and she heard the desperateness in his voice. Dora still could feel the way dryness gripped her throat that night. She'd hung up and drank glass after glass of water, unable to quench the horrible thirst. Before she hung up she'd told him that she would pay for treatment, if that's what it took. She told him it was about time he'd realized where Melinda had led him. "If you leave her," she'd said, "you can come back here and start over. You can even bring the boy." It wasn't until a week later, when she got the call that he was dead, that Dora regretted all she hadn't said that night. She hadn't said she was proud of him for finally realizing he needed help. She hadn't told him she loved him.

"Gran!" Peter shouted and he ran over to her.

That was when Dora felt the hot butter on her leg, burning her as it dripped from the pan. She let the boy take the fish from her and lead her to a chair. Already an ugly blister appeared on her calf, and smaller ones ran down to her ankle like a trail of tears.

"I'm all right," she said.

But she stayed seated, feeling the hot pain surge through her as Peter grabbed a dishtowel and ice cubes. She watched him move through the kitchen as if she were watching a movie. His own strong calves under khaki shorts, the golden hair on his arms. A stranger, kneeling at her feet, pressing a cool cloth to her burns.

"Thank you," she said.

He nodded.

Dora took her hand and placed it on his bent head. She kept it there until he looked up, searching for a clue that she was fine. The thing was, Dora did not want him to go away from her. She didn't want to let go.

"Another minute," she lied. "Just another minute." Again Dora rested her hand on his head.

Check the children. Stumbling, Dora pulled on her robe and walked barefoot down the dark hallway. She should get a nightlight, she thought as she pushed open the door to Tillie's room. A nightlight to keep everyone safe. Tillie's bed was a mess, the summer quilt in the tumbling blocks pattern was on the floor, the sheets a knot beside it. Not at all like Tillie, Dora thought, her heart racing. She took another step into the room before she remembered. Tillie was in California. That's where she lived. Dan's boy slept here now.

Her heart still beating fast, Dora dropped onto the chair at Tillie's old desk, where photographs of Tillie as a teenager stared back at her. She had taken ballet forever, then without warning switched to modern dance. Even though Dora never really enjoyed those later performances, she'd enjoyed watching her daughter. In one of the pictures, Tillie sat on the grass at Roger Williams Park, strumming a guitar, grinning. Braless, the outline of her nipples poked through the cotton tee shirt. Dora lifted the picture to look closer.

Right after Dan had died, that very next winter, Tillie had a breast cancer scare. They'd done a lumpectomy, some radiation. Dora had flown out to San Francisco to be with her, had driven her through the maze of unfamiliar streets to doctors and hospitals, keeping her tone upbeat even as her gut ached with fear. When Madeline Dumfey drove Dora to Logan Airport for her flight to San Francisco, she asked her if she felt life was being unfair to her. Bill gone. And Dan. And now Tillie sick. Dora had been surprised by the question. Life unfair? She had known three big loves, she had borne two children, she had traveled as far as China, she was old and alive, she had her own health. She had listed these things to Madeline. "But to lose everyone," Madeline had said. "Really, Dora, you must let yourself get angry. You must." Someone, Dora no longer remembered who, had once said that one death was a tragedy, but many deaths were a statistic. Dora told Madeline this and Madeline had blinked back at her in that way she had, part disbelief, part disgust. "Really, Dora. That's a terrible thing to say."

Now here was Madeline, dead, and Tillie fine except for a small ugly scar on her left breast. Dora did not feel equipped to understand any of it. What of all those boys she'd held who'd been killed in the Pacific, at Omaha Beach, at sea? What of the other men she'd loved, dead now too, both of them. Bill's partner had died right at the Museum of Fine Arts in Boston, in front of a Winslow Homer painting, of a massive heart attack. If that hadn't happened, it was possible that she would have run off with him.

Standing, Dora heard the low hum of a voice downstairs. She followed it, carefully holding the banister as she walked. There in the kitchen, hanging up the telephone, was Peter. He looked at her, weary.

"It could be any day now," he said. "She's dilated two centimeters. Her back hurts."

Dora allowed herself to ask the question that had been on her lips since Melinda had first called back in the spring.

"Why the hell didn't she get an abortion?" Dora said.

"She's Baptist. You know; Super religious. She thinks she'll go to hell for something like that."

"That's plain stupid," Dora said. She sat across from Peter. "What kind of nincompoop is this girl?"

He laughed. For the first time it did not sound like a harsh bark. Dora laughed too.

She took him to lunch at the Rue de L'Espoir. "You can't sit waiting by the phone," she told him as she hustled him into the car. "Having a baby can take a very long time. I was in labor twenty-eight hours with your father."

Dora ordered her martini with her lunch. She always enjoyed a good martini.

"May I ask," she said to her grandson, "how all this came to pass?"

"Come on, Gran," he said, narrowing his eyes. "You know how girls get pregnant."

"I'm not sure I know how teen-aged girls get pregnant by boys who don't even love them," she said. The martini was perfect, dry and cold.

"Love," he said, practically spitting out the word. "What good is loving someone? Then they die, or leave, or don't love you back. Big deal."

"Well," Dora said, "everyone is going to die. Even you. That's one of humankind's most foolish ideas, that everyone will die except you."

"You know what my mother says about you?" Peter said, narrowing his eyes again. "She says you're a tough old bird. Cold-hearted too."

Dora rolled her eyes. "How would Melinda know anything about me at all? As far as I can tell she was in a drug-induced haze until my son died. Then she got scared enough to straighten herself out, go to law school, and join the real world." She leaned across her sandwich and added, "Am I cold hearted because I call things as I see them?"

Peter smiled. She was almost starting to like the boy. "Not at all." He sighed. "I guess maybe I do love Rebecca a little. I mean, I love being with her and everything. Touching her and stuff."

"Yes, well, that's obvious," Dora said, blushing a little. "You know, Tillie, your Aunt Tillie, I mean, got herself in similar trouble. Of course, she was older, in college, and she came home for Christmas with the news. I said, Tillie, you are far too young and immature to have a baby. I'll arrange an abortion for you and that was that. Of course, Tillie agreed."

Peter said, his mouth full of hamburger, "I thought she was . . . you know . . ."

"A lesbian. Yes. Apparently that wasn't always the case."

Peter swallowed and then looked at Dora, all seriousness. "Boy, you've had a sad life, haven't you?"

Dora finished her martini. "Not at all. If you asked anyone about their life when they were seventy-eight years old it would be full of the same sorts of stories. I guarantee you. This baby of yours that's getting born is just one of many many blips in your lifetime."

"But it breaks my heart," Peter said.

"What does?" Dora asked him, surprised.

"That I'll never even lay eyes on it. That I'll grow old with a child in the world that I don't even know. That I'm losing something important."

Without warning, Dora felt tears spring to her eyes. Hastily, she closed them and pressed her fingers to her eyelids, hoping her grandson did not see her do it.

"I thought you said it took forever!" Peter shouted.

Dora was surprised to see his cheeks wet with tears, surprised that he would cry so freely.

"I'm sorry," she said, and her own voice sounded weak and feeble.

Peter stood in the middle of the kitchen, still rumpled from sleep. His thin cotton striped pajamas and the way his cowlick stood straight up like a miniature bale of hay made him seem like a child rather than a young man who had just become a father.

"Sorry? That's all you can say?"

His hands were placed on his hips, his jaw jutted out. Dora thought of Dan, how he would stand in this very spot in this very way and challenge her. The thought made her dizzy enough to drop, sighing, into a chair and hold her head in her hands.

"Her mother said she had it yesterday afternoon," Peter was saying, his voice bordering on shrill. "The kid's already like a day old practically."

Dora shook her head. He would never see this child of his anyway. Hadn't he told her that the girl wasn't even going to hold it? That the adopting parents would be right there, waiting, ready to take the baby away with them?

"What can it possibly matter," Dora said evenly, "that you got the news twelve hours after the fact?"

"Almost a day later!" he insisted.

Slowly, Dora stood and made her way to the stove to put on the kettle. She didn't like noise and discussion before she'd had her cup of Earl Grey. She never had. When the children were still at home she would wake up early, make her tea, then slip back into bed to drink it quietly. Now here she was at a time in her life when she should not have to get screamed at and be accused right in her own kitchen, before she'd had her tea.

She concentrated on the kettle, the way it shook slightly as the water began to heat.

"You haven't told me what she had," Dora said.

A puff of steam rose from the spout, then the low whistle began.

Peter's voice was soft now. "A boy," he said, as if he couldn't believe it himself.

A sharp pang of regret shot through Dora's gut. A baby boy. Her Dan's grandson. Her own great-grandchild. She tried to keep her hand steady as she poured the boiling water into her mug, a lumpy thing that Tillie had made in a pottery class some years ago. For an instant Dora believed that she would turn around and find *her* children there: Dan's face still creased from sleep, his frown deep, Tillie's sunnier self humming tunelessly. She would turn, Dora let herself think, and her children would ask for French toast and quarters for treats after school and their mittens and erasers for their pencils and hair ribbons and papers that needed signing. She took a breath and spun around expectantly. But of course there was just this other boy. Peter. Still crying, his face blotchy and swollen now, he waited for something from her, something she could not possibly give him.

Dora did not know what to do for Peter, who moved around the house noisily, slamming cabinets shut, muttering to himself. He called the girl constantly, as if she could give him answers. Dora heard him say: "But they were cool, right? Like in their pictures?" And: "They seemed in love, right? Like they're not going to get divorced, right?"

Another time she heard him asking softly: "Did he have any hair? Did he look at you or anything?" It took Dora a moment to understand Peter was asking about his baby, not the man who adopted him.

After several days of this, Peter appeared in front of her as she dozed over a mystery novel.

"I've got to do something," he said.

Dora stared at him, trying to sort out who exactly he was and why he was standing in her parlor.

"Peter," she said finally.

"Yeah. Right." He was jumping up and down a little. "I've got to do something."

"Let's go to dinner," Dora said, getting to her feet, even though a small roasting chicken was defrosting in her kitchen sink.

Once in the car, she couldn't think of where to go. She drove around the city, confused. She didn't really like all this renovation that was going on, the way they rerouted the entire river and made all the roads go in new directions.

"Maybe I should have talked her into keeping it," Peter was saying. "Maybe I should have married her. I mean, I will never see that kid. Ever."

Dora nodded politely. Weybosset Street, Washington, Dorrance. None of them seemed to be in the right place. It was twilight now, and the lights came on unexpectedly, out of nowhere.

"I mean," Peter said, "it's like he vanished."

"Yes," Dora said. "Well."

Then a thought occurred to her. She and Bill used to take the kids to The Blue Grotto, up on Federal Hill, for special occasions. It had white tablecloths, good martinis, chicken marsala and spaghetti with bolognese sauce. Tillie liked to get a Shirley Temple there and Dan had a Roy Rogers, both with extra cherries.

"Do you like Italian food?" Dora said, getting her bearings.

"Like the Olive Garden?"

Dora sighed. She didn't know what the boy was talking about most of the time. "I suppose," she said.

Federal Hill, at least, had not changed: it was still impossible to get a parking space. After circling a few times, Dora suggested they park and walk the six or seven blocks to the restaurant.

"Whatever," Peter said.

It was one of those summer nights where in the country you would hear crickets, where the air is so still it makes a person move slower. On the sidewalk, Peter took Dora's arm. His chivalry surprised her.

"Maybe I do love her," he said, his voice full of the resignation a man three times his age might have.

Out of the car, Dora noticed that indeed Federal Hill had changed after all. Now there were Thai and Cambodian restaurants everywhere.

"Let's go in here," Peter said. "What do you say?" He stopped abruptly.

Dora glanced up at the sign, the squiggly lines for letters, the red dragon on the window. She had read once that they ate dogs in Cambodia. She thought of the Blue Grotto, the smell of garlic and tomato.

But Peter was tugging her arm.

"Not there," he said. "Here."

She only had a moment to see where he was leading her before they were inside, and in that moment Dora read the words: Buddy's Tattoos.

Melinda had said nothing about tattoos. That was what Dora told herself as Peter explained what a good idea this was. He would commemorate his son's birth. He would have a reminder of him every day for the rest of his life. And if the boy ever decided to try and find him, there would be the proof of his fatherhood right on his arm. Dora listened and looked around. It was exactly what she might expect—a little seedy with its peeling paint and hastily washed linoleum floor, the iron smell of blood mingling with an antiseptic that reminded Dora of hospitals, and an array of customers in leather and metal. The lighting was florescent.

"I'll get his name and maybe like a little heart or something," Peter said, jabbing his finger at the wall where available tattoos were displayed.

Dora's eyes drifted past cupids and dolphins and vaguely familiar cartoon characters.

"A heart is nice," she said. She sat on a folding chair, her purse on her lap. Like an old lady, she realized, and tried to strike a more casual pose. "But I didn't know there was a name. Or rather, that we knew the name." She crossed her legs at the ankle, the way she had learned in charm school back in the thirties.

Peter studied a variety of hearts. Broken, intertwined, chubby, pink, red. "It's Daniel," he said, without looking at her. He pointed to one of the hearts and said, "This one's good."

A fat hairy man came into the room from one of the curtained off cubicles. He wore farmer overalls with no shirt underneath. "Who's next here?" he said.

"I am," Dora said firmly. She stood up and smoothed her skirt. "I'm getting the same as him."

The man looked from Dora to Peter. "Fifteen each or two for thirty," he said. He laughed at his own joke, then wiggled his fingers at them. "Come on."

Dora and Peter followed him into one of the cubicles.

"You show him," she told her grandson.

Again Peter pointed to a heart and explained the lettering he wanted for the name. He answered questions about color and size. The man nodded thoughtfully, not unlike a painter Dora had once watched in Paris who sat by the Seine with his easel and tubes of paint. Even when the tattoo man—*tattoo artist,* Dora silently corrected herself—prepared his tools, the needles and dyes and medicated swabs, Dora thought of that French painter, how his nose was peeling and pink from sunburn, the yeasty way he'd smelled, his serious concentration. She had wanted to buy that painting; it had filled her with a longing for things she would never have but always want. Bill had laughed at her, claiming it was simply bad art. They had continued their stroll along the river, Bill reading from the guidebook, pointing at this bridge and that monument, while Dora kept glancing over her shoulder at the man painting.

"You need to take off your sweater," the tattoo artist told Dora gently.

She had put on her jade green cashmere twin set for dinner. Now she slipped off the cardigan almost casually, tossing it on Peter's lap.

Dora closed her eyes and offered the man her arm. She thought of nothing. The first prick of the needle startled her with its burning pain.

"Oh," she said, her eyes flying open.

"The outline's the worst part, Gran," Peter said.

Dora took a breath and closed her eyes again. But each prick of the needle sent fresh tears down her cheeks. She heard herself panting, the way she had when she'd waited too long to get to the hospital to have Dan and arrived crouched on the floor of their Impala, like a wild animal.

"Usually people have a few drinks before they come," the man told her.

"It hurts," Dora managed to say between needlepricks and tears. "It hurts so much."

The pain took over her body, her mind, it invaded every part of her: hot, sharp, constant. Until she was no longer separate from it. Only then could she stop crying, open her eyes, and continue.

OTHER

Richard Bausch

Riches

Mattison bought the lottery ticket on an impulse—the first and only one he ever bought, in fact. So when, that evening, in the middle of the nine o'clock movie, the lucky number was flashed on the television screen and his wife, Sibyl, holding the ticket in one hand and a cup of coffee in the other, put the coffee down unsteadily and said, "Hey—we match," he didn't understand what she was talking about. She stared at him and seemed to go all limp in the bones, and abruptly screamed, "Oh, my God! I think we're rich!" And even then, it took him a few seconds to realize that he had the winning ticket, the big one, the whole banana, as his father put it. Easy Street, milk and honey, the all-time state lottery jackpot—sixteen million dollars.

Later, standing in the crowd of newspaper photographers and television people, he managed to make the assertion that he wouldn't let the money change his life. He intended to keep his job at the Coke factory, and he would continue to live in the little three bedroom rambler he and his wife had moved into four years ago, planning to start a family. Their children would go to public schools; they were going to be good citizens, and they wouldn't spoil themselves with wealth. Money wasn't everything. He had always considered himself lucky enough: he liked his life. Maybe—just maybe—he and Sibyl would travel a little on vacation. Maybe. And he said in one television interview that he was planning to give some to charity.

A mistake.

The mail was fantastic. Thousands of letters appealing to his generosity—some of them from individuals, including a college professor who said she wanted time to complete a big study of phallocentrism in the nineteenth century novel. Mattison liked this one, and showed it to friends. "Who cares about the nineteenth century?" he said. "And—I mean—novels. Can you imagine?"

But he was generous by nature, and he did send sizable checks to the Red Cross, The United Way, Habitat For Humanity, and several organizations for the homeless; he gave to The March of Dimes, to Jerry's Kids; he donated funds to The Danny Thomas Foundation, Save the Children, The Christian Children's Fund, Project Hope, The Literacy Council, The Heart Association, The Council for Battered Women, DARE, The Democratic Party, The Smithsonian, Mothers Against Drunk Drivers, the Library Association, the American Cancer Society, and the church. They all wanted more. Especially the Democratic Party.

He kept getting requests. People at work started coming to him. Everybody had problems.

His two older brothers decided to change directions in life, wanted to start new careers, one as the pilot of a charter fishing boat down in Wilmington, North Carolina, the other as a real estate salesman (he needed to go through the training, to get his license). The older of them, Eddie, was getting married in the Spring. They each needed a stake, something to start out on. Twenty thousand dollars apiece. Mattison gave it to them; it was such a small percentage of the eight hundred-fifty thousand he had received as the first installment of his winnings.

A few days later his father phoned and asked for a new Lincoln. He'd always hankered for one, he said. Just forty thousand dollars. "You're making more than the football players, son. And with what you're getting at the Coke Factory—think of it. Your whole year's salary is just mad money. Thirty-eight thousand a year."

Mattison understood what was expected. "What color do you want?"

"What about my father?" Sibyl said. "And my mother, too." Her parents were separated. Her mother lived in Chicago, her father in Los Angeles. Mattison was already footing the bill for them both to fly to Virginia for Thanksgiving.

"Well?" she said.

"Okay," he told her. "I didn't know your father wanted a Lincoln."

"That's not the point, Benny. It's the principle."

"We have to see a tax lawyer or something."

"You can't buy a Lincoln for your father and leave my parents out."

"What about your grandparents?"

Sibyl's father's parents were alive and well, living in Detroit, and they already owned a Cadillac, though it was ten years old.

"Well?" Mattison said.

Sibyl frowned. "I guess, if you look at it that way—yes. Them, too. And us."

"Well, I guess that covers everybody in the whole damn family," Mattison said.

"Do you begrudge us this?"

"Begrudge you."

"I don't understand your attitude," she said.

"We could buy cars for the dead, too. A new Lincoln makes a nice grave marker."

"Are you trying to push me into a fight?" she said.

Christmases when he was a boy, his father took him and his brothers out to look at the festive decorations in the neighborhoods. They'd gaze at the patterns of lights and adornments, and when they saw particularly large houses—those mansions in McLean and Arlington—Mattison's father would point out that money doesn't buy happiness or love, and that the rooms behind the high walls might very well be cold and lifeless places. They did not look that way to Mattison, those warm tall windows winking with light. And yet over time he came to imagine the quiet inside as unhappy quiet, and saw the lights as lies: the brighter the decorations, the deeper the gloom they were designed to hide.

The idea had framed a corollary in his mind: people with money had problems he didn't have to think about. It was all over there, in that other world, the world of unfathomable appetites and discontents; the world of corruption, willfulness and greed. He had worked his way up to supervisor at the Coke factory, after starting there as a stock boy, and he didn't mind the work. His wife was a lovely dark-haired girl from Tennessee, who had been a flight attendant for a year or so before walking into his life at a dance put on by the local Volunteer Fire Department. They had gone into debt to buy the little rambler, and for the first year, she worked as a temporary in the front offices of the factory, so they could make the payments on the mortgage. She was home now, and for the last couple of years they'd been trying, unsuccessfully, to get pregnant.

Their life together had come to an awkward place regarding her failure to conceive: there were hours of avoiding the subject, followed by small, tense moments circling it, with a kind of irritability, a mutual wish that the problem would go away, the irritability fueled by the one suggestion neither could come out and make: that the other should go in for tests to see if something might be wrong. They were in love, they had begun to doubt themselves, and they were not dealing with any of it very well, and they knew it.

This was the situation the day he purchased the lottery ticket. He had walked into the convenience store and bought an ice cream bar and an apple, on his way home. The ice cream bar was for Sibyl—a little peace offering for the words they had exchanged in the morning. He was standing at the store counter waiting to pay, his thoughts wandering to their trouble—they had argued about plans for dinner, but of course the real argument was about the pregnancy that hadn't happened—when a man stepped in front of him.

This was the sort of thing he usually reacted to: he had a highly developed sense of fair play, and he believed with nearly religious fervor in the utility, the practical good, of graciousness, of simple courtesy. Because, like his father, he expected these virtues of himself, he also tended to require them of others. He might have said something to this rude man who had butted into the line. But he merely stood there, deciding on the words he would use to apologize to Sibyl, feeling low and sad, worried that something might really be wrong with him, or with her. The man who had stepped in front of him bought a pack of cigarettes and a lottery ticket. So as Mattison stepped up to pay, he asked for a ticket, too, and dropped it into the bag with the ice cream and the apple.

Sibyl ate the apple. She didn't want the ice cream bar, and

expressed surprise that he had considered she would, anxious as she was now about her weight.

"I bought a lottery ticket," he told her. "Here, maybe it'll being you some luck."

That night, late, after the magnitude of his winnings had been established, after the calls to friends and family (several of whom thought the excitement was that Sibyl was pregnant), after the celebrating and the visits of the news media and the hours of explaining what he felt, he lay in the dark, with Sibyl deeply asleep at his side, and fear swept over him, a rush of terror that hauled him out of the bed and through the little rooms of the house—the kitchen, littered with empty bottles of beer and unwashed dishes; the nursery, with its crib and its cherubs on the walls; the spare room, the room they planned to put her mother in whenever the baby came. The only light came from the half moon in the living room window. He looked out at the lunar shadows of the houses along his street; everyone in them knew by now what had happened to him. His life was going to change, now, no matter what. He fought the idea, walked into the kitchen, poured himself a glass of milk, and tried to think of anything else.

Sibyl found him there an hour later, sitting at the table, trembling, his hands clasped around the base of the half-empty glass of milk. "Honey?" she said, turning the light on.

He started. "I'm scared," he said. "I feel real scared." She walked to him and put her arms around him. "Silly," she said. "Now you're scared?"

He had been right to be scared. He understood this, now. At work, he couldn't take a step without someone approaching him for money, or reproaching him—with a look, a gesture of avoidance—because of the money. Everyone had changed, while he remained essentially the same. Even Sibyl had changed.

She wanted a new house, a bigger house, and the new Lincoln; all new clothes. She yearned to travel, and said he should quit the Coke factory. And, worst of all, she'd decided to stop trying to get pregnant. "Let's see the world," she said. "We can just spend the whole year going around to all the places in the magazines."

"Maybe I'll take a long leave of absence," he said, without being able to muster much enthusiasm. He was worried that he might be getting an ulcer.

"Honey," he said one evening. "You really don't want to start a family now?"

"We could do that," she said. "But just not now. I mean, come on, baby. We've got all this money. Let's use it."

"I thought we weren't going to let it spoil us?"

"Don't be ridiculous," she said. "That stuff about getting spoiled by money is what rich people say to make poor people think it's better to be poor. We're rich, and I don't feel a bit different, except I'm a whole hell of a lot happier."

"Are you?"

"Oh, don't be cryptic, Benny. Yes, I'm happy as a clam. Come on, let's spend the money the way we want to."

"And what way is that?"

"Gee," she said. "I don't know. Duh, I'll try to figure it out though."

She bought a Lincoln for her father, a Cadillac for her mother, and another for her grandparents, who then decided that they wanted one each, since they were not getting along all that well, and would rather have separate cars. They already had separate bedrooms, and to them it seemed reasonable, since there was so much money in the family now, to ask for the two cars. Sibyl's grandmother said she would settle for a smaller car—a BMW, perhaps, or a Miatta. Something like that. Something sporty. Sybil, worried about her in traffic with a smaller car, said, "You'll take a Cadillac and like it."

Mattison said he'd have to keep his job, because the lottery money would run out, paying as he was for a corporation-sized fleet of luxury cars, and Sibyl accused him of being sarcastic.

"I'm not being sarcastic," he said. "You forget—we gave some money to charities."

They were in the bedroom, moving back and forth past each other, putting their clothes away before retiring for the night.

"I know," said Sibyl, hanging her new blouse up in the closet. "And the whole family thought you were crazy for doing it, too."

He had just put his pants on a hanger, and he paused to look at her. "You—you said you wanted to—you said you were proud of me—"

"I'm tired." She crossed to the bed, pulled the spread back, and stood there in her slip, such a pretty young woman. "I don't see why we have to give money to anyone outside the family. This room is so damn small."

"You're the one who wanted to give an expensive car to everybody."

"No—you started that. With your father."

"My father asked for the damn thing."

"And you gave it to him."

"I did. And then you asked for five cars—five of them—and you got them. Now who's crazy?"

"Are you calling me crazy?" she said.

"You said everybody thought I was crazy."

She got into the bed, and pulled her slip off under the blankets, then dropped it on the floor.

"Honey," he said. "Listen to us. Listen to how we sound."

"I'm going to sleep. The whole thing's silly, We're rich and that's all there is to it. There's nothing complicated or threatening about it."

"You don't see the unhappiness this is causing us?" he said.

She didn't answer.

"We were going to start a family. We were in love—"

"Stop it, Benny. Nobody said anything about not loving anyone. We all love you."

"I'm talking about you and me," he said. "Look at us, Sibyl. You don't even want to have a baby anymore."

"That has nothing to do with anything. Come to bed."

He went into the bathroom and cleaned his teeth. She'd bought things for the walls. Prints, mostly, in nice frames, which they could never have afforded before the lottery. And even so it was all junk. Cheap department store crap.

"Are you going to stay in there forever?" she said sourly. "Close the door, will you? You're keeping me awake."

The rooms of his house had grown so discouragingly quiet, even as possessions and outward signs of prosperity and warmth were added; he no longer felt comfortable there. He no longer felt comfortable anywhere.

Over the next few days, Sibyl kept talking about where she wanted to go, and she had evidently dropped the assumption that he might wish to accompany her. He went to work and got drubbed, every day, with veiled insults, bad jokes about money, hints at his failure to be the friend he ought to be, if only he were inclined to spend his treasure on something other than what he was spending it on, meaning the charities. Though one co-worker, a woman whose husband had a drinking problem and was inclined to violence, had made a comment—jokingly but with a stab of bitterness nonetheless—that Sibyl was certainly loading up with all the trappings of the well-to-do.

This woman's name was Arlene Dakin. And one morning, perhaps a week after she'd made that remark, she asked him for enough money to buy a one-way ticket on a plane bound far away, so she could start over. She spoke so directly that it threw him off and caused him to hesitate.

"I was only half serious," she said sadly. Something in her eyes went through him. He tried to speak, but she turned and walked away.

Thanksgiving, Sibyl insisted that both her parents be flown in from their separate cities; her mother had a new beau (Sibyl's expression) and this person was of course also invited. Her father would rent a car at the airport, and drive everyone in. He wanted to do some touring in the area. Mattison was miserable, his favorite day ruined with these elaborate and costly arrangements. In midmorning, Sybil looked up from a phone conversation with a friend and said, "Benny, for God's sake go do something, will you? You're driving me crazy."

He drove to the firehouse, where the local Red Cross Chapter had used his donated money to set up a turkey dinner for the elderly. There didn't seem to be anything for him to do, and he saw that he was making everyone uneasy, so he cruised around town for a while, feeling lost. He ended up at Arlene Dakin's house. The day was sunny and unseasonably warm. Yesterday he had taken two thousand dollars, two packets of fifties, out of the bank, intending to give it to her when he saw her at work. But she had not come in on Wednesday.

Her house was at the end of a tree-lined street (he'd attended a cookout there, a company function, last summer. The husband had been sober, then. A gregarious, loud man with a way of rocking on the balls of his feet when he talked). Mattison pulled along the curb in front and stopped. In the front yard, a bare tree stood with all its leaves on the ground at its base. He wondered how he could give

Arlene Dakin the money without her husband knowing about it. Then he imagined himself trying to talk through or over a drunken man. He did not get out of the car, but drove on, then turned around and came back. The windows of the house reflected daylight sky. He felt odd, slowing down to look. Finally, he sped away.

A rental car and a caterer's truck were parked in the driveway at home. Mattison pulled in beside the rental car and got out. There was no legitimate reason to remain out here. His father and brothers were sitting in the living room watching a football game. Sibyl's father was with them. He had drunk something on the airplane, and held a cold beer now. In the kitchen, Sibyl and her mother stood watching the caterers work. They had arrived with the almost-finished meal under metal lids. Her mother's new friend sat drinking a beer of his own. Sibyl introduced him as Hayfield. "Nice to meet the winner," Hayfield said, rising.

Mattison shook hands. Sibyl's mother put her arms around his neck and kissed him, then stood aside and indicated him to Hayfield. "Can you believe this boy? Never gambled a day in his life. Buys one ticket. Bingo. Come on, Hayfield, you're the math teacher. What're the odds?"

"Something like one in 53 million, isn't it?" Hayfield said.

Mattison had lain awake nights with the feeling that since this extraordinary thing had happened to him, he was open to all other extraordinary things—the rarest diseases, freak accidents. Anything was possible. He recalled that the frustration out of which he'd bought the ticket in the first place was the difficulty he and Sibyl had been having over not being able to get pregnant.

The jackpot had ruined that for good, now, too.

He was abruptly very depressed, and tired. He looked at the careful, sure hands of the two Arabic-looking men who were preparing the meal, slicing a large breast of turkey, and wished that he could find some reason to be elsewhere.

Sibyl said, "Let's go on into the living room and get out of these people's way."

"Honey," Mattison said. "You hired caterers? On Thanksgiving?"

She put one hand lazily over her heart. "Did you want me to slave all day in here?"

In the living room, the men sat in front of the TV. Mattison's brothers argued in angry murmurs about the relative merits of foreign and American luxury cars. Chip, the middle brother, wanted a motorcycle, and spoke rather pointedly about how he'd been saving like a dog for the last three years. Recently, he'd had his left eyebrow pierced, and was wearing a stud there; it looked like a bolt to keep parts of his skull together. Mattison stared at it, and felt a little sick. "What?" Chip said. "Did I say anything? Did I ask you for any more money?"

Sibyl's mother said. "Who mentioned money? Don't you know that's vulgar?"

Apparently Chip hadn't heard the joke. "I think people expect too much," he said.

And Mattison found himself telling them about Arlene Dakin and her bad husband. It was odd. He heard the urgency in his own voice, and he was aware that they were staring at him. "It's hard to turn each individual case down," he said. "When only a little money would help."

"Another woman?" Sibyl's mother said. "You can't save the world."

"I agree," Mattison's father said.

Hayfield said, "I think it's admirable, though."

Mattison's oldest brother, Eddie, said, "If you ask me, I think it's stupid."

Sibyl laughed. "Don't pussyfoot around it like that, Eddie."

He turned to Mattison. "Why give the money to strangers?"

"No man is an island," Hayfield said.

Sibyl's mother made a sound in the back of her throat, "You're so big on quoting the Bible."

"I don't think that is the Bible, is it?"

"Why in the world are you so concerned about this woman with two babies?" Sibyl asked her husband.

"It's got nothing to do with that," Mattison said. "It's just each individual case."

"You feel sad for everybody, lately. I swear, I think my husband wants to be Albert Einstein."

"I think that's Schweitzer," Hayfield said, gently. "Albert—uh, Schweitzer."

"Give the lady a yacht," Chip said. The eyebrow with the stud in it lifted slightly.

They all sat down to dinner, and Mattison's father said the grace. "Lord, we thank you for this feast, and for the big bless-us-God jackpot, which has made it possible for us all to be together, from such distances . . ." He paused and seemed to lose his train of thought, then shrugged and went on. "In thy name, amen."

Sibyl's mother said, "Every man for himself." She meant the food. But Mattison's father gave her a look.

"Marge," Hayfield said, low. "That's a strange sentiment to express."

"I used to say it every Thanksgiving," Sibyl's father said. He had been very quiet, drinking his beer.

"You never said it," Sibyl's mother broke in. "That was my saying."

"Sibyl, you remember, don't you?" her father said.

"Let's all just be thankful," said Hayfield.

Sibyl's father looked down the table at him. "You must be especially thankful. You hit the jackpot big-time, there, didn't you?"

Mr. Hayfield seemed too confused to respond.

"Well," Chip said addressing everyone. "I think at the very least we ought to be able to quit working. I mean eight hundred fifty thousand dollars. If it hasn't all been given to the lame and the halt."

Eddie said, "I'm not ashamed or too proud to admit that I'd like hair transplants and some lyposuction, too. Get rid of this beer gut. Hell, Dad got forty thousand dollars."

"You begrudge your old man?" Mattison's father said cheerfully. "Look, the boy's still got his salary, don't forget that. He's getting money like a freaking bonus baby."

"The caterers stood against the far wall, each with a bottle of wine. Sibyl's father signaled them to pour, and they went around the table, asking if people wanted white or red. Sibyl's father said, "Here's to wealth."

"I want a house in the Florida Keys," Sibyl said, holding up her glass of wine. "And I want servants. A whole staff." It was as though she were offering this statement as a toast.

"Maybe, in time, we could each have a house," said her mother.

"The chicken's good," Hayfield said, rather timidly.

"It's not chicken," said Sibyl. "My God, how could you mistake this for chicken?"

"Did I say chicken?"

Sibyl's father drank his wine, then finished the last of his beer. "It's quite a feeling," he said. "Economic power."

"Nothing but the best," Chip said. "For us and the lame and halt."

Mattison said. "You got all you need, didn't you?"

"I'd like a house, too," said Eddie. "Why not? But I'm not begging for it, that's for damn sure."

"Who's begging?" Chip said. He looked down the table. "Do you all know that right now there's a bunch of old people eating a turkey dinner on us? Right this minute over at the firehouse?"

"That's immaterial to me," said Eddie. "I've learned my lesson. I'm not asking for any charity."

"I always liked the skin," Hayfield put in. "I know it's not healthy."

"What the hell is he talking about?" said Sibyl's father.

"The chicken," Sibyl said, and smirked.

"I make Thanksgiving better than this," her mother said. "I must admit."

"Why do you have to suggest that I'm asking for a handout?" Chip said suddenly to Eddie. "You always put things in a negative light. You're the most negative son of a bitch I ever saw."

"I tell the truth," Eddie said.

"I didn't see it stop you from taking twenty grand for yourself when the time came."

"Whoa," their father said. "Let's just stow that kind of talk. You got a new boat, Eddie, didn't you?"

"God," Mattison said, standing. "Listen to us. Look what this has done to us. It's Thanksgiving, for God's sake."

For a moment, they all regarded him, the one with the money.

"It's brought us together," Sibyl said. "What did you think it would do?"

"A little family discussion," said her mother. "We're all thankful as hell."

Chip said, "Did anybody say anything about not being grateful?"

Mattison's father said, "Nobody's being ungrateful. We just

thanked the Lord for our luck. Your luck, son. God knows I spent most of my damn life trying to contend with bad luck."

"But you had happy times, didn't you? Sweet times."

His father considered a moment. "Well, no. Not really. I worked my ass off is what it all amounted to."

Mattison had an abrupt, and painful memory of him walking down the long sidewalk in front of the house on Montgomery Street, bags of groceries in his arms—a cheerful man with nothing much in the bank, and a family that seemed to make him happy, a house he liked to come home to. It was what Mattison always wanted, too, he thought: a family. He gazed at his father, who was dipping a roll into the hot turkey gravy, and said, "Dad, remember how it was—those Thanksgivings when we were small—those Christmases you took us to see the big houses. . . ."

But his father was arguing with Chip about twenty thousand dollars. "You begrudge twenty thousand dollars to your own father," he said. 'I'm damn glad you didn't buy the winning ticket. None of us would see diddly-squat."

They were all arguing now, Sibyl's mother and father talking over each other about the houses they might own or not own; Sibyl chiding Eddie about being greedy, how unattractive it was. "You should see how ugly it makes you," she said. "Look at yourself in a mirror."

Poor Hayfield sat chewing, a man unable to decide which conversation to listen to, or try mediating. He said to Mattison, "Prosperity can be as hard on good spirits as anything else." He turned to Sibyl and repeated this, even as she raised her voice to gain Chip's attention. "Consumers," she said. "That's all either of your two ever have been."

"Excuse me," Mattison murmured, standing. Nobody heard him. He went into the other room, past the caterers, who were smoking, standing at the open kitchen window, talking quietly. He went out, and along the side of the house, to the street. The caterers watched him, and when he looked back at them, they continued to stare. He got into the car, turned the ignition, and pulled slowly away.

The sun was low now, winter-bright through the bare trees. He drove to the main highway, then headed east, away from the Coke factory, toward Washington. There was almost no traffic. All the families were gathered around festive, polished tables, in warm light. No one in any of these dwellings was thanking the Lord for sixteen million dollars. He repeated the number several times, aloud; it felt unreal, oddly harrowing. Driving on, he passed the road down to Arlene Dakin's house, and then looked for a place to turn around.

She was standing on the stoop in front as he pulled up, her coat held closed at her throat. He got out of the car and walked to her, hurrying, his heart racing. This meeting was somehow his destiny, it seemed, a tremendously meaningful coincidence. Looking beyond her for her husband, he saw the open front door, and part of a disheveled living room.

"What do you want here?" she said.

"Where—" he began. "Did you see me before—I came by . . ."

"He took them," she said. "My babies. He took them. I don't know where." She began to cry. "I was trying to find a way—and he just rode away with them."

"Here," he said, approaching. He put his hands on her shoulders and gently guided her toward his car.

"Leave me alone," she said, pulling away. The violence of it astonished him.

"I'm sorry." He walked dumbly after her. "Let me take you somewhere."

"No." She was crying again. She made her way across the street, got into her little red car and started it. He hurried to his own, watching her. She drove to the end of the street and on, and he kept her in sight. A few blocks down, she stopped in front of a small row of shops, flanking a restaurant.

This part of town was already decked out for Christmas. There was a sign in the restaurant window:

OPEN THANKSGIVING; TURKEY FEAST; BOBBY DALE TRIO.

She went in. Mattison followed. It was a narrow, high-ceilinged place. At the far end a man was singing with the accompaniment of a bass and piano. Some people sat at tables surrounding the bandstand, eating plates piled high with turkey, dressing, and potatoes. She had taken a table near the entrance to the kitchen. Apparently, she knew someone here—a woman who paused to speak with her, then reached down and held her hands.

Mattison walked over to them.

"I said to leave me alone. Jesus Christ," she burst out at him, crying.

"I—I just wanted to help."

"I don't want your help. I told you."

The friend seemed wary. "Who is this character, anyway?"

"Oh, he's the big winner," Arlene Dakin said. "Didn't you know?" She looked at Mattison. "Can't you see I don't want your money now? I don't want anything to do with you."

He moved to the other end of the room, where several people were seated, talking loud above the sound of the Trio. He saw her get up and enter the kitchen with her friend. It wasn't his fault about the money; he had ravaged no forests, taken no wealth by exploiting others, nor plundered anyone or anything to get it. He was not a bad man. If she would only let him, he could show her. He could make her see him for what he was. The idea seemed distant, far away, as the idea of riches once had seemed. She came back from the kitchen and went on to the doorway and out.

He ordered a drink, finished it and then ordered another. He would have to go back home soon. They would wonder where he'd gone. Bobby Dale, of the Bobby Dale Trio, was a compact man in a silvery-blue double-breasted suit. He ended a long, incongruously bright version of "House of the Rising Sun," and then, talking about his own heavy drinking and widely adventurous love-life, launched into "Don't Get Around Much Anymore." It wasn't very good singing. As a matter of fact, it was rather annoying—this bright, cheerful rendition of a song about being lost and alone. Mattison had still another drink. When the song ended there was scattered applause. He stood and approached Dale, reaching into his pocket. As his hands closed on the first packet of fifties, it struck him that he had never felt more free, more completely himself.

"Yes?" said the singer.

"This is a thousand dollars," Mattison told him. "I want you to sit down and shut up."

"Pardon me?" Bobby Dale said, almost laughing.

"I want you to stop singing. I'll pay you to shut up and sit down."

"You asking for trouble, Jack?"

"Just quit for the day." Mattison held the money out to him. "It's real," he said. "See? One thousand dollars."

"Man, what the hell're you trying to do here?"

"Hey, Bobby," the bass player said. "Chrissakes take it if it's real. Fool."

Dale said, "Man, you think I won't?" He snatched the packet from Mattison's hand.

"Thank you," Mattison said, and returned unsteadily to his seat.

"Okay folks. It takes all kinds, don't it. I guess the show's over for a time. The man with the money says we should take a little time off, and we're very happy to oblige the man with the money."

"That's me," Mattison said, smiling at the others, all of whom quite frankly stared at him. "Hi, everyone," he said. He felt weirdly elated.

"I recognize you," said one woman. Her lipstick was the color of blood. "You're the guy—you won the big jackpot. I saw it on the news." She turned to her friends. "That's him. And look at him. Throwing money around in a bar on Thanksgiving day."

"Hey," a man said. "How about letting us have a little of it?"

"I can't think of a single solitary thing I'd rather do," Mattison said. "Why not?" He began to laugh, getting to his feet. He stood before them, their frowning faces, the wrong faces, no one he knew or loved. He reached into his pocket for the other thousand.

Robert Olen Butler

Carl and I

Three nights after I married Carl Peterson, we watched Sarah Bernhardt die of consumption on a bed strewn with camellias. She was very beautiful, her face a sad white mask, her eyes enormous and dark, her voice rising from the stage and filling the Lyric Theatre, though as the courtesan Marguerite Gautier she was capable of barely a whisper, dying as she was from the tubercular bacilli breeding in her lungs. Her sins had been cleansed, Marguerite Gautier's, by her suffering and by the goodness of her heart and by the sacrifice she had made, giving up for his own sake the one man she had ever loved. I grasped my Carl's arm on the seat next to me as Marguerite died, for he was the one man I had ever loved and now we were married, on the previous Saturday, December 16, 1905, and the church was filled with red camellias. The newspapers said that Sarah Bernhardt slept in her own coffin, transporting it with her wherever she went, and she had died nearly twenty thousand times in her life, just as she was dying before us, and she took a cloth from her bosom as she lay on her deathbed, and she coughed terribly into it.

Now Carl has written to me from Attleboro that he is dying. He left for the sanitarium barely a month ago and he has lost hope. So quickly. The death is coming upon him very quickly. This sometimes happens. Like John Keats, who wasted and died at the age of twenty-six. The British writer Robert Louis Stevenson, on the other hand, resisted for decades before being overwhelmed. As Dr. Gilbert would say, the bacilli have found "fertile ground" in Carl's body. Oh, had you only been as barren as I, my Carl.

He did not send me a view of the sanitarium. None of his postcards have been of this place I have never seen, where he will die. He says it is vast and made of gray stone the color of our birdbath. He could not resist a romantic postcard, even considering. Two lovers sitting at the edge of the sea and she has raised her parasol to shield what they are doing, but their silhouettes are visible. They are about to kiss. He put the postcard in an envelope so the postal carrier would not share his words. "Dearest Sweetheart," he said to me. I grew weak at this. And he tried hard to put his bravery down on the card, going quite formal for a moment. "A line or two hoping they will find you all in good health," he said. All in good health. Wholly in good health. Completely in good health. As I seem, in fact, to be, which gives me no comfort. "As for me," he said, "I am getting worse. I don't think I will live long enough to see your dear face again."

He turned his face to me when we tucked the quilts around him in the back seat of the automobile that came to take him. He was as white as Sarah Bernhardt dying in the Lyric Theatre. As white as Marguerite Gautier. As white, I'm sure, as John Keats. I gave out John Keats' book of poems this very morning to a sallow-faced boy at the library. I am a Carnegie Maid, dispensing the words of all the writers of the world, some still living, but destined to die at last, and most who have died already, some of this disease, some not.

One in seven who dies in the world, dies of this White Death. Some leave words behind, some do not. I have kept all the postcards Carl has sent to me. They are in a teakwood box. He wooed me with postcards. And he continued to write them even after we were married. He would be at work and I would come home from the library before him, and waiting in the mailbox would be a card from him. "Oh you sweetheart," he wrote, in his love of a good catchphrase. This was not so very long ago. "Oh you daisy field and up along the creek on that log or under the big tree. Oh you. I wish I could go there now and pick daisies with you." His face was white and his eyes were terrible dark when he left for Attleboro.

I must write him now in return. He will not let me come to visit. He says I've been exposed long enough to the contagion, he could not bear for me to get sick. And he doesn't say it, but he's ashamed of how he's grown weak, how he's lost so much weight. He has always been a man to take off his coat and roll up his sleeves and have at some physical thing. My only recourse is a penny postcard that lies before me now in the center of the little flat top desk in our bedroom. I've chosen a card from among the romance cards with all the come-hithering and the oh-no-not-now-sirs, but this is of a woman sitting with her hands clasped around a knee and her eyes are cast down and beneath her is the printed word "heartbroken." I'm regretting the choice. The card was intended for a woman whose beau has not written to her, has not asked her to the dance. But I am, in fact, heartbroken. Carl will understand.

I look out the open window and across the yard to the sugar maple and to the laundry I'd hung this afternoon, the sheets and my nightgowns and underskirts and two of his dress shirts and I cannot look at his shirts. They lift slightly in a wisp of breeze and I cannot look. I'm finding more things I cannot look at in this house. The overstuffed arm chair in our front room where he would read his newspaper of the evening. The porch swing. The cotton handkerchief near my feet. I wish I'd found it before I'd done the laundry. It was caught in the narrow dark space between the wall and his bed, near the headboard. It is folded tightly over the things he brought up from his lungs in his last days in our home. I can see the stains, the color of dried camellias. I found it an hour ago and dropped it at once and I washed my hands, as Carl would wish me to do.

I have filled my fountain pen.

I turn the card over.

I look at it for a long time, its blank, divided back. Finally I take a stamp from the folder in the drawer, a green, one-cent Benjamin Franklin, the image of a man who died when he was eighty-four and who wrote a poem, which I was compelled in school to memorize, that said,

Death is a fisherman, the world we see
his fish-pond is, and we the fishes be.

I lick the stamp and put it on the card, and then I sit for another long time, feeling irritated with this old man, for him to live to such an old age and to say this vapid thing about death. This man our country reveres, an old fool is.

But I no better am. I've written nothing yet to my husband. My mind is seizing idly on this and that. The chased hard rubber of my Waterman pen. The ticking of the clock from the front room. The faint snap of the sheets in the breeze. The stirring of the maple tree. We first kissed under a vast maple tree, Carl and I. Decoration Day, 1904. We had met in a late March snow that year. I came out of the general store and I had my shopping bag clutched to my chest. The air was unexpectedly full of snow and I was dazzled by this. I lifted my face as I stepped out and turned and I even closed my eyes to let the flakes fall on my eyelids and I ran into Carl Peterson, a great tall oak of a man whose arms went around me even before I had looked into his face, though he was a perfect gentleman, Carl was always a gentleman and his arms were there simply to keep me from falling. As soon as I was steady on my feet he withdrew and we looked into each other's face and he did not seem particularly handsome to me in those first moments. I am an overly critical sort, I think. It is my nature. His eyes were rather too close together and his face too round and too ruddy and though he was clearly a young man, he had a deep-shadowed furrow across his brow above his nose and defining his cheeks from nose to lips. I would come to love these places on his face. I would run my fingertip in these soft grooves of his face. Even when I had long prayed for that ruddiness to return, and when his face had begun to go gaunt, I would lie beside him and run my fingertip in these places and he would close his eyes and perhaps dream of how we met.

He suddenly bent forward and I took a step back, startled. Then he rose up with the tinned milk that had fallen from my bag. "I make these," he said.

"Yes?" I said, not comprehending at first, though the new Pet Milk factory was a source of civic pride in our town. Flakes of snow were clinging to his kersey cap.

"Well, so to speak," he said, lifting the can and considering it, his lower lip pushing up thoughtfully. Too thoughtfully to be serious.

"I'd say cows made those," I said, surprised at myself that I'd suddenly banter with a strange man.

The deep furrow across his brow dipped down sharply, but not for a moment did I think I'd made a mistake. We knew at once, both of us, what we were doing. He said, "Well now, miss, do you think the cows run all the kettles and vacuum pans and heating chambers and cooling tanks to make this stuff pure and safe?"

"So the cows work for you?"

"And then there's the canning." He lifted the tinned milk high. "No cow can do a double seam on a tin can."

"All right," I said. "I'm prepared to give you credit . . . You own the company, do you?"

He drew up to full height and he laid the can in the center of his chest. "Please," he said. "I'm a proud member of the working class, which does the real work. Neither cow nor tycoon can usurp our importance." He paused to let that sink in for a moment and I duly stood there looking up at him, agape. Then he winked at me and said, "I *am* a foreman, however."

And that was how we met, Carl Peterson and I. And we kissed under a maple tree up along a creek where we lingered, sitting on a log, and we talked, and there were daisies all around and then we kissed under the big tree, and this was on Decoration Day, 1904, the Pet Milk factory picnic, and all the working men tipped their hats to Carl and he was dressed in coat and collar and tie and I wore my lingerie dress and I carried a parasol, and without a fuss we walked away from all the others, and on the log, before we got to the maple tree, we sat silent for a long while, a few daisies drooping in his large hand that rested on his knee, and he was unaware of them, he had picked them thinking, I'm sure, to give them to me, but something else had come to his mind and he'd forgotten. I was feeling very tender about this absent-mindedness in him and I was watching that hand, its stillness, the yellow flower faces leaning there. He was thinking hard. And then he said, with no preamble, no clearing of his throat or shuffling around, without that hand and the daisies stirring even a little bit, he said just straight out, having quietly worked up the courage, "I love you."

"Well," I said after only a single quick breath, "I love you, too."

I slept in the yard last night in a reclining chair, my body swaddled like Carl's. I want to share this sanitarium life of his. Yesterday I ate raw eggs and milk and did exercises, moderately, morning and evening, and I lay in that chair under the sky all day long, trying to think of nothing, resting my body and mind, resting completely and activating my body's own defenses out in the fresh pure air. On the day we found out for sure that our worst fears about his persistent cough, his afternoon flush, his weakness were true—this was still before the blood—on that day, Dr. Gilbert, who has always looked pale and gaunt himself, truth be told, sat behind his massive desk and his glasses hung round his neck on a cord and he told us straight out. "Mr. Peterson, you have tuberculosis of the lungs."

I was calm, at this. And, of course, Carl was calm. We had known for a while, though the words had never been spoken between us. But Carl, even from the first, would smother his coughs in some bit of cloth or other, and he would rise up abruptly and walk out of the house to a corner of the yard to spit. Carl and I held hands before Dr. Gilbert, who was going on in a voice tainted with sarcasm about "that German germ hunter who has made us imagine the very air full of contagion." Then Dr. Gilbert shrugged and said, "These bacilli, though they may well exist, must necessarily fall on favorable soil, fertile soil, to grow and live. So we must build up the soil."

He had used the same metaphor—apparently the only one he knew—when he'd told me the year before that my ovaries were not properly formed and my womb was tilted. So I cannot have children? I said, not really a question. You have no fertile soil, he said. I imagine him bending over a man suffering a heart attack to say, Your heart lacks fertile soil for beating. He is a fool with his words. I held Carl the night we discovered my barrenness and for several nights thereafter. I held him till morning, my arms around him as if to cradle him. We both shed tears, though with no sounds, no words about this turn of events. There would be no children for us. Though so many die young, anyway. When yellow fever and cholera and small pox aren't going around, there's always influenza and pneumonia and typhus and scarlet fever and measles and whooping cough and diphtheria, to name a few, and there is always a bit of poisoned meat or milk or something else that a child can eat and die from, and, of course, there is tuberculosis. Let *us* die then, Carl and I, but not a child. It's better for us not to have a child than to bear a child that will die young, is it not?

It is not. But I have no other consolation.

I rise up from my desk. The postcard is still blank, except for my husband's name and his final address in this world, the Attleboro Sanitarium, Attleboro, Massachusetts. I turn away from the desk. I cross the room and stand in the doorway from the bedroom to the living room. I look at his arm chair by the window. I turn and face into the bedroom. I look at our bed. He wrote me a postcard from Attleboro soon after he arrived to say that the nurses all admired him, how he followed procedures. He wrote, "I will surely win next month's Careful Consumptive Award for sputum management." I wrote and asked if there was money for that. I knew he would laugh. He knew I had laughed. I will soon lose this house to the savings and loan. I can go to Worcester and live with my mother. Carnegie has put a library there, I'm sure.

I wait for another thought. I wait for words to say to my husband.

We were so careful. He was always a careful consumptive, even at home, and I let him. I regret that. Standing now looking at our bed I understand that I should have kissed him more. I should have turned his face to me when he was coughing so terribly in the night and I should have taken his face in my hands and kissed him in that moment when he needed something no one could give. I should have kissed him on the lips.

I move to the desk now. I sit. I pick up my pen. I think to call him sweetheart. I think to say, My darling I love you and always will. I kiss your dear face, your darling lips. But I write none of this. These are foolish words. True, perhaps, in their way. But foolish in their bland abstractedness. They have nothing to do with the life Carl and I now share.

And then I know what to say.

I remove the cap of my pen, and I angle the card just so, and I write: "We'll meet in death."

And I know what to do. I put the pen down and I push my chair back and I bend to the handkerchief on the floor. I hold it with my two hands, Carl's handkerchief, and I unfold it. I expose the remnants of his tortured breath and I lift it to my face. And I breathe in, deeply. I breathe into myself my husband's life, and I pray that I am fertile soil.

Roy Parvin

Betty Hutton

He was a big man who looked like trouble, even with his glasses. A cruel fact of nature that made Gibbs a prisoner of his own body long before he became an actual one, at Toms River or the various and lesser security county facilities before that.

He'd been back in the world for months now and had few things to show for it, chiefly a girlfriend and a parole officer, neither of whom was able to give Gibbs what he really needed or wanted, and, truth be told, Gibbs himself hadn't the clearest idea of what that might be either.

"I guess I'm waiting for opportunity to suggest itself to me," he'd explained to his parole bull. "I think it's one of those little-birdy-will-tell-me type situations."

"A birdy," O'Donoghue echoed, a stick of a man with a third-act sort of look to him. "Now I've heard it all. I guess a birdy beats grifting antiques, though."

"I'm not expecting a bird to actually speak to me," Gibbs had said. "Unless it's a parakeet or something." He was not stupid though it often seemed the world was telling him otherwise. All he knew about was old things or how to make a thing look old. During his last bit in the can he'd seen killing and what struck him about it was how easy it was. Anybody could do it.

From the deck of Jolie's second-story flat he could glimpse the Atlantic, if he craned his head, perching on tip-toes. It was October, the year beginning to die more than just a little, the Jersey shoretown of Barnegat wearing the season like a down-at-the-heels beauty queen, the summer crowds vacating after Labor Day, neon glaze of the arcades finally switched off, revealing a pitted sweep of a beach with all the charm and color of dirty concrete, the slack Atlantic crawling ashore, an old pocket watch winding down.

But it was what stood at his back, the ocean of land behind Gibbs, that pulled at him like a tide. He'd never been farther west than the eastern fringe of Pennsylvania, had never been anywhere. He'd heard about Montana, though, a place that sounded like everything hadn't yet been decided, where there still might be some time left. A cellmate had told him of the chinooks, the southerly winds capable of turning winter into spring in a matter of hours, sometimes a ninety-degree temperature swing, and it had seemed to Gibbs lying in their dank cement crib, it seemed if such a thing as the chinooks were possible, anything was.

It was a sand-blasted fall morning that he happened on the Chrysler, a rust-scabbed Newport parked along a dead-end of bungalows clapped shut for the season, the car blue and about the size of a narwhal, its white vinyl roof gone to peel, a whip antenna for a CB the car no longer owned. It looked like the beginning to a thought that Gibbs couldn't see his way to the end of.

Staring at the car, two things came to mind. That Jolie had been hiding her squirrel's stash of mad money in a coffee can on a high kitchen shelf. And the practical knowledge gleaned from his time at the wall of how to jack an automobile which indeed proved easy enough, a matter of popping the door, taking a screwdriver to the steering column, touching off the appropriate wires, and then, like some low-grade miracle, the car rattling awake, exhaling an extravagant tail of blue smoke.

That was how it started: with two wrongs. After a lifetime of wrongs, what were two more? Nothing, Gibbs told himself, nothing. It was just possible he'd finally stumbled on the two wrongs that actually might produce a right.

He didn't take much with him: a leather satchel swollen with a few changes of clothes, his shaving kit, sundry effects; a paper sack of sham works: jades and Roman carnelians and open-work medallions; and, shoved between both on the backseat, an antique pistol, a keepsake handed down in his family, more a piece of history than an actual piece, the only article of legitimate value among the lot. Out the back window, Barnegat framed like a diminishing postcard. That was where trouble would come from when it did, from behind. He tugged on the rearview mirror, yanked it free from its mooring, and then there was only the gray road ahead.

A tattered map inside the Chrysler's glove box ran as far as Harrisburg. After that, Gibbs imagined himself, past the banks of the Susquehanna, falling out the other side of the country, running free, into territory unbound by statelines or the iron sway of laws.

He drove clear around the circle of hours, until all the license plates on the road read Wisconsin. Gibbs pulled off to refuel, him running on fumes as much as the car. A gas jockey shaped like a butterball stepped out of the office and Gibbs stood to stretch his legs, to take measure on the endless table of land fleeing to every point of horizon. At the far corner of the lot, tethered to a pole, was the strangest animal he'd ever seen, looked like he didn't know what, devil eyes set high on his head.

Gibbs said, "What kind of dog is that?"

"It's a goat," the gas jockey told him.

Gibbs nodded heavily. "I didn't think it was a dog."

"Michigan," the jockey said and it took Gibbs a few beats to catch his meaning and then he remembered swapping plates the evening before at a reststop outside Franklin, Pennsylvania, with a listing Travel-All bearing Michigan tags.

"Yeah, the Lions and Tigers. Motor City."

The jockey asked what he wanted, couldn't have been any more than seventeen, all pimples and baby fat. Over his heart: Hank stitched in script. Gibbs glanced around for anybody else and there was no one. Back at Toms River, a whole class of inmate specialized in burgling gas stations, called it *striking oil.*

"What do I want," Gibbs laughed. "Well, Hank, I want it all."

"I meant gas."

"Right. Good man. Fill it with regular. Knock yourself out."

Hank propped the hood. On the pump, the scratchy spinning of the gallon dial. The roll of money that Gibbs had filched from Jolie bulged the pocket of his trousers, the size of a baby's fist. He considered the goat as it grazed leggy plants in a flower box.

And then a strange thing.

It was as if the person who was Gibbs vanished altogether and he could see the entire scene like it was in front of him, a big man standing in the filling bay, a teenager under the hood of a car wiping the dipstick with a rag, the numbing horizontal of land on all sides. And he watched to see what the big man would do, waiting for the squeal of the hood's hinges as it dropped, the blackjack crunch of it slamming the jockey on the crown of his head, laying him out on the oil-splotched concrete, peaceful as an afternoon nap.

It was the pump boy's hand reaching over the lip of the hood that brought Gibbs back to the there and then, the hood gently closing, Hank leaning on it till the catch held fast. Gibbs stared off at a windbreak of buckeye chestnuts, his heart throttling, the dry rattle of the few leaves still on the branches.

Hank pulled a part from a pocket, massaged it with a rag as if trying to screw it into his palm. "You're missing a rearview mirror, you know."

Gibbs said, "I guess I've seen enough of what's behind me."

Nothing left to do but pay. He was spooked yet. Hank appeared none the wiser, doling out change slowly, making sure to get it right.

Gibbs folded himself into the Chrysler. In a few moments he'd be back on his way. For the time being, though, all he was was afraid. A close call, he told himself. Easing out of the filling bay, he rolled down the window. "It's a funny world, Hank," he said gently, pointing at the goat. "Things aren't always what they seem. You know the one about wooden nickels, don't you?"

"Yes sir."

"Good man."

Two days later, and it was Montana.

Thus far it wasn't entirely what Gibbs had expected. The sky was indeed big and everywhere. But Hokanson, his cellmate from Toms River, had mentioned mountains. He'd told about mining, too, the strikes of gold and silver. "An occupation," Hokanson had promised, "where nothing's required, other than doggedness and luck." Gibbs had liked the sound of that.

For a distance of miles the road banded the tracks of the Great Northern and he raced a train with a string of cars long enough almost to be considered geography. There were no posted speed limits, so Gibbs could open the Chrysler up.

He drew a high line through the eastern end of the state,

motoring through flat prairie grasslands and fields already disked for winter wheat, through one-horse towns so small they hardly rated as towns at all, a grain elevator at the outskirts, then a short business strip, usually a grange hall and a church or two and a cross-hatching of streets off the main, the neat rows of side-gabled houses at the edge of the frontier.

It was not until after Devon had spread across the front windshield and out the back, after Ethridge and Cut Bank had come and gone, not until Blackfoot that he saw the mountains. They rose before him, out of the west and yellowed plain like a wave, a sea of mountains, and Gibbs drove toward them, his expectation gathering like a wave itself.

He made Glacier as the sun was emptying from the sky. The calendar still said October though it felt later than that now, the mountaintops webbed in snow, switchbacked roads cut high onto the white shoulders, as if with pinking shears. A different world than the one he'd left behind: wilder and somehow older.

It was late enough in both the day and season that the guard at the gate to Glacier just waved him through and Gibbs wheeled the Chrysler down a park road lined with the tall green of Englemann spruce and Doug fir, pulling up at a lake a couple miles on.

It was lovely—he had no other words to match up with the landscape—only lovely and cold. The lake looked even colder yet and it stretched out before him glassy as a marble, the smudge of twilight already descending, the surround of mountains holding a few clouds within their spires like a cage. A solitary bird flew low over the water, the lake reflecting sky and bird so that it looked like two birds on the wing. Off in the distance, he could see the road following the contours of the shore.

In the foreground: a beach of fine pebbles, a woman and a little kid seated at water's edge. Gibbs couldn't remember his last real conversation that hadn't concerned gas or lodging, and with the day guttering like a candle all he wanted right now was to share the moment with someone, an exchange of pleasantries that he associated with regular life.

He skimmed through what he had to say for himself. So many places and things in the last few days, the mad rush out, but all the hours and miles of driving bled in a dreamy smear now.

The kid didn't look more than a year and change, just a tyke scooping handfuls of stones, flinging them into the shallows with both arms, exclaiming a pleased trill of gibberish with each throw.

"He has all the earmarks of a major leaguer," Gibbs said, coming up from behind.

The woman started like a gun had been fired over her shoulder.

Gibbs smiled at her as harmlessly as he could, showing his impossible teeth, wideset as old tombstones in a cemetery. "Just look at him," he said softer, indicating the boy, "throwing with either arm, swinging from both sides of the windmill."

The woman regarded Gibbs, a shielding hand over her eyes to block the last light, like an explorer gazing off into a great distance. Her surprise resettled into a pleasant face, her hair not blonde or red but falling somewhere in between, the kid's coloring pretty much the same and it suited them both. Gibbs guessed she was younger than him, though not by a lot, a bit late for family rearing. That was how it was done these days, sometimes not even a man in the picture, which could have been the case here.

"I never know what to call them at that age," he said. "Babies or toddlers."

"Elliot," the woman said and smiled herself.

The kid held up another handful of rocks. Gibbs winked and the boy tossed them, pockmarking the skin of water.

"A handsome little man," Gibbs told her. "A crackerjack. I'm sure you get tired of hearing that."

"Oh, I don't think so," the woman said.

"No, I wouldn't think so either," Gibbs said. He liked her smile, how it closed the space between them, held nothing back, no room for anything but it. It made him feel more than who he was.

A diving platform a hundred yards off bobbed and slapped at the water, the far rim of the lake now more an idea than a physical thing.

"They say you can see two hundred miles," the woman said. "On a clear day. That's hard to believe."

"That's something," Gibbs agreed. "Two hundred miles."

"I read it in a brochure."

"Well, then it must be true."

In rapid strokes the day dimmed, clouds blacking out, pinprick of stars here and there. The wind kicked up a chop on the lake, like pulled stitching. Gibbs watched the woman button the kid against the evening chill, the coat ill-fitting, perhaps a hand-me-down or from the church donation bin. The kid squirmed worse than an eel, wanting no part of it, wanting only the rocks. The woman persisted as if nothing was more important than this, than making sure the kid was warm, her face tired yet burnished with devotion, a face that said to Gibbs that things might not have been the easiest but if she got this simple task right, then maybe life might tell a different story for the boy, a hope that attached to her like a shine.

Gibbs felt he was spying on them. He drifted back to the car, sat behind the big circle of steering wheel. In the dark, the woman's face stayed with him. A raven flapped over the windshield, like a hinged W; across the way, twin pearls of headlights throwing cables into the black. Gibbs would have bet down to the green felt of the table that the boy was an accident, all she had to show for bad times and worse memories.

There was still her hope, so much it seemed to extend to Gibbs as well. She could have gathered up the kid back there, turned tail, the daily papers full of accounts of what could happen to a woman and a child alone in the night. A face that held that much trust—Gibbs would have stolen another auto, driven another nineteen hundred miles just to look into another such face.

He reached for the paper sack on the backseat, withdrew a jade piece he could identify by touch alone, stood out from the car and double-timed back to the lakeshore, fearing the woman and Elliot might have moved on but they were still there, turning to Gibbs as he approached, as if waiting.

He bent to show what was in hand, told about the fish which was green and long and slender, fashioned with incised fins and a squared mouth. "From the Shang dynasty," he said. "It dates back to well over a thousand years before Jesus. Something this ancient—in its own way, it's a lot like seeing two hundred miles, isn't it?" Gibbs was tempted to hand the jade over to the boy but thought the better of it because it just might wind up in the drink and gave it to the woman instead.

She turned it with a careful finger. "It's pretty," she said and it was. In some circles it wouldn't amount to more than a passable imitation, but it was still pretty; he'd even gone to the trouble of filing and edge off one corner of the tail. By his lights, all that should be worth something.

"For the boy's college fund," Gibbs explained. He'd not see her after tonight, would never see her again, but maybe they'd remember him for that.

The woman switched her gaze from the jade to him.

"How do you like that, bub," Gibbs said, poking the boy in his tight round of belly. The kid ducked behind the woman, peeked out.

"I'm Claire," she said.

"Gibbs," he told her. "My name's Gibbs."

He expected her to beg it off, a gift from a stranger, but she curled her hand around the jade, shook it like dice. She swept her other arm back behind her to bring the boy forward. "Look at this, Elliot," she said, then considered Gibbs, a face like a question. "Well, we thank you Mr. Gibbs."

"No, it's just Gibbs," he said. "There's no mister about it."

It was full night when he quit Glacier. The road wound amidst close hills and, high above, cold points of stars flashed. He had everywhere and nowhere to go.

He thought the random thoughts of a man behind the wheel of a car. He considered his kid brother, hadn't in the longest time and now he did. Miles was a scientist; he studied genes. The last time Gibbs had seen him was the old man's funeral, before Toms River. After the burial, Miles had talked about his work, the fact of DNA carrying the code of a person's make-up, down to the soul practically. Gibbs followed the spiral of explanation the best he could, nodding like a woodpecker, until all the talk of markers sounded only like poker. Miles grew increasingly fidgety and Gibbs had wondered if maybe there wasn't something else his brother was trying to tell him. In the end Miles had said maybe it wasn't such a good idea for Gibbs to contact him for a while, his forehead crumpling like paper. "It's just that I have a wife now and there's the kids," he said, leaving the thought unfinished, for it to spin in the air between them like flies. "It's O.K., Miles," Gibbs had assured him. "If I were related to me I wouldn't want to know me either. No harm, no foul."

As it turned out, it'd been like mourning two deaths for Gibbs, that of the old man and Miles, too. And he was the only one left.

There'd been Hokanson, the sole opportunity for fraternity that custody had afforded. Hokanson was a nasty piece of work, a transfer from a distant facility out west, his crimes so monstrous that he was remanded thousands of miles back to the tidal flats of Jersey for his own safety. None of the other numbers could say exactly what he'd done, only talk, but even the hardest cases swung wide of him.

Hokanson and Gibbs, though, had got on without incident. After lights-out, he'd tell Gibbs stories of Montana, that eerie, raspy voice, almost like metal-on-metal, the trail of words leading into the nameless hours.

The facility at Toms River was erected on marshy land, hard by the steady rustle of the Atlantic. On nights of particular full moons the water table rose, the floor of their matchbox quarters awash in brine, and on those nights Hokanson's words were of unique comfort. As long as he talked, that barred world went away, the sad murmurings down the cellblock row of dangerous men crying and praying and talking in their sleep, the stories sticking with Gibbs long after Hokanson had gone, tales of a place big enough that there still might be room for someone like him.

He stayed that night outside Glacier in a town called Hungry Horse, in an efficiency unit at a motel, a room with mismatched burners on the gas stove and a stale ammonia odor, like a convalescent home. Gibbs suspected he was the only guest for the evening but later heard a car trunk slam and the scrabble of a key finding the lock, then the door to the next room swinging open on creaky hinges. A woman's throaty voice carried through the shared wall. "You *already* told me more than I want to know," it said and then a deeper voice answering, unintelligible, little more than a grunt.

Gibbs woke during the middle of the night to a train whistle or perhaps just a dream. A picture came to mind, an old-timey locomotive chug-chugging through the folds of hill, a plume of smoke mingling with the feathering evergreens, a soothing image.

Sleep seemed like another place he'd left behind. There was a light outside the curtained window, the moon, the same moon shining over the shore town in Jersey he'd fled although it didn't feel that way. He mulled over what he knew about motels, how they were largely a charge card business these days, whatever cash on hand probably secured in a strongbox. And he could sense the old impulses edging in, as familiar and thick as blood and he tried to think of something else. He thought about the Claire woman from earlier, from the lake, how her hope seemed to flow as easy as instinct, as easy as breathing, a gift. Gibbs would have given almost anything for such hope. Years before, he'd forsaken drink and at the time it'd seemed like the hardest thing in the world but he now understood it wasn't.

A dog barked out on the road and down the way another answered it, back and forth, and he could imagine the chorus being picked up in houses further down the line, the call and response carrying all through Montana, as long as the road stretched, and he suddenly felt far away from anything he'd ever known. Gibbs dropped into sleep, dreaming of the locomotive from before, a mare's tail of smoke over a steel trestle bridge and a bottomless gorge below, the warm sensation that he was arriving at some destination but wasn't quite there yet.

For the next few days, Gibbs was content to stay put, operating without purpose, letting the hours assume their own shape. He had money in his pocket and he put up in motels and ate as if he'd the key to the king's larder.

He whiled away an afternoon in Kalispell watching planes wing in to the airport. In Whitefish he found a park with a lake that was not as big or majestic as the lake in Glacier, and along the rocky beach, a canoe. Nobody was around and Gibbs paddled out.

A cloudy day, gray mountains ringing the horizon and merging with sky, the lakeshore vacation homes perched on stilty legs, dark and empty. From experience he knew one couldn't count on finding anything of value in such places but you never really knew—sometimes you got lucky. Gibbs idly considered the steep A-frames like possibilities, then paddled back.

Happy hour: sounds of drinking, lively discussion about if it might snow wafting out of the avenue bars. He walked to the older end of town, suppertime in the boxy hall-and-parlor houses. He watched in the dark as he would a TV with the sound off, tried to picture himself inside among them.

He used to taunt his prey, in the prickly moments before hands got thrown, used to ask, "Do you know physics? Do you know what happens when and object comes up against an immovable object?" To a man they'd been more chump than victim, would have done the same to him if they could have—that was what he told himself then, what he repeated now. And he watched the cheery scenes on the other side of the glass, brothers and sisters passing servings around kitchen tables, Gibbs taking it in like something he needed, almost like food.

So far it'd all been fine and good but Gibbs had no further clue about that place that might have him.

He drove north one morning, the road following the river which fattened into a reservoir, at one end a dam straddling the shores like a giant ship. He crossed a bridge to the other side, the road snaking in the green of fir and spruce, turning into a hill, a bit of snow skiffed in some places, then more, then everything coated, the evidence of a recent plow, the oil-and-gravel surface still navigable.

Gibbs hadn't encountered another vehicle since gaining the woods. He wondered how close he was to Canada. At the crest of a hill, a pocket alpine lake iced over and in the middle of it, a plywood shanty. Woodsmoke pulled out a stack on the top and a pair of window squares were glazed in mist, a tiny house on the ice. He'd never seen a house on the ice before.

He wasn't prepared for the cold outside the Chrysler which struck like a hammer. He rapped on the door, heard a shuffling inside, then the door opening, a blocky, lumpish fellow in gumboots and nylon pants blinking up, a pile of white hair on his head like a tornado funnel. Behind, a lantern glowed. Gibbs could not get over the tidy cubby—wood benches on opposite walls, shelves all around, a little hinged table that dropped down, a kerosene heater, the floor covered in board except for a few circles cut away to expose the ice below.

"Shoot fella, you gave old Ernest here quite a scare," the man said. "Thought you might be the missus. I'm taking me one of those mental health days."

Gibbs explained himself the best he could.

"Jesus, man. You must be catching the death of it." Ernest stepped back to admit Gibbs into the shanty. "So you never been hard water fishing is what you're telling me."

Gibbs allowed that he'd not.

"Then you're in for a treat. Gibbs you said it was? A name you don't hear everyday. I guess that's your business." He considered Gibbs, then handed a spoon augur over, demonstrating how to bore into the ice. "You're a big enough man to handle it yourself. Good Lord, look at your feet. Must make buying shoes a trial. You know what they say about big feet, don't you. Big feet, big shoes. You can tell me to shut up any time."

He outfitted Gibbs with a tip-up equipped with a bell that jingled when a fish was on the take. Ernest managed a jig pole, a rod so small it looked like gear for a pygmy. He told Gibbs about himself, blinking rapidly the whole time, about his panel truck, how he hauled trash for a number of the homes dotting these hills. Winters he fit a blade on the front-end and did some plowing. "A lazy man who's always had the curse of having to work hard. Married twice. First time was poison, the second, the cure. Wife number one accused me of being Ernest in earnest, and vice versa."

Gibbs smiled. "I bet you are."

A whiff of kerosene hung in the interior. Ernest cracked a window, cold entering like a knife but still cozy in the ice bob.

Gibbs realized it was his turn. "I guess I'm between things," he said.

"Good for you. Sit one out and think about it."

"I'm currently on a ramble."

Ernest chewed at the corner of his mouth. "I'd say we're about the same vintage. What are you, forty-seven or thereabouts?"

"Forty-three." Gibbs offered an abridged version of his run west leaving out the parts that a man alone in an ice shanty with an ex-con might not care to know. There wasn't much to say.

"Hold on there, friend," Ernest said. He jiggered the rod, sang out, "Fish on the line!" He reeled in smoothly, eventually pulling a perch up through the gray water which he smacked smartly about the head. "Let's put this in the fridge." Ernest opened the door, dropped the fish on the ice. "Cold enough to turn shit blue out there. You were saying."

"A crony of mine used to tell me stories. I figure I had to see this place for myself before it was all said and done. Just to see if he was jerking my chain or not." Considering what had come of Hokanson, some of the stories were no doubt hogwash and prison fiction. He'd even told one that included the motion picture actress

Betty Hutton. But he'd said other things, too. Gibbs could get behind the idea of mining gold.

"Ah, the lure of the west," Ernest said. "Not the first man to be seduced by it and won't be the last. But it's a true thing, the promise of it all. Else they wouldn't say it."

"I hope so," Gibbs said. "You're throwing a rope to a drowning man."

"Just look at you," Ernest said. "A tall stranger riding into town. Like what you used to hear off the old radio serials, the shoot-em-ups. How did it go? 'His skin is sun-dyed brown, the gun in his holster is gray steel and rainbow mother-of-pearl, its handle unmarked.' "

From deep memory Gibbs recalled the rest, joined in, " 'People call them both the Six-Shooter.' "

They laughed, Ernest dabbing his eyes with the heel of his palm. "We are such old farts, we don't even smell anymore."

They discussed what the world was coming to. Ernest talked about growing up in these woods. "That river you seen on your way up here. We used to tie one end of a length of rope around a stout tree, the other end around your waist. The spring melt would be spilling down gangbusters and we'd jump in the water like that, snap to the end of the line like a fish. The ride of your life. And *cold.* I swear you could sneeze ice cubes. When we got a bit older we used to take girls out there, have them climb on our backs. I tell you, a girl on your back in a cold river that's yelling watery death in your ears. It was like. . . ." He ran a hand through his hair. "Well, like a young girl on your back in the cold water."

"It sounds like a time," Gibbs agreed. He could remember tuning into the serials with his father, the console about as big as a Stutz Bearcat, tubes bluer than any sky. He thought again of his brother Miles, the authorities having already phoned him, informing him that Gibbs had jumped parole.

The bell on his tip-up rang like a telephone.
"Heigh ho, friend. Hop to. Fish on the line."

Gibbs fell asleep after reeling in the fish, the heat of the shanty, and roused to the ice pack expanding like a crack of a gun. He couldn't at first place where he was, the echo from the depths jarring loose memories of the sharpshooter's rifle sounding in the boggy scrublands outside the wall.

He woke to himself idly sizing up the immediate world of the shanty, eyeing the contents of the ice bob, the surprise of finding amid the crowded shelves what appeared to be a small, primitive bear terra-cotta handwork of pre-Columbian origin, possibly a tomb figure not worth much. From where he sat he couldn't make it out any better than that. It could have just been an odd-shaped rock. But it got Gibbs wondering anyway, if it was a piece Ernest might have encountered along his trash route, a case of someone not knowing what they had. He wondered, too, what other items of interest the hut might contain. Perhaps Ernest kept a gun for the grizzlies. Even so, Gibbs didn't expect too much fight from the chatterbox. He considered the patchwork of clouds quilting the blue; he himself had the antique sidearm back in the Chrysler.

Ernest crouched over a gas Coleman, a *whooshing* of its jets. "You got quite the snore, friend, that and the whistling sound from your nose. A bigger commotion than a brass band."

Outside a wind swirled from the empty, wooded hills, shaking the shelter down to its two-by-four blocks and for a time that's all Gibbs heard, the rushing air. He closed his eyes again, thought of Hokanson's chinooks, the fact that all it took was a favorable wind, the possibility of everything turning in a moment.

He sensed the opportunity for action slipping away and let it, the fading prospect of knocking over Ernest leaving a taste of iron in his mouth, cramping his insides like a vise. He'd heard of cons back at Toms River shitting themselves like babies after losing the nerve and fire for the business and maybe a bit of that was beginning to happen to him now.

Ernest diced a slab of bacon, cooked it over a low flame, the bacon popping like Chinese firecrackers. He decanted the grease into a jar, added a can of kernel corn to the bacon, a chopped bell pepper and five eggs, then fired another burner, gilled and boned two of the perch and broiled them, using the ice skimmer in lieu of a pan.

"It smells like Thanksgiving in here," Gibbs said, voice thick with sleep, not quite sure he could manage food.

"I wouldn't know about that. The last few years my nose has gone deaf on me. At least you can die saying you had some of old Ernest's apache corn."

The two men in the tight confines of the shack—it reminded Gibbs of Toms River.

"Don't be bashful," Ernest said. "A growing boy like you."

Gibbs dug in and it was good, the chow, its heat momentarily jabbing a nerve in a tooth.

"You were looking a little indisposed back there," Ernest said. "Girl trouble, right?"

Gibbs reddened. "I was thinking about my brother," he lied. "Haven't seen him in a long time. His two kids wouldn't know me from Adam."

"Family problems," Ernest said, setting a coffeepot on a burner. "Biggest tragedy of them all. Shakespeare would have been out of business if it weren't for families."

Gibbs stared into the ice holes, like deep-set eyes. "My brother—a scientist. He used to tell me how the littlest drop of blood could tell you all about a person. A lot of things change in life but some don't."

Ernest emptied the grounds directly into the boiling water. "What, like a disease?"

"Maybe," Gibbs said.

Ernest screwed up his face. "I don't know anything about that. Unless it's a cat he was talking about. Nothing you can do with a cat. An established fact of nature." The smell of brewing rose in the shack. "It's a big life, though. Full of surprises. Just look at you."

"Just look at me," Gibbs said.

"One day, you never been ice fishing. The next day, you have."

Ernest retrieved two mugs hanging on hooks and poured out the coffee. He opened a cabinet on the wall, withdrew a pint. "How about some sweetener? Guaranteed to wash away the blues."

"My drinking days are over," Gibbs said. "If I have a whisky, it makes me feel like a new man. The only problem is, pretty soon the new man starts wanting a whisky, too."

"I hear you. Stuff will kill you." Ernest added a splash to his mug. "Ah me, it'll be my funeral." He helped Gibbs with the tip-up, this time rigging a topwater spool, baiting the lure with mousie grubs, and into the afternoon they fished.

A light snow snicked and whisked against the windows, the day darkening, sun dipping behind the hills, only past four in the afternoon but good as night. Ernest suggested taking a sweat in the sauna he'd built, snugged in a swale onshore, its rough-hewn boards, a door that looked like the portal to an elf's house.

It was cold enough to freeze the stuff in Gibb's nose when they quit the fish house. He'd brought only a greasy mac from Jersey and he folded his arms, balled his hands under his armpits. Out on the road, the Chrysler sat collecting flakes.

The building consisted of two rooms. Gibbs ducked into the outer room's soupy dark, a slip of a space with hooks on the wall, a narrow bench, wooden slatwork over a stone foundation. A door opened onto a second chamber and this was larger, a steel tub containing granite stones situated to one side. Underneath this, a woodstove which Ernest mended with splits of piss fir and lodgepole pine. Two tiers of wooden benches were fastened against the wall across from the stove. In the corner of the room, Ernest had sunk a tub into the floor, an overhead shower above the drain, a contraption that stored water which could be heated from the fire for a proper shower.

Gibbs whistled. "You're a busy little booger, aren't you?"

"Idle hands," Ernest said. "One head, a lot of hats."

The two men stripped down in the anteroom. The sauna chamber was hotter than before, smelled of wood. "Engelman spruce," Ernest said, indicating the benches and walls. Gibbs's glasses misted over and he removed them, the room softening. Ernest poured a dipper of water seasoned with red cedar onto the hot granite stones which sizzled, a greenish scent rising. "The Indian influence," he explained. "The sweat lodge tradition." He proffered a cigar. "I don't have a peace pipe but I do have these."

The men smoked and dripped.

Even without his glasses, Gibbs noticed Ernest staring at his arm, his biceps, his tattoo, an interlocking design from a Grecian urn, the number thirteen and a half, the handiwork of a con at Toms River who'd adapted an electric razor and length of guitar string for the purpose.

"You put the pin to the skin," Ernest said.

"It seemed like a good idea at the time."

"Twelve jurors, one judge, and one half-assed chance. I've done that, too. The house of pain. My hellcat days. Mostly drunk and disorderlies."

Gibbs said, "I'm basically and antique dealer gone bad. Once upon a time, I worked the legal end of the trade but that never amounted to much more than pin money."

He explained how he liked old things. Put an old thing in his hand and it spoke to him, told a story, had always been this way. Back as a little kid, his old man had somehow come into a handful of pieces of eight, reales from the Petosi mines in Bolivia, the first mint in the new world. Even before Gibbs could read he sensed the magic in the coins, sat for wordless hours studying them. And later, they held his interest in a way school never did, the rogue accounts of Pizarro in the steeps of the Andes, amazing that so much could be bound in those rough, tarnished circles of silver.

"Counterfeits carry a different sort of story," Gibbs said. "Actually two stories." There was the one that got recounted to customers and then the actual truth of the work's pedigree, each intertwined around the other, snakes coiled on a scepter. The trick had been hawking a piece authentic enough and he'd been cunning in that end of it, ferreting out jewelers on the downside of their careers, individuals with too few scruples and too many bills, who'd not think twice about using their craft to disguise their cast marks on a mold for a phonied-up bronze. But it was the other half of the equation, conjuring a history equally true, that had from time to time tripped him up. Gibbs owned an erratic gift of blarney: it came and went. There was more he could have told, the occasions he'd had to employ his hands rather than his mouth to see a deal through, but he left all that in the shadows.

Ernest said, "Sounds like you put the tits on the monkey."

"The what?"

"You did it up right. I can respect a man who does it up right even if it's a wrong thing he's doing." Ernest rubbed his jawline. "You're a betting man. That's how I read you. A man who relishes a ticklish situation."

"I do have the danger gene," Gibbs agreed. He pulled on the cigar, exhaled smoke out the side of his mouth, waving a hand to disperse it. "There was this dealer once," he said. "A hundred years ago. In London." He couldn't recall the fellow's name, only the boys he used to send into the Thames: mudboys, they were called—Billy and Charley. The story went that these mudboys would emerge from the river with artifacts of ungodly value. Coats of arms in open-work medallions. Oil lamps from the Roman era. Bronze Medusas.

"Here's the thing," Gibbs said.

Ernest nodded. "There's always a thing."

"The dealer, he made a tidy fortune on the stock and word spread and then, wouldn't you know, somebody was always finding something on a piece that didn't quite make sense, shouldn't have been there. Turns out the whole lot is a trove of fantasy pieces. The mudboys just made for a more convincing story."

The fire ticked in the stove.

"It's crazy," Gibbs continued. "The pieces the mudboys excavated—there's actually a market for them now. Called Billy-and-Charley's."

"You're shitting me."

"I shit you not."

Ernest ladled water onto the fire and the granite stones spat. "I guess if enough time goes by, you can expect anything. You should live so long. We both should."

Outside it was dark and only that. The lantern cast a sallow shine, their indistinct shadows on the walls.

"I would like to think that part of my life is over," Gibbs said.

Their sweat hitting the benches: like a light rain.

Ernest stuck the cigar in the corner of his mouth. "You were thinking of taking me down," he said evenly. "Before. Back in the shanty. In the afternoon."

Gibbs took the cigar from his mouth, placed it on the bench, felt the other man's eyes on him. He inspected the back of his hands, his face flushing from shame, from the dry fire of the sauna. "I didn't though," he said. "That should be worth something."

"It wouldn't have been sporting. Me teaching you fishing."

"No, it wouldn't have been." It was somehow worse without his glasses. He wiped the lenses on the end of a towel, fit them on, found Ernest considering him more than carefully and removed his glasses again. "I guess I should go," he said.

The men dressed in the anteroom, Ernest like a fever blister in his red union suit. "But you're right, pal," he said. "You didn't do it. You didn't roll me. Far be it from me to hold you accountable for a thing you didn't do."

It was cooler in the dressing room. Gibbs leaned against the back wall, could feel the cold from the outside but remained hot from the sauna.

"The Finnish people," Ernest said, "typically roll in the snow after taking in a sauna." He smiled. "I could always use another hand for my trash hauling business. A good back. You just might happen on some diamonds in the rough. I could tell you stories."

"You shame me, Ernest."

"You're not such a bad man."

"Sometimes I don't know."

"Take it from old Ernest then."

"There's this place I still want to get to," Gibbs said.

Out on the ice, steam ascended from their heads.

"That would be you up there," Ernest said, pointing to the Chrysler. A moon had lifted above the timbered hill, its light thrown across the lake and snowy ground, a sky with more stars than Gibbs had ever seen, the night stippled with them.

"I jacked the car," Gibbs said. "Back in Jersey."

Ernest blinked. "You didn't kill anybody."

"No."

"There you go. I'd say you're rehabilitated."

They laughed, the sound of it carrying across the frozen water. It was cold, the effects of the sauna wearing off.

"Fish on the line," Gibbs said.

"Right-o," Ernest said and they shook on it.

On his way back to the Chrysler, Gibbs glanced over his shoulder, Ernest in his union suit, a reddish blob against a white field of hills but nothing that might look like a mine.

"Hey!" he yelled. "What is this place?"

"Here?" Ernest puffed on the last of his cigar. "This is officially nowhere."

Gibbs threw a wave, like a man erasing a blackboard, then continued toward the snow-clad vehicle.

Gibbs felt so cheap after the ice fishing he could have been bought all day long for a penny. He'd hoped that he'd put distance between him and his old self, that it was left back there, along the road, like so much other trash but his afternoon with Ernest had chased more than a little of that optimism.

He thought about Jolie. He'd not suffered a minute's remorse before then for making off with her mad money, sailing out of her life, not so much as a note. These were people—Jolie and Ernest, too—who'd cared for him, taken him in, and look how he'd acted.

He'd known her from the bars where he'd once bent elbows though it was only after he'd stopped drinking, after his last stint at the facilities, that they hooked up. A little thing: blonde hair from one bottle, tan skin from another, a tattoo along the bikini line of her hip that read DO YOU WANT TO DANCE. It'd been hunky-dory for a while, his early days out from the wall, Jolie returning home from the graveyard shift at the bakery, a flecking of maple frosting still on her. Outside, the sun hoisted over a gray ocean and Gibbs licked her like a postage stamp from stem to stern.

His thieving past had excited her. She also liked things on the rough side and for a while he liked that, too. "Isn't that how they did it in the pokey?" she'd tease him. "Isn't this how it was done?" It was new and seemed like kicks but over time it'd only reminded him of all he cared to forget, didn't feel like any love he'd ever hoped for, only one more wall in his life, one more thing he didn't have use for any longer.

Now, Gibbs recalled the thrumming animal rush of his run. Aside from the two wrongs—stealing the car and Jolie's money—he'd not done anything else wrong since. His thoughts were a different story. But as Ernest had said, you couldn't hold a man accountable for ideas that never grew legs.

Gibbs decided he still needed to road dog until he happened on the right situation. Luck couldn't avoid him all his life.

He fired the Chrysler, drove to the south and west and Montana remade itself, the bunched, scoliotic spines of mountains spreading out until they were bookends on the sides of far valleys, the nameless habitations in the lee of distant hills. Rails shadowed the road for a while and then not.

He motored the Bitterroots, then mining country, the towns that got fat a century ago, the avenue buildings constructed of brick, made to last. He lodged in seedier accommodations, a nod to economy, fearing the day when his roll would unpeel to zip. He'd not counted the money—it felt like bad luck to do so—but he'd steadily nibbled away at it like a holiday roast, didn't know what would happen after he reached the bottom of pocket.

At the edge of town the high plains met the main, the mountains on the western horizon hooded in snow, not unlike the sugar-dusted crullers Jolie sometimes brought back from the bakery. Gibbs studied them, as if the place he still hankered to get to might blow in from there. The locals hurried about their business, pickups loaded down, townspeople walking the streets bent with purpose, all of it a world unconnected to his own. It was only the wind that blew in from the mountains and if it spoke of anything, it was winter.

And then one morning Gibbs woke to a crown going off in his head. His teeth were never any good and ham-fisted prison dentistry hadn't improved matters any. The nerve howled like an alarm, like it was jerked on a string all the way back to Jersey, and he took it as an omen.

He made for the mountains on the western horizon, a blustery day, a sky like bleach. It must have snowed up high during the night, certainly chill enough, the mountains now entirely covered in an enamel of white and he drove toward them for the better part of the day. Nearing the foothills, the road began to climb and, off to one side, a weather-beaten mining flume girding the shoulder of hill.

A sign along the shoulder of road indicated the continental divide ahead, the falling snow not much at first, spokes of bluestem grass still sticking out the spotty carpet that had accumulated. And then more, the air a white screen. A few more sheer miles and he was in the chowdery thick of it, the blizzard splitting the season like a frozen maul.

Late afternoon and then twilight. Both Gibbs and the Chrysler running feverish, the infection in his sick tooth, the car missing every now and then. The road rose in a ladder of switchbacks, only the mess of horizontal weather, everything else erased in the swirl. Gibbs stood on the pedal, the engine hammering more than a tinker's workshop.

It was only when he crested the pass that he saw them—the horses. They ran ahead, somewhere beyond the throw of the headlights. A dream, he thought at first, a snow mirage. Then he caught them again in the television static of the storm: a kick of hooves, flickers of rumps big as ship sterns. Gibbs was on the western side of the divide now, where the rivers flowed to the opposite end of the continent, to a different ocean, and it seemed possible he could be chasing a gang of wild mustangs through a stone-blind snow.

The roadway tipped down and momentum carried the Chrysler forward. The scratch of wipers on the windshield. He strained for another glimpse but they were gone, his glasses not of much help anyway, two prescriptions behind what they ought to be. After a few miles of descent, the living world came into view: treeline, aspens plumb as flag-poles, then clumps of red willow, and then an occasional buck-and-rail fence stapling the snowfields.

Gibbs more sledded than drove. Rounding a bend, his beams locked on a lone horse in a paddock, not one of the stampede, but a roan so emaciated it could have been a stick-figure drawing. He stopped. No house or barn, only the horse in white up to its knees, its tumble-down pen. The two regarded each other for several cold minutes. Gibbs debated whether to set it free. It could get hit by a car, not any kinder fate than freezing to death right here.

The Chrysler sounded like it was eating itself. At first he assumed the glinting lights were constellations of stars, so faraway. But they couldn't have been: Gibbs was above them. Flakes fell out of the course night and he stared at the winking bracelet, at the lights in the valley below.

The Chrysler seized up for good in the flats at the outskirts of town and he plodded the remaining distance on foot. A sign read LADLE and beyond that another, of homemade variety, GO AWAY.

Wind scared up snow ghosts, the town like something out of a Lionel train set, a run of buildings of board-and-batten construction on either side of the street. A string of lights shook the yaw of a gooseneck lamp on its mooring.

He pitched through the drifts like a man on stilts. It was only when circling nearly back to the far end of the other side of street did he spot the dry goods store in an alley, the faint amber of a burning bulb behind a fogged shop window. The door opened onto a dusty room, two runs of deep wooden shelves for aisles, burlap sacks of rice and grain along the wall as well as tack and feed. A graying woman behind the counter, a dreamy face that said she might have been expecting him for ages. A fire cracked in a potbellied stove. Gibbs tracked snow across the floor scuffed the color of tobacco.

"The first storm of the season," she said, as if the answer to a question he might have asked and maybe he had.

The shelves contained a motley assortment—tins of kippers and jellies, sourdough mix. He'd not thought of his tooth for a long time and now he did, its spiking twinge. He must have looked ridiculous, snow capping his hatless head, epaulets of it across the shoulders of his mac. Gibbs told her of the white-knuckle ride down the divide. The last miles of the descent the heater had surrendered, then the wipers and power steering and he'd the sensation of going down in a plane, searching for the best place to ditch.

As he talked, he noticed, high on a shelf above the woman's head, a bronze known as Christ of the Tender Mercy if he could trust his eyes, a highly prized collectible. He himself had traded in a counterfeit of the piece, coating it with varnish to fake the patina of age.

"Is there a dentist in town?" he asked.

"Brownie might be of help with the car," the woman told him.

"Brownie," Gibbs said, as if a name he should know.

"He's the only one left in Ladle who can figure cars. Brownie would be the one." She glanced at her watch. "He's probably at the Silver Cloud. The roadhouse." She gave directions, through the alley, behind the shuttered-up buildings on the main. "You'll see the red from the beer signs."

The lights dimmed, a brown-out, then the electricity catching, the click and whir of refrigeration starting up.

"Thank you," Gibbs said, feet clomping toward the door which opened with a shiver of bells. He turned, squinted up at the high shelf. "You know, that's a Christ of the Tender Mercy," he ventured before leaving, gesturing up at the bronze. He'd have liked to take the step-ladder over, to make sure.

The woman smiled, eyes nearly closed. "Yes," she said. "Yes, He certainly is."

On the outside the Silver Cloud appeared normal enough. The inside, however, was fashioned after a maritime passenger ship, the tavern in the front done up like a quarter-deck: a railing on one side of the room, an oceanscape painted beyond it; a row of portholes that looked out onto the snowy world: in one corner, a lifeboat slung to davits, a web of standing rigging held fast in lanyards and dead-eyes; over by the billiards table, a ventilator cowl, upthrust like a brass mushroom.

It was in the back room where he found Brownie, playing poker with three others. Gibbs stood in the doorway and watched, the quarters modeled after a stateroom, its walls bloodied burgundy, streaky with water stains, a fire blazing away in the hearth. Overhead, a pendant lamp of flash copper, the plaster ceiling in a couple of areas eaten away, the tin roof above as well, and snow fell through the gap, shaking out like rock salt down into cookpots.

Much later it would all seem a dream to Gibbs, like the four could have been playing cards for days, or quite possibly forever, this strange, beached ship in the high mountains, the sea of snow.

The storm raged like an animal that wanted in.

"I'm looking for someone called Brownie," Gibbs said.

A sprite of man, a beard like a waterfall, said, "That would be me."

"I got some business with a car," Gibbs said.

"Maybe you care to join us. Our little kitchen table game."

The dying nerve in Gibbs's mouth banged away, a nail being driven into his head. There was no place else for him to go and he could do with extra funds, not down to scared money but close. Gibbs listened to the wolf wind, as if that could decide it for him, but to his eyes, there was only trouble inhabiting this room. He told them thanks but no thanks, told this Brownie he'd wait up front for him.

At the bar in the quarter-deck tavern, he allowed the lady bartender to pour a club soda. In the corner by the lifeboat, a jukebox all lit up like the county fair. A small crowd was in from the storm, their talk largely speculation regarding its severity and duration, a few having snowshoed, their gear leaning by the door, cakes of snow melting on the deck flooring, mostly men, canvas coats still on their backs.

Gibbs sat amidst the gabble of conversation, a mongrel aroma of smoke, sweat, booze. From behind someone said, "It'll be a bumpy ride." And then from another end of the room, as if answering it, "You got the soul of a fat woman."

A few stools down the line, a couple of smart alecks getting pleasantly stinko, arm-wrestling for drinks and cigars. Gibbs considered his options and there wasn't much to consider. He thought about the poker, the open seat at the table tempting him like an open bottle.

He was relieved when somebody took the seat next to him. "It's cold," he found himself saying.

"A good blow," the fellow agreed and told Gibbs it was nothing like Alaska where he once worked, running gravel for the oil concerns. Gibbs had heard about that, the money to be made and was glad to think about something else besides the pull of the other room.

They carried on. Gibbs recounted seeing some fool in a bear costume waving customers to a diner in Battle Lake, Minnesota, during his run out, and they laughed about how crazy the world was. They reached the bottom of their glasses at roughly the same time and Gibbs offered the next round.

"Oh no, you don't," the fellow said. "You don't pull coin in my town."

"O.K., club soda then," Gibbs said.

"The wagon?"

"Afraid so."

"Sobering," the other man said. "Sounds an awful lot like 'so boring,' doesn't it?"

After a while, he left Gibbs at the bar alone. All the forward motion of the run collected within, like a hunger, nowhere else to go. He thought of Hokanson, the lights-out stories, one feeding to another until what bobbed to the surface was the one that concerned Betty Hutton.

It'd occurred during the war. She'd been on some sort of tour to spur the boys in the ore drifts, give them cheer for their end of the effort. If Gibbs remembered it right, there'd been a storm then, too. Betty was only supposed to visit an afternoon, a few hours, but wound up weathered in for days, this the first blush of her fame, and she glowed brighter than anything the mines would ever excavate, like magic, the days snowbound in town, the world lost behind the storm, only Betty and a hundred lucky souls.

There was the usual that one might expect, Betty giving her heart—and perhaps a bit more—to some of the local men. But what remained glued in Gibbs's mind was not that. "She promised she'd be back," Hokanson had rasped. The presence of Betty in the town had lent the place a quality it'd not owned before, given it hope, made it somehow bigger. On her last night, she'd stood atop the bar in the saloon, blonde hair shiny as bullion, and belted *Let's Not Talk About Love,* her hit song of the time, stopping shy of the big ending in the final verse, telling the gathered people she'd finish it properly for them upon her return. "One more reason so you don't forget me," Betty had said, winking at the lot of them.

According to Hokanson, though, she never visited again, only word of her motion pictures making their way to town from time to time, her snapshot in magazines. "She said she'd be back," Hokanson had said. "People are still waiting for her."

Listening to the story in the narrow raft of his bunk, Gibbs had thought maybe Betty Hutton was dead and that explained it but he said nothing. Later, after Hokanson had flown, he ran across a story on her in an old *Life Magazine,* in the prison library, and she was indeed alive. It'd been a tough life, more disappointment than joy perhaps, a bad marriage and a stalled career, a brief comeback in the fifties, a stage show where she fired six-shooters and sang a medley of her motion picture hits, but it didn't last. And Gibbs could understand why she might have broken the promise. And it seemed sad to him, the saddest thing, what age and life could do, that Betty Hutton wasn't even Betty Hutton anymore and if she had returned, would anybody have recognized her even so?

Gibbs surveyed the tavern now. He could not recall the name of that town but it struck him that this could have been it, the beaten, lined expressions on the folks around him, faces that said that they might be waiting out more than just the end of a blizzard. He searched the walls, the flotsam of nautical gewgaws—standing blocks and capstans and running lights—but no evidence of Betty, no autographed, fading glamour shot, and Hokanson had never mentioned a bar that looked like a ship anyway.

It snowed and snowed.

Hours later the game broke for refreshment, the four men walking up from the backroom. There was a fat man, perhaps the fattest Gibbs had ever seen, and he took a seat in a corner booth. The two players besides Brownie were mouthy types, one with an ill-advised mustache like a push broom, the other, older and a little worse for the wear, limped like he had a sack of nails in his shoe, a *pop-siss* that Gibbs realized must be a prosthetic leg. Both were done up in checked cowboy shirts and looked like idiots.

From up at the bar, Gibbs observed the four with interest. He did not need to be in the game to understand what was going down, had sat in on enough poker to know the story. The idiots were obviously a couple of rammer-jammers who'd blown into town before him, had the good fortune of catching the heater of their life, every card falling their way; they were invincible. Perhaps, too, they were riding more than a hot streak—from their antics at the pool table, Gibbs would have guessed cheap trucker speed.

He could not get a read on the fat man in the corner or Brownie who'd settled into a nearby booth. Gibbs walked over, sat down without invitation, told the little man about the trials of the Chrysler.

"That's a real sad story," Brownie said when Gibbs was done, his own eyes sad-looking—red-rimmed and small as scattershot.

Gibbs did not want to be there. The game would turn, as it always did, and then there'd be hell to pay one way or the other and he wanted to be miles distant by then.

Brownie said, "There's nothing I can do, seeing as I'm conducting business back there."

The lady bartender asked for food orders and Brownie simply nodded at her and Gibbs ordered a dish called red flannel hash because it sounded like something he could choke down without much chewing. He'd not eaten since his tooth went off that morning, since his flyer into the mountains.

The two men watched the flakes spill down on the other side of the porthole, the evening lost in tatters of white.

"What is this place anyway?" Gibbs asked.

"What is this place," Brownie said and then told him and Gibbs leaned forward to hear it, hoping maybe it'd be the Betty Hutton story but it wasn't.

"Believe it or not this used to be somewhere," Brownie said. "A company town. Mining. They own everything here down to the nails. This establishment included."

Gibbs tried to imagine it but couldn't. All he could see was a forgotten nest in the mountains.

"They're closing us down," Brownie said. "Once was thirteen thousand of us, during the boom years. Now hardly a handful left. An end to a life." He smoothed the table cloth. "Welcome to Ladle, mister."

Gibbs thought the little man might cry. A shelf of snow slid off the tin roof: a deep rumble, like continents shifting.

"It's not been a good year," Brownie continued. On top of it all, his dog up and died on him, a Heinz 57. He pulled a photo from his shirt pocket. "One of those supermarket dogs, the kind they have out front. So gentle it wouldn't bite its own fleas." He'd buried and dug it up five times, not wanting to believe, hoping it was just a seizure or something. "Friends—they come and go. But a dog is a dog."

The talk of Brownie's mutt reminded Gibbs of the spectral run of the horses he'd seen after topping the divide and they galloped through him again. "I saw some horses," he said. "On my way in before the car died. Wild horses."

Brownie considered him balefully. "I don't know anything about that."

From over at the billiards table, the ruckus of the two jokers in checked cowboy shirts, the rammer-jammers. Brownie and Gibbs glanced over, Brownie lifting an eyebrow.

"You could still buy into the game," he said and told Gibbs that they'd all agreed to play until the snow stopped.

The bartender conveyed a tray of food down to the fat man in the corner, so many platters it could have fed a small battalion.

"You want to know about Tap," Brownie said. Gibbs did not care to know, only wanted out. Brownie told him anyway, about a terrible mining accident years ago concerning a fraternal twin brother, this Ladle seeming to be somewhat peopled with more sad stories than actual souls, as far away from that place he'd dreamed of reaching as the moon.

Across the table, the little man, flinty as a prospector or at least what Gibbs thought a prospector should look like. He suspected he'd encountered Brownie's sort before, that they might not have been very different men at all, his wrist bearing a spidery tattoo with all the earmarks of prison scratch: old, but like it might have been still bleeding.

Gibbs held up both hands, as if in surrender. "I'm doing my best here to be a standup citizen. The hardest thing in the world sometimes."

Their food arrived, the red flannel hash the consistency of prison chow, a brick-colored slurry, but tasted better, Brownie's fare a slab of unspecified meat, orange as neon. Gibbs stared at it.

"What," Brownie said, "you never seen elk before?"

"What is that," Gibbs said, "some kind of deer?"

They busied themselves with their food. The men, Gibbs knew, would return soon to the card table, the stateroom drawing on him like a tide or gravity. He sucked on his fouled tooth, the pain offering something else to focus on. From out of the blue, he remembered that Claire woman from Glacier, her kid Elliot, his first day in Montana, the trust she'd extended. It felt like long ago to Gibbs, like an antique he still wished he owned.

After Hokanson had escaped Toms River the entire cellblock was put under lockdown, Gibbs thrown into the hole once the battery of interrogation had run its course. He'd nothing to tell, could have told any of a hundred stories, the scrape of Hokanson's voice covering the scrape of his jerry-built file across the heating vent above his upper bunk, the one word note left under his pillow, *Smile.*

He thought of this after the four cardplayers resumed the game. It was just possible that the Chrysler was hale again, that all it needed was to cool down after the ordeal of climbing the divide. Cars had their own agenda and Gibbs never fully understood them.

The world on the other side of the door was unlike any he'd ever witnessed, the midnight sky flinging lightning now in addition to snow, forks walking in the shoulders of mountain, illuminating the ghostly peaks. With the drifts piled waist-high and higher, it was more like swimming than striding, the cold cracking the left lens of his glasses, numbing his extremities into clubs, boring a hole through the inflamed nerve in his jaw, up into his head.

Somewhere, a bell ringing or maybe just the clanking wind.

It was a fight to keep on and what Gibbs thought about to hold off the cold were all the various brawls he'd been in. He would like to have said he didn't like hitting people although he had certainly done that. A fight had sent him to Toms River, the result of a ruinous transaction of no-good works of figurative jewelry he couldn't move, Gibbs resorting to strong-arm methods to setting things aright. The subsequent fact of fraud, a broken nose and a shattered cheekbone had made it aggravated circumstances and, as a matter of course, he'd graduated to a new level of convict. It was not the first time he'd relied on such tactics in a business dealing. Sometimes it hadn't even been called for but he'd done so anyway because he felt it'd been expected from a person like him. And, of course, the scuffles in his drinking days. Whisky used to turn him into someone else. He remembered one time breaking a bottle over a man's head for the crime of telling a joke wrong.

Every freezing step, another fracas. Gibbs had walked clear of Ladle, the buildings on the main appearing over his shoulder in a snap of lightning. Back as kids, he'd beat on Miles for the sport of it, because he could. And Gibbs gasped at it all, the icy intake of air, wind tearing a hole in his face.

The Chrysler was nowhere to be seen. Gibbs spun a tight circle in the drifts. The signs had disappeared, the one that read LADLE and the other, GO AWAY. It occurred to Gibbs then that perhaps he was on the top of the car, that it'd snowed that much, and he spotted the last of the whip antenna sticking out of the white like a hank of unruly hair, dug down with bare hands, located the backdoor, clearing around so it could swing open, the dome light still working but nothing else, like a coffin inside.

Gibbs sat in the backseat. He could remain, allow the blizzard to pile up over the car, a prison of snow. He tried to keep his teeth from chattering but it was no good, a feeling like someone twirling his failing crown by the root. Hokanson's chinook winds blew into mind except the process seemed to be working the other way, fall turning to winter in a matter of hours, this the other side of the coin he realized, like some law of physics, that if a life could be redeemed in a moment, it could go south just as fast.

Next to him on the seat, between his satchel of effects and the sack of counterfeit works, the familiar wooden handle of the sidearm which looked like two handles, the refraction of his cracked lens. He pulled it out, took it in hand, considered the piece like an answer to a question he'd not yet asked, the bluing on the barrel gone to pitch, the curly filigrees above the trigger. The old man used to finger it idly when they listened to the serials, a few splashes in his glass to chase the hours of operating the elevator, the up and down and never going anywhere, all of it held at bay for a time by whisky and dreams.

Gibbs mulled it over but there was really no other option. He gathered up the phonied works, tucked the gun into his waistband of his slacks, left the satchel where it was, and stepped out into the riot of flakes. He retraced his footprints, the occasional glint of lightning, boom of thunder. Along the way, he peered in the window of the dry goods store he'd stopped in earlier. No lights burning, no bronze of Christ of the Tender Mercy on the high shelf, only dust cloths shrouding every surface, like it'd been closed for years.

He sat down to a different game from before. There was the spiral of snow threading through the gap of roof and the four other men at the table, the bench to the upright piano in the corner broken up for firewood.

But it was a different game. Nobody'd bothered to tell the pair in the checked cowboy shirts, that the heater they'd caught like a rocket was fast crashing back to earth. They tried to bull the action even so, their chips rapidly traveling across the table, some to Gibbs but mostly the other two, the fat man Tap wagering in the softest voice, oily as tallow, Gibbs recalling the mining accident story that Brownie'd told about the twin brother, a loss that Tap appeared to be grieving yet.

They played cards—Omaha and lowball, stud and draw. Sometime in the little hours, the lights blacked out. "The weight of snow on the lines," Brownie said, lighting a lantern.

The hours swam as in Gibbs's drinking days of old. When they broke for food one last time, he visited the bathroom instead, lit a match to see himself in the mirror, retracted his cheek to inspect the angry red of his gumline, a haggard face staring back at him from the dark, worn as a shoe. He was up in the game but couldn't count on it lasting and the thought of what lay ahead only made him tired. He retreated to the stall toilet, sat on the can, propped his feet on the metal partition and dozed.

He woke to the two clowns banging lines on the sink counter, hatching a plan for what would come next.

"We should sack these boys," the one with the push broom mustache said. "I tell you, they'll never know what hit."

"I don't know," the peg leg answered.

"Then why don't we just hand over all the rest of our money?" Mustache had a voice like a needle.

"What about the stranger?" Peg Leg wanted to know.

"The lummox?" Mustache said. "The lummox concerns me."

Gibbs didn't move for a long time after the boys quit the restroom, sat there, felt his legs going back toward the room even before they were under him, as inevitable as overflow.

• • •

All the crazy games walked out of the deck once the poker reconvened, the pot limits thrown through the holes in the ceiling, what Brownie and the fat man had been waiting for all along, the rash play of losing men wanting to once more own the universe. The cards circled the table—hands of southern cross, wild widow, butcher boy—the lantern's modest cast on the bloody walls, like the inside of Gibbs's mouth, like the deer meat that Brownie had supped earlier, elk he'd called it. The two rammer-jammers began fortifying their toot and resolve with grain alcohol, operating on full tilt. Gibbs played like a leather ass, mucking his cards more often than not, no longer concerned with the outcome of hands, waiting only for the pair to do something stupid, then he would do something, the gun barrel of the six-shooter sticking the shank of his hip like an insistent idea.

It didn't happen like that. The burn Mustache had been riding finally consumed him, knocking him out flat, stranding his pal in the game. And then dawn. They didn't notice at first, the storm having blown out, leaving in its wake a white-swept expanse, a sapphire sky through the ceiling, the last flakes sifting in like talc.

It was Gibbs's deal and he heard again Hokanson, the scratchy voice: "She said she'd be back." And it would all come down to this, the two words he'd utter next. "Betty Hutton," Gibbs said. "Some of you might know Kankakee. Betty Hutton is fives and nines wild." They would play the final hand blind, the cards dealt face down, unseen by the players, a contest of chicken to determine who'd be standing last, Gibbs tired and desperate enough to resign his fate to the disposition of kings and queens.

They wagered after each card, raised in giant steps, beyond reason, until everything was heaped in the middle, four men with nothing else to lose.

Seventh street, the final card. The fat man pulled a creased deed from a pocket, let it flutter in, the family claim he told them. Brownie tossed in the key to his Willy's jeep. Peg Leg scoured himself so thoroughly it seemed he might even unhitch his prosthetic leg and offer that, too. He ransacked Mustache's pockets instead, once his own were down to lint, went as far as disengaging the massive rodeo belt buckle from his slumped confederate, unlooping it, dropping belt and buckle into the pile like an exotic three-foot snake wearing a gold helmet.

Gibbs unpeeled the last of Jolie's mad money, emptied his sack of fantasy works, the gaudy carnelians and jades. He knew from the old radio serials what a fellow was supposed to do in such a circumstance and reached in his mouth, pulled the offending crown until it broke loose, a jolt as clarifying and sharp as a white flame.

A small lifetime—his years in rooms overcrowded with men. From outside, chiming voices, kids cavorting in the morning's untracked drifts. He thought of Miles, not the scientist, but them as boys, riding bikes like a couple of cowboys roving the range, a cocked hand all that was needed to convey a gun. And even with his rotten glasses, Gibbs saw it clearer then, what he'd been driving at all this time, since jacking the car and before, not a place, only a feeling, the understanding of what his body could do and had done, the difference between what ran in his blood and resided in his heart. It was an awful truth, just how much his arms had kept the world at a distance, a lonelier confinement than any prison he'd ever know. And for the briefest moment, the wild horses blew through him again, more like a scavenging wind than the roll of hooves this time, then the hopelessness of the immediate situation returning.

He smiled, a new space among the composition of his teeth, the eyes of the others traveling on a wire between the bloody stub of porcelain and gold on the green felt and Gibbs, each of them with a different variation of the same look, like they might have drunk milk that had turned bad.

It would be so easy. If it came to it, he figured he could squeeze off two shots and maybe that would be enough, the ancient sidearm just as liable to blow up in his face as shoot true, which might've been O.K., too.

Later that morning, Gibbs thought maybe Brownie was trying to welsh on the jeep, the little man bent on showing him the town after that last hand was on the books. He was glad to see the place anyway, all that he'd missed under the cover of dark and weather, the evening before. A morning of sunshine, jeweled glimmer of snow, a sky the color of a pretty girl's eyes.

It was situated in the bottom corner of a canyon, Ladle, and the mine, the old Silver Cloud, located where the sheer walls met, behind the run of main. With the crust of white, the squared angles of rock, the land reminded Gibbs of an ice box.

Brownie showed him the tailing carts rusting on narrow gauge tracks, piles of waste rock and slag from the operation. They ducked through the adit and walked a distance into the drift, the sides closing in on Gibbs and inside the mine he thought not of Hokanson's pie-in-the-sky stories but of Tap, the accident with his twin, that there were worse things that could be visited on a pair of brothers.

Gibbs was unprepared for what he found at Brownie's house. It was a string of structures actually, the old assay office, pay and samples, boiler shop and hoist house cabins, the tin roofs rusted to a fine brown stubble, wood beams silvery with age, Brownie evidently an unofficial caretaker for the dead mine. The buildings contained a staggering collection of antiques—mica windows, walls of painted oil cloth, sinks adapted from the lacquered wood of whisky barrels, like a seashell clasped to his ear, the life Gibbs could hear breathing out. A wall calendar said the right month but the wrong year. The newspaper stuffing the stove in one of the cabins dated 1941. In one of the buildings, toys of first World War vintage, in another a lunch bucket left on a counter from forty years before.

He'd the sense of strolling through a museum, a place frozen in cold storage, something even more of a miracle than that last hand of Betty Hutton. A hard-bound copy of Zane Grey's *Twin Sombreros* sat on a shelf and Gibbs again remembered listening to the shoot-em-ups on the radio with his old man and it came to him thumbing the yellowed pages, that perhaps Miles somehow had it wrong, that maybe blood wasn't quite as fixed as he'd said, that what ran in them stepped back through their father, back to the oldest living things, that there was still room for possibility, enough to have produced the both of them.

"I try to keep it how it was," Brownie said.

Gibbs nodded. He stopped cataloging the items when he reached a turn-of-the-century Marvel cookstove, bygone kitchen utensils hanging from the close rafters, stopped guessing the value and just took it in, the buildings ticking like a heart, a time when the outside world had beat a path to Ladle, when it had been a place; Brownie's life, too, his untold days of preserving a thing nobody had use for anymore.

It was real and he had no words for what he saw but it seemed important, Gibbs among the last to hear what the town had to say for itself. He toured the cabins, studied their contents like something he needed to memorize, to get right.

He stood on Brownie's covered porch before taking claim on the Willy's and shoving off. From the incline of hill, the town spread out below, the high crated sides of rockwall, the mountains behind everything, like gears of a terrible machine. It was cold, but not so bad. A faint sickle moon had attached itself in the low blue.

"I thought you might have been a mechanic with the cards," Brownie said. "I watched you deal, though, and it wasn't that. All the fives and nines. Just lucky."

Gibbs leaned over the railing. In the front yard, the snow-capped shape of a '55 De Soto which Brownie told him he'd stopped driving ever since the Arabs monkeyed with the gas prices.

"Lucky," Gibbs said. "I wouldn't have said so." He considered the word, how it matched up with his life, trying it on like some new hat. "Maybe," he said.

Brownie squinted. "The gems and curios you threw in. They real?"

"Does it matter?" Gibbs said. He considered the avalanche chutes on the slopes ascending back in the direction of the divide. He had gotten someplace, only part of the way to where he had to go, and the remaining distance—he couldn't guess how long that might take. "I suppose it does matter," he said.

From somewhere in the valley, the sound of a radio, a big band tune from the forties, the bell-like tones of a songbird carrying like a breeze, filling up the canyon. The western end of the rock-face seemed close enough for Gibbs to reach out and touch, like touching the other side of the earth.

"What are you going to do?" Gibbs asked. "This place."

"We're running out of time," Brownie said. "There's hardly any left."

Gibbs watched the little man, noticed that part of one ear was chewed off, the hangy-down of his lobe, and the idea occurred to him that perhaps Brownie might have been dying. "So what happens after?"

"There's talk of a theme park. Tearing all this down to erect a ghost town theme park," Brownie said.

Gibbs shook his head. "The world is a broke-dick operation." He reached into a pocket, found the slip of paper, pulled out the mining claim. "You can give this back to that Tap fella," he said. "I have no use for blood money. I myself have a brother."

Brownie smiled more hard-won than happy. "The clutch will stick on you but you won't be unsatisfied."

They looked at the boxed landscape of snow, rock, sky. Gibbs thought of the buried Chrysler, how next spring when the white receded it'd reveal itself again, one door open, a hulk of metal, and the rest, mystery.

"I expect you'll be going though you don't have to," Brownie told him.

"Oh, I might come back," Gibbs said.

Brownie kicked a mantle of snow from the porch. "O.K. but I won't hold you to it."

Late afternoon. Gibbs drove west, following a cleft in the canyon, like a roofless tunnel through the mountains. The Willy's motored with a constant shout, a body square as an old flivver, its backseat containing the contents of the last round of poker; a sack with more money than he might have ever held and the various other spoils.

He climbed in altitude and the landscape unfolded ahead, a dashing stream on one side, rapids white as shaving soap. He had enough scratch to pay Jolie back and still live fat, though he probably wouldn't. He thought about calling his brother Miles, another thing he'd not do.

On the approaching slope, treeline, the dense network of aspens frosted in new snow, the hills lit in the alpenglow of impending twilight. It was then that he saw them again, the animals. They indeed had the hind quarters of horses but the forequarters were something else entirely. They looked like deer on steroids, that big and chesty. They ran in a clattering herd ahead of him and he followed, goosing the accelerator, attempting to close the distance.

And then the word came to him. “Elk,” Gibbs said and laughed, the teeth and gumline around the space in his mouth where his crown was once, twanging like a guitar string. *Elk,* like the first word of a new language he was only now beginning to learn.

Pam Durban

Rowing to Darien

March 1839, just after midnight on the Altamaha River, and it's cold, the thin, watery cold of spring on the coast of Georgia. Fluky breezes blow, smelling of silt and fish and woodsmoke. The hoot of a horned owl carries across the water, a heron's croak, the creak of oarlocks and the splash of oars. The moon is up, one night past full; it throws a bright track on the water and across this track, Frances Butler rows a boat with a lantern set on the thwart. Out under the moon which lights up the whole sky, the lantern flame looks small, a small brightness crossing the river to safety. That's how she thinks of it as she rows—a mission, not a flight—to dignify the journey and to keep the fear at bay.

Fear of the river to begin with. The Altamaha only looks slow because it is wide and deep, coiling through the Georgia swamps. But the Altamaha is a tidal river; the whole river moves as the tide pushes inland for twenty miles, then flows out again. On a tidal river, lacking strength and will, you go where the water goes which is—it occurs to her now as she rows away from her husband's rice swamp—what Mr. Butler expected of her once they were married. He the river and she the boat, carried on his tide. Whither thou goest; wives be subject to your husbands and all the other trappings of this world in which she has found herself, down here in the dark pockets of his wealth, the flood and drain of his profitable estuary.

Now, as her husband's boatmen have taught her to do, she sweeps the oars back, dips them deep, pulls with all her strength, all of this done quickly, for in the pause between strokes, when the oars are lifted, she feels the current grab the boat and pull it downriver. She is an accomplished horsewoman, a hiker in the Swiss Alps; she is no flower, but this is hard, nearly desperate, work. The sleeves of her dress are pushed up over her elbows; her hair straggles out of its twist. She rows steadily away, but someone rowing a boat across a river has to face the shore she's leaving. One last trial, she thinks and would have laughed if she'd found the breath for it: to watch the scene of her downfall dwindle and disappear, though in this endless flat landscape that might take all night. So be it, she thinks, because once Butler Island is out of sight, she will be free. It is only a matter of time.

Back on Butler Island, the tall cane and grasses stir and hiss. She sees the landing from which she'd untied the boat, the rice dike and beyond it their house, then the kitchen house and rice mill and the cabins of the nearest slave settlement beyond the mill. Smoke pours out of many chimneys there and flattens like a ceiling, so that the whole scene lies under a smokey haze lit by the bright moon. Otherwise all is still. No torches move along the dike that separates the river from the rice fields; no light shines on the water, as it would if someone on shore held up a lantern and looked into the river. No one is searching for her yet. Across the Altamaha lies a wide marsh island, General's Island, and beyond that island, the town of Darien, a line of two-story warehouses, glimpsed over her shoulder, standing white as salt in the moonlight. In Darien, she thinks as she rows, in Darien, she will get on a ship and sail away north, then home to England and become again the woman she was before she married Pierce Butler and came down to Georgia—mistress to no Negroes, no slaveholder's wife.

Seven years earlier she'd come to America with her father, the actor Charles Kemble, on a tour to raise money for the Covent Garden theater in London. The two of them performing scenes from *Hamlet, Romeo and Juliet, Much Ado About Nothing,* at theaters in New York, Philadelphia, Boston. The newspapers in those cities called her *glorious, sublime,* and everywhere they went people shouted her name, threw yellow roses onto the stage until she stepped out from behind the curtain to curtsy again and speak a few more lines.

Still, she found acting demeaning, a kind of drudgery. A nightmare, really, for a woman of her sensibilities. Standing among the dusty drapes and props, the shabby backstage clutter, waiting for her cue. Then out onto the stages of those packed and stifling theaters where in winter, tin stoves blazed in the aisles, and candles cast wavering shadows across the rows of upturned faces. She was a writer, a poet, a published diarist, sister in soul to Byron and Keats. Byron above all, that reckless hero poet-man of the tragic limp and the swagger, whose poetry had moved her, she once wrote, like an evil potion taken into my blood.

They had not been in America long when an English friend, another conoisseur of women, wrote to Pierce Butler at his home in Philadelphia: You must go and see this Frances Kemble perform. Her eyes flash with passion, he wrote, and when, as Juliet, she flings her head back in love's tormented ecstacy, you will be deeply stirred.

The day after their first Philadelphia performance she walked into the outer room of their hotel suite to find Pierce Butler sitting down to tea with her father. He wore fawn colored trousers, a green coat and pale yellow satin vest over a creamy shirt. As she entered the room, he stood and bowed, then kissed her hand, held it tightly between both his own. His eyes were deep, soft, and brown; they'd flown to her when she'd walked into the room and stuck to her when she smoothed her hair, and when she spoke they watched her lips. "Please do sit down," she said. He wore three gold rings on one hand and carried a cane with a silver handle. He had a child's brown curls; his mouth was small, moist, pouting; his chin was weak. He lounged when he sat, as though expecting to be served. In this luxurious room where yellow brocade swags and fringed drapes framed the tall windows, he seemed completely at home. "Miss Kemble," he said in his buttery voice, soft and broad of vowel, "I hope that in the future you will number me first on the list of your greatest admirers." He sat with his back to the window, sunlight pouring in around him.

She sat across from him, next to her father, in the circle they'd made with their chairs. "I might consent, Mr. Butler, had I such a list," she said, smiling at him as she sipped her tea. "Though in America I fear I shall be judged a traitor should I encourage such undemocratic ranking."

"Then allow me to keep that traitor's ledger for you," he said. "I shall be honored to take the blame as fair exchange for being listed first in your favor."

She learned that he was rich and that he would be richer when his father's last sister died and he claimed his share of the family's Georgia rice and cotton plantations. He was waiting for that day, passing time in a rich man's way: cards and music, the racetrack, the theater. Rich enough to follow her from Philadelphia to New York to Boston, to take rooms in the hotels where she and her father stayed, to buy a seat at every performance. He slid into her life that way and she let him come. Every night from the stage she'd skim the front row faces, and there he'd be, smiling up at her, the silver handle of his cane shining. In New York, he filled her dressing room with yellow roses; in Boston, bottles of old port and madeira appeared backstage. In Philadelphia his carriage waited at the stage door to drive her to his house on Chestnut St. for a late supper. Once she returned to her dressing room, exhausted, after three curtain calls. Her face ached from smiling; her throat felt raspy raw; her legs ached from striding and curtsying. On the dressing table she found a pair of cream-colored leather gloves tied up with a narrow, rose ribbon, gloves so soft, so warm, they seemed to melt like warm wax on her hands.

This went on for two years. The American tour. Flowers and port and gloves and candlelight. *Get this for Miss Kemble. Take that away. Quiet, please. Bring the carriage.* Mr. Butler the first on his feet when the curtain came down, leading the applause, pressing money into her father's hand. "For the theater," he would say, "for Covent Garden, Mr. Kemble." Riding in his carriage with the curtains drawn, falling into his arms. Deep kisses in the deep night, his words breathed into her ear: "Marry me, Fanny, marry me, marry me," until, resting in his arms, she began to feel the whole tiresome weight of herself, her vividness and intelligence, this life of roles and exile, and to imagine how it would be to shrug it off like a heavy coat and rest lightly, cherished, in his care.

So what has gone wrong, five years and two daughters later? Why is she fleeing now, without coat or bag or money, across this dangerous river? In January, they'd traveled south from Philadelphia to the Georgia coast: herself and Mr. Butler, leaving Sarah and Francis back in Philadelphia in the care of an Irish girl, Margaret.

He'd come to inspect his properties and to oversee the rice planting at Butler Island and the planting of cotton at Hampton, a short distance down the coast on St. Simon's island. She had come for her own reasons.

They'd arrived at Butler Island on New Year's Day, on a sloop breasting upriver from Darien under full sail on the incoming tide. Sun a white disk in the palest blue sky she'd ever seen. The river had looked dark as strong tea and the winter marsh was a rippling palette of brown, red, gold, where flocks of red-winged blackbirds wheeled and settled in the grasses. After the pleated, rocky folds of New England, the landscape had looked startling: flat all the way to dim, distant trees or open to the horizon where the sky came down and met the land, like a seal. A world of grass and water and sun, clouds piled high in towers.

As the Butler Island landing came in sight, they'd stood at the rail together. He'd taken her hand, and feeling its warm pressure, she'd smiled up at him and renewed the vow she'd made to herself. She would rescue her husband's soul from the darkness in which it now lived and kindle within it the light of moral conscience. Her friend and mentor, Dr. William Channing, had often preached that it was the duty of the Christian opponent of slavery to accomplish this waking and kindling, for it was by this persuasive pressure of one soul upon another that slavery would be abolished, one slaveholder at a time. Sailing for Butler Island, she remembered listening to Dr. Channing speak as light poured in through the tall, clean windows of his Boston church, and how she'd imagined Mr. Butler's soul bathed in such a light, imagined it freed and rising to meet her own. She'd never loved her husband more than she did that morning as she sailed toward his rice swamp, imagining his salvation.

As the sails were furled and the sloop tied up for the first time at the Butler Island landing, the people swarmed out to them, weeping, dancing, clapping, crying *Massa* and *Missis,* kissing the hem of her dress, stroking her hair, until, frightened, she'd called out for Mr. Butler, who was also being plucked at, spun, wept over. Up at the house, long after the noisy, happy mob had gone away and all the doors were closed, the shutters latched over the windows, she sat with her hand pressed to her chest to quiet her pounding heart. She found herself in a long, bare room furnished with a pine table and a sofa with a dull green baize cover. Candles flickered in sconces along the walls and on the table. At one end of the room there was a fireplace, and as she waited for her heart to slow, he began to build a fire. When she found her voice again, she said, "This is idolotry, Pierce, or something very like it."

He knelt on the hearth, pushing sticks into the fireplace. "You are their mistress now, Fannie," he said over his shoulder.

"I will not be worshipped," she said. "I will not have them groveling before me."

Already he was weary of her intensity, her forceful mind. "You will understand," he said. "After you've been here for a while you will acclimate yourself to their feeling for you."

"I never shall," she said, "not if I live a thousand years here."

It had only felt like a thousand years since she'd come to this place. A thousand more to leave it. From the river where she rows, their house on Butler Island looks peaceful. A whitewashed, square, wooden box of a house squatting on brick pillars behind the river dike. The rice fields begin behind the house and run for miles, from the house to the river and across the river and out of sight. In January the people had moved into those fields. They'd chopped and hoed the boggy ground; in late February, they sowed and tamped the rice seed. They opened the trunk gates and flooded the fields, squatted under trees at noon, scooping food out of cedar piggins with their fingers. Their children ran around half-naked, and when they were sick they laid down on the floor of the sick house and recovered or died. Seeing them lying under their wretched scraps of cloth on the sick house floor she'd decided: if she must be their mistress, she would raise them up; she would teach them their worth. She went down to the slave settlements with lessons on cleanliness and order. She bought glass for the sick house windows, new blankets for the sufferers there.

All winter, she went out in the long plantation canoe, up and down the Altamaha in any kind of weather. Primus, Quash, Hector, Ned, and Frank rowed, and Kate's John, the foreman of the boat crew, rowed and shouted orders and led the singing that thrilled her to hear, wild songs on the wild water. She went out on horseback with Renty, Jack, and Ben moving ahead of her, machetes in hand, cutting trails through thick stands of oak and pine, through nets and loops of vines and creepers, and for these services (until he found out and forbade her to do it) she paid small wages to Mr. Butler's men, to teach them the value of their labor. That winter, from Darien to St. Simon's, their plantation neighbors talked: Pierce Butler could not control his wife, that English actress, that scribbler, that abolitionist on a mission to their country, to her own husband, as though he were the one in need of civilizing. Every day, so they heard, every waking hour, she lectured him on the evils of slavery, on the will to power that corrupts master and slave alike.

A breeze comes up and cools her scalp and her face which is hot with the work of rowing. Flying fast, a flock of swifts skims the water. She is one of them, she thinks, flying away. She thinks: you row and the distance widens between you and the place you are leaving. There is comfort in this simple, physical fact of distance and how it grows if you keep moving in the direction you want to go. She's almost to General's Island now. Back on Butler Island, the dwelling house and kitchen house and the cabins behind the kitchen house look smaller, as though the distance were at last restoring order and scale, reducing Butler Island to a small place under an enormous sky. As she rows she sees light—a torch? two?—moving from the slave quarters toward the house. Perhaps the women are coming back, a dozen of them trooping in to sit in front of the fire; it makes her smile to think of it. And only Pierce to listen to them now or to send them away.

Two weeks after they'd come to Butler Island, she'd invited the women to bring their needs to her, and every night as she sat writing at her table at one end of the long, barnlike room, they came, asking for cloth and meat. Nancy. Judy. Sophy. Sally. Charlotte. Sukey. House Molly. "How de, Missis," they said, and sat or squatted in front of the fire.

One night last week, she'd asked: "How many children have you had, House Molly?" thinking to record their histories in her journal so that one day the world would look into slavery's face as she had done.

House Molly was a tall, thin, light brown woman with a long neck and golden eyes. She sat on the floor in front of the fireplace, legs straight out in front of her, massaging her knees. "Six, Missis. Four in the earth now," the woman said, staring into the fire.

"Charlotte?" she asked the tall woman with the broad, flat, face who squatted next to House Molly.

"Three, Missis, all in the earth."

In the earth? She'd sat back in her chair, put down her pen. She thought of her own children in Philadelphia. She imagined them in the winter garden with Margaret, rolling hoops and rattling the seeds in the brown pods there. When someone asked how old they were, she did not feel it necessary to add that they were still alive.

Sukey, who was short and very black, had four, and two still walking this earth. A terrible mathematics. She covered pages with the sums and stories which they told in the plainest way, a series of facts. The women worked, they worked in the fields with the men, into the last weeks of pregnancy and went back to the fields three weeks after the children were born. Chopping weeds around the new rice shoots, up to their ankles in the gray muck of the fields, skirts tied up between their legs. Shovelling out the rice field ditches in winter, out in the cold mud and the scouring wind. An occasional piece of fatty bacon or fish. Thin milk in their breasts, or none.

A dozen times a night her heart was broken by their stories, and she took their stories to Mr. Butler in hopes that his heart would be broken as well, for the chastened heart, the broken heart, is the heart prepared for salvation. But his heart would not be broken, it would not be touched. He lost the pages that she brought him; he folded and stuffed them in his pockets and never mentioned them again. He was planting a rice crop on Butler Island, cotton at Hampton. Surely his own wife could see that he was busy and not trouble him with the complaints of malingering women. Finally, last week, he'd forbidden her to bring him any more grievances. "You must no longer call me Missis," she said to them that night, after she'd told them that her husband would hear no more their troubles from her. Who was this mistress they cried out to? Surely it was not she. She could not think of herself as mistress of this world in which children went into the earth and their mothers called to her for help and she could not help them. House Molly had stood up then. "Night, Missis," she said, and the rest followed. "Night, Missis," they said, one by one, curtsying as they filed out. Now she is fleeing them, fleeing them all, their faces and their voices, the children in the earth. But their voices follow her as she rows, calling *Missis, Missis* across the water.

Looking over her shoulder across the marshes of General's Island, she sees the flickering light of candles in the upper story windows of the warehouses that line the Darien waterfront. She's that close. A short pull through the canal across General's Island that connects the Altamaha with the Darien River and she'll be there. She works one oar, then the other, steering toward the opening in the grass that marks the canal. As she rows she feels her heart lighten and lift. Soon, she thinks, soon she will be free of the river's hold and Butler Island will drop from sight as though it were a ship that sank, carrying her husband and his people to the bottom.

No sooner does she row into the canal than the bottom of the boat scrapes mud, the boat stops. It has taken her too long to cross the river and now the tide is dead low, the water all drained out of the canal. She knows the tide will turn; it will fill the canal and lift the boat, and on the other side of General's Island the tide will be coming up the Darien River; it will sweep her upriver, toward the town. But for now, there is nothing to do but pull in the oars and wait. Her dress is soaked halfway up the skirt and drapes heavily across her legs. She is tired and chilled, and her heart pounds, her arms tremble from the rowing. Worst of all, the lighted windows and the chimney smoke of Butler Island still hang above the horizon, and she can still see the glow of a fire inside the kitchen house from which she had fled.

Tonight she'd been sewing in front of the fire when Mr. Butler came in, dressed in a clean white shirt, his hair damp and combed back from his face. He'd poked up the fire then leaned over her shoulder, testing the cloth between finger and thumb.

"Fanny," he'd said, "oh, Fanny," in the fond, punctilious, and lordly voice she bristled at the sound of these days, "on whose behalf are you straining your eyes and laboring over this cloth?"

She'd stabbed the needle through the cloth, pulled another stitch tight, tight, "For Judy, your cook, Mr. Butler," she'd answered, "who is in need of these trousers to ease the pain in her knees." In the fire, a log collapsed in a shower of sparks. She heard Mr. Butler breathing, she felt his hands tighten on the back of her chair.

"But what you must recognize by now, Fanny, is that there is no need for you to do this work when there are women always within the reach of your voice who will sew if you tell them to sew, as they are to us as my fingers are to my hand." As he spoke, he held out his hand to her, the seamless joining of wrist to palm, palm to fingers, illustrating the relationship he wished her to grasp.

"They will never be the fingers of any hand of mine, Mr. Butler," she said, head bowed over her sewing.

Words had flown between them then, about Judy's flannel trousers, then hotter words about the fact that his own wife felt free to match words with him at all. And in the middle of the shouting, she'd sewed the last stitch and bitten the thread, she'd stalked out of the house to find Judy.

The moon had risen then, fat and white, and smoke from the kitchen house chimney feathered out on the breeze. Just over the dike, she heard the river sweep by, its eternal windy rush, and from the kitchen house she heard Judy singing, a sharp, wailing song that slid up and down a mournful scale. She'd walked toward the sound. Outside the kitchen house door, in a wooden tub, she saw hooves and legs and the head of a sheep, dead eyes staring up into the sky. She stopped for a moment, stood on the round, flat stone outside the door and looked in. In the middle of the room, in front of the fire, Judy stood behind the chopping block, knife in hand. At the sight of Judy's bowed head, the sound of her voice, Frances Butler's heart had grown quiet. She had come with the soothing garment; knowing her fondness for mutton, Judy was cutting up a sheep. She had never felt it before, the exchange by which her husband swore they all lived here: kindness or a favor given, work and gratitude returned. She smoothed the trousers, and Judy looked up, beckoned her with the knife: "Oh, Missis, come for see."

She stepped up into the kitchen house, into the smokey heat, the reek of blood, the thick, familiar smell of mutton. As always, the smell brought a picture to mind: sheep grazing on green hills under old castle walls, the tinkle of bells. England. The trencher on the corner of the wooden block was stacked with meat. "Look, Missis," Judy said, and she put down the knife and wiped her hands on her apron, "I be for cut the beautifullest mutton you ever see." She held the trencher up in front of Frances Butler's face, smiling. She was a tall, stooped woman with a long, puckered welt across her forehead where the iron arm that held pots over the fire had swung out and burned her.

"Oh, Judy, thank you," she said. Then she looked down. The platter was stacked with strips, ragged diamonds, thick squares of bloody meat. Twice, three times, she'd tried to teach Judy to cut a sheep into proper pieces. She and Mr. Butler had laughed about the first platter of bizarre, roasted shapes that had come to their table; the second time, only Mr. Butler had laughed while Judy smiled and smiled and curtsied as though she'd handed Frances a plate of gold. She'd repeated the lesson a third time, tracing for Judy with a carving knife on a sheep's body the shapes of brisket, saddle, leg and joint. Three lessons and now the meat still looked as if it had been torn from the sheep by a wild animal and spat onto the platter.

"Oh, Judy, now you must really tell me" she said, trying to wipe that image from her mind, "is it so difficult to cut up a simple sheep?" Her voice had come out sharper than she'd intended. She felt her smile tremble, her heart begin to pound, and she saw in Judy's eyes a moment's cringing fear.

"Oh, Missis," she said quickly, twisting her hands in her apron. "I so sorry."

"Look at me," she said to Judy's bowed head. "I said look at me." The woman raised her head; the fear had cooled now, changed to something watchful. She must be gentle, have patience. "You spoiled this meat again, Judy," she said, and then she waited.

Outside, the marshes croaked and sang; inside, the fire crackled. Judy watched the floor, pushed at the dirt with a bare toe. "Sorry, Missis," she said, again, flapping a rag at flies that had begun to settle on the meat.

As soon as she heard it, she knew it was not what she'd wanted to hear. The tone was wrong, there was something quick and heedless about it, as if, in apologizing, the woman had simply recited something learned by rote. It meant nothing. Now she would have to wait. If she'd learned anything in her time in this place, it was patience with these poor, wretched people who sometimes required many lessons to learn the simplest task. She would wait, and when Judy was truly sorry she would forgive her, and then it would be finished and they would go on. That was all she wanted; it was little enough to ask and when enough time and silence had passed, Judy would realize that and give her what she wanted. And so she waited, and the longer she waited the more she wanted what she was waiting for until it began to seem that the apology she wanted belonged to her and unless Judy gave it back, it was stolen.

But Judy did not speak, the mutton lay on the trencher, and as the silence went on the idea of theft began to take hold in her. And as she thought of the respect that was being withheld from her, kept from her willfully, cunningly, with a great dumbshow of humility, she found herself studying the tools that hung on the kitchen house walls—the pokers and the heavy tongs. It seemed that she could feel the weight of each one in her hand, feel it brought down hard to break this unrepentant silence. That is when she'd dropped the trousers and run, climbed into the boat, lit the lantern and started rowing, each stroke carrying her away, away from Pierce Butler and from the rice fields and the kitchen house and the sorry-making weight of those tools that hung so close at hand. That is what she remembers from her perch in the mud of General's Island with the night almost gone and Butler Island still in sight.

Next morning in Darien she will find no ship going anywhere, no ship expected for days. She will be hungry and stiff and so tired all she wants to do is to curl up and sleep in the sun on the wharf among the bales of cotton and barrels of rice. The white men who pass her, sitting at the edge of the wharf on a trunk, staring into the river, will touch their hat brims and turn away. The black people will not look at her at all. "Missis," they will say and slip past her, heads down. Pierce Butler's wife. Before noon, the long plantation canoe will arrive and the six oarsmen will row her silently back to Butler Island, her own boat in tow.

Their separation will be long and bitter. She will leave him, and he will take her children, sell her favorite horse, Forrester, to a livery stable so that she will have to go back onstage to make the money to rescue him. They will try for a while to live together again and each time, before she moves back into Mr. Butler's house, his lawyers will draw up agreements for her to sign. *I will observe an entire abstinence from all references to the past, neither will I mention to any person any circumstances which may occur in Mr. Butler's house or family. I will not keep up an acquaintance with any person of whom Mr. Butler may disapprove.* Their divorce will be famous, the details printed in the Philadelphia newspapers. She will threaten scandal and he will swear she knows no names, has returned all the letters that she found. He will publish a statement in the Philadelphia paper offering evidence of her irrational anger, her refusal to yield to him, all the refusals that had corroded their marriage from the inside out.

Still later, in 1859, after Pierce Butler has gambled and speculated most of his fortune away, the Butler Island people will all be sold. *The weeping time,* they will call it. A three day auction at the race track in Savannah in a steadily falling rain, where Pierce Butler will walk among them, carrying two canvas bags of twenty-five-cent pieces fresh from the mint, handing out to each of them a dollar's worth of new coins.

So the details will be reported in *The New York Tribune.* By then she will be Frances Kemble again, herself alone, reading the paper on the porch of her house in Lenox, Massachusetts. It will be a bright, cool morning in May that smells of cedar and balsam. Goldfinches everywhere in the purple thistles. Down a long meadow in front of her house and through a gap between two low hills, a lake will shine in the sun. Her American home, "The Perch," where her girls spend their summers and Emerson comes to call. She will read the story three times through, then drop the paper in her lap, close her eyes. And what she will feel then will follow her for the rest of her life. Not the sorrow. She's ready for the sorrow; it sweeps through her whenever she remembers the faces of House Molly, and Renty and Quash or Kate's John, standing solemnly in the back of the boat, or when she thinks of the children, the women who bore them and the men who carried them, small bundles wrapped in cloth, to their graves. When the sorrow comes, she lets it carry her. She welcomes the sorrow because by it she knows that the light of her conscience has not been snuffed out. What catches her by surprise and holds her is the satisfaction she feels, such as a person feels when a hard job is finished, at the thought of Judy the cook standing humbly in the rain, holding out her hand for Mr. Butler's coins.

Daniel Wallace

Town of Sarah

There's always a joke, and the joke now is that if this is what dying looks like, she's glad she won't be around to see what she looks like dead.

"Because you know it's got to be worse," she says.

She holds the mirror in the air with both of her twig-brittle hands.

"How though?" she asks, studying her pale reflection as though it were the face of someone she knew a long time ago. "Could I possibly become any less attractive?"

"Yes," he says.

She looks at him.

"Was that a compliment?"

"I think so."

"Good," she says. "I feel better now, somehow."

She lays the mirror on the quilt, suddenly still. He's moving his fingers slowly down her forearm to her fingers, and back, then down again. She closes her eyes and smiles. The tips of his fingers barely touch her they move so lightly, but she says she can feel it even when they don't touch, some pre-sensory magic she's developed in her last days. She tells him she knows things she didn't know before, too, things about life and what happens after, and sometimes he thinks she's serious, and sometimes he thinks she's kidding. Like when she says she can now predict the weather, she just doesn't know where the particular weather she's predicting will take place. No reason to predict only local weather. In Paris, she says, it's probably a beautiful day. But here it's been raining for three days.

Her basement is flooded.

"I mean," she says, taking up the conversation where they left it five minutes ago. "I would think you could only get so sallow, or so hollowed-out looking. Dried out, withered up. Scruffy, bony, callused. And then . . ."

"What?"

"After you get as wretched as you possibly can?"

"Yeah. What happens?"

"Well, I can tell you this much," she says in her quiet, conspiratorial tone, so he has to move his ear close to her lips. "Angels are really, really ugly. That's why we never see them."

"Makes sense," he says, and she nods.

"When you get that ugly, becoming invisible is very important."

This is a love story. At least it is to Ray, who loves Sarah. Sarah doesn't love Ray because she's dying and most of her energy is used up just living a little longer, and doing last things: last letters to old friends, last telephone calls, last thoughts, last laughs. She doesn't have room for a last love, though she appreciates Ray to a point which you could almost call love. She says she loves him sometimes but what she really means is that she appreciates him intensely. *I appreciate you intensely* doesn't sound right, though, and that's why, when he says I love you, sometimes she says I love you, too.

For Ray, though, this thing with Sarah is about as good as it gets. This is what he has always wanted, whether he knows it or not. It was bound to happen, to come to this, it made sense in a way but who would ever have guessed it, really? Who would have ever guessed a dying woman would become the love of his life?

Not even Ray himself.

Before Sarah, they were all alive—not that she isn't. She is very much alive: she just isn't going to be that way for long. The others before her had no set expiration date, though in his defense Ray would tell you that you never really knew what might have happened. Accidents happen. People get run over. Cynthia (the one before Sarah) almost died, for instance, in the fire. Although that would have been after the fact, whereas Sarah here was dying when they met, perfectly wonderful in every other way, but just this one little thing, the fact that she was officially temporary to this world, his world. To many, perhaps to most, this wouldn't be seen as a virtue; to Ray it's positively fetching.

So the joke now is angels. Angels and their ugliness.

"They are butt ugly," she says later that evening. "You see me?"

He does. She's the woman with the colorful scarf on her head, with the pronounced cheekbones and deep green eyes, with the oddly full lips. She's resting against the down pillows in her bedroom. Sure, he sees her. He sees her better than she sees herself and—though he can't say it, especially now—he thinks she's beautiful. Really beautiful.

"If I were an angel, looking the way I do now, I'd be like the Heidi Klum of angel society. Every male angel would want me, and every woman angel would hate me. That's how ugly they are."

Ray laughs. There is something truly amazing in her ability to make him laugh.

"How do you think angels got to be thought of as being so cute?" he asks her.

"Marketing," she says, without skipping a beat. She needs Ray to keep the joke alive. She won't force it herself. He feels secure as her straight man. She needs him more for this than for anything else.

"And God," she says.

"What about Him?"

"God can hardly stand to look at them, even though—"

"What?"

"God's no prize himself," she says.

"You can't be serious."

"But I can," she says. "He's sort of plain, actually. With a weak chin."

"Explains the beard."

She looks up at him and smiles bravely. He takes her hand. Their eyes meet.

"Be careful what you say about God," he says.

"Or what? What's He going to do to me?"

He laughs, and she laughs, because it's true, there's not much left to do to Sarah that hasn't already been done. He could kill her, blow her up, turn her to dust, strike her with lightening, but then that would be sort of anti-climactic.

"Bring it on, God!" she says, as loud as she can toward the ceiling, raising her tiny hands and her tiny arms out and upward, pitiful little weapons, too small to be taken seriously. "You and your butt-ugly angels. I'll take on all of you!"

But the fight is suspended for a coughing spell. It only lasts three minutes or so but feels much longer. It feels like an eternity.

By the end of it her face is sunset red and her breathing comes shallow and light.

"What brought that on, I wonder?" he asks her when it's safely over, and she just looks at him, and sneers.

Time is weird at this house. How it passes, what happens when. Sometimes lunch is at twelve, sometimes it's at three, depending on lots of things, like naps and general bad feelings. Ray lives with Sarah, but not in the way a lover does. He lives with her the way a nurse does, in another room. He still has his own apartment, but it's on the other side of town, and he only goes there occasionally to get a book or some clothes or a present for Sarah. Then he rushes back. Time is weird and it's precious, because who knows when she's going to die, and though he's not sure he actually wants to see her die—he doesn't know what it would be like, if he could even bear it—missing it because he was getting another pair of socks is a feeling he could never life with. So he rarely leaves her house.

For her part, Sarah wishes she had a little more time to herself, but doesn't know how to tell Ray this. He has given up so much just to be with her—a normal life, even his job, which, though it wasn't much of one really (he managed a kitchen at a natural foods store), was still work. She has secretly put him in her will, to posthumously cover his costs. He'd never accept money while she was alive, but what's he going to do after she's dead? He won't have much choice.

The odd thing is, she thinks he actually loves her—is in love with her, the way normal people fall in love with each other, but she can't understand or explain it. They haven't known each other that long, and, of course, she's terminal, which he's known from day one. But she wonders about him. Is he crazy? Other than his love for her, he doesn't seem insane. Hard to be sure, of course, but in every other way he appears rational. Which is good. She just wishes she had a little bit more time to herself.

They have never had sex, though they have kissed twice for minutes at a time.

That night, before bed, Ray is right there beside her with a glass of water and his steno pad.

"I thought we could go over our schedule," he says.

She looks at him crossly.

"We have a schedule?" she says.

"Well . . ."

"Shouldn't we be taking it easy? All things considered? I mean, a schedule is kind of like work, isn't it?"

"It's more like, Let's plan something to do so we don't go crazy sitting here doing nothing at all."

"Oh," she says, "that kind of schedule. Okay."

He cocks his head to one side, not sure where she's coming from.

"So in the morning," he says, "if it's pretty, we'll go for a roll. I oiled the wheelchair by the way, so it doesn't make that awful squeak. Then back for a nap and *Oprah*. Then lunch. Then—"

"Hey," she says.

"Yeah?"

"This sounds more like a plan. I don't think making plans is a good idea."

"It's not a plan," he says. "It's a schedule."

"Sounds like a plan to me."

"It's a schedule."

They look at each other, soundlessly.

"Oh," she says, the word not so much a word but an extension of the breath she just exhales. "Are we having an argument, Ray?"

He rubs his chin. He hasn't shaved recently and it's a little scratchy. It makes him look like an artist who has been up all night painting.

"I guess we are," he says, smiling: it's their first. "But it's over now."

"So who won?"

"I think," he says, stroking her arm, "that I did."

"But it was a Pyrrhic victory."

She breathes, smiling, and her eyes flash like the afterglow of fireworks, and Ray can see passing through her a version of the woman she once was, when she was fully alive and not scheduled to die.

"This is great," she says, and her legs move slightly below the covers. "I've been trying to use that word for days."

Happy, she falls asleep without brushing her teeth. Sarah doesn't care about cavities anymore. It's something she's crossed off her list of things to do. Like mowing the lawn, picking up after herself, being kind to telephone salesman. She's trying to turn dying into a vacation, into a holiday. She wants the good stuff that comes with it. And Ray wants her to have it. That's why he's here.

They met just three months ago in the hospital parking lot. He was there visiting a friend who had just had sinus surgery; she was there getting her last dose of chemo. She had dropped her cane getting out of her car, and Ray had rescued her; he had picked up the cane, at least. It was a nice cane, too. Blond wood studded with bright jewels and laced with a golden wire; a cane with style, maybe even a sense of humor. Anyone with a cane like that, he thought as he handed it to her, had to be worth knowing; one look at her and he knew she was. She was his type. Loose, beautiful, smart. He didn't know she was dying then, but he sort of got that feeling from the cane and the scarf and the hollowed-out cheeks and remarkably, it wasn't a problem for him: it was a plus. Because this was the kind of woman he'd always been drawn to, the sad, lovely, damaged girls with broken hearts, some of them slightly—sometimes immensely—insane. He had a special sense, a nose for these women, and when he saw one he went to her quickly, and brought her close, as if it were her distance from him all these years which had made her who she was. Hey: I've got the antidote to your life, he might as well have declared, and it's me! This is what he believed, even if he never put it into words. It's what his heart felt. He would fix her, he thought, whoever she was. He would fix her right up.

Sarah, of course, having this terminal cancer thing, made it a real challenge, but he didn't count on success. He just liked to try. He wasn't going to fix Sarah because he never fixed anyone. Not even Cynthia, who had had little more than a bad childhood. Cancer was on another level entirely, but that didn't stop him. She had and has that forlorn, hollow-eyed beauty, that tragic aura and poetic sensibility he is powerless in the face of. The fact that she's dying only makes it better—in that way. For him.

It is a look he likes.

"How are we doing?" he asks her the next morning. He doesn't sleep with her because she gets so hot she needs that cool spread of sheet where his body would be. This is what he tells himself, anyway. He's in the next room, not really sleeping himself but listening to her breathe. He's an attentive listener.

"We're fine," she says, shifting her hips beneath the sheets, grimacing. "You feel good, I feel bad. So we average out to fine."

"Well, feeling good is a huge responsibility," he says. "But if it keeps our average up."

"You're a trooper," she says.

"And brave. Don't forget brave."

"Health is a burden only you could shoulder. I'm glad it's not my problem anymore."

"Way to count your blessings."

"Actually, I'm multiplying them now. I'm up into the thousands."

Laughs all around. This must be the joke for the day.

But they cancel their roll for the morning. The first nap and the second blend together, and they even miss Oprah.

So much for a schedule. So much for a plan.

Sarah drifts wildly from consciousness to unconsciousness, sometimes not really sure where one ends and the other begins. But every time she opens her eyes, even for a second, Ray is there, in his chair beside her bed, reading, or smiling at her. Soon she begins to feel him, his presence, even when she is unconscious. And though, if she told him this, it would make him happier than almost anything—that she could actually feel him there—it is driving Sarah pretty crazy. She has too many feelings already. She doesn't want any more. It became so serious so fast, this thing with Ray. She's starting to think that maybe a mistake has been made. And this makes her sad. And tired. Which might explain the extra nap.

Ray doesn't see Sarah as just another woman, of course, or even as logical evolutionary step on his romantic ladder. But she is. Before Sarah was Cynthia, and Cynthia nearly killed him. Not really, he would say. Not really really. But you could still smell the smoke from the fire she set in his clothes. His whole post-Cynthia manner now had a singed effect. He walked around gingerly, and he touched things as though the tips of his fingers were extra-sensitive. The look in his eyes was sort of pitiful as well: it was the abused animal look. But who could blame him? It was difficult to come home and find the woman you love—loved—presiding over a bonfire. On your bedroom floor. Consisting of every papery thing—from photos to journals to letters, even books—which held value for you. Flames leaping toward the ceiling while she cried, while the tears glowed rolling down her cheeks, and all Ray could think of, in the moments before he realized he had to put the fire out, was, Isn't she pretty?

She was always pretty—prettier—when she cried. And he would have gone to her, even then, even after realizing what she had done. But there was a fire in his way.

Cynthia was volatile.

Before Cynthia was Petra (he was also fond of the odd name, the offbeat spelling, the weird pronunciation). She had stolen from him. Money, brass candlesticks, his favorite ballpoint pen. She later became a heroin addict, or so Ray had heard. Good thing he never saw her then. She had the longest of long brown hair, and the deepest, darkest most troubled eyes you could imagine. And nice bangs. On heroin, she was probably irresistible. Petra was before Cynthia and before Petra was Max, who moved in with Ray and then slept with the next-door neighbor. Et cetera. Making lists like this is depressing. But Cynthia was probably the worst of them all. Cynthia had poetic tendencies. And asthma. And then of course she had almost killed him—which, when you think about it, is pretty incredible for a girl. But what's even more incredible is that Ray never broke up with her, even after the fire. He broke up with none of them, after all of the things they did to him. They were the ones who eventually left him, one after the other. Ray sees this as a temporary trend; it's actually a hallowed tradition.

Finally, the next day, things look good for a roll. The weather and Sarah's condition coincide, and so Ray gets out the wheelchair.

There's this park they go to, and there're lots of dogs there who run after Sarah's wheelchair as though it were a small, slow-moving car, barking and nipping at the wheels. This is what Sarah and Ray do for fun.

Sarah applies her makeup in bed. She has a basket of stuff beside her, a portable mirror balanced on her lap. The makeup is getting thicker and thicker—she insists on it every time they go out—but Ray doesn't like it. He would never tell her this, because clearly, she thinks she looks better with the lipstick, the base, the rouge, the eyeliner. But she doesn't. She looks made up. She looks created. He actually prefers the rings beneath the eyes, the chalky skin, the hollow cheeks, because it's her. He loves her. She's beautiful. But maybe that's just him. The makeup is like an admission that Sarah doesn't like the way she looks, that her imminent death doesn't become her. It's just one thing, of course, one difference between them, but it leaves Ray feeling unsecured. Where there's one, there could be many.

And now she reads his mind. She's getting good at that, too good.

"Promise to kill me if I am still alive and get yet uglier than I am right now."

He tries to laugh, but can't.

"Please, Sarah," he says. For the first time, possibly ever, he actually thinks she is not funny. "You're not ugly. It can't happen."

He moves in closer to get a good look. He sits beside her on the bed.

"At least put a bag over my head," she says. "And I don't mean the plastic kind."

"Sarah."

"Obviously that would defeat the purpose. They're see-through. I mean a brown grocery bag with little holes cut out for the eyes and nose and mouth and—"

"I like the way you look, Sarah."

And then he touches her. This is something she discourages, because she doesn't want to be touched, by anybody. It hurts, among other things. But as he says this he takes her hands in his own, and the lipstick, which she had been holding, falls to one side, and lightly smears the white cover red. Her face is only half done now. It's something from a low-rent horror movie. She glances at it in the mirror, and then back at him.

She has no joke now.

"You can't like the way I look, Ray," she says.

"Yes I can."

"I'm dying," she says to him, but says it as though it's just another fact of life. "I'm part dead already. Parts of me are dead. Seriously. This is death you're looking at, Ray, the preview. You can't like it."

"I like you. I love you."

"I'm cancerous. I'm full of cancer. Is that the part of me you like?"

"This sounds like a trick question."

"It isn't. If you had met me when I was healthy—and I was, once. Normal, strong, pretty average actually. No emotional problems—no really big ones anyway. I had a nice childhood. Politically: conservative democrat. Art: I like the Impressionists, especially Mary Cassatt. I could have fun playing miniature golf. I would eat veal occasionally, even though I knew what a terrible life they led. And I had hopes of becoming a microbiologist, meeting another scientist, and making a little family."

"A microbiologist?"

"If you had met me then, do you think you would have liked me? Do you think you would have even looked at me?"

"Of course," he says.

"You're lying."

"Yeah, so?"

And he kisses her. She lets him kiss her but she doesn't kiss back. Her face is placid, without emotion. He doesn't know how to say what he wants to say so he just has to say it the way the words come together in his mind.

"Let's make love."

"My goodness," she says, and he can see the unmade half of her face deepen in a blush. "How did we get from miniature golf to sex so quickly?"

"Make love with me."

"No," she says.

She smiles at him, because she knows this must hurt. But how could she say yes? Desire was one of the first things to go. Which is odd because she used to be terribly frisky, but that's so far gone now as to hardly be a memory. She doesn't miss it anymore because she can't conceive of it. She can't conceive. Another joke. A sense of humor thank God is the last thing, the very last thing to go. She would rather have that, too. She would rather laugh than fuck. Who would have ever thought it.

But she can't tell Ray this. It's too late for that.

"You know what, Ray? Sweet Ray, you know what?"

And he knows because he's heard that voice before, those words, this tone. He tries to pre-empt them though he knows he can't. It's like trying to stop a flood.

"Sarah."

"You know, it's just not working, Ray. I mean, I can't—I can't have this. I can't have to think about someone wanting what you want. I would say I can't live with this, but I really mean the opposite. It's just not how I want to be the last however long I've got."

"Loved? You don't want to be loved?"

"Stop it, Ray."

"I love you, Sarah."

"And I—" But she can't say it, the words won't come. She knows that means she's right. "I wish things were different."

"You're breaking up with me?"

"I am."

He sits beside her, still, stunned, and yet somehow at home, in a familiar place. His heart isn't breaking now because it was broken already. It's just opening a little wider, making room for the new boarder.

II

When Cynthia, the fire girl, left him, Ray became pathetic. He sulked, drank, never returned phone calls from his friends. There was a dark burn circle on the bedroom floor which he stared at constantly, this cold dark symbolic space where a fire used to be. Now every time he smelled smoke he thought of her. This is the way it would be forever, he thought; the rest of his life, he would not be able to smell smoke without the image of this incomparable if somewhat emotionally unstable woman coming to mind. How he wished it were a rarer smell she'd left behind, something like brie, or wild rabbit.

It's not that much different with Sarah. Every time he hears the words death or dying or cancer he thinks of her, if he's not thinking of her already, which he probably is. Every time someone tells a joke he thinks of Sarah's jokes. Every time he sees a wheelchair, or watches television, or wakes up in the middle of the night not hearing her breathe because he doesn't live with her anymore, he doesn't sleep in the guest room at her house, he thinks of her. Every time he sees a pair of lovers, every time he sees a woman or a man, alone or together, sick or healthy, happy or not, pretty, ugly, fat, thin, black, white, brown, he thinks of Sarah. And he imagines that it will be this way forever. Because he always knew she was going to leave him, but he thought this would happen when she left the rest of the world. He didn't think he would be singled out to be left while she was still alive. Still, in the end it's the same: all he figured on being left with was a memory. He just got it earlier than expected.

The days immediately afterwards, he waits for her call. Then he realizes that's not the call he's waiting for, really. He's waiting for The Call. He's waiting for her mother, or a friend, or one of her faraway sisters to find his name on the phone tree, to tell him the inevitable news. But it doesn't come, that day or the next. So after three days he goes back to the health food kitchen and gets his old job back. Lucky for him they're so slack. He gets right to work. It helps him not think of her as he schedules the baker's shifts, and determines how many sandwiches get made that day. After a week a whole hour goes by when he does not think of her, even once. Then he does think of her. He looks back at that empty hour as though from a great distance. Like a trip to some exotic foreign country, he can't believe it actually happened.

Sarah thinks of Ray only occasionally. She has a lot on her mind. Among other things she wonders how much longer she'll be alive, how many days, weeks, months. In between this thought and some others, the thought of Ray unbidden swims through her mind. Then it's back to her own mortality, to TV, the long phone calls with her mother, who is on her way down to be with her. No one really knows how long she has, all they know is that it can't be long. The day she met Ray she had gone into the hospital to tell her doctors that she'd had enough of it all, the radiation and chemotherapy, and they'd tried to talk her out of it, but couldn't. Finally they told her that it was her decision, of course, but that she might want to think of it this way: that the treatments she was receiving were like sandbags stacked up against the rising river of her illness: perhaps it was futile, inevitably, but it allowed a little bit more time before the town of Sarah was completely washed away.

She understood this.

The river is rising.

By now the cancer has metastasized so much that she's probably having a little cancer party almost everywhere, top to bottom. She forgets things, like her mother's telephone number, and sometimes slurs her words, so she knows it's working full-time on her brain now. But, as she says, mostly to herself, she tries not to think about it.

That's a joke. Get it?

Anyway, there's this drama in her life from moment to moment, not knowing if she'll breathe again, not knowing if she'll speak, feel another feeling. Or just be dead.

So she doesn't think about Ray all that much. But it is on her list of things to do.

Three weeks later, she calls him. Not because she really wants to but because she knows he wants her to, is dying for her to. So she does.

Her voice to him is the sweetest sound in the world.

"How are you?" he asks her, meaning those words more than he has ever meant them in his life. He wants to know.

"Well, I'm looking pretty angelic," she says.

"Really," he says, and he can only imagine.

"This is good though," she says. "None of that angel animosity now. I think I'll fit right in."

"Oh, please," he says, his voice cracking, watching his words now because the last thing he wants to say is the wrong thing, and lose her. It's like in hostage negotiations. He just wants to keep her on the line.

"Ask me how ugly I am," she says.

He doesn't want to but he does. For old time's sake.

"How ugly are you, Sarah?"

"I'm so ugly," she says after a moment, "even the dogs won't play with me."

And suddenly, he's jealous. This means she's getting out. Someone is wheeling her around the park: but who? He can't believe he is jealous of a dying woman in a wheelchair, but he is. By the end of the call her voice is sleepy and weak, and he listens for every last sound, the phone fumbling into the receiver.

She calls him again, the next day, but this time is not so talkative. "In Heaven," she says at one point, "there's an unlimited supply of carbonated beverages."

A little later she says, "Bye."

And that, of course, is the last time he speaks to her, hears her voice. She dies the next day. The Call comes from one of her sisters, Francine, and he can tell he isn't the first person she's called, and he won't be the last. Ray never met the family. They all lived far away, and Sarah wasn't very close, had insisted they stay away. She told Ray once she didn't want to be a part of any death-bed conversions, religious or familial. And now he tells himself that's why she never loved him, because she didn't want to take advantage. She didn't want to take advantage of death, knowing how attractive her condition was to him. This is the story he tells himself, but even he doesn't buy it, not anymore. He knows she would have loved him if she could. That's just the way love goes. Not even death is a match for love. And it was the same with all of them,

Sarah and the women who came before her, all those crazy dames: they could have loved him if they'd wanted to, but they didn't. In fact, he is starting to see, that this is what he looks for in a woman, the special quality he yearns for most: her inability to love him. He could really go for a woman like that.

But Sarah was the last, he tells himself. How could there be another after Sarah? Things happen for a reason, Ray is learning. Because even on the day she dies, the darkest of all days, he feels himself getting better, healthier, becoming a stronger man.

The next woman he loves will be a tall, sturdy Nordic type, and she'll live to be a hundred.

They'll build a house together, farm land.

He'll sire a clan of Rays and Raylettes, and the animals of the forest will sit in his lap, perch on his shoulder, warn him when strangers approach.

This is what he wants. This is what he really believes he wants until her funeral, when he looks around him as he stands beside her grave, and his heart sings, he is overflowing with joy, to be surrounded by so many sad and beautiful women.

Madison Smartt Bell

Parallel Lines

"Beryl," she told him, when he asked her name. In full it was Beryl Cornelia Fallsworth. She had an aunt who went by "Con." "Beryl" was her father's fancy, and in grade school the other kids had jeered at it, so that she came home complaining, wreathed in tears. Why couldn't she have had some ordinary name? Her father, tipsy as he always was by six, had said half-mockingly, *Did you want to be another Jennifer—Jennifer number eight-hundred-and-forty-two?* Knowing he meant to jolly her out of it, she'd flown into a rage and wept much harder. Later, older, now for instance, she'd recognized the name as an asset.

Karl, whose name she had not quite caught, repeated the word in a savoring tone, *Beryl,* as if he weighed upon his tongue a morsel of the stone it designated. At once she was moved by his air of recognition, removed some small distance from the mobbed ballroom with its clang of shouting voices and wedding music fractured by the bad acoustics. She could feel it in the bottoms of her feet, so powerfully that later, that same night, she'd let him touch and tongue her secret pearl.

That was unlike her. But what was she like? At the office they called her "Ms. Fallsworth," to be sure. She dressed severely, as young lawyers must, accenting her good looks by repressing them in her garments—a tactic she thoroughly understood. There were no casual Fridays at "Wiley, Craven, Snivel, and Cringe" (as Karl had rechristened the firm, playing on the actual initials). Sometimes the joke would surface in the midst of a tedious meeting with some client, so that she'd have to struggle not to burst into inappropriate laughter, and often she was truly afraid that she might address the senior partner, Cranston, as Mr. Craven . . . She was a strawberry blonde, petite, flat-chested. Karl could lift her and manipulate her like a doll. She'd worn, the night they met, a sort of doll's ballgown, a blue which set off her beryl eyes, skirt extravagantly flared, the low and square-cut bodice drawing a straight line across the honey-toned skin of her chest, where someone else might have displayed *décolletage.* "You have *no breasts,*" Karl said, when he peeled it down—but with fascinated rapture, and she was thrilled, since all her other lovers, infrequent as they were inept, had passed this feature over without comment.

Her days were disciplined, nothing like this. Her nights too, usually. She never had the name of a grind—was always popular enough and certainly more than pretty enough. On a good day, more than pretty . . . But she launched herself at a certain target and stayed on trajectory till the target was struck. *Summa* in politics at Princeton, a somewhat less brilliant record at Columbia Law. She passed the New York bar, soared over it, on her first try. The nights made long with study were now stretched out by work. She did the necessary to keep her life in balance: played a hard fast game of squash three mornings a week before the office, caught a weekend film or play with a college friend or a group of them. On the rare occasions when she danced she did it with enough abandon that it counted as aerobic exercise. She was mostly vegetarian, nonideological; she'd eat bites of chicken and even beef were it served to her in a social situation. She drank socially, no more than that. At night when she got into her bed her mind was clear and she'd position herself behind a boulder, her back covered by some red cliff, imaginary rifle snug in the cradle of her arms, and for fifteen or twenty minutes gun down the men or savages or beasts which vainly assailed the security of her position, and then she slept.

"Hey, cowboy," the black girl said, that first morning when Karl ushered Beryl down to the predawn mist of Delancey Street. Beryl did not mean to miss her scheduled squash game, no matter how unexpected the night had been. There was no reasonable way to notify her partner, and it was a matter of mind over matter after all.

"Yolanda," Karl said, briefly though he didn't seem self-conscious. "Beryl." The black girl had her hair in a hundred tight long slender braids. Half a head taller than Beryl and much fuller in the bosom, her almond eyes slanted down on her, acute. Beryl felt the tingle of her interest starting as a blush. The party dress was folded in a shopping bag under her arm and in Karl's rolled chinos and drooping T-shirt she knew she looked like a castaway. Her hair was damp from the quick shower she couldn't face the street without (though of course she'd need another after squash), and both sets of her lips were glowing from the recent friction. She felt the black girl was aware of this. Yolanda. Beryl stopped the blush before it reached her surface. With her fair skin she'd learned the technique long ago: halt the internal process before its symptoms showed. She smiled and nodded, more primly than she meant—her client smile—and the moment passed.

Karl kissed her lingeringly at the stair rail, but Beryl heard the rumble and galloped down the steps to catch her train. Dash to her apartment to collect her clothing, then a two-stop ride to the club. She slept, hanging on her strap, her eyes half open, and thought nothing of Yolanda, whose image returned to her in flashes like the squash ball rebounding from the too-white wall: details she hadn't known she'd registered, the thigh-high boots, the stamp-sized miniskirt, smell of smoke blurred by perfume. Of course the girl had to be a streetwalker in that get-up at that hour, half a block off the Bowery. The black ball throbbed in the web of her racket, then smashed hard against the wall.

"What got into you today," her partner said. The game was over and Beryl, as usual, had won. "I mean, you're always hungry, but . . ." Rueful, though he was used to losing, he rubbed the patch at the back of his head where the bald spot would emerge in ten years' time. She only smiled at him enigmatically; the smile she used to keep such partners at their proper distance. She didn't think of Yolanda again till many weeks had passed, perhaps two months, when things had advanced much faster than she had anticipated and Beryl found herself debarking from a cab on Karl's corner, a late night, a work night, some time after midnight.

"Girlfriend," and it was like the voice itself had coiled around her shoulders to draw her in. "Beryl," Yolanda said, as if to make things clear. Beryl was startled but not alarmed, even when Yolanda dexterously plucked a pin from the back of her head, releasing her hair from the chignon she generally wore to work to fall down over her shoulders. Yolanda's fingers were long and slim; they drew out a lock of the strawberry hair and held it against a snaky black braid.

"I be Y and you be B," Yolanda said. She was on something, Beryl could see that for sure, but she felt no resistance. Yolanda raised her arm with Beryl's, palm to palm, elbow to elbow, the flesh of their forearms connected in a firm, magnetic adhesion. There was a tang of sweat and semen in the air and behind it the smell of Chinese garbage discharged by the groceries and noodle shops across Delancey Street toward the glittering lights of the bridge. *Crack whore*—the phrase arose in Beryl's mind, but it didn't seem pejorative; she wasn't even sure to whom it referred. Plump glossy black against the honey, their joined arms were a ribbon flowing in the street light.

"I be next to last," Yolanda pronounced with her slight lisp. "And you be next to first."

Karl cut cocaine on a plastic CD case. Beryl watched him with consent, her heart already racing slightly. In school she'd done that shit sometimes, more often for work than for recreation, liking the keenness it would give her for the last cramming hours before dawn. At Wiley, Craven, &c, it obviously wasn't done. You drank more coffee and soldiered on. She lowered her head, her nostril flaring around the straw, and sucked it up. The image on the album partly emerged, then completely when Karl cleaned the last crystals with a dampened fingertip and rubbed them into his gums. Another wedding party, it might have been, a hipper one: the blonde girl hard-edged in white satin, flanked by her bachelors in black suits. Behind them hard flat vertical bars of black and white. She straightened, feeling the acrid drip at the back of her throat already, and with the rush she became aware of the music.

> *i'minnaphoneboothitwasawunnaacrosshall* . . .
> *ifyoudontanswerljustringitoffawall* . . .

The rush of snare and cymbal pressed all the words together till they blew, breaking into shards of fractured light. Beryl spun on the balls of her bare feet—she'd kicked off the torturing high heels the second she'd walked into the loft. It wasn't *so* big, maybe six hundred square feet her eye had automatically measured from the doorway, but now it was space, light and air and sound, room to let her doll's skirt flare as he twirled her and the music ran faster, faster still. Go with it. He was a reasonable dancer, but she was leading, she was a long way out in front. So very quickly she'd come from that to this: his praises for her body—she wasn't troubled by the expertise with which he'd laid it bare. First time for her that love had ever felt as good as dancing.

Walking the richly carpeted halls of Wiley, Craven, et al., coolly reserved in her trim business suit, she felt the space he'd stretched inside her; it felt something like desire. She drew it up into herself, encapsulated, squeezing her thighs under her skirt as she smoothed it down. The client sat across the polished surface of the table, while Snivel (no! it was Mr. Smythe . . .) was supervising, just to Beryl's left.

"Ms. Fallsworth will explain to you the various types of . . ." Normally she worked with Mr. *Cranston,* but he was absent—two weeks honeymoon with his new trophy bride. Cancun, if she remembered right, or maybe it was Rio. It was his wedding, where she'd found Karl; she'd been added as an ornament to that occasion, as to this one. She could hear her voice rolling like a tape, was aware, at a very long remove, of the accompanying gestures and turns of phrase meant subtly to charm. They used her as a showpiece, as a mouthpiece. She understood the contract and did not object. She was appreciated, yes, for other qualities besides her intellect and training, but no one dared to think of carrying it too far. The firm specialized in estate planning, but the recent rules of sexual harassment were thoroughly well understood. Beryl could demolish the junior partners at morning squash and none of them would risk an indiscreet glance. Mr. Cranston exercised his libido far, far away from these darkly paneled chambers of law. He could afford it, and he knew where to go. Beryl had done a little work on his prenup, in fact—rather a sordid document, yet it had taught her a new thing or two about the mechanics of holding back.

Today it was Mrs. Warrington, a widow fidgeting with her will. It was their second meeting, but the lady was quite deaf and a little senile and had difficulty making up her mind. Sometimes Beryl didn't do so well with old ladies as old gentlemen, as some of the ancient dames still harbored veins of jealousy. Mrs. Warrington, however, was well captivated, following Beryl's every movement with her weak and watery blue eyes. There would most probably be lunch, perhaps some presses of that liver-spotted, ringworn hand. Beryl felt Snivel relax beside her; he pushed back from the table and crossed his legs, dangling his two-hundred-dollar shoe.

That night a great black dog assailed her where she lay snug in her cockpit of heaped stones. This time she had a shotgun, not a rifle, the barrel heavy and long, somehow warm and slightly pulsing on its underside beyond the pump. She waited to fire till the dog's hot breath was practically on her face. The wound expanded behind the black shoulder, a bloodless ogive welling with light. The ribbon flowed, lights of cars drawing red and white lines down the broad avenue, oiled with rain. Multiply strapped in high-heel sandals, her feet were damp and chafing. *Got to get off the street,* the voiceover said. Familiar voice, though new to her dreams. A car door opened as if by its command. The dream thing: she was Beryl still, riding in a Checker cab up Eighth Avenue from the Film Forum, and still this other sinking to her knees in Roosevelt Park, nursing the latex-sheathed sausage. Shin splints when she was freed to rise—from those high heels. *The first shall be the last,* the voice whispered. Suddenly shelter, warmth of the hotel hallway. Scuffling behind the doors, but it didn't matter, only the flare of the lighter flame reflected from the lip of the glass pipe. Huff, hold, relax, redemption. Nothing mattered. *The last shall be first.*

By daylight, beneath, shall we say, the jeweler's loupe, Karl presented certain problems. Nothing which nakedly met the eye. Karl took his body seriously: weights, Pilates, Tai Chi. There was plenty of definition, beneath a milky skin delicious as her own. He still had all his hair and wore it rather long, a sheet of dirty blond always available to drop across the roughly chiseled features of his face. In younger days he'd worked occasionally as a model. Now he designed album covers, did some cabinet work, sold (Beryl knew it though she didn't see it) small quantities of drugs. He'd appeared at Cranston's wedding as a friend of the bride; Trisha had once been a model too, and Karl sometimes sold her coke.

A *bad boy.* Beryl had seen that right away, more or less at the same moment that he'd registered whatever he'd discerned beneath her friction-free surface of *good girl.* Still, a bad boy who'd circumscribed himself with certain limits, as she came to know. Beryl was wary at the start. She made him call first, which he did promptly. She would not change herself for him, not much, not permanently. Nor was she fool enough to think she would change him. Was there so much in him that wanted changing? A bit of a gypsy lifestyle certainly—and at his age. That late-seventies New Wave record collection, all the stuff that went so well with coke, even if it was the CD reissues he played now . . . surely he must be pushing forty, even past it maybe, as well as he did manage to look ten years younger. Well, he couldn't have been so self-destructive, could he? Or more would show in that much time. She saw no sign of real addiction. The cocaine was an occasional treat; it didn't appear every time she did. He kept a package of Russian cigarettes ziplocked in the freezer for freshness—he smoked that seldom, only sometimes after sex. All his vices had such epicurean restraint surrounding them. Beryl liked that. His drafting table, by the light of the tall, south-facing windows, was always neat, dust-free, and when he had graphic work he did it with a meticulousness which she could admire and even almost envy. Just once there'd been a pistol on the windowsill. Her hand went to it like a magnet, though it was mostly plastic, surprisingly light when she picked it up. Beryl had some familiarity with firearms, for her father collected them in a small way. She'd done some real-life shooting as a kid, amassed a row of riflery badges from a series of camp summers. This was different, one of those nine-millimeter murder weapons popular with gang-bangers, as she knew from law school friends who'd gone with the DA or the public defender. She handled the gun with sufficient confidence, keeping it pointed at the gritty window pane, her finger curled outside the trigger guard, while Karl watched, interested but not alarmed, his nicely manicured hands composed at the edge of the drafting board.

The dog's eyes were golden, its tongue juice red. She compressed the trigger with extraordinary care. The report was a silent shock between her ears; the dream door unfurled its inner labia. Yolanda, lying on her back, compressed the shotgun barrel between her heavy breasts. The darker, richer chocolate shade of her wide aureolae. *May be a little surgery involved,* Karl's voice reported on the soundtrack. *You know, professional expenses . . .* Beryl, on her neighboring track, could feel his connoisseur's touch, feathering the small strawberry of her nipple. Her breath sighed inward. The gun-metal blue of the shotgun pumped and when it fired, Yolanda turned her face sharply aside, to catch the sticky burst on her left cheek and lower jaw.

Beryl didn't see the pistol again. It went unexplained, unmentioned. Other things too. They ran into people when they went out together: junkies, musicians, artists, fags. The other women ran from rock chick to model—some whose good looks might have unnerved Beryl. They kissed in European fashion, on both cheeks. Beryl never let herself be bothered. She didn't mean to throw her weight where the support could be withdrawn. Those other women always seemed to see her standing there. They smiled, showing their top teeth only, simpered pleasantly enough. A few of them made real talk in her direction. Yolanda, whom she passed often on the street, began to call her Girlfriend with a capital, in tones that recognized her status and respected it.

Beryl held to her own schedule, much as it had always been. She worked late several nights a week, kept up her theater dates with friends, and dated other men sometimes, although they bored her. Throughout all this, Karl remained constant. He was seldom unavailable to her. Their pleasure in each other was unflagging. It was a nonintrusive thing.

There was a small and slightly inconvenient matter of a key. Karl said he only had just one. He'd lost the magic number that would replicate it. Moreover, there was no doorbell in his building. She'd have to call on her cell phone, from the cab or the unpropitious street, where she waited for the key to flutter down, pocketed in a cotton sock or finger of a glove. One day she noticed a metal tag push-pinned to the bulletin board where he kept delivery menus and a schedule of graphic assignments. She memorized the number long enough to jot it down on the back of a business card. Sure enough it created a key when she took it to a locksmith, but she didn't know for sure what door it fit. She held it secreted in her purse and never tried it in Karl's door. After all she'd never keyed him into *her* apartment—a place he'd scarcely ever been. But somehow, once she had the key, the relationship seemed to have stepped to a new level. When had she used the word *relationship* for Karl? But maybe she wasn't wrong about that, because it was only two or three weeks later that he popped the box on her: a modest but respectable diamond ringed with chips of beryl.

They flew to Saint Louis to meet with a passive lack of resistance on the part of Beryl's mother. Beryl paid for both their tickets and didn't care. It was her father, right here on East 74th Street, who made trouble. "You've known this man for what, six months? He is *forty-four years* old—Beryl, that's almost *twenty years*. . . ."

"What," Beryl said. "Did you get his rap sheet?" Her father had been a prosecutor back in the day, and still had the pull to have done it. Beryl also felt annoyed because, till now, she'd remained a little vague on the point of Karl's exact age.

"I looked up his license on the internet," her father said. "That's kid stuff, nowadays. As far as I know he doesn't have a rap sheet. He doesn't have much of a résumé either. What we have here is an over-the-hill underwear model who still plays with his crayons and did well in shop."

"Dad." Beryl was thinking about when she'd brought Karl over for last Sunday lunch. Her father had done martinis before the meal, mixing them up in his dented chrome shaker. A couple apiece, and strong as ever. By the second round, Karl and her father were clapping each other on the back and getting on like a pair of old sailors.

"Of course he's a nice guy," her father said. "Of course he's charming." Beryl never quite knew if she liked it or not when he read her mind. "He's got to be charming. It's how he gets by. Do you think that makes him marriage material?"

Her father stood up and walked to the wet bar and with a touch of ostentation poured himself another glass of seltzer. For this important interview, he was making a point of not getting half-crocked.

"I don't think you do," he told her, with a trace of the prosecutorial tone, raising the water glass slightly in her direction. "I don't think so, or I would have met the man sometime before he'd sprung the ring. Every Sunday you come over for lunch—alone. Or once in a while with some punk from your office. And no, I don't think you should marry them either."

He took a long drink of the fizzy water, sat down in the wingback chair next hers.

"It's fun now, I know," he said. "You don't notice the difference. Give it twenty *more* years, you'll be changing his diapers."

"Dad."

"Okay." He turned his glass so the crystal fluting glittered. "That was low. I admit it. But still, think it over. Have fun with this guy. I think that you should. Screw around, *live* with him—I won't say a word. Just don't marry him."

Beryl didn't answer. He turned her way, his eyes looking fainter. "So what does your mother have to say about it?"

She looked at the unlit gas logs in the fireplace. "About what you think."

"I know, I know," her father said. "But . . . you don't have to do all of our mistakes."

He was looking at the gas logs too. The mantel clock ticked on the library shelf. He reached for her hand and cradled it in a way that let her know how very special she was to him, how infinitely superior to Karl. She was wearing the ring and he was looking at it, admiring the lay of the little stones and the excellent craft of the goldsmith.

"He's got good taste, I'll give him that," he said. "But you ought to be asking yourself those questions."

Then all of a sudden he let her hand go. "Ah, what the hell, Baby. Let's have a real drink."

Beryl *had* asked herself the questions, even some her father had not voiced. She thought about them, padding the hushed corridors of Wiley, Craven, Snivel, and Cringe. She knew how little she knew about Karl. Also she did wonder if he might not be at least a little bit attracted by her comparatively humongous and regular paycheck. It might be that she was being set up as a sugar mommy of some kind. She had this thought, but she couldn't get it to bother her. Day and night, her clients thought of nothing else, all the old gents and old dames trying to express in their estate planning everything they'd never said or done in their lives. Mrs. Warrington took her to the Russian Tea Room and ordered six kinds of caviar. Beryl was wearing the ring, and Mrs. W. caught up her hand and held it to the light.

"Oh, my dear," she said, vicariously ecstatic. "I know you will be *very* happy."

All at once she clawed off one of her own gigantic rings, gold flowing lavaly around a huge rock, and pressed it into the palm of Beryl's free hand. Beryl's alarms all went off at once, and this time she didn't think to stop herself from blushing.

"I mustn't," she said, almost in a stutter. "I can't—"

"Oh," Mrs. Warrington said, her weak eyes looking right through her. She folded Beryl's fingers down over the ring. "But you will."

The dog's steaming breath lapped over Beryl's face, so near she saw quartz-like flakes floating in the golden irises. She fired, and passed shuddering through the dream portal's membrane. Yolanda leaned toward a cloudy mirror, cleaning goo from her face with a wet clump of toilet paper. She wiped something from the corner of one eye, touched up the edges of her lipstick. She cooked up in a blackened spoon and tied off with a shoelace. When the dope hit the vein, Beryl sighed into a relaxation deeper than she'd ever dreamed. Why, oh why had this been withheld from her? She hadn't even known she'd been in pain.

Finally it came down to something stupid, the most minor and trivial oversight. A Saturday, and Beryl was on her way to a girlfriend's place with some swatches of fabric and a couple of patterns for bridesmaid's gowns. That's what she thought. When she checked her tote she remembered she'd left the stuff at Karl's the night before. With a muttered curse, she gave the cabbie new directions. On the way downtown, she tried to call. The machine; she didn't leave a message. The cabbie pulled up to the corner, twisted to look at her over the seatback as she punched the number into her flipphone another useless time.

"Just wait right here," Beryl sighed as she slid out of the cab door. "I've got a key."

Still, she hesitated on the threshold. Practical or not, it felt a little like a trespass. But it *was* practical, and then she thought that Karl would never need to know. The key went in and turned smooth as butter. The inside of the loft was all one space, and Beryl's eye flew straight to the rumpled futon. She must have made some sort of sound, for Karl jerked backward, detaching from the other, darker body, clawing up the sheet to cover his erection.

Beryl's hand went to her throat, where she wore Mrs. W's ring on a gold elastic cord. The ring pulsed into her hand with her heartbeat. Karl had sense enough not to try to start talking, though a blush was spreading from his navel to the roots of his hair. Yolanda sat up easily, coiling her long braids over her shoulder with one hand. Beryl watched how her breast lifted with the movement of her arm, and thought that she must be very good at what she did. Yolanda was looking at Beryl quite calmly. The petals of the dream door lay open between her legs and there was an amazing brown warmth in her eyes. It occurred to Beryl that Karl might not be so essential after all. The heavy ring pushed harder against the lifeline in her palm. She didn't know if it was the end or a beginning.

Ann Beattie

Cat People

Mrs. Eugenie Nestor and her husband, Old Nestor, live next door to us in Key West, behind a tall bamboo fence with several shoebox-size rectangles cut in it so their cats can prowl in our yard. Key West has changed a lot during the twenty years my husband and I have been renting a winter house here. For one thing, these days you can throw away your alarm: if it's not the crashing clatter of the recycling truck twice a week—this beast can come at three in the morning, by the way—it's the daily whine of buzzsaws. No one needs an alarm anymore. The renovation has drowned out the roosters, machines screech more piercingly than any of the birds, and motorcycles let you know how frustrated the riders feel, having to zig and zag through so much traffic. The main street, Duval, is, during the height of the tourist season, entirely blocked off, being bulldozed and jackhammered. Everyone takes the next street over, Simonton, which means traffic pours by day and night. My husband refuses to drive the car and has even abandoned his bicycle because of the many ruts in the road, and because tourists have recently been reaching out their windows to try to topple the cyclists. It's a new sport, malevolent, but a direct response, people think, to the number of cyclists who frighten them by riding at high speeds on the right and sideswiping them or cutting them off. Yesterday I saw a woman in a convertible using a shopping bag like a big flyswatter. You used to see amusing, interesting things in Key West: men riding along in bikini trunks with their dogs in baskets on the front of their bikes, or adults pulling other adults in wagons on the sidewalk. And the gay people were quite flamboyant; leftover masks from Fantasy Fest might appear pushed to the top of their heads like one of those old lady pancake hats, or they'd wear masks on the street, nothing particular going on except that they were escorting some friend in chains down Duval, and the one who wasn't bound in chains would have on a mini-skirt with a T-shirt with something outrageous written on it, and over his eyes, a mask made of peacock feathers. AIDS took its toll in the '80s, though, and now most of the birds are in the trees, or snatching expensive goldfish out of people's little garden pools. Yesterday my husband saw a crane walking up the steps of a recently opened gift shop. Amazed tourists were giggling and gawking and photographing it. The storekeeper said, "Let it come in. Maybe it has a credit card."

Inevitably, the Conch Republic has changed. Even the conch is now imported. The tourists still come in droves and hurtle around the island on a big caterpillar with an awning called the Conch Train. My husband and I hear the punchline of the recorded jokes as it passes, about every half hour. One of the drivers moonlights for my husband, coming on Monday and Wednesday nights to stand in our pool with some other models, clothed and unclothed. He recites the canned jokes to make them groan, and they roll their eyes or splash water on him. My husband understands that modelling can be very boring, and he expects to be talked to, but pretty quickly the models understand they won't be getting much feedback except for an occasional "pardon me?" or "you think so?" Inevitably, the models who have been in analysis come to love my husband. If he could remember ten percent of what they tell him, I could spend my whole life amazed by people's bizarre lives and problems. One of the drivers, Lem Rupert, is not only a Conch Train driver, but also a weekend waitperson, as well as a part-time model. Lem grew up in Wales, in a little place called Hay-on-Wye, which he calls Ham-on-Rye. Apparently the place is famous for its bookstores; some shops are so large they spill out onto the street and only awnings keep the books from getting rained on. Lem's mother was a maid in one of the inns and his father was away at sea for most of the years Lem was growing up. Lem has a sister, Daphne, who also models for my husband when she needs extra money. Like her mother, she works in a hotel, but it's the Hyatt in Key West: quite large and new and grand. Daphne has auburn hair and a ruddy complexion that my husband has speculated may be protective coloration, a way of disappearing while working in a big hotel that is primarily pink.

Last Wednesday night my husband had the two of them posing in the pool, Daphne on a raft, Lem holding a palm frond and pretending to be fishing out leaves, when Old Nestor had what my husband calls "an episode" with one of the cats. The cats seem to disappoint him in many ways. They do something that makes him bang a spoon on a pan—that is the very worst cat punishment for all of us—though other times the Nestors throw fruit or simply clap their hands and curse. But this night the orange cat did something that really set Old Nestor off. Even from inside the house, I could hear distinctly the metallic beat of the tom-tom, with Old Nestor's wife shrieking in falsetto. A banana was the first thing to end up in our pool, followed by the orange cat's darting through one of the shoebox holes in a state of wild agitation and making a mad dash so intense that it overshot the yard entirely and ended up in the water. An apple and several starfruit flew after it, and the apple smacked Daphne on the head, causing her to scream as she toppled off the raft into the pool. To make matters worse, the orange cat was terrified and attempted to scramble up Daphne, which was the first time anyone realized quite how afraid of cats Daphne was, though anyone might have been afraid of some wildly circling animal in fear for its life, with its eyes bugging and its claws extended. As I understand it, Lem was immediately possessed of enormous strength—such a surge of power that he dismantled part of the fence with his bare hands, and clomped into the Nestor's yard cursing every bit as obscenely as Eugenie and Old Nestor. Meanwhile, Daphne was shrieking in the pool, and the cat was swimming in circles around her like a shark, so my husband peeled off his shirt, stepped out of his sandals, and rushed into the water, swatting the cat toward the shallow end with the palm frond, where it quickly found the steps and clambered out. Daphne was in tears, really going crazy. She started whacking at Andy, accusing him quite irrationally of "offering no protection" or something like that, her hand on top of her head where the apple had hit it, the string on her bikini top having broken, so that she clutched one little triangle of fabric over one breast, while trying to elbow the other triangle over the other breast . . . well: it was pandemonium, and furthermore, the orange cat had run right through Andy's pallet, and there were blue pawprints everywhere. The cat's mad dash had triggered the other neighbor's new security system, so suddenly, amid the three-way cursing at the Nestors', a voice you knew did not originate from a human being announced: "You have entered a secured area. You have five seconds to leave the premises." If the neighbors had been home, they could have come out to investigate, but they weren't home, so the alarm system went off, resulting in earsplitting noise which only ended when the police arrived. They obviously knew the code and had little trouble deactivating the alarm, but in their haste, in the dark, they knocked over the birdcage, and the door opened and the Minichiellos' parrot flew off into the night, which made one of the cops completely exasperated and furious, as his partner laughed and laughed, grabbing hold of our back gate to keep himself upright. Then his eyes drifted to Daphne, with the string and triangles dangling around her neck, standing and screaming after Andy, because by then he, too, had disappeared into the Nestors' backyard. Though none of us knew it that moment, he had embarked on a plan to uproot every bush and tree he could find there that was without thorns.

"Fucking idle rich!" Daphne screamed, climbing out of the pool. "It's exploitation! Seven dollars an hour doesn't entitle you to slam-dunk me. I want that monster arrested. I want to press charges because he could have bloody well killed me, him with his rabid cat and his stinking bloody violence, I want whoever threw that rock *arrested!*"

"You miserable low-life," Eugenie Nestor screamed. Which one of them she meant, I had no idea, but when an enormous bird of paradise plant was heaved over the fence into our yard, Old Nestor followed after it, through the newly broken fence, and as he attempted to scoop it up, Lem kicked him from behind and he went sprawling, and that was when the police finally did intervene—with the parrot staring down from high up in the palm tree, calling out: "Margaritaville! Margaritaville!" Like the bird, the laughing cop only got out individual words, but the address did get through, and within a matter of seconds there were sirens in the distance, and two police cars converged in front of our house, where Daphne now stood, topless, screaming that someone had tried to murder her. The upshot of it was that Old Nestor and Lem had to be restrained, and it took Andy quite a long time to disabuse the cops of the notion that a porn movie was being shot in the back yard. "Why do you keep asking, when you don't see any camera?" Andy said repeatedly to the cop. "Look at this. Look here. This is what was happening, when our neighbors began throwing things after their cat. I was painting a painting. That's what I do for a living. I've been coming to Key West for twenty years. I'm a painter. I'm a painter." If he weren't so tall, he could have been mistaken for Rumpelstiltskin, jumping up and down. I was a great help in giving a balanced view of the whole situation. By ten P.M. they were gone—with Lem in custody, and Daphne weeping in a butterfly chair on our front porch, dabbing her eyes with a tee-shirt, saying that it was their father Lem had gotten his ungovernable temper from, and hadn't he been wonderful, going after the people who had tried to kill her? The Minichiellos' parrot had flown away. When Daphne stopped sniffling and put on her in-line skates to follow after Lem to the police station, we put on the evening news and took comfort in hearing how cold it was elsewhere.

On Thursday, quite unexpectedly, Eugenie Nestor appeared at the door, carrying a paper plate covered with Saran Wrap. "Father Donegan said you would let me in," she said. It took a moment to register. First of all, though I'd heard her screaming and beating pans for years, I'd rarely seen Eugenie Nestor, and when I had, she hadn't been wearing black wrap-around glasses and a big sunhat with a calico bow. "Father said not to drown the kittens. To ask if you would take one. To ask all my neighbors," she said.

It registered. She had been to see the priest. He had told her—

"Bless you for enduring our struggles with the cats," she said. "I would like us to be friends. People should be friends with their neighbors, as Father says. He says there's a chance you might want one of the kittens. The key lime cookies are a present, whether or not you care to take a kitten."

"You know, this is very nice of you, Mrs. Nestor," I said. "Please come in. Would you like an iced tea?"

"Do you have Coca-Cola?" she said, handing me the cookies. They slid around on the paper plate. There seemed to be only a few of them.

"Yes, I think we do. Come into the kitchen."

"This is a rental house, isn't it?" she said. "Very nice. I've looked through the fence. Of course, today that wouldn't be any problem, would it? My husband says the hole reminds him of *Ghostbusters*."

"We rent from a couple in Vero Beach."

"How would you feel about a cute kitten?" she asked, changing the subject.

"We don't have any pets. It would make it too difficult to travel," I said.

"Without ice, please," she said.

I poured the Coke into a glass. I poured some Perrier into a glass for myself.

"Father has taken one of the kittens," she said. "My husband's dentist might take one for his daughter. One way or another, I have to find people."

"An ad in the paper?" I suggested.

"He already drowned four. My husband, I mean. He said that regardless of what Father said, the cat was as much his as mine, and what he wanted to do with his four kittens was drown them." She cleared her throat. I moved toward the front porch. She followed. "Of my four, one has been spoken for, and there's a chance the dentist might take another."

I nodded.

"You wouldn't take one?" she said.

"I really can't, Mrs. Nestor. My husband and I travel a lot. It's very difficult to find places that will—."

"You can sneak them in," she said.

"Mrs. Nestor, I'm really not going to take one of the kittens. I realize you would like me to do that. But I'm not going to be able to."

"The Minichiellos are heartbroken about the parrot," she said. "They haven't heard about any sightings of it. They had that bird for years. They think it will die."

"That would be a shame," I said.

"I asked them to take a kitten, but she doesn't feel a kitten is a good replacement for a parrot that could count to fifteen. It always said good morning to her. She's heartbroken."

"I can understand that," I said.

"Father put up a note on the church bulletin board. It's been up for a week," she said. She had never taken off her black sunglasses. She had pushed the hat back on her head. She had drained her glass. She said: "The mother cat was upset he'd drowned the kittens. She knew it was him. She peed in his hammock."

"Perhaps we can talk another time," I said. "I have some things I need to do before it gets any later."

"Housework," she said.

"Errands," I said.

"If on your errands you think someone might be interested in a kitten, could I give you our phone number?"

"Absolutely," I said.

"We're in the book, but people are too lazy to look. You'd have to give the number to them," she said.

"Let me get a piece of paper," I said.

"And a pen," she said.

I went into the kitchen, forcing myself to be patient. Soon she would be gone.

"I was a lapsed Catholic," she said. "I regret those years away from the church."

"Just jot down your phone number," I said. "And thank you for the cookies."

"Do you think there's any chance you'll change your mind?" she said.

"No," I said.

"Because if you do, you could call over the fence. Or just walk through the broken part and let me know."

"I won't change my mind," I said.

She put her face in her hands and began to cry, using the piece of paper she'd written her number on as a tissue. "Nobody ever changes their mind," she said. "My husband hasn't changed his mind once in forty years. He said he hated cats when we got married. I gave away my cat. Then when we moved to Florida a cat followed me home one day and I thought he'd change his mind, because it was such a pretty cat. But he didn't change his mind about that cat or about any of the others. For forty years, he's drowned kittens. What do they say? 'Always a bridesmaid, never a bride.' With me, it's always a cat, never any kittens." She wiped tears from her eyes. She said: "I agreed with that woman who was screaming the other night. She came here to give us a message, do you realize that? She was sent from on high with a message. It's true: no one protecting anyone else. It's my right to have kittens if I want them, but would anyone protect my rights? Nobody would. Father says give away the kittens because my husband will drown them. I don't even know if they're alive now. I could go home and find them all in a bucket."

"Mrs. Nestor," I said, "this is not anything I can help you with. Do you understand?"

"You're a monster," she said. "Some people aren't cat people, they're dog people. I can understand that. But you—you're just selfish. You just want to travel. It's what that woman said. That woman was an angel, who'd come to speak to you. Did you hear her say that you were the idle rich? You are. You and your husband are monsters. You have friends who go on rampages, and you turn them loose like wild beasts, like other people's yards were the jungle. My plants were all pulled up. The same day he drowned the kittens, my whole yard was destroyed. You are horrible, violent, selfish people. I never want to see you again."

"That's wonderful," I said. "All you'll have to do is leave, then."

"Where can I find that angel?" Mrs. Nestor said.

"Cleaning rooms at the Hyatt, as a matter of fact. Go home and call the Hyatt and ask to speak to the angel Daphne Rupert. She works the afternoon shift. You can reach her."

Which she did, and here is what followed: Daphne exited a recently cleaned room, having no idea Eugenie Nestor was the one who had left three kittens in an Easter basket with a towel draped over the handle. It was there, wedged between the miniature shampoos and the rolls of toilet paper: a purple and pink wicker basket with three kittens curled inside. She took it to the manager's office, and the manager of course couldn't understand it, except that she knew a dirty trick had been played on the hotel. Daphne felt there was some suspicion that she knew more than she did—that perhaps they were even *her* kittens, which she was trying to foist off on the Hyatt. Well: thank god it was not a baby; they had all agreed on that. Really, it could have been much worse if a baby had been abandoned on the cleaning cart. The whole episode upset Daphne so much she blurted out the whole story to Andy, who had given her an extra two hours pay for the trauma she had undergone and who was therefore now back in her good graces, painting her floating in the pool in a new bikini he had reimbursed her for—a rather nice little blue and white checked cotton suit. He was able to be amazed, and to listen sympathetically, because I had told him nothing about Eugenie Nestor's visit. He'd been teaching at the community college, and when he came home I was on the phone, and by the time I was off, Daphne was in place in the pool, and I could hear, through the open window, that she was telling him a story that wasn't all that surprising to me. She thought something had been fated, though she barely understood what. Just a sense she had, she told Andy: first the cat jumping in the pool and circling, circling. Then, coming out of a room and seeing something on top of her cart that turned out to be kittens. She was no kitten lover, but one of the cooks at the hotel had taken a fancy to one of them, and the manager had taken the other two to her vet, who had agreed to try for a week to place them, before turning them over to the animal shelter. On and on Daphne went, about how peculiar she found life in Key West. "I want to go to Tortola next year instead of coming here," I heard Andy say wearily. The fence had been repaired by the gardener, who was very handy. Things were again calm at the home of Eugenie and Old Nestor. He was probably in his hammock, the orange cat having forgiven him—where else was she going to live?—curled in his lap. Eugenie was probably in the kitchen, baking another three (if it turned out to be only three) cookies. I thought about the many places Andy and I had travelled during our marriage, and how many of those places had seemed magical, for a while. Key West lasted longer than most: the Atlantic breezes, the lush foliage, the amazing light that Andy captured so well, painting paintings that sold at the New York gallery that represented him for enough money that by ordinary standards, we really had become the idle rich.

As I mulled over our good fortune, Lem passed by, driving the

Conch Train. Once again, as he sped by, I caught the tail end of a joke dissipating in the breeze, like the string of a kite blowing quickly out of reach. I opened the front door and stood on the porch, looking at the bougainvillea spilling off a balcony across the way. Then I looked at the two young men skating in sync, with their arms around each other, their bodies toned and tanned. Key West was a place that encouraged people to be childish, and I found that atypical, and delightful.

I was startled from my reverie when the Minichiellos' parrot began its count-down from the royal palm in the front yard. It was there! It had returned—or at least it taunted with the possibility of its return. It looked well, and seemed to be enjoying its freedom. Counting "one, two, three," it spoke looking directly at me, and then—though I may have seen too many Walt Disney movies—I would swear that it winked. The moment it said, "fifteen" it flew away, having a more distinct idea than most of us when it should leave and perhaps even where it should fly.

Frederick Busch

Manhattans

He drove though he wasn't supposed to. According to the tiny print of the pamphlet that came with his medications, he must not operate heavy machinery or drive a car. He steered in the passing lane before his courage failed and he wobbled back to the right and slowed to forty-five.

"I'll get better," he had promised his wife, sick with his conviction that his sickness was the only truth and health was a lie.

"But I might not," she'd said. She had said it flatly and evenly, as it she was telling the time.

He understood her anger, he thought. She had spoken to him, before leaving, in the sorrow of her understanding that nothing was left for her but leaving him. If she didn't, she would have to face him during all the hours of every day of the weeks of his medical leave of absence—it would never be long enough—and even Green himself knew the bleakness of the prospect of living with him. He found it impossible to live with himself, he thought, speeding up, then slowing down, blinking in the bright, watery light that poured around trees and over the face of an iron-stained high, white cliff at the side of Route 17, a hundred miles from his city. New York. Was that thought, about not being able to live with himself, a thought about not living at all? Was he talking to himself about suicide? He didn't much care, he thought, and he knew that such considerations might be called ominous, though disguised in something like unpleasant, or a warning shot, let's call it, by Marcy Bellochio, his therapist. Dr. Xin, who wrote his prescriptions, didn't speak English well enough to suggest synonyms. He would call a suicide just that.

Bess, his wife, was angry at his disorderly disease—angry at him for giving in to the illness and angry at herself for failing to understand that he hadn't chosen to suffer it. And she knew it, he knew. Still, something in her fury at him, which left her trembling at times as hard as he always did, suggested to him that maybe a broken segment of his character had made him get sick, or had kept him entangled in what he thought of as its thousands of tiny branches that grew through his body and couldn't be torn away unless the body were torn apart.

They'd been right to marry, he thought, speeding up. They'd always understood each other, even now, while her energy for sustaining the knowledge, the plain bad news, ran out.

Tearing the body apart to root it out would be classified by Marcy Bellochio, he knew, as a suicidal ideation.

"We'll have none of that," he instructed the car, slowing it at an exit that he thought he remembered and driving, according to the rental-car dashboard compass, due north. "Let's really try and have none of that."

He passed a diner and thought of hot coffee with a lot of sugar and milk. He saw his hands shake as he gripped the cup with both of them. He saw the coffee spill, the mess of sugar crystals and milk drops and dark tan coffee stains on the napkins he would wetly wad as he scrubbed at his paper placemat.

He said, "Let's try having none."

At first, Bess called them The Shakes. Then, when she understood that calling it A Case of The Shakes suggested that sometimes he didn't suffer them, she stopped referring to them at all. "It's a side effect," he'd told her, although she knew it was, and he knew that she did. "Pharmacological side effects may include sexual dysfunction, palsied trembling, and being unable to gauge the distance between the self and the world or the pain inflicted on the world by the presence of the self. It's the price one pays for ingesting psychotropics in what I think we could call large quantities."

"I think we could call them frighteningly large quantities," she said. "It's part of the treatment, though. I say treatment because I suppose we shouldn't call it the cure, there apparently not being one."

"My trembles and the little dysfunction business and your tears."

"Never mind my tears, thank you."

"And never mind my trembles or the other," he said.

She smiled a broad, false smile that made her lean, patrician face look cruel, and she said, "There. Haven't we managed our little crisis?"

He remembered that while they parried, he had very powerfully felt that he might start to cry. It wasn't until she had left the room, turning to walk away as if she'd suddenly been frightened, that he wiped at his cheeks and felt the moisture of his tears.

It would be best to be strong and resolute and comforting by the time he got there, he thought. Jerry and Nancy Stradling were old people in a cul-de-sac of distress, whereas Green was only middle-aged, merely rocked breathless, from time to time, by sorrow. Everyone in the world gets sorrow, he knew. You hadn't a right to complain when you did. But distress, he thought, was another matter. Distress was a complaint of a higher order. The Stradlings were very old people alone in the world except for others like themselves in their circle. By now, it had to be the smallest of circles. He imagined drawing it on the sand of a hot Rhode Island beach, or in chalk on the cloudy, gray board of a Fordham Law School classroom, or with a brush dipped in whitewash on the liver-colored stone of a three-story town house around the corner from lower Fifth Avenue. It would be closer to a big dot than a circle. The old couple's son lived in Europe, and he flew from Brussels to New York and drove this same route up to them in a rented car whenever he could. Jerry Stradling's partners were dead, and his remaining associates in the Syracuse firm conducted a cold, lucrative legal practice that had nothing to do with his former clients or him; at Christmastime, the firm sent a basket of cheeses out in a van, Nancy had told him. She had also told him that her sister sometimes visited, but she was as old as Nancy and Jerry, and she had to be driven from Concord, Massachusetts by her daughter, who seemed not to have too much time for her mother, much less her ancient uncle and aunt.

That apparently left Green as the one to call, and as he drove under the dwindling flare of dusk he imagined a little circle inside of which was a doodle resembling his face. He had been a summer intern for Jerome Stradling several decades before, and then for nearly six years he had practiced law as a junior colleague while learning what Jerry could teach him about pleading in the Second District of the federal bench and the New York State Supreme Court. Jerry was a gent, a cordial maverick, a slick litigator, and an accomplished scholar of the law. In the office, he'd worn excellent Donegal tweed sport coats with slacks of bright primary colors such as golfers wore on the links. In court, he wore rich sharkskin suits with muted stripes and neckties that cost a hundred dollars each.

His little moustache had sat heavily on a mouth that frowned more often than it smiled, and that rarely was still. His nose was hawkish, his forehead high, his body broad. He was a decorated naval officer who had served on destroyers in World War II, and in the long winters so common to this part of the state, he liked to talk about some weather making, and how they might see a little action on the deck. Now, backed into the last available corner of his old age, Jerry was alone with Nancy, once a great giver of dinner parties and cocktail parties and even high teas—cucumber sandwiches on homemade bread, Green remembered, and slices of salty Southern ham and real scones, butter-cream layer cakes. She had been rumored to have been a debutante in Rochester, New York. She had been a fine skier, trained by professionals after World War II. She could sit much of the day without complaint in a duck blind and bring down more than most of the men who shot with her. It was Nancy who had telephoned after so many years of silence between them to say, "Can you come for a weekend visit, Jim? Well. It's actually—could you come up here and lend us a hand?"

The Stradlings' house was 200 miles from New York City. He felt as if he'd come a thousand. He was probably the fifth or even tenth she had called, Green thought. He could imagine her sitting with their very old book of telephone numbers and addresses, many of them perhaps crossed out. He couldn't bring himself to efface the names and numbers of the dead who had begun to accumulate in his life. He saw it as a coming on, a kind of dusk, an ashen light that would grow dull and then dim and then dark. As if he were not giving in to the failing light, he kept the names of friends and acquaintances who had died. Their telephone numbers were there to consult among the numbers of those who had greeted him with pleasure when he called. But he didn't call them anymore, and he suspected that they wouldn't be smiling at the sound of his voice if he did. And Nancy, hearing reason after reason for the failure of their past to assist them, had at last come upon his name and had called him for help.

They had exchanged holiday greetings every year. They hadn't spoken since he'd left to practice in New York City. But you have to say yes when they call, Green thought, because when you stop responding to something like that, you're controlled by the darkness. It owns you. All you have a right to expect, after not saying yes when they call, is the purchase of a newspaper every day, and a meal if you can keep it down, and the medication, and then television with everyone laughing, and nights of not sleeping followed by what is sometimes called the light of day but which Green and others knew was darkness with its name changed.

Although it was spring, the low-ceilinged Colonial house was cold. Nancy Stradling wore a man's bulky gray cardigan over a dark blue polka-dotted dress. She greeted him with a smile that appeared to raise each crease of her seamed, small face. Her hair was thick and silky, purely white and twisted into a bun. He remembered it as a shade of light chestnut, or maybe even a honey blonde. She was proud of it, he could tell, because she drew the eye to it with a filigreed silver pin bearing small garnets that protruded from the bun and caught the light. As soon as she let go of his hands, he stuck them in his trouser pockets and followed her to the kitchen, where she insisted on his drinking a cup of coffee.

"I forget how you take your coffee," she said. "Of course, some days, I forget how I take mine."

"It's been a good many years, Mrs. Stradling."

"Oh, you call me Nancy, for heaven's sake, Bill."

"It's Jim."

"Jim. God. Jim! Of course. Forgive me. Tell me the truth, now. Do you think the house has grown shabby after all these years?"

"Well, no, actually. No. It's always been lovely. I remember wanting to live in a house like yours—when I was working for Jerry, in the early days. I even insisted that we buy a table like this one. Curly maple, right? I remember you telling me it was curly maple at, I think it was, one of your parties. Maybe at some Christmastime."

"And did your wife agree when you insisted? She's called—"

"Bess."

"Perhaps next time she can come with you."

He smiled. He had to look away from what her face did when he tried to smile. "Maybe so," he said. "Jerry's pretty low these days?"

"If he were any lower," she said, carrying the coffee to him in the dim chilliness of the narrow kitchen with its unlighted wood stove and windows with crazed panes that made the daylight look smeared, "he'd be flat on his back." She set the coffee before him. "Of course, he is on his back. Oh, he's very pleased that you're coming. He'll be up and about later. I wouldn't be able to keep him from dressing smartly and greeting you. Later on, he'll be out."

"Nancy, you said you needed a hand."

"I did?"

"Over the phone. You asked if I could come here and give you a hand. Is there a specific problem? You know, something concrete I could tackle for you?"

Sitting in the junction made by the side of the table and the kitchen wall, she opened her hand to reveal some small silver spoons that were tarnished nearly black. "You must remember these," she said.

He didn't. He nodded and smiled, and Nancy looked away.

"Would you like the one celebrating the Erie Canal, the lovely Stuttgart, the—ah!—the Cipriani in Venice, and this is Mexico, this is Taos, and here's Niagara-by-the-Lake. We've collected dozens. Pick whichever one you want."

Suddenly, he did remember them, from an evening's cocktails, with Jerry very carefully measuring out small shots of bourbon for what he called highballs, though he served them in low glasses, and excessive portions of vermouth for weak martinis on the rocks. He recalled candles scented with vanilla and someone playing "Moonlight in Vermont" on the huge, Victorian upright piano in the front sitting room, as he now remembered their calling it. He remembered his broad pleasure, Green recalled, as he'd thought that night of the woman who was flying in to wait for him at the Hotel Syracuse: Bess, he said to himself as his stomach twisted and his face felt filled by a surging of blood. It had been their first hotel together at the start of what was a very short courtship and a marriage that had lasted at least a year too long for her. And he had come to the senior partner's party without her because her plane was arriving late and because he knew how little she would want to be among the braided rugs and old, dark furniture inherited by Jerry from his mother in Kansas, and the worried junior lawyers, and of course the polished commemorative spoons arrayed beside the glasses for stirring drinks. He remembered how Stradling and his wife had made them select a souvenir spoon that then was served protruding from their drink. Perhaps he was inventing it, he thought, his recollection of the young lawyers standing and sipping with one hand while holding with the other a purposeless, shiny, small spoon.

He paddled tiny circles through his coffee with Niagara-by-the-Lake and lifted his cup with both hands. She had the grace to turn her attention to her cup while he tried to drink from his.

"The firm frowned on our living here, you know."

"No, I never did. Of course, the junior associates only speculated about the senior partners. We called them The Gods."

"I had heard that," she said. "Look at us. Some gods."

"But why? The frowning, I mean."

"They wanted all of him they could get, and that included time spent in commuting. The partners found it difficult to understand that it was his therapy—the cars, I mean, and the drive. It cleared his mind."

"Good cars," he said. "I remember that now: excellent machines."

"The Studebaker Silver Hawk," she said. "And the little Spitfire. And the Jaguar, of course. He always complained about the carburetion in the Jag. But he adored the Hawk. And now we aren't allowed to drive. We can't. But we kept a little white Ford, very bland, and I can get us around by going slowly. It's not so easy in winter, you remember our icy roads. I'm not supposed to operate a car. But you have to live."

He felt himself about to argue with the proposition that living was imperative, and he said, "But Jerry would let himself relax when he drove, you're saying? It would clear his mind?"

"Exactly. He remembered you as being sympathetic, he said. And there you are. You can put yourself in the other fellow's shoes."

"Shoes are easy," he said. "But about my being useful to Jerry and you. . . ."

She cocked her head and took a noisy breath. She said, "It gets very hard."

"Yes."

"Aging. Illness. He's quite ill."

"Yes."

"And that gets hard."

"Yes, it must."

"I'm as healthy as a dray horse," she said, laughing without any apparent pleasure. "I have normal cholesterol and my blood pressure's rather good for someone my age. All my tests are always rather good. And poor Jerry, the military hero. He's the one who crossed the North Atlantic four times on a World War I–vintage tin can. He's the one who was always splitting wood and mowing the lawn, for gosh sakes, with a hand-powered mower. He's the one people used to call on to help them take up tree stumps in the town, or put together a pipework scaffolding to lay down a roof. He hasn't barely got a pulse some days, Jim. His blood pressure's so low. It's affecting the—well—"

She turned away as if to look at someone seated beside her. She shook her head, then faced him again.

"All that's left is indignity," she said. "The best of it's frustrating, or embarrassing, and the worst of it's as bad a humiliation—an affliction, I'm tempted to call it—as you could imagine. He can't see very much at all. He can't read anymore. It affects his brain, I think. I don't mean the memory. That's gone most days, or going, though he still remembers events from the office or the court room. So that's that. But his reasoning. He was the most sensible man, wasn't he?"

"A good lawyer's as analytic as a chemist—as an accountant. Even his feelings have to be mostly cold thought. Or so his wife would say." He barked a laugh too loudly, and she recoiled.

She moved her cup away and clasped her hands on the table before her. She said, "He isn't thinking well. I wondered if someone from the old days, coming into the house, into his mind, I suppose I mean, might jolt him. Do you know? That kind of jolt you sometimes can get from the past? Even when you might not be remembering well? Do you and your Bess have children, Jim? I should have asked you right away."

"We have a son and a daughter, yes."

"And where are they?"

"One's in the Army and the other is either a partner in a dot-com in Eugene, Oregon, or he's on unemployment, we aren't sure which because neither is he."

"So your girl's the soldier. It's a new world."

"Sarabeth is a captain. She flies helicopters in frightening places. Like her mother, she is very brave."

"How wonderful for you."

"Yes," he said, "it's wonderful."

"And do you think I was right to ask you all the way up here from Manhattan?"

"Right?"

"The jolt," she said. "Like the—you know. Oh, what's it called? Electric shock, for crazy people? It's supposed to bring them to their senses, or something. Do you know?"

"Electroconvulsive therapy," he said. "It's called ECT."

"The little jolt," she said.

"The little jolt. I believe it's thought of as the last resort for certain patients."

"Is it really? I'm afraid I know nothing about it."

He said, "I know about the jolt is all."

"Yes," she said. "And do you think we might try that with Jerry?"

He saw himself leaping from behind a curtain with his arms outspread, providing the sudden little jolt. He saw Jerry, in liver-colored Donegal tweed jacket paired up with lime green golf slacks, standing still, paralyzed with terror, then going pale, then falling to the hardwood floor with his heart stopped.

"Maybe telling him first that I'm here."

"Yes," she said. "Of course. He knows that already."

"Then maybe a gentle, small prod more than a jolt."

"I knew you'd know what's best," she said.

"You did?"

"Well, of course, Jim." They nodded like the little figures on an old German clock who spring out to chase each other when the hour tolls. "That's why I called you up," she said. And then, as if it had been the topic of conversation all along, Nancy asked him, "Do you have photographs of you and your Bess at your wedding?"

"I think we do," he said. "Yes. I think we have a scrapbook's-worth, a lot of them. We never look at them," he said. "Like most people, I suppose."

"Not us," she said in a flat, hard voice. "Not us. We were married by one of Jerry's professors, a philosophy teacher at Lehigh. He was a Lutheran pastor and because I was Catholic and Jerry was a rather exotic species of Baptist, the teacher was our way of bridging the gap. A Christian, but not a sectarian, marriage, I suppose you would call it. We were very independent, and no one in his family knew about marriages. That is, the planning, you know, and catering and all of that. My people, if we'd have let them, they'd have taken it over and staged a quiet little affair with the Rockettes and the Notre Dame marching band. So we just drove out to the professor's farmhouse, near Easton, and we got married. Well, we had set the date, mind you. We had an appointment with the professor, we didn't just show up. But it was more or less 'Hello, let's have the wedding, now you're married, congratulations, good-bye.' His wife was very unhappy. She was our witness. I mean, I think they were unhappy together. At first, I was frightened that it was an omen for us. But we did pretty well for a very long time. I can't complain about that. It's the pictures."

"Pictures of you and Jerry at your wedding."

"We don't have any. The unhappy wife never thought to take them. I never thought to ask for them. Maybe she enjoyed knowing that some day we'd want them and there wouldn't be any. Maybe that was the omen part of the ominousness that I felt. She was all pale and doughy and slope-shouldered and quiet, and she frightened me. She had a wen or some sort of thick, fleshy protrusion under her lower lip. She never said a word. She didn't even say 'Congratulations.' She never hugged either of us. She shook my hand. Her hand was as cold as a stone from the river. And now there isn't a picture of us from the day we were married. It's as if the day didn't happen. Of course, it did, and I know it. But I would love a little proof. You and Jerry understand proof. It's what you deal in."

"You make me want to drive home and look at our photos and feel lucky," he lied.

"You do that. Don't rush off, of course. But count your blessings."

"I will," he said. "I do."

"Good," she said, "because you've a sad expression etched into your face, Jim."

"That's what my mother always warned me," he said.

She laughed, and she was a little bit of a pretty girl. " 'Make that face too much, and your face will freeze that way.' God. Didn't they all tell all of us that?"

"And all of them were right," he said.

She nodded, and he nodded back. He thought again of the dark, high wooden clocks in Europe when, as the hour was struck, the figures chased other figures in jerky motions across the base of the broad, white dial. It was often someone wielding a scythe in pursuit of maidens, he thought he recalled.

While Nancy went in to Jerry, Green walked, on his toes, like an intruder, through the front of the house—the living room that led to the foyer that led to the sitting room with its piano and its broad bureau that they used as the sideboard for drinks. The living room was furnished with comfortable chairs and deep sofas, and the walls were dressed with paintings by artists Green had never heard of.

The pictures were mostly of snowy scenes, although there was one portrait that bore a likeness to what Jerry looked like thirty years before. In the sitting room the furniture was dense, more black than brown, heavily worked—the worst of proud Victorian decoration—and the walls were hung with murky prints. On the sideboard were bottles and glasses and, of course, more small commemorative spoons. In the back of the sitting room on the wall was hung a plaque that celebrated Jerome Stradling for his selfless service to the Bar Association of Central New York. Beside it was a photo, in a hardware-store frame, of a smiling, athletic young Nancy Stradling in a strapless gown who held the arm of Jerry, in his late twenties, who was wearing a dress shirt and cummerbund with his tie undone, his eyes a little glazed with drink, Green assumed, and the two of them about to take possession of a lot of the known world.

He went quietly back to the kitchen to drink cooled coffee. He slopped some over the side of the cup and onto the floor. He was mopping it with a paper napkin when she brought Jerry in. He had shrunk in height and breadth and had become her size, Green thought, and he wobbled a little from side to side as he moved forward. His face was bony and pale, and his nose seemed all the more like a beak. It was naked-looking, and Green took a minute to understand that the bristly moustache was gone. The waxy skin around the nose was blooming small suppurations, some of which had formed red-and-white scabs. His light blue eyes looked clear, though his vision was nearly gone. He gripped Nancy's upper arm and appeared, at first, to be looking directly at Green. But he didn't see much, Green thought, because he focused on the space between them, no matter how close he came, until they were nearly toe-to-toe.

Jerry stuck his small hand before him and said, in a slightly hoarse voice that had little of the baritone resonance Green remembered, "Bill!"

"It's Jim," Nancy said.

Stradling leaned his head back, as if trying to remember something. Then he said, "Of course. Of course, it's Jim. You must forgive me."

"I'm happy to see you, Jerry. Any name you want to use is fine."

"You're as elegant as ever," Stradling said, smiling uncertainly.

He looked like an ancient child who made an appearance at the grownups' party. He was dressed in pale yellow golf slacks tightened high on the waist by a brown leather belt. The pants hung loosely about his legs and broke in a puddle over his black-and-red checked cloth bedroom slippers. His corduroy shirt was a dark olive green worn with a loosely-knotted golden silk tie such as Jerry might have worn to court forty years before. Green felt a surge of affection for her effort to dress Jerry as he might have dressed himself.

They sat in the kitchen, Jerry at the head of the maple table, where Nancy served him Postum while she reheated their coffee. "Perhaps you'd care to tell us about your practice," Jerry said, looking to Green's left. Green moved in that direction and Jerry said, "My eyes, as you can tell, have suffered. I'm not blind. I am debilitated. But of course you can see just fine, so you see that for yourself. Jim, why is it that I am tempted, steadily, to call you Bill?"

Green knew. It was because Nancy must have told him that she was phoning up Billy Grossman, who overlapped with Green for three or four years before Green left to work at the firm on Pine Street in lower Manhattan.

"A lot of people have told me I look like a Bill."

Nancy said, "But not a counterfeit bill. Nor a two-dollar bill. Nor a bill of lading?"

"You do crossword puzzles," Green said.

"I do," she said with pleasure. "You're a canny lawyer, aren't you?"

"I do them too," he said. "On the subway, coming down from our apartment, going to work."

" 'Six-letter word for a sixteenth-century lunatic Spanish ruler?' " she said, giggling. "Joanna. She was known as Joanna the Mad. I love any kind of game."

"It's the word part that I like," Green said, or would have, when Jerry cut in by saying angrily, "I enjoyed the billing letters. I itemized everything to the tenth of an hour. I included the sharpening of pencils, the steeping of a pot of tea. I dared them to object. And there was somebody, always, who did. Those were the conversations I enjoyed. 'I just kept you from a whopping fine for tortuous interference, you maladroit boat jumper, and you quibble with me over tea leaves?' I used to have the girl make them with an infuser. We brewed first-rate tea that I sent her to buy over on Townsend Avenue. She had to scald the pot and use a cozy that Nancy purchased in Harrod's. And they paid for the leaves, for the water to pour on them, and for the breath the girl expelled when she poured it into good china cups."

They sat in silence.

"That was an outburst, I'd say," Nancy announced. "What got into you, Jerome Stradling?"

"Some things need to be said," he told her.

She looked at Green. "But what I really want to know," she said, "is what in heaven's name is a—what was it? A boat jumper. What's that?"

Jerry raised the fingers of each hand, one after the other, and held them against the table. "What's that? Ten? A ten-letter word for an illegal immigrant," he said. "You're welcome to make whatever use of it you wish."

Green noted how steady Stradling's hands and fingers seemed, and how he did not spill his Postum when he sipped it. The table in front of Green was spotted with sugar and coffee and milk. He saw Nancy notice it and he placed his hands in his lap.

"His wife's name is Bess," Nancy said to Jerry. "Did you ever meet her?"

"I regret that I did not," he said. "Not having met Bill, I could hardly have encountered his wife, given the unfolding of circumstances."

"Jim," she reminded him.

Stradling nodded and stared off. Green suspected that Nancy would be thinking that now, as Jerry wore out after a few minutes of conversation, now Green ought to deliver the little jolt for which she had made him responsible. It was almost five o'clock, and he thought of taking his medication while they watched and then excusing himself to go upstairs to nap. He hadn't slept for many hours of the past three days. When you've spent a good number of hours of the night in not sleeping, and you walk without purpose through your apartment to pause, finally, at a window, and you look at the city at night from eight stories up, and you wait—you're waiting, by then, for anything at all to approach through the thick nothing that wraps you—you begin to feel the pressure one remove from you in the air above New York. You sense the chill, you hear engine noises thinned to tinny rattles, and you see the lighted windows of office suites and apartments, the dampered intensity of distant lives nearby.

Then, let's say, you lie down again to close your eyes again and try. Your head is filled with the lights you saw against the nighttime sky, but now it's a different New York City that's inside you. After a while, instead of seeing bright, rectangular windows pulsing on the dark buildings framed against the dark sky, you're teeming with fragments of conversation and scraps of ideas and small shreds of image you can barely identify before they leave your head to be replaced by frightening pictures, whole sentences spoken to you years before by forgotten speakers. For people who cannot sleep at night for many nights, this other city is what you have instead of nightmares.

Even now, at this table in the kitchen lit by smeared, declining light, he heard his wife say as he had heard her say during so many of his hours of not sleeping, "Sure, it could be your mother's death. It could be your father dying eight years before her. It could be my father, or because we never got a dog and the—the undogginess just hit home. Maybe it's our daughter living like a man and our son is living like some over-privileged boy. Just because you give it a name, just because you name something, doesn't mean you know it. I don't care what it is. Call it whatever you want to, you know? But how selfish can I be? How unfeeling can I be after you've been living in hell for a year, for more than a year? Right? I am so sorry. I am. I really am. But I want you to just not be like this. Jimmy, get us back our life!"

"Jim," Stradling said.

"Sir?" he said.

"You argued the Oneida Board of Education matter, didn't you? Before the state appellate?"

"What an excellent memory you have," Green said. "Yes. I did. I won."

"I remember the victory. The head of the board actually kissed me on the cheek. He was that relieved. He smelled, I remember, of cheap deodorant. I ordered in chilled champagne from Liquor Square. It cost us a pretty penny. But then we delivered the bill. And they paid, of course. And we had our pretty penny back. So you can see that my mind is unaffected by the advance of—what would you call it?"

"I wouldn't," he said, waiting for Nancy to rescue him.

"Your complaint," she said.

"My complaint," Stradling said. "My broken-down heart. The heart isn't sad," he said, "but it doesn't pound away as sturdily as it used to. And of course there's the eyesight problem."

"But he sees well in his mind," Nancy said to Green.

"Try a—" Stradling counted his fingers. "Try a nine-letter word for hectoring blabbermouth," he said.

"Jerry!"

"Termagant," he said. "Seeing well in the mind, my Irish ass."

And so much for the little jolt, Green thought.

"I'm going to put the stew on," said Nancy. "It's a daube, actually, a stew of lamb that's been flavored with white wine, although one would drink some light-bodied red with the meal. We'll have to see what bottles are out in the pantry. I always prepare this meal in advance to let the flavors marry. It's a jolly springtime dish. I'm going to add some green peas, and it already has pearl onions and carrots. So I'll get to that, Jim, if you'll make us our highballs? Do you remember where the liquor is?"

Stradling said, "How many guests did you invite?" His nostrils were white and flared. The eruptions around his nose seemed to darken. His bony face seemed even more drawn. He said, "Gatherings and gatherings, with our backs still against the wall from the *last* time you invited so many strangers in."

"Jerry Stradling, you will lie down before dinner, even if it's only for a minute or two," Nancy said.

"I suppose I ought to. I suppose I will. Otherwise she'll knock me down is what she'll be telling me next. You remember." Then he said to Nancy, "Does he remember what drinks we want?"

She said, "I'm sure he does. He *knows* us, Jerry."

She looked at Green as if now, at last, he could deliver the necessary jolt. But then she turned to Stradling and moved him out of the kitchen. He went obediently, wobbling. Green took a tray of ice cubes from the freezer compartment of the refrigerator and went along to the sitting room to make them their drinks.

He remembered the care, the miserliness, with which Stradling at that party given so many years before had measured the shot of liquor he'd put in each drink. As if retaliating, Green dropped ice cubes into heavy, cut-crystal glasses and carelessly poured plenty of bar-whisky bourbon into cheap sweet vermouth that looked and smelled like Mercurochrome. Green doubted that Jerry Stradling was supposed to drink liquor any more than he was. He used the same spoon—from a hotel in British Columbia—to stir each drink. Then he worked at opening a crusted, small bottle of maraschino cherries. He used the British Columbia spoon to place a cherry in every drink. He had to use his fingers to pick up two that his shaking spoon had let fall to the surface of the sideboard. He ate them both and then found purple-and-gold paper cocktail napkins in the first drawer he opened. He used a napkin to wipe his fingers and then to scrub the cherry syrup from the sideboard. He wanted to telephone his wife. He knew he made her sad. But he wondered whether she was as miserable without him as she'd been in their life together. He was afraid that she felt too much better away from him. He had a real malady, he knew, but to his wife he *was* the disease. He would have loved her to tell him otherwise, but he wouldn't ask. Even he, because he loved her and sometimes could remember that he did, would prescribe for her a life without him. He sucked at his sticky fingers like a child.

"Ladies and gentlemen," Jerry Stradling said.

He stood in the doorway of the sitting room. He moved his head as if surveying a crowd of guests. He smiled with the taut confidence of a capable attorney about to deliver his opening argument. "I want to thank you very much for coming tonight, and I apologize for the delay. If you will be patient a moment longer, my junior colleague will see to your drinks. And I will return to join you shortly." He smiled with no sincerity and said, "If you'll take over from here, Bill?"

Stradling nodded to no one with great courtesy, then turned in the doorway and, pushing at the door frame as if to launch himself, he lurched lightly down the corridor and out of sight.

Green looked at the empty doorway for a while. Then he took a small oval metal tray from the sideboard. It was decorated with the faded head of a terrier, painted in white and black on a red background. He put the Manhattans on the tray, and then he selected for each drink a spoon that was a forgotten commemoration—the British Columbia for one, an Allentown Fair for another, and a Red Lion in Salisbury, England for the last. Two of the tarnished spoons were stubby and broad, and the third was longer, slimmer, with a narrow, dull brass band around the handle, souvenirs stolen by a healthy, confident young couple who were starting to take their ease in the world. He folded three napkins and set them on the tray, and then he squeezed his trembling fingers around and under its edge. He lifted and wheeled and set off to follow Jerry Stradling down the dark corridor. He knew that he must not spill a drop.

ACKNOWLEDGMENTS

I wish to thank everyone at Georgia State University who has fostered *Five Points* from the beginning: Lauren Adamson, David Blumenfeld, Robert Sattelmeyer, Matthew Roudané, and Carl Patton. I am forever grateful to founding co-editors David Bottoms and Pam Durban for their constant support and faith, and to Sheri Joseph and Beth Gylys, for their talent and friendship, and many thanks to our devoted student editors for all their hard work over the years.

Additional thanks to our Editorial Board Members and Donors, especially Mike Easterly and Anne Deeley Easterly, and Bud Blanton and Karen Vereb, and to our Editorial Consultants Edward Hirsch and Richard Bausch.

To the all of the authors included here, they have made all the difference.

I'm especially grateful to Philip Turner for taking us under his wing.

To Maria Carvainis, my agent and angel, for her tenacity and vision.

And to Michael, Nora, and my family for their daily mercies and love.

ABOUT THE CONTRIBUTORS

RICHARD BAUSCH's novels include *Hello to the Cannibals, The Last Good Time, Mr. Field's Daughter*, and *In the Night Season.* His stories have appeared in numerous anthologies, including Best American Short Stories, O'Henry, and Pushcart, and have won two National Magazine Awards—one for *The New Yorker* and one for *The Atlantic Monthly.* He is the co-editor of *The Norton Anthology of Short Fiction* and the recipient of the Lila Wallace Reader's Digest Writer's Award and the Award in Literature from the American Academy of Arts and Letters.

ANN BEATTIE is the author of seven novels, including *Chilly Scenes of Winter, My Life Starring Dara Falcon,* and *The Doctor's House*, and eight short story collections, most recently *Follies: New Stories*, a collection of nine stories and a novella. Her many honors include the Award in Literature from The American Academy of Arts and Letters, a Guggenheim Fellowship, the PEN/Malamud award for Excellence in Short Fiction, and the 2005 Rea Award for the Short Story. She is the Edgar Allan Poe Professor of Literature and Creative Writing at the University of Virginia.

MADISON SMARTT BELL is the author of twelve novels, including *The Washington Square Ensemble, Waiting for the End of the World, Straight Cut, The Year of Silence, Doctor Sleep, Save Me, Joe Louis, Ten Indians, Master of the Crossroads, Anything Goes, The Stone That The Builder Refused*, and *Soldier's Joy,* which received the Lillian Smith Award in 1989. Bell has also published two collections of short stories: *Zero db* and *Barking Man.* His novel *All Soul's Rising* was a finalist for the 1995 National Book Award, the 1996 PEN/Faulkner Award, and winner of the 1996 Anisfield Wolf award for the best book of the year dealing with matters of race. Since 1984 he has taught in the Goucher College Creative Program, where he is currently Professor of English, and is Director of the Kratz Center for Creative Writing at Goucher College.

FREDERICK BUSCH "wrote poetic novels and stories that delved into the seemingly unspectacular but ultimately profound," as described by the *New York Times.* He received numerous honors and awards, including the National Jewish Book Award in 1984, the American Academy of Arts and Letters Fiction Award in 1986, the PEN/Malamud Prize for achievement in the short story in 1991, and the Award of Merit of the American Academy of Arts and Letters, for "a writer's lifetime achievement," in 2001. In 2001, Busch was elected a Fellow of the Academy of Arts and Sciences.

ROBERT OLEN BUTLER has published ten novels, including *A Good Scent from a Strange Mountain*, which won the 1993 Pulitzer Prize for Fiction. He has received many awards, including a Guggenheim Fellowship in fiction, a National Endowment for the Arts grant, the Richard and Hinda Rosenthal Foundation Award from the American Academy of Arts and Letters, a National Magazine Award in Fiction, and was a finalist for the PEN/Faulkner Award. His stories have appeared widely in such publications as *The New Yorker, Esquire, Harper's*, and have also been chosen for inclusion in four annual editions of *The Best American Short Stories* and seven annual editions of *New Stories from the South*. He is the Francis Eppes Distinguished Professor holding the Michael Shaara Chair in Creative Writing and is Director of the Creative Writing Program at Florida State University in Tallahassee, Florida.

ALICE ELLIOTT DARK is the author of the short story collection *Naked to the Waist*, and has been published in numerous literary magazines and anthologies. Her short story "In the Gloaming" was recently adapted into an HBO film starring Glen Close and Robert Sean Leonard, and was included in the *New Yorker* collection of love stories titled *Nothing But You*. Her writing has appeared in *Harper's, DoubleTake, The New Yorker*, and in many anthologies, including *Prize Stories: The O. Henry Awards* and *The Best American Short Stories of the Century*.

PETER HO DAVIES's short fiction is widely anthologized, including selections for *Prize Stories: The O. Henry Awards* (1998) and *Best American Short Stories* (1995, 1996, and 2001). His own first published collection of short stories was *The Ugliest House in the World* (1998), which won the PEN/Macmillan Silver Pen Award and the Mail on Sunday/John Llewellyn Rhys Prize. His second collection, *Equal Love*, was published in 2000. He is a recipient of fellowships from the National Endowment for the Arts and the Fine Arts Work Center in Provincetown. In 2003, he was named by *Granta* magazine as one of twenty "Best of Young British Novelists."

MICHAEL DOWNS teaches journalism at the University of Montana. His short fiction has appeared in *The Gettysburg Review, The Georgia Review, Michigan Quarterly Review, Witness*, and other literary reviews. He was born in Hartford, Connecticut, where he sets all his stories.

PAM DURBAN has written several highly acclaimed short story collections and novels, including *All Set About with Fever Trees and Other Stories* (1985), *The Laughing Place* (1993), and *So Far Back* (2000). She has received numerous literary awards and honors, including a fellowship from the National Endowment for the Arts, a Lillian Smith Award, the Rinehart Award in Fiction Writing, and a Whiting Writer's Award. She is a founding co-editor of *Five Points* and is currently the Doris Betts Distinguished Professor of Creative Writing at the University of North Carolina at Chapel Hill.

LESLIE EPSTEIN has published nine books of fiction, including *P.D. Kimerakov, The Steinway Quintet Plus Four, King of the Jews, Regina, Goldkorn Tales, Pinto and Sons, Pandaemonium, Ice Fire Water: A Leib Goldkorn Cocktail,* and, most recently, *San Remo Drive*. In addition to the Rhodes Scholarship, he has received a Fulbright and a Guggenheim fellowship, an award for Distinction in Literature from the American Academy and Institute of Arts and Letters, a residency at the Rockefeller Institute at Bellagio, and grants from the Ingram Merrill Foundation and the National Endowment for the Arts. He has been the director of the Creative Writing Program at Boston University for more than twenty years.

STEPHEN GIBSON is author of a poetry collection, *Rorschach Art* (2001), as well as the story collection *The Persistence of Memory,* a finalist for the Flannery O'Connor Award and the Spokane Prize. His work can also be found in *Epoch, McSweeney's Internet Tendency,* and in The People's Press anthology *Familiar.*

STACY GRIMES is currently at work on a collection of short stories.

ALICE HOFFMAN has published sixteen acclaimed novels, two books of short fiction, and six books for children. *The Ice Queen,* published by Little, Brown and Company, is her most recent novel, and *The Foretelling*, also by Little, Brown and Company, is her most recent teen book. Her work has been published in more than twenty translations and one hundred foreign editions. Her novels have received mention as notable books of the year by *The New York Times, The Los Angeles Times, Library Journal,* and others. The movie *Aquamarine,* adapted from her novel, was released this year from Fox 2000.

ANN HOOD is the author of seven novels, including *Somewhere Off the Coast of Maine, Waiting to Vanish, Three Legged Horse, Something Blue, Places to Stay the Night,* and *The Properties of Water.* She has won both the Pushcart Prize and a Best American Spiritual Writing Award. Her essays and short stories have appeared in *DoubleTake, The New York Times*, and *The Paris Review*, among other publications.

HA JIN has published two volumes of poetry, *Between Silences* and *Facing Shadows,* as well as two books of short fiction, *Ocean of Worlds,* which received the PEN Hemingway Award, and *Under the Red Flag,* which received the Flannery O'Connor Award for Short Fiction and was a finalist for the Kiriyama Pacific Rim Book Award. He also published a novella, *In the Pond,* which was selected as a best fiction book of 1998 by the *Chicago Tribune*. His short stores have been included in *The Best American Short Stories* (1997 and 1999), three Pushcart Prize anthologies, and *Norton Introduction to Fiction* and *Norton Introduction to Literature,* among other anthologies. *Waiting*, Ha Jin's first full-length novel, was the winner of the 1999 National Book Award for Fiction and the 2000 PEN/Faulkner Award for Fiction, and a finalist for the Los Angeles Times Book Award for fiction. His most recent book is *War Trash.*

ROY PARVIN is the author of two works of fiction, *In the Snow Forest* and the short story collection *The Loneliest Road in America.* He received a National Endowment for the Arts Fellowship Grant and was featured in *The Best American Short Stories.* Parvin has also been awarded the Katherine Anne Porter Prize in Fiction. His work was a Book Sense 76 selection and part of the Barnes & Noble Discover a Great Writer series. He lives in northern California with his wife, Janet.

NANCY REISMAN is the author of *House Fires,* a short story collection that won the 1999 Iowa Short Fiction Award, and *The First Desire,* a novel. Her work has appeared in *The Best American Short Stories* (2001), *Tin House*, and *The Kenyon Review*, among others. She has received fellowships from the National Endowment for the Arts and the Fine Arts Work Center in Provincetown. She currently teaches creative writing at Vanderbilt University in Nashville.

HEATHER SELLERS is the author of *Georgia Under Water,* which won a place in the Barnes and Noble New Discovery Writers Award in Summer 2001. Her work has been collected in anthologies such as *New Stories From the South,* and her recent fiction, poetry, and nonfiction appear in many journals and magazines. She teaches at Hope College.

DANIEL WALLACE is a writer and illustrator. His books include *Big Fish,* which was made into a feature film; *Ray in Reverse,* published in 2000; and *The Watermelon King*, published in 2003. Wallace teaches at UNC at Chapel Hill.